Praise for Harlan Coben

'It is always satisfying to discover a new crime writer – and this is the business . . . this book will keep you up until 2 a.m.' *The Times*

'Harlan Coben. He's smart, he's funny, and he has something to say' Michael Connelly

'An increasingly frightening conspiracy with an unguessable ending . . . hard to put down' *Sunday Telegraph*

'At last a British publisher has given British readers the chance to discover something every US mystery fan already knows – that Harlan Coben is one of the most entertaining and intriguing crime writers around'
Val McDermid, *Manchester Evening Guardian*

'What sets Harlan Coben above the crowd are wit and . . . an entertaining plot' *Los Angeles Times Book Review*

'Fast action, snappy dialogue and plenty of insider hoops material make this a fast, enjoyable read' *Toronto Star*

'Coben . . . scores a hole in one! The characters are deftly etched and the details keenly observed'
Publishers Weekly

'Coben is still one of America's masters of the hook, the twist and the surprise ending' *Literary Review*

'Intelligent and gripping, this is a real white-knuckle read of a thriller' *Daily Mail*

Harlan Coben is one of the most exciting talents in crime writing. He is an international number one bestseller, gracing the charts of the *Sunday Times* and the *New York Times*. His books are published in more than forty languages and there are more than fifty million of his novels in print worldwide. Harlan lives in New Jersey with his wife and four children. Visit his website at www.harlancoben.com

Fade Away

HARLAN COBEN

An Orion paperback

First published in Great Britain in 2000
by hodder & Stoughton
This new paperback edition published in 2014
by Orion Books,
an imprint of The Orion Publishing Group Ltd,
Orion House, 5 Upper St Martin's Lane,
London WC2H 9EA

An Hachette UK company

Published by arrangement with Dell Publishing,
an imprint of The Bantam Dell Publishing Group,
a division of Random House, Inc.

A CIP catalogue record for this book
is available from the British Library.

Printed and bound by the CPI Group (UK) Ltd, Croydon, CR0 4YY

The Orion Publishing Group's policy is to use papers
that are natural, renewable and recyclable products and
made from wood grown in sustainable forests. The logging
and manufacturing processes are expected to conform to
the environmental regulations of the country of origin.

www.orionbooks.co.uk

For Larry and Craig,
the coolest brothers a guy could ever have.
If you don't believe me, just ask them.

Acknowledgements

The author wishes to thank the following for their help: Anne Armstrong-Coben, MD; James Bradbeer, Jr, of Lilly Pulitzer; David Gold, MD; Maggie Griffin; Jacob Hoye; Lidsay Koehler; David Pepe of Pro Agents, Inc.; Peter Roisman of Advantage International; and, of course, Dave Bolt. Any errors – factual or otherwise – are totally their fault. The author is not to blame.

Chapter 1

'Just behave.'

'Me?' Myron said 'I'm always a delight.'

Myron Bolitar was being led through the corridor of the darkened Meadowlands Arena by Calvin Johnson, the New Jersey Dragons new general manager. Their dress shoes clacked sharply against the tile and echoed through empty Harry M. Stevens food stands, Carvel Ice Cream carts, pretzel vendors, souvenir booths. The smell of sporting-event hot dogs – that sort of rubbery, chemically, yet nostalgically delicious aroma – wafted from the walls. The stillness of the place consumed them; there is nothing more hollow and lifeless than an empty sports arena.

Calvin Johnson stopped in front of a door leading to a luxury box. 'This may all seem a bit strange,' he said. 'Just go with the flow, okay?'

'Okay.'

Calvin reached for the knob and took a deep breath.

'Clip Arnstein, the owner of the Dragons, is in there waiting for us.'

'And yet I'm not trembling,' Myron said.

Calvin Johnson shook his head. 'Just don't be an ass.'

Myron pointed to his chest. 'I wore a tie and everything.'

Calvin Johnson opened the door. The luxury box faced midcourt. Several workers were putting down the basketball floor over the hockey ice. The Devils had played the night before. Tonight was the Dragons' turn. The box was cozy. Twenty-four cushioned seats. Two television monitors. To the right was a wood-paneled counter for the food – usually fried chicken, hot dogs, potato knishes, sausage and pepper sandwiches, that sort of stuff. To the left was a brass cart with a nicely stocked bar and minifridge. The box also had its own bathroom – this so the corporate high rollers would not have to urinate with the great unwashed.

Clip Arnstein faced them, standing. He wore a dark blue suit with a red tie. He was bald with patches of gray over both ears. He was burly, his chest still a barrel after seventy-some-odd years. His large hands had brown spots and fat blue veins like garden hoses. No one spoke. No one moved. Clip glared hard at Myron for several seconds, examining him from head to toe.

'Like the tie?' Myron asked.

Calvin Johnson shot him a warning glance.

The old man made no movement toward them. 'How old are you now, Myron?'

Interesting opening question. 'Thirty-two.'

'You playing any ball?'

'Some,' Myron said.

'You keep in good shape?'

2

'Want me to flex?'

'No, that won't be necessary.'

No one offered Myron a seat and no one took one. Of course the only chairs in here were the spectator seats, but it still felt weird to stand in a business setting where you're supposed to sit. Standing suddenly became difficult. Myron felt antsy. He didn't know what to do with his hands. He took out a pen and held it, but that didn't feel right. Too Bob Dole. He stuck his hands in his pockets and stood at a weird angle, like the casual guy in the Sears circular.

'Myron, we have an interesting proposition for you,' Clip Arnstein said.

'Proposition?' Always the probing interrogatory.

'Yes. I was the one who drafted you, you know.'

'I know.'

'Ten, eleven years ago. When I was with the Celtics.'

'I know.'

'First round.'

'I know all this, Mr Arnstein.'

'You were a hell of a prospect, Myron. You were smart. You had an unbelievable touch. You were loaded with talent.'

'I coulda been a contenda,' Myron said.

Arnstein scowled. It was a famous scowl, developed over some fifty-plus years in professional basketball. The scowl had made its first appearance when Clip played for the now-defunct Rochester Royals in the forties. It grew more famous when he coached the Boston Celtics to numerous championships. It became a legendary trademark when he made all the famous trades ('clipping' the competition, ergo the nickname) as team president. Three years ago Clip had become majority owner of the New

3

Jersey Dragons and the scowl now resided in East Rutherford, right off Exit 16 of the New Jersey Turnpike. His voice was gruff. 'Was that supposed to be Brando?'

'Eerie, isn't it? Like Marlon's actually in the room.'

Clip Arnstein's face suddenly softened. He nodded slowly, giving Myron the doelike, father-figure eyes. 'You make jokes to cover the pain,' he said gravely. 'I understand that.'

Dr Joyce Brothers.

'Is there something I can do for you, Mr Arnstein?'

'You never played in a single professional game, did you, Myron?'

'You know very well I didn't.'

Clip nodded. 'Your first preseason game. Third quarter. You already had eighteen points that game. Not bad for a rookie in his first scrimmage. That was when fate took over.'

Fate took the form of big Burt Wesson of the Washington Bullets. There had been a collision, a searing pain, and then nothing.

'Awful thing,' Clip said.

'Uh huh.'

'I always felt bad about what happened to you. Such a waste.'

Myron glanced at Calvin Johnson. Calvin was looking off, arms crossed, his smooth black features a placid pool. 'Uh huh,' Myron said again.

'That's why I'd like to give you another chance.'

Myron was sure he'd heard wrong. 'Pardon?'

'We have a slot open on the team. I'd like to sign you.'

Myron waited. He looked at Clip. Then he looked at Calvin Johnson. Neither one was laughing. 'Where is it?' Myron asked.

4

'What?'

'The camera. This is one of those hidden camera shows, right? Is this the one with Ed McMahon? I'm a big fan of his work.'

'It's not a joke, Myron.'

'It must be, Mr Arnstein. I haven't played competitive ball in ten years. I shattered my knee, remember?'

'All too well. But as you said, it was ten years ago. I know you went through rehabilitation to rebuild it.'

'And you also know I tried a comeback. Seven years ago. The knee wouldn't hold up.'

'It was still too early,' Clip said. 'You just told me you're playing again.'

'Pickup games on weekends. It's a tad different than the NBA.'

Clip dismissed the argument with a wave of his hand. 'You're in shape. You even volunteered to flex.'

Myron's eyes narrowed, swerving from Clip to Calvin Johnson, back to Clip. Their expressions were neutral. 'Why do I have the feeling,' Myron asked, 'that I'm missing something here?'

Clip finally smiled. He looked over to Calvin Johnson. Calvin Johnson forced up a return smile.

'Perhaps I should be less' – Clip paused, searched for the word – 'opaque.'

'That might be helpful.'

'I want you on the team. I don't much care if you play or not.'

Myron waited again. When no one continued, he said. 'It's still a bit opaque.'

Clip let loose a long breath. He walked over to the bar, opened a small hotel-style fridge, and removed a can of

Yoo-Hoo. Stocking Yoo-Hoos. Hmm. Clip had been prepared. 'You still drink this sludge?'

'Yes,' Myron said.

He tossed Myron the can and poured something from a decanter into two glasses. He handed one to Calvin Johnson. He signaled to the seats by the glass window. Exactly midcourt. Very nice. Nice leg room too. Even Calvin, who was six-eight, was able to stretch a bit. The three men sat next to one another, all facing the same way, which again felt weird in a business setting. You were supposed to sit across from one another, preferably at a table or desk. Instead they sat shoulder to shoulder, watching the work crew pound the floor into place.

'Cheers,' Clip said.

He sipped his whiskey. Calvin Johnson just held his. Myron, obeying the instructions on the can, shook his Yoo-Hoo.

'If I'm not mistaken,' Clip continued, 'you're a lawyer now.'

'I'm a member of the bar,' Myron said. 'I don't practice much law.'

'You're a sports agent.'

'Yes.'

'I don't trust agents,' Clip said.

'Neither do I.'

'For the most part, they're bloodsucking leeches.'

'We prefer the term "parasitic entities,"' Myron said. 'It's more PC.'

Clip Arnstein leaned forward, his eyes zeroing in on Myron's. 'How do I know I can trust you?'

Myron pointed at himself. 'My face,' he said 'It screams trustworthiness.'

6

Clip did not smile. He leaned a little closer. 'What I'm about to tell you must remain confidential.'

'Okay.'

'Do you give me your word it won't go any farther than this room?'

'Yes.'

Clip hesitated, glanced at Calvin Johnson, shifted in his seat. 'You know, of course, Greg Downing.'

Of course. Myron had grown up with Greg Downing. From the time they had first competed as sixth graders in a town league less than twenty miles from where Myron now sat, they were instant rivals. When they reached high school, Greg's family moved to the neighboring town of Essex Fells because Greg's father did not want his son sharing the basketball spotlight with Myron. The personal rivalry then began to take serious flight. They played against each other eight times in high school, each winning four games. Myron and Greg became New Jersey's hottest recruits and both matriculated at big-time basketball colleges with a storied rivalry of their own – Myron to Duke, Greg to North Carolina.

The personal rivalry soared.

During their college careers, they had shared two *Sports Illustrated* covers. Both teams won the ACC twice, but Myron picked up a national championship. Both Myron and Greg were picked first-team All-American, both at the guard spots. By the time they both graduated, Duke and North Carolina had played each other twelve times. The Myron-led Duke had won eight of them. When the NBA draft came, both men went in the first round.

The personal rivalry crashed and burned.

Myron's career ended when he collided with big Burt Wesson. Greg Downing sidestepped fate and went on to become one of the NBA premier guards. During his ten-year career with the New Jersey Dragons Downing had been named to the All-Star team eight times. He led the league twice in three-point shooting. Four times he led the league in free-throw percentage and once in assists. He'd been on three *Sports Illustrated* covers and had won an NBA championship.

'I know him,' Myron said.

'Do you talk to him much?' Clip Arnstein asked.

'No.'

'When was the last time you spoke?'

'I don't remember.'

'Within the last few days?'

'I don't think we've spoken in ten years,' Myron said.

'Oh,' Clip said. He took another sip. Calvin had still not touched his drink. 'Well, I'm sure you heard about his injury.'

'Something with his ankle,' Myron said. 'It's day to day. He's in seclusion working on it.'

Clip nodded. 'That's the story we gave the media anyway. It's not exactly the truth.'

'Oh?'

'Greg isn't injured,' Clip said. 'He's missing.'

'Missing?' Again the probing interrogatory.

'Yes.' Clip took another sip. Myron sipped back, not an easy task with Yoo-Hoo.

'Since when?' Myron asked.

'Five days now.'

Myron looked at Calvin. Calvin remained placid but he had that kind of face. During his playing days, his nickname had been Frosty because he never displayed emotion. He was living up to his name now.

Myron tried again. 'When you say Greg is missing—'

8

'Gone,' Clip snapped. 'Disappeared. Into thin air. Without a trace. Whatever you want to call it.'

'Have you called the police?'

'No.'

'Why not?'

Clip gave him the wave-off again. 'You know Greg. He's not a conventional guy.'

The understatement of the millennium.

'He never does the expected,' Clip said. 'He hates the fame. He likes to be on his own. He's even disappeared before, though never during a playoff drive.'

'So?'

'So there's a good chance he's just being his usually flaky self,' Clip continued. 'Greg can shoot like a dream, but let's face facts: the man is a couple of sandwiches short of a picnic. You know what Downing does after games?'

Myron shook his head.

'He drives a cab in the city. That's right, a goddamn yellow taxi cab in New York City. Says it keeps him close to the common man. Greg won't do appearances or endorsements. He doesn't do interviews. He doesn't even do the charity thing. He dresses like something out of a seventies sitcom. The man is a nut job.'

'All of which makes him immensely popular with the fans,' Myron said. 'Which sells tickets.'

'I agree ,' Clip said, 'but that just underlines my point. If we call the cops it could damage both him and the team. Can you imagine the media circus if this got out?'

'It would be bad,' Myron admitted.

'Exactly. And suppose Greg is just hanging out in French Lick or whatever hickville town he goes to in the off-season, fishing or something? Christ, we'd never hear the end of it. On the other hand, suppose he's up to something.'

'Up to something?' Myron repeated.

'Hell, I don't know. I'm just talking here. But I don't need a goddamn scandal. Not now. Not with the playoffs coming up, you know what I'm saying?'

Not really, but Myron decided to let it go for now. 'Who else knows about this?'

'Just the three of us.'

The work crew rolled in the baskets. Two extras were kept in storage in case someone pulled a Darryl Dawkins and shattered a backboard. They then began putting down additional seats. Like most arenas, the Meadowlands holds more seats for basketball than hockey – in his case around a thousand more. Myron took another sip of Yoo-Hoo and let it roll around his tongue. He waited until it slid down his throat before he asked the obvious question. 'So how do I fit in?'

Clip hesitated. His breathing was deep, almost labored. 'I know something of your years with the FBI,' he said finally. 'No details, of course. Not even vagaries really, but enough to know you have a background in this kinda stuff. We want you to find Greg. Quietly.'

Myron said nothing. His 'undercover' work for the feds, it seemed, was the worst kept secret in the continental United States. Clip sipped his drink. He looked at Calvin's full glass, then at Calvin. Calvin finally took a sip. Clip turned his attention back to Myron. 'Greg's divorced now.' Clip went on. 'He's basically a loner. All his friends – hell, all his acquaintances – are teammates. They're his support group, if you will. His family. If anyone knows where he is – if anyone's helping him stay hidden – it's got to be one of the Dragons. I'll be honest with you. These guys are a major pain in the ass. Spoiled, pampered prima donnas who think our purpose in life is to serve them. But they all have one thing in common: They see management as the enemy. Us against the world and all that crap. They won't tell us the truth. They won't tell reporters the truth. And if you approach them as some, uh, "parasitic entity," they won't talk to you either. You have to be a player. It's the only way to get on the inside.'

'So you want me to join the team so I can find Greg.'

Myron heard the echoes of hurt in his voice. It was unintentional, but he saw that both men heard it too. His face flushed in embarrassment.

Chip put a hand on his shoulder. 'I meant what I said, Myron. You could have been great. One of the greatest.'

Myron took a deep swig of his Yoo-Hoo. No more sipping. 'I'm sorry, Mr Arnstein. I can't help you.'

The scowl was back. 'What?'

'I have a life. I'm a sports agent. I have clients to tend to. I can't just drop it all.'

'You'll get the player's minimum prorated. That's two hundred thousand dollars less whatever. And there's only a couple of weeks left until the playoffs. We'll keep you on till then no matter what.'

'No. My playing days are over. And I'm not a private investigator.'

'But we need to find him. He could be in danger.'

'I'm sorry. The answer is no.'

Clip smiled. 'Suppose I sweeten the pot.'

'No.'

'Fifty-thousand-dollar signing bonus.'

'I'm sorry.'

'Greg could show up tomorrow and you'd still get to keep that. Fifty grand. Plus a share of playoff money.'

'No.'

Clip sat back. He stared at his drink, dipped his finger into it, stirred. His voice was casual. 'You say you're an agent, right?'

'Yes.'

'I'm very friendly with the parents of three guys that will go in the first round. Did you know that?'

'No.'

'Suppose,' Clip said slowly, 'I guarantee you that one of them signs with you.'

Myron pricked up. A first round draft pick. He tried to keep his expression cool – to do like Frosty – but his heart was thumping. 'How can you do that?'

'Don't worry about how.'

'It doesn't sound ethical.'

Clip made a scoffing noise. 'Myron, don't play choirboy with me. You do me this favor and MB SportsReps gets a first round draft pick. Guaranteed. No matter how this thing with Greg plays out.'

MB SportsReps. Myron's company. Myron Bolitar, ergo MB. Representing sports people, ergo SportsReps. Add it together: MB SportsReps. Myron came up with that name on his own but still no offers came in from major advertising companies to use his services.

'Make it a hundred-thousand-dollar signing bonus,' Myron said.

Clip smiled. 'You've learned well, Myron.'

Myron shrugged.

'Seventy-five thousand,' Clip said. 'And you'll take it so don't bullshit a bullshitter.'

The two men shook hands.

'I have a few more questions about the disappearance,' Myron said.

Using both armrests Clip rose and stood over Myron. 'Calvin will answer all your questions,' he said with a nod toward his general manager. 'I have to go now.'

'So when do you want me to start practicing?'

Clip looked surprised. 'Practicing?'

'Yeah. When do you want me to start?'

'We have a game tonight.'

'Tonight?'

'Of course,' Clip said.

'You want me to suit up tonight?'

'We're playing our old team, the Celtics. Calvin will make sure you have a uniform by game time. Press conference at six to announce your signing. Don't be late.' Clip headed toward the door. 'And wear that tie. I like it.'

'Tonight?' Myron repeated, but Clip was already gone.

Chapter 2

After Clip left the box, Calvin Johnson allowed himself a small smile. 'I warned you it would be strange.'

'Serious strange,' Myron agreed.

'Finished with your nutritious chocolate beverage?'

Myron put down the can. 'Yeah.'

'Come on. Let's get you ready for the big debut.'

Calvin Johnson walked fluidly, back straight. He was black, six-foot-eight, thin but not gawky or disproportionate. He wore an olive Brooks Brothers suit. Perfectly tailored. Perfectly knotted tie. Perfectly shined shoes. His tightly kinked hair was receding, making his forehead overly prominent and shiny. When Myron matriculated at Duke, Calvin had been a senior at North Carolina. That made him around thirty-five years old, though he looked older. Calvin had enjoyed a solid pro career over eleven seasons. When he retired three years ago, everyone knew he'd end up in the front office. He started off as an assistant coach, moved to player personnel, and just recently was promoted to vice president and general manager of the New Jersey Dragons. These however were just titles. Clip ran the show. General managers, vice presidents, player personnel, trainers, even coaches all bent to his will.

'I hope you're all right with this,' Calvin said.

'Why wouldn't I be all right?'

Calvin shrugged. 'I played against you,' he said.

'So?'

'You were the most competitive son of a bitch I ever faced,' Calvin said. 'You'd stomp on someone's head to win. Now you're going to be a pissant bench-warmer. How's that going to sit with you?'

'I can handle it,' Myron said.

'Uh huh.'

'I've mellowed over the years.'

Calvin shook his head. 'I don't think so.'

'No?'

'You may think you've mellowed. You may even think you've got basketball out of your system.'

'I have.'

Calvin stopped, smiled, spread his arms. 'Sure you have. Just look at you. You could be the poster child for life after sports. A fine example to your fellow athletes. Your whole career crashed down around your ears, but you rose to the challenge. You went back to school – at Harvard Law nonetheless. You started up your own business – a growing company in the field of sports representation. You still dating that writer?'

He meant Jessica. Their togetherness seemed to always be an iffy thing but Myron said, 'Yes.'

'So you got the education, the job, and the gorgeous

girlfriend. Yep, on the outside you're happy and well adjusted.'

'On the inside too.'

Calvin shook his head. 'I don't think so.'

Everyone's Dr Joyce Brothers. 'Hey, I didn't ask to be put on the team.'

'No, but you didn't argue much either – except to up your price.'

'I'm an agent. That's what I do. I up the price.'

Calvin stopped and looked at Myron. 'Do you really think you have to be on the team to find Greg?'

'Clip seemed to think so.'

'Clip is a great man,' Calvin said, 'but he often has ulterior motives.'

'Like what?'

Calvin did not respond. He started walking again.

They reached the elevator. Calvin pressed the button and the doors immediately slid open. They stepped inside and began to descend. 'Look me in the eye,' Calvin said. 'Look me in the eye and tell me you never think about playing again.'

'Who doesn't *think* about it?' Myron countered.

'Yeah, but tell me you don't take it one step further. Tell me you never drift off and dream about making a comeback. Even now, when you're watching a game on TV, tell me you don't sit there and do a slow burn. Tell me you never watch Greg and think about all the adulation and fame. Tell me you never say, "I was better than him," because it's the truth. Greg is great. One of the top ten players in the league. But you were better, Myron. We both know that.'

'Long time ago,' Myron said.

Calvin smiled. 'Yeah,' he said. 'Right.'

'What's your point?'

'You're here to find Greg. Once he's found, you're gone. The novelty will be over. Clip will be able to say he gave you a chance, but you weren't up to the challenge. He'll still be the good guy with the good press.'

'Good press,' Myron repeated, remembering the upcoming press conference. 'One of his ulterior motives?'

Calvin shrugged. 'Doesn't matter. What does matter is that you understand you don't have a chance. You're only going to play during scrub time and we rarely win or lose by a lot so that doesn't happen and even if it does, even if you play spectacularly, we both know it's scrub time. And you won't play well because you are such a competitive son of a bitch, you need the points to mean something to the outcome of the game or you don't play your best.'

'I understand,' Myron said.

'I hope you do, my friend.' Calvin looked up at the numbered lights. The lights flickered in his brown eyes. 'Dreams never die. Sometimes you think they're dead, but they're just hibernating like some big old bear. And if the dream has been hibernating for a long time, that bear is going to wake up grumpy and hungry.'

'You should write country songs,' Myron said.

Calvin shook his head. 'Just giving a friend fair warning.'

'Much obliged. Now why don't you tell me what you know about Greg's disappearance?'

The elevator stopped and the doors opened. Calvin led the way. 'Not much to tell,' he said. 'We played against the Sixers in Philly. After the game Greg got on the bus with everybody else. When we got here, he got off the bus with everybody else. The last time anyone saw him he was getting into his car. The end.'

'How did Greg seem that night?'

'Fine. He played well against Philly. Scored twenty-seven points.'

'And his mood?'

Calvin thought about it. 'Nothing I noticed,' he said.

'Anything new going on in his life?'

'New?'

'Changes, that kind of thing.'

'Well, the divorce,' Calvin said. 'It's been nasty. I understand Emily can be quite difficult.' He stopped walking again and smiled at Myron. The Cheshire cat smile. Myron stopped but did not return the smile.

'Something on your mind, Frosty?'

The smile spread a bit farther. 'Weren't you and Emily an item at one time?'

'A lifetime ago.'

'College sweethearts, if I recall.'

'Like I said, a lifetime ago.'

'So,' Calvin said, starting to walk again, 'you were even better with the women than Greg.'

Myron ignored the comment. 'Does Clip know about my so-called past with Emily?'

'He's very thorough.'

'So that explains why you chose me,' Myron said.

'It was a consideration, but I don't think it's too important.'

'Oh?'

'Greg hates Emily. He'd never confide in her. But since this whole custody battle started there's definitely been a change in Greg.'

'How so?'

'For one thing, he signed a deal with Forte sneakers.'

Myron was surprised. 'Greg? An endorsement deal?'

18

'It's very hush-hush,' Calvin said. 'They're supposed to announce it end of the month, right before the playoffs.'

Myron whistled. 'They must have paid him a bundle.'

'A bundle and a half, I hear. Upwards of ten million a year.'

'Makes sense,' Myron said. 'A popular player who has refused to endorse any products for more than a decade – it's an irresistible draw. Forte does well with track and tennis shoes, but they're fairly unknown in the basketball world. Greg gives them instant credibility.'

'That he does,' Calvin agreed.

'Any idea why he changed his mind after all these years?'

Calvin shrugged. 'Maybe Greg realized he wasn't getting any younger and wanted to cash in. Maybe this whole divorce thing. Maybe he got whacked on the head and woke up with an iota of sanity.'

'Where's he been living since the divorce?'

'In the house in Ridgewood. It's in Bergen County.'

Myron knew it well. He asked for the address. Calvin gave it to him. 'What about Emily?' Myron asked. 'Where's she staying?'

'She and the kids are with her mother. I think they're in Franklin Lakes or thereabouts.'

'Have you done any checking yet – Greg's house, his credit cards, bank accounts?'

Calvin shook his head. 'Clip thought this thing was too big to trust to an agency. That's why we called you. I've driven past Greg's house a few times, knocked on the door once. No car in the driveway or garage. No lights on.'

'But no one's checked inside the house?'

'No.'

'So for all you know he slipped in the bathtub and hit his head.'

Calvin looked at him. 'I said, no lights on. You think he bathed in the dark?'

'That's a good point,' Myron said.

'Some hotshot investigator.'

'I'm a slow starter.'

They arrived at the team room. 'Wait here,' Calvin said.

Myron took out his cellular. 'Mind if I make a call?'

'Go ahead.'

Calvin disappeared behind the door. Myron turned on the power and dialed. Jessica answered on the second ring. 'Hello?'

'I'm going to have to cancel dinner tonight,' Myron said.

'You better have a good excuse,' Jessica said.

'A great one. I'll be playing professional basketball for the New Jersey Dragons.'

'That's nice. Have a good game, dear.'

'I'm serious. I'm playing for the Dragons. Actually, "playing" is probably not the right word. Might be more accurate to say I'll be getting fanny sores for the Dragons.'

'Are you for real?'

'It's a long story, but yes, I'm now officially a professional basketball player.'

Silence.

'I've never boffed a professional basketball player,' Jessica said. 'I'll be just like Madonna.'

'Like a virgin,' Myron said.

'Wow. Talk about a dated reference.'

'Yeah, well, what can I say. I'm an eighties kinda guy.'

'So, Mr Eighties, you going to tell me what's going on?'

'No time now. Tonight. After the game. I'll leave a ticket at the window.'

Calvin stuck his head back in. 'What's your waist? Thirty-four?'

'Thirty-six. Maybe thirty-seven.'

Calvin nodded and withdrew. Myron dialed the private line of Windsor Horne Lockwood III, president of the prestigious investment firm of Lock-Horne Securities in midtown Manhattan. Win answered on the third ring.

'Articulate,' Win said.

Myron shook his head. 'Articulate?'

'I said articulate, not repeat.'

'We have a case,' Myron said.

'Oh yippee,' he drawled in that preppy, Philly Main-Line accent of his. 'I'm enthralled. I'm elated. But before I completely wet myself, I must ask but one question.'

'Shoot.'

'Is this case of your customary charity persuasion?'

'Wet away,' Myron said. 'The answer is no.'

'What? No moral crusade for brave Myron?'

'Not this time.'

'Heavens be, do tell.'

'Greg Downing is missing. It's our job to find him.'

'And for services rendered we receive?'

'At least seventy-five grand plus a first round draft pick as a client.' Now was not the time to fill Win in on his temporary career change.

'My, my,' Win said happily. 'Pray tell, what shall we do first?'

Myron gave him the address of Greg's house in Ridgewood. 'Meet me there in two hours.'

'I'll take the Batmobile,' Win said and hung up.

21

Calvin returned. He held out a purple-and-aqua Dragon uniform. 'Try this on.'

Myron did not reach for it right away. He stared at it, his stomach twisting and diving. When he spoke his voice was soft. 'Number thirty-four?'

'Yeah,' Calvin said. 'Your old number at Duke. I remembered.'

Silence.

Calvin finally broke it. 'Go try it on.'

Myron felt something well up in his eye. He shook his head. 'No need,' he said. 'I'm sure it's the right size.'

Chapter 3

Ridgewood was a primo suburb, one of those old towns that still calls itself a village, where ninety-five percent of the students go on to college and no one lets their kids associate with the other five percent. There were a couple of strips of tract housing, a few examples of the mid-sixties suburban explosion, but for the most part Ridgewood's fine homes dated from an earlier, theoretically more innocent time.

Myron found the Downing house without any problem. Old Victorian. Very big but not unwieldy, three levels with perfectly faded cedar shingles. On the left side there was one of those rounded towers with a pointy top. Lots of outdoor porch space with all the Rockwellian touches: the kind of double swing where Atticus and Scout would share a lemonade on a hot Alabama night; a child's bicycle tipped on its side; a Flexible Flyer snow sled, although it hadn't snowed in six weeks. The required basketball hoop hung slightly rusted over the driveway. Fire Department 'Tot Finder' stickers glistened red and silver from two upstairs windows. Old oak trees lined the walk like weathered sentries.

Win hadn't arrived yet. Myron parked and rolled down a window. The perfect mid-March day. The sky was robin-egg blue. The birds chirped in cliché. He tried to picture Emily here, but the picture would not hold. It was far easier to see her in a New York high rise or one of those nouveau-riche mansions all done in white with Erté sculptures and silver pearls and too many gaudy mirrors. Then again he hadn't spoken to Emily in ten years. She may have changed. Or he may have misjudged her all those years ago. Wouldn't be the first time.

Funny being back in Ridgewood. Jessica had grown up here. She didn't like coming back anymore, but now the two loves of his life – Jessica and Emily – had something else in common: the village of Ridgewood. That could be added to the list of commonalities between the two women – stuff like meeting Myron, being courted by Myron, falling in love with Myron, crushing Myron's heart like a tomato under a stiletto heel. The usual fare.

Emily had been his first. Freshman year of college was late to lose one's virginity, if one were to listen to the boasts of friends. But if there had indeed been a sexual revolution among American teenagers in the late seventies/early eighties, Myron had either missed it or been on the wrong side. Women had always liked him – it wasn't that. But while his friends discoursed in great detail on their various orgylike experiences, Myron seemed to attract the wrong girls, the nice girls, the ones who still said no – or would have had Myron had the courage (or foresight) to try.

That changed in college when he met Emily.

Passion. It's a word bandied about quite a bit, but Myron thought it might apply here. At a minimum, unconfined lust. Emily was the type of woman a man labels 'hot,' as opposed to 'beautiful.' See a truly 'beautiful' woman and you want to paint or write a poem. See Emily and you want to engage in mutual fabric-ripping. She was raw sexuality, maybe ten pounds bigger than she should have been but those pounds were exquisitely distributed. The two of them made a potent mix. They were both under twenty, both away from home for the first time, both creative.

In a word: *kaboom.*

The car phone rang. Myron picked it up.

'I assume,' Win said, 'that you plan on having us break into the Downing residence.'

'Yes.'

'Then parking your car in front of said residence would not be a sound decision, would it?'

Myron glanced about. 'Where are you?'

'Drive down to the end of the block. Make a left, then your second right. I'm parked behind the office building.'

Myron hung up and restarted the car. He followed the directions and pulled into the lot. Win leaned against his Jaguar with his arms crossed. He looked, as he always did, as if he were posing for the cover of *WASP Quarterly*. His blond hair was perfectly in place. His complexion slightly ruddy, his features porcelain and high and a little too perfect. He wore khaki pants, a blue blazer, Top-Siders *sans* socks, and a loud Lilly Pulitzer tie. Win looked like what you'd picture a guy named Windsor Horne Lockwood III to look like – elitist, self-absorbed, wimpy.

Well, two out of three ain't bad.

The office building held an eclectic mix. Gynecologist. Electrolysis. Subpoena delivery service. Nutritionist. Women-only health club. Not surprisingly Win was standing near the entrance to the women-only health club. Myron approached.

'How did you know I was parked in front of the house?'

Keeping his eye on the entranceway Win motioned with his head. 'Up that hill. You can see everything with a pair of binoculars.'

A woman in her early twenties wearing a black Lycra aerobics suit walked out carrying a baby. It hadn't taken her long to get her figure back. Win smiled at her. The woman smiled back.

'I love young mothers,' Win said.

'You love women in Lycra,' Myron corrected.

Win nodded. 'There's that.' He snapped on a pair of sunglasses. 'Shall we begin?'

'You think breaking into that house will be a problem?'

Win made his I'll pretend-you-didn't-ask-that face. Another woman exited the health club; sadly, this one did not warrant a Win smile. 'Fill me in,' Win said. 'And move away. I want to make sure they can see the Jag.'

Myron told him all he knew. Eight women came out in the five minutes it took to tell the story. Only two of them were awarded The Smile. One wore a tiger-striped leotard. She was treated to the Full-Wattage Smile, the one that almost touched Win's eyes.

Win's face did not seem to register anything Myron said. Even when he told him about taking Greg's temporary slot on the Dragons, Win went on staring hopefully at the health club door. Normal Win behavior. Myron finished up by asking, 'Any questions?'

Win bounced a finger against his lip. 'Do you think the one in the tiger-striped leotard was wearing any underwear?'

'I don't know,' Myron said, 'but she was definitely wearing a wedding band.'

Win shrugged. Didn't matter to him. Win didn't believe in love or relationships with the opposite sex. Some might take this for simple sexism. They'd be wrong. Women weren't objects to Win; objects sometimes got his respect.

'Follow me,' Win said.

They were less than half a mile from the Downing house. Win had already scouted it out and found the path with the least chance of being seen or arousing suspicion. They walked in the comfortable silence of two men who had known each other a long time and very well.

'There's one interesting aside in all this,' Myron said.

Win waited.

'Do you remember Emily Shaeffer?' Myron asked.

'The name rings a bell.'

'I dated her for two years at Duke.' Win and Myron had met at Duke. They had also been roommates for all four years. It had been Win who had introduced Myron to the martial arts, who had gotten him involved with Feds. Win was now a top producer at his Lock-Horne Securities on Park Avenue, a securities firm that had been run by Win's family since the market had first opened. Myron rented space from Win, and Win also handled all money-matters for MB SportsReps' clients.

Win thought a bit. 'Is she the one who used to make the little monkey noises?'

'No,' Myron said.

Win seemed surprised. 'Who was the one who made the little monkey noises?'

'I have no idea.'

'Maybe it was someone I was with.'

'Maybe.'

Win considered this, shrugged. 'What about her?'

'She used to be married to Greg Downing.'

'Divorced?'

'Yep.'

'I remember her now,' Win said. 'Emily Schaeffer. Built.'

Myron nodded.

'I never liked her,' Win said. 'Except for those little monkey noises. They were rather interesting.'

'She wasn't the one who made monkey noises.'

Win smiled gently. 'The walls were thin,' he said.

'And you used to listen in?'

'Only when you pulled down the shade so I couldn't watch.'

Myron shook his head. 'You're a pig,' he said.

'Better than a monkey.'

They reached the front lawn and proceeded to the door. The secret was to look like you belonged. If you scurried around back, hunched over, someone might take notice. Two men in ties approaching the door does not normally lead one to think thief.

There was a metal keypad with a little red light. The light was on.

'Alarm,' Myron said.

Win shook his head. 'Fake. It's just a light. Probably bought it at Sharper Image.' Win looked at the lock and made a tsk-tsk noise. 'A Kwiktight brand on a pro basketball player's salary,' he said, clearly disgusted. 'Might as well use Play-Doh.'

'What about the dead bolt?' Myron asked.

'It's not locked.'

Win already had out his strip of celluloid. Credit cards are too stiff. Celluloid worked much better – known as 'loiding the lock. In no more time than it would take with a key, the door was open and they were inside the front foyer. The door had a chute and the mail was all over the place. Myron quickly checked some postage dates. No one had been here in at least five days.

The decor was nice in a fake-rustic, Martha Stewart sort of way. The furniture was what they called 'simple country' where the look was indeed simple and the price outrageous. Lots of pines and wickers and antiques and dry flowers. The smell of potpourri was strong and cloying.

They split up. Win went upstairs to the home office. He turned on the computer and began to download everything onto floppy disks. Myron found the answering machine in a room that used to be called a 'den' but now went by such lofty titles as the 'California room' or 'great room.' The machine announced the time and date of each message. Awfully convenient. Myron pressed a button. The tape rewound and started playing. On the first message, which according to the digital voice was received at 9:18 P.M. the night Greg vanished, Myron hit bingo.

A shaky woman's voice said, 'It's Carla. I'll be in the back booth until midnight.' Click.

Myron rewound and listened again. There were lots of noises in the background – people chatting, music, glasses clinking. The call had probably been placed from a bar or restaurant, especially with that back-booth reference. So who was this Carla? A girlfriend? Probably. Who else would call that late to set up a meeting for even later that night? But of course this had not been just any night. Greg Downing had vanished sometime between the time this call was made and the next morning.

Strange coincidence.

So where did they meet – assuming Greg had indeed made their back-booth liaison? And why did Carla, whoever she might be, sound so shaky – or was this just Myron's imagination?

Myron listened to the rest of the tape. No other messages from Carla. If Greg hadn't shown up at said back booth, wouldn't Carla have called again? Probably. So for now, Myron could safely assume that Greg Downing had seen Carla sometime before his disappearance.

A clue.

There were also four calls from Martin Felder, Greg's agent. He seemed to grow more perturbed with each message. The last one said, 'Jesus, Greg, how can you not call me? Is the ankle serious or what? And don't go incommunicado on me now, not when we're wrapping up the Forte deal. Call me, okay?' There were also three calls from a man named Chris Darby who apparently worked for Forte Sports Incorporated. He too sounded panicked. 'Marty won't tell me where you are. I think he's playing a game with us, Greg, trying to up the price or something. But we had a deal, am I right? Let me give you my home number, okay, Greg? How bad's this injury anyhow?'

Myron smiled. Martin Felder's client was missing, but he was doing all he could to turn it into a positive lever. Agents. He pressed the mode button on the answering machine several times. Eventually the LCD screen scrolled to reveal the code number Greg had set to call in for messages: 317. A fairly new trick of the trade. Now

30

Myron could call in anytime, press 317, and hear what messages had been left on the machine. He hit the redial button on the phone. Another fairly new trick. Find out who Greg called last. The phone rang twice and was picked up by a woman saying, 'Kimmel Brothers.' Whoever they were. Myron hung up.

Myron joined up with Win in the upstairs office. Win continued copying onto computer disks while Myron went through the drawers. Nothing particularly helpful.

They moved on to the master bedroom. The king-size bed was made. Both night tables were cluttered with pens and keys and papers.

Both.

Curious for a man who lived alone.

Myron's eyes swept the room and landed on a reading chair that doubled as a dressing dummy. Greg's clothes were strewn over one arm and the back. Normal enough, Myron guessed – neater than Myron, in fact, though that wasn't saying much. But looking again, he noticed something a tad strange on the other arm of the chair. Two articles of clothing. A white blouse and a gray skirt.

Myron looked at Win.

'They might belong to Miss Monkey Noises,' Win said.

Myron shook his head. 'Emily hasn't lived here in months. Why would her clothes still be on a chair?'

The bathroom, too, proved interesting. A large Jacuzzi on the right, a big steam shower with a sauna, and two vanities. They checked the vanities first. One contained a can of men's shaving cream, a roll-on deodorant, a bottle of Polo after-shave, a Gillette Atra razor. The other vanity had an open make-up case, Calvin Klein perfume, baby powder, and Secret Roll-On. A sprinkling of baby powder was on the floor near the vanity. There were also two disposable Lady Schick razors in the soap dish next to the Jacuzzi.

'He's got a girlfriend,' Myron said.

'A professional basketball player shacking up with some nubile lass,' Win remarked. 'Quite a revelation. Perhaps one of us should cry out, "Eureka."'

'Yes, but it raises an interesting question,' Myron said. 'If her boyfriend had suddenly vanished, wouldn't said lover have reported it?'

'Not,' Win said, 'if she were with him.'

Myron nodded. He told Win about the cryptic message from Carla.

Win shook his head. 'If they were planning on running away,' he said, 'why would she say where they were meeting?'

'She didn't say where. Only in a back booth at midnight.'

'Still,' Win said. 'It's not exactly the kind of thing you do before you disappear. Let's say that for some reason Carla and Greg decide to vanish for a little while. Wouldn't Greg know where and when to meet her before the fact?'

Myron shrugged. 'Maybe she was changing their meeting place.'

'From what? Front booths to back booths?'

'Damned if I know.'

They checked the rest of the upstairs. Not much doing. Greg's son's bedroom had racing-car wallpaper and a poster of Dad driving past Penny Hardaway for a layup. The daughter's room was done in Early American Barney – dinosaurs and purple. No clues. In fact there were no other clues until they reached the basement.

When they turned on the lights, Myron saw it right away.

It was a finished basement, a brightly colored playroom for the kids. There were lots of Little Tikes cars and big Legos and a plastic house with a sliding board. There were scenes from Disney movies like *Aladdin* and *The Lion King* on the wall. There was a television and a VCR. There was stuff too for when the kids got a little older – a pinball machine, a jukebox. There were small rocking chairs and mattresses and knock-around couches.

There was also blood. A fair amount of it in drips on the floor. Another fair amount smeared on a wall.

Bile nestled in Myron's throat. He had seen blood many times in his life, but it still left him queasy. Not so with Win. Win approached the crimson stains with something akin to amusement on his face. He bent to get a better look. Then he stood back up.

'Look at the bright side,' Win said. 'Your temporary slot on the Dragons may become more permanent.'

Chapter 4

There was no body. Just the blood.

Using Glad sandwich bags he found in the kitchen, Win collected a few samples. Ten minutes later they were back outside, the lock on the front door reengaged. A blue Oldsmobile Delta 88 drove past them. Two men sat in the front seat. Myron glanced at Win. Win barely nodded.

'A second pass,' Myron said.

'Third,' Win said. 'I saw them when I first drove up.'

'They're not exactly experts at this,' Myron said.

'No,' Win agreed. 'But of course, they hadn't known the job would require expertise.'

'Can you run the plates?'

Win nodded. 'I'll also run Greg's ATM and credit card transactions,' he said. He reached the Jag and unlocked it. 'I'll contact you when I have something. It shouldn't take more than a few hours.'

'You heading back to the office?'

'I'm going to Master Kwon's first,' Win said.

Master Kwon was their tae kwon do instructor. Both of them were black belts – Myron a second degree, Win a sixth degree, one of the highest ranking Caucasians in the world. Win was the best martial artist Myron had ever seen. He studied several different arts including Brazilian jujitsu, animal kung fu, and Jeet Kun Do. Win the Contradiction. See Win and you think pampered, preppy panty-waist; in reality, he was a devastating fighter. See Win and you think normal, well-adjusted human being; in reality, he was anything but.

'What are you doing tonight?' Myron asked.

Win shrugged. 'I'm not sure.'

'I can get you a ticket to the game,' Myron said.

Win said nothing.

'Do you want to go?'

'No.'

Without another word, Win slipped behind the wheel of his Jag, started the engine, peeled out with nary a squeal. Myron stood and watched him speed away, puzzled by his friend's abruptness. But then again, to paraphrase one of the four questions of Passover: why should today be different than any other day?

He checked his watch. He still had a few hours before the big press conference. Enough time to get back to the office and tell Esperanza about his career shift. More than anyone else, his playing for the Dragons would affect her.

He took Route 4 to the George Washington Bridge. There was no waiting at the tolls. Proof there was a God. The Henry Hudson however was backed up. He swung off near Columbia Presbyterian Medical Center to get on Riverside Drive. The squeegee guys – the homeless men who 'cleaned' your windshield with a mixture of equal parts grease, Tabasco sauce, and urine – were no longer at

35

the light. Mayor Giuliani's doing, Myron guessed. They had been replaced by Hispanic men selling flowers and something that looked like construction paper. He asked once what it was and had gotten an answer back in Spanish. As much as Myron could translate, the paper smelled nice and spruced up any home. Maybe that was what Greg used as potpourri.

Riverside Drive was relatively quiet. Myron arrived at his Kinney lot on 46th Street and tossed Mario the keys. Mario did not park the Ford Taurus up front with the Rolls, the Mercedes, Win's Jag; in fact, he usually managed to find a cozy spot underneath what must have been a nesting ground for loose-stooled pigeons. Car discrimination. It was an ugly thing, but where were the support groups?

The Lock-Horne Securities building was on Park Avenue and 46th, perpendicular to the Helmsley building. High-rent district. The street bustled with the doings of big finance. Several stretch limos double-parked illegally in front of the building. The ugly modern sculpture that looked like someone's intestines stood pitifully in its usual place. Men and women in business attire sat on the steps, eating sandwiches too hurriedly, lost in their own thoughts, many talking to themselves, rehearsing for an important afternoon meeting or rehashing a morning mistake. People who worked in Manhattan learned how to be surrounded by others yet remain completely alone.

Myron entered the lobby and pressed the button for the elevator. He nodded to the three Lock-Horne Hostesses, known to everyone else as the Lock-Horne Geishas. They were all model/actress wanna-bes, hired to escort high rollers up to the offices of Lock-Horne Securities and look attractive while doing it. Win had brought the idea home after a trip to the Far East. Myron guessed this could be more blatantly sexist, but he wasn't sure how.

Esperanza Diaz, his valued associate, greeted him at the door. 'Where the hell have you been?'

'We need to talk,' he said.

'Later. You've got a million messages.'

Esperanza wore a white blouse – an absolute killer look against her dark hair, dark eyes, and that dark skin that shimmered like moonlight on the Mediterranean. Esperanza had been spotted by a modeling scout when she was seventeen, but her career took a few weird turns and she ended up making it big in the world of professional wrestling. Yes, professional wrestling. She'd been known as Little Pocahontas, the brave Indian Princess, the jewel of the Fabulous Ladies of Wrestling (FLOW) organization. Her costume was a suede bikini, and she was always cast as the good guy in the morality play that was professional wrestling. She was young, petite, tight-bodied, gorgeous, and though of Latin origin, she was dark enough to pass for Native American. Racial backgrounds were irrelevant to FLOW. The real name of Mrs Saddam Hussein, the evil harem girl in the black veil, was Shari Weinberg.

The phone rang. Esperanza picked it up. 'MB Sports-Reps. Hold on a moment, he's right here.' She flashed the eyes at him. 'Perry McKinley. It's his third call today.'

'What does he want?'

She shrugged. 'Some people don't like dealing with underlings.'

'You're not an underling.'

She looked at him blankly. 'You going to take it or not?'

Being a sports agent was – to use computer terminology

– a multitasking environment with the capability of performing a variety of services with but a click of a button. It was more than simple negotiating. Agents were expected to be accountants, financial planners, real estate agents, hand-holders, personal shoppers, travel agents, family counselors, marriage counselors, chauffeurs, errand boys, parental liaisons, lackeys, butt-kissers, you name it. If you weren't willing to do all that for a client – to be what is known as a 'full service agency' – the next guy would be.

The only way to compete was to have a team, and Myron felt he had assembled a small yet extremely effective one. Win, for example, handled all the finances for Myron's clients. He set up a special portfolio for each player, met with them at least five times a year, made sure they understood what their money was doing and why. Having Win gave Myron a big leg up on the competition. Win was a near-legend in the financial world. His reputation was impeccable (at least in the financial world) and his track record unmatched. He gave Myron an instant 'in,' instant credibility in a business where credibility was a rare and heady concoction.

Myron was the JD. Win was the MBA. Esperanza was the all-purpose player, the unflappable chameleon who held it all together. It worked.

'We need to talk,' he said again.

'So we'll talk,' she said in a dismissing tone. 'First take this call.'

Myron entered his office. He overlooked Park Avenue in midtown. Great View. On one wall he had posters of Broadway musicals. On another there were movie stills from some of Myron's favorites: the Marx Brothers, Woody Allen, Alfred Hitchcock, and a potpourri of other classics. On a third wall were photographs of Myron's clients. The client wall was a bit sparser than Myron would have liked. He imagined what it would look like with an NBA first rounder in the middle.

Good, he decided. Very good.

He strapped on his headset.

'Hey, Perry.'

'Jesus Christ, Myron, I've been trying to reach you all day.'

'Good, Perry. And you.'

'Hey, I don't mean to be impatient but this is important. You get anything on my boat?'

Perry McKinley was a golfer on the fringe, no pun intended. He was a pro. He made some money, but he wasn't a name anyone but big golf fans would recognize. Perry loved to sail and was in need of a new vessel.

'Yeah, I got something,' Myron said.

'What company?'

'Prince.'

Perry did not sound thrilled. 'Their boats are just okay,' he whined. 'Nothing great.'

'They'll let you trade in your old boat for a new one. You have to do five personal appearances.'

'Five?'

'Yep.'

'For a Prince eighteen-footer? That's too many.'

'They originally wanted ten. But it's up to you.'

Perry thought about it a moment. 'Ah, shit, okay the deal. But first I want to make sure I like the boat. A full eighteen-footer, right?'

'That's what they said.'

'Yeah, all right. Thanks, Myron. You're the best.'

They hung up. Bartering – an important component in

the agent's multitasking environment. No one ever paid for anything in this business. Favors were exchanged. Trading products for some form of endorsement. Want a free shirt? Wear it in public. Want a free car? Shake hands at a few car shows. The big stars could demand serious payments in exchange for their endorsements. The lesser-known athletes happily seized the freebies.

Myron stared at the pile of messages and shook his head. Playing for the Dragons and keeping MB Sports-Reps afloat – how the hell was he going to pull it off?

He buzzed Esperanza. 'Come on in here please,' he said.

'I'm in the middle—'

'Now.'

Silence.

'Gosh,' she said, 'you're so macho.'

'Give me a break, huh?'

'No, really, I'm very frightened. I better drop everything and immediately do your bidding.'

Her phone fell. She sprinted in, feigning fear and breathlessness. 'Fast enough?'

'Yes.'

'So what is it?'

He told her. When he came to the part where he'd be playing for the Dragons, he was once again surprised to see no reaction. This was strange. First Win, now Esperanza. The two of them were his closest friends. They both lived for ridiculing him. Yet neither one of them had taken advantage of the obvious opening. Their silence on the subject of his 'comeback' was a tad unnerving.

'Your clients aren't going to like this,' she said.

'*Our* clients,' he corrected.

She made a face. 'Does it make you feel better to be patronizing?'

Myron ignored the comment. 'We have to turn this into a positive,' he said.

'How?'

'I'm not sure,' he said slowly. He leaned back in his chair. 'We can say that the publicity of all this will help them.'

'How?'

'I can make new contacts,' he said, the ideas coming to him even as he spoke. 'I can get closer to sponsors, learn more about them. More people will hear about me and indirectly my clients.'

Esperanza made a scoffing sound. 'And you think that's going to fly?'

'Why not?'

'Because it's bullshit. "Indirectly my clients." Sounds like trickle-down economics.'

She had a point. 'What's the big deal really?' he asked, palms to the ceiling. 'Basketball will only be a couple of hours a day. I'll be here the rest of the time. I'll have the cellular phone with me all the time. We just have to emphasize that I won't be there long.'

Esperanza looked at him skeptically.

'What?' he asked.

She shook her head.

'No, I want to know. What?'

'Nothing,' she said. She looked him straight in the eye, her hands resting on her lap. 'What does the bitch say about all this?' she asked sweetly.

Her pet name for Jessica. 'Will you please stop calling her that?'

She made a suit-yourself face, for once not arguing.

There had been a time – long, long ago – when Jessica and Esperanza had at least tolerated each other. But then Jessica left, and Esperanza saw what it did to Myron. Some people held grudges. Esperanza internalized them. It didn't matter that Jessica had come back.

'So what does she think?' Esperanza asked again.

'About what?'

'About the prospects for peace in the Middle East,' she snapped. 'What do you think I mean? Your playing again.'

'I don't know. We haven't had a chance to talk about it much. Why?'

Esperanza shook her head again. 'We're going to need help in here,' she said, closing the subject. 'Someone to answer the phones, do some typing, that kind of thing.'

'You have someone in mind?'

She nodded. 'Cyndi.'

Myron blanched. 'Big Cyndi?'

'She could answer the phone, do some odd jobs. She's a good worker.'

'I didn't even know she could talk,' Myron said. Big Cyndi had been Esperanza's tag-team wrestling partner, fighting under the name of Big Chief Mama.

'She'll take orders. She'll do shit work. She's not ambitious.'

Myron tried not to wince at the thought. 'Isn't she still working at the strip joint as a bouncer?'

'It's not a strip joint. It's a leather bar.'

'My mistake,' Myron said.

'And she's a bartender now.'

'Cyndi's been promoted?' Myron said.

'Yes.'

'Well, I'd hate to sidetrack her burgeoning career by asking her to work here.'

'Don't be an ass,' Esperanza said. 'She works there nights.'

'What,' Myron said, 'Leather and Lust doesn't do a big lunch crowd?'

'I know Cyndi. She'll be perfect.'

'She scares people,' Myron said. 'She scares me.'

'She'll stay in the conference room. No one will see her.'

'I don't know.'

Esperanza rose smoothly. 'Fine, you find somebody. I mean, you're the boss. You know best. Me, I'm just a pissant secretary. I wouldn't dare question how you handle *our* clients.'

Myron shook his head. 'Low blow,' he said. He leaned forward, his elbows on his desk, his hands holding up his head. 'All right,' he said finally, releasing a deep breath. 'We'll give her a try.'

Myron waited. Esperanza stared back at him. After several seconds passed, she said, 'Is this the part where I jump up and down and say thank you, thank you?'

'No, this is the part where I leave.' He checked his watch. 'I got to talk to Clip about those bloodstains before the press conference.'

'Have fun.' She headed for the door.

'Hold up,' he called out. She turned and freed him. 'Do you have class tonight?' Esperanza took night classes at NYU Law school.

'No.'

'You want to go to the game?' He cleared his throat. 'You can, uh, bring Lucy, if you'd like.'

Lucy was Esperanza's latest love. Before Lucy she had

dated a man named Max. Her sexual preference seemed to vacillate. 'We broke up,' she said.

'Oh, I'm sorry,' Myron said, not knowing what else to say. 'When?'

'Last week.'

'You didn't say anything.'

'Maybe because it's none of your business.'

He nodded. True enough. 'Well, you can bring a new, uh, friend, if you'd like. Or you can go yourself. We're playing the Celtics.'

'I'll pass,' she said.

'You sure?'

She nodded again, left the room. Myron grabbed his jacket and headed back to the lot. Mario tossed him his keys without looking up. He took the Lincoln Tunnel and hopped onto Route 3. He passed a huge and fairly famous appliance and electronics store called Tops. The billboard featured a giant nose jutted out over Route 3. The caption: Tops Is Right Under Your Nose. Very lifelike. The only thing missing were the giant nose hairs. He was only a mile or so from the Meadowlands when the car phone rang.

'I have some preliminaries,' Win said.

'Go ahead.'

'None of Greg Downing's accounts or credit cards have been accessed in the past five days.'

'Nothing?'

'Nothing.'

'Any cash withdrawals from his bank?'

'Not in the past five days.'

'How about earlier? Maybe he grabbed out a lot of money before he vanished.'

'It's being worked on. I don't know yet.'

Myron took the Meadowlands exit. He considered what this all meant. So far, not much, but it wasn't really good news. The blood in the basement. No sign of Greg. No financial activity. It wasn't really promising. 'Anything else?' Myron asked.

Win hesitated. 'I may soon have an idea where dearest Greg had that drink with fair Carla.'

'Where?'

'After the game,' Win said. 'I'll know more then.'

Chapter 5

'Sports is folklore,' Clip Arnstein told the room full of reporters. 'What captures our imagination is not simply the winning and losing. It's the stories. The stories of perseverance. The stories of sheer will. The stories of hard work. The stories of heartbreak. The stories of miracles. The stories of triumph and tragedy. The stories of comebacks.'

Clip looked down at Myron from the podium, his eyes properly moist, his smile his most grandfatherly. Myron cringed. He fought back an intense desire to duck under the conference table and hide.

After a proper pause Clip turned back to the front. The reporters were silent. An occasional flashbulb burst forth. Clip swallowed several times as though summoning some inner resolve he'd need to continue. His throat slid up and down. He raised his moist eyes to the audience.

A little hammy, Myron thought, but all in all a fine performance.

The press conference was more crowded than Myron would've thought. Not a free seat and many reporters standing. Must have been a slow news day. Clip took his time, regaining his seemingly lost composure. 'A little over a decade ago, I drafted an exceptional young man, a player I believed was destined for greatness. He had a great jumper, a well-honed court sense, mental tenacity, and on top of all that was a fine human being. But the gods had other plans for that young man. We all know what happened to Myron Bolitar on that fateful night in Landover, Maryland. There is no reason to dredge up the past. But as I said when I opened this press conference, sports is folklore. Today the Dragons are giving that young man a chance to weave his own legend into the lush tapestry of sports. Today the Dragons are allowing that young man to try and recapture what was so cruelly snatched away from him all those years ago.'

Myron started squirming. His cheeks flushed. His eyes darted about, seeking a safe haven and finding none. He settled for looking at Clip's face, as per the media's expectations. He zeroed in on a cheek mole, staring so hard his vision began to mercifully blur.

'It won't be easy, Myron,' Clip said, turning now and addressing Myron directly. Myron kept his vision locked on the mole; he couldn't meet the gaze. 'No promises have been made to you. I don't know what happens from here. I don't know if this is the culmination of your story or the commencement of a brave new chapter. But those of us who love sports can't help but hope. It is in our nature. It is in the nature of all true combatants and fans.' Clip's voice started to crack.

'This is reality,' he went on. 'I have to remind you of that, Myron, much as I'd rather not. On behalf of the

New Jersey Dragons I welcome you, a man of class and courage, to the team. We wish you nothing but the best. We know that no matter what happens to you on the court, you will bring honor to the entire Dragon organization.' He stopped, tightened his lips and managed a quick, 'Thank you.'

Clip held out a hand to Myron. Myron played his part. He stood to shake Clip's hand. Clip however had other ideas. He put his arms around Myron and pulled him toward him. The flashbulbs increased to the point of being a disco strobe. When Clip finally pulled back, he wiped his eyes with two fingers. Sheesh, the man put Pacino to shame. Clip held out an arm, ushering Myron to the podium.

'How does it feel to be back?' one reporter yelled out.

'Scary,' Myron replied.

'Do you really think you have what it takes to play at this level?'

'No, not really.'

The moment of honesty stopped them for a second. But only a second. Clip laughed and everyone else in the room followed suit. Figuring it was a joke. Myron didn't bother correcting them.

'Do you think you still have three-point shooting range?' another asked.

Myron nodded. 'I have the shooting range,' he said. 'I'm just not sure I have the making range.' A stolen joke but what the hey.

More laughs.

'Why the comeback so late, Myron? What convinced you to come back now?'

'The Psychic Friends Network.'

Clip stood and warded off further questions with a

raised hand. 'Sorry, gang, that's it for now. Myron has to get suited up for tonight's game.'

Myron followed Clip out. They hurried down the corridor and into Clip's office. Calvin was already there. Clip shut the door. Before he sat down Clip asked, 'So what's the matter?'

Myron told him about the blood in the basement. Clip visibly blanched. Frosty's fingers tightened against the armrest.

'So what are you trying to say?' Clip snapped when he finished.

'Say?'

Clip gave an elaborate shrug. 'I don't get it.'

'There's nothing to get,' Myron said. 'Greg is missing. No one has seen him for five days. He hasn't used his ATM or credit card. And now there's blood in the basement.'

'In his kids' playroom, right? That's what you said before. The kids' playroom.'

Myron nodded.

Clip looked a question at Calvin then turned his palms to the sky. 'So what the hell does that mean?'

'I'm not sure.'

'It doesn't exactly add up to foul play, now does it?' Clip continued. 'Think it through, Myron. If Greg were murdered, for example, where is his body? Did the killer or killers take it with them? And what do you think happened here? The killers – what? – surprised Greg? Alone? In his kids' playroom where, I guess, Greg was playing with his little dolly? Then what happened? They killed him down there and dragged him out of the house without leaving traces of blood anywhere but in the basement?' Clip spread his hands. 'Does that make sense?'

The scenario had bothered Myron too. He sneaked a glance at Calvin. Calvin seemed deep in thought. Clip stood.

'For all we know,' Clip went on, 'one of Greg's kids cut himself playing down there.'

'Hell of a cut,' Myron said.

'Or a bloody nose. Christ, those things gush like mad. Could be nothing but a bloody nose.'

Myron nodded. 'Or maybe they were slaughtering chickens,' he said. 'Could be that too.'

'I don't need sarcasm, Myron.'

Myron waited a beat. He glanced at Calvin. Nothing. He glanced at Clip. Nada. 'It's getting opaque in here again.'

'Pardon?'

'You hired me to find Greg. I'm tracing down a major lead. Yet you don't want to hear it.'

'If you mean I don't want to hear that perhaps Greg has met with foul play—'

'No, that's not what I mean. You're afraid of something and it's not just that Greg may have met with foul play. I'd like to know what.'

Clip looked over at Calvin. Calvin nodded almost imperceptibly. Clip sat back down. His fingertips drummed the desktop. The grandfather clock in the corner ticked an imitating echo. 'Understand,' Clip said, 'that we have Greg's best interests at heart. We really do.'

'Uh huh.'

'You know anything about hostile takeovers?'

'I was alive in the eighties,' Myron said. 'In fact, someone recently remarked on what an eighties kinda guy I am.'

'Well, I'm undergoing one now.'

'I thought you were a majority owner.'

Clip shook his head. 'Forty percent. No one else owns more than fifteen percent. A couple of the minority shareholders have gotten together and are trying to oust me.' Clip made two fists and put them on his desk like paperweights. 'They say I'm too much a basketball mind and not enough a business mind. I should only be handling players and the on-court affair. They vote in two days.'

'So?'

'So right now the vote is very close. A scandal and I'm done.'

Myron looked at both men and waited a beat. Then he said, 'You want me to sit on this.'

'No, no, of course not,' Clip said quickly. 'I'm not saying that at all. I just don't want the press going berserk over what might be nothing. I can't afford to have anything unsavory uncovered now.'

'Unsavory?'

'Right.'

'Like what?'

'Hell if I know,' Clip said.

'But Greg might be dead.'

'And if that's the case, a day or two isn't going to help – cold as that might sound. And if something did happen to Greg, there might be a reason.'

'A reason?'

Clip threw up his hands. 'Hell, I don't know. You lift up a corpse or even a man in hiding and worms start to crawl out. You know what I mean?'

'No,' Myron said. But Clip went on.

'I don't need that, Myron. Not now. Not till after this vote.'

'Then you are telling me to sit on this,' Myron said.

51

'Not at all. We just don't want an unnecessary panic. If Greg is dead, we can't do him any good now anyway. If he's vanished, well, then you are his best hope to avoid media glare or to save him.'

They were still not telling him everything but Myron decided not to press it just now. 'Do you have any idea why someone would be watching Greg's house?'

Clip looked puzzled. 'Someone is watching his house?'

'I think so, yes.'

Clip looked over to Calvin. 'Calvin?'

'No idea,' Calvin said.

'I don't know either, Myron. Do you have any thoughts?'

'Not yet. One more question: did Greg have a girlfriend?'

Again Clip looked toward Calvin.

Calvin shrugged. 'He played around a lot. But I don't think there was anyone special.'

'Do you know any of the women he played around with?'

'Not by name. Some groupies, stuff like that.'

'Why?' Clip asked. 'You think he ran off with a broad?'

Myron shrugged and stood. 'Guess I better get to the locker room. It's almost game time.'

'Wait.'

Myron stopped.

'Please, Myron, I know it sounds like I'm being cold, but I really do care about Greg. Very much. I want him found alive and well.' Clip swallowed. The wrinkles in his skin looked more pronounced, like someone had just pinched them out a bit. His color was not good. 'If you can honestly tell me that revealing what we know to the public is best, I'll go along with it. No matter what the costs. Think about it. I want to do what's best for Greg. I care about him very much. I care about both of you. You're both fine young men. I mean that. I owe you both a great deal.'

Clip looked like he was about to cry. Myron wasn't sure what to make of all this. He decided to nod and say nothing. He opened the door and left.

As he approached the elevator Myron heard a familiar, husky voice say, 'If it isn't the Comeback Kid?'

Myron looked over at Audrey Wilson. She was wearing her customary sports-reporter garb: dark blue blazer, black turtleneck, what they called 'stone-washed' jeans. Her makeup was either light or nonexistent, her nails short and unpolished. The only splash of color could be found on her sneakers – bright aqua Chuck Taylor Cons. Her looks were completely unspectacular. There was nothing wrong with her features but nothing particularly right about them either. They were just there. Her straight black hair was cut short in a pageboy with bangs. 'Do I detect the scent of cynicism?' he asked.

Audrey shrugged. 'You don't really think I buy all this, do you?'

'Buy what?'

'Your sudden desire to' – she checked her notes – 'weave your own legend into the lush tapestry of sports.' She looked up, shook her head. 'That Clip can sure talk some shit, huh?'

'I have to get dressed, Audrey.'

'How about giving me the lowdown first?'

'The lowdown, Audrey? Gee, why not ask for a "scoop"? I love it when you reporters say that.'

She smiled at that. It was a nice smile. Full and open. 'Kinda defensive, aren't we, Myron?'

53

'Me? Never.'

'Then how about – to coin yet another cliché – a statement for the press?'

Myron nodded, put his hand to his chest in dramatic fashion. 'A winner never quits, and a quitter never wins.'

'Lombardi?'

'Felix Unger. It was on *The Odd Couple*, the one where Howard Cosell guest starred.'

He turned and walked toward the locker room. Audrey followed. She was probably the top female sports reporter in the country. She covered the Dragons for the East Coast's biggest newspaper. She had her own radio show on WFAN in a coveted time slot with huge ratings. She had a Sunday morning round-table talk show called *Talking Sports* on ESPN. And yet, like almost every other female in this male-dominated profession, there was something tenuous about her station, her career always a half-step from toppling over no matter how big she became.

'How's Jessica?' Audrey asked.

'Good.'

'I haven't spoken to her in a month,' she said with a singsong tone. 'Maybe I should give her a call. Sit down and have a heart-to-heart, you know.'

'Gee,' Myron said, 'that won't be transparent.'

'I'm trying to make this easier on you, Myron. There's something strange going on here. You know I'm going to find out what it is. Might as well just tell me.'

'I really don't know what you're talking about.'

'First Greg Downing leaves the team under mysterious circumstances—'

'What's mysterious about an ankle injury?'

'—then you, his old nemesis, takes his place after being

54

out of commission for the better part of eleven years. You don't find that strange?'

Great, Myron thought. On the job five minutes and already someone was voicing suspicion. Myron Bolitar, master of the undercover. They reached the door to the locker room.

'I gotta go, Audrey. We'll talk later.'

'Count on it,' she said. She smiled at him with a gentle mocking sweetness. 'Good luck, Myron. Knock them dead.'

He nodded, took a deep breath, and pushed open the locker-room door.

Show time.

Chapter 6

No one greeted Myron when he entered the locker room. No one broke stride. No one even looked at him. The room did not go quiet like something out of an old Western where the sheriff pushes open the creaking door and sashays into the saloon. Maybe that was the problem. Maybe the door needed to creak. Or maybe Myron had to work on his sashay.

His new teammates were sprawled about like socks in a college dorm. Three of them were draped over benches, semidressed and seminapping. Two were on the floor, a leg being held in the air by assistants, stretching quads and calves. A couple others were dribbling basketballs. Four were hobbling back to their lockers after getting taped. Almost all were chewing gum. Almost all were also listening to Walkmans, the tiny speakers jammed in their ears and blaring so loudly that they sounded like competing floor models at a stereo store.

Myron found his dressing area pretty easily. All the

other lockers had bronze plaques with a player's name engraved on it. Myron's did not. It had a piece of white adhesive tape above it, the kind used to tape ankles, with the letters M. BOLITAR scrawled in black marker. It hardly inspired confidence or spoke commitment.

He glanced around for someone to talk to, but the Walkmans were the ideal room dividers. Everyone was in their own private space. Myron spotted Terry 'TC' Collins, the team's famed whining superstar, sitting alone in a corner. TC was the media's newest poster boy for the spoiled athlete, the guy 'ruining' the genteel world of sports 'as we know it,' whatever that meant. TC was a hell of a physical specimen. Six-ten, muscular, wiry. His cleanly shaven head glistened in the fluorescent light. Rumor had it TC was black though it was hard to see any trace of skin through the work of his tattoo artist. The obscure ink images blanketed almost all available somatic sites. Body piercing too appeared to be more of a lifestyle with TC than a hobby. The man looked like a nightmare version of Mr Clean.

Myron caught TC's eye, smiled, and nodded a hello. TC glared daggers and turned away. Making chums already.

His uniform was hung where it should be. His name had already been sewn on the back in block letters. BOLITAR. He stared at it for a moment or two. Then he quickly snatched it off the hanger and put it on. Everything caused bouts of déjà vu. The feel of the crumbly cotton. The shoelacelike tie-string on his shorts. The slight elastic tug at the waist when he put them on. The slight tightness of the top as it went over his shoulders. The practiced hands tucking in the tail. The lacing up of his high-tops. It all caused pangs. It was getting harder to breathe. His eyes blinked something back. He sat and waited until the feeling went away.

Myron noticed very few of the guys wore jock straps anymore, preferring those tight, Lycra shorts. Myron stuck with old dependable. Mr Old Fashioned. Then he strapped a contraption onto his leg that was loosely labeled a 'knee brace.' Felt more like a metal compressor. The last thing he put on was his warm-ups. The bottoms had dozens of snaps up and down the legs, so a player could dramatically rip them off when called to go into a game.

'Hey, kid, how's it going?'

Myron stood and shook hands with Kip Corovan, one of the team's assistant coaches. Kip wore a plaid jacket that was about three sizes too small. The sleeves inched up to the forearms. The gut jutted out with great defiance. He looked like a farmer at the semiannual square dance. 'I'm doing fine, coach.'

'Great, great. And call me Kip. Or Kipper. Most people call me Kipper. Sit down, relax.'

'Okay.' Kipper?

'Great, happy to have you with us.' The Kipper pulled over a chair, turned it so the back faced Myron, and straddled it. His pants inseam didn't look happy with the move. 'I'll be honest with you, Myron, okay? Donny wasn't thrilled about this. Nothing personal, you understand. Just Donny likes to pick his own players. He don't like interference from upstairs, you know what I'm saying?'

Myron nodded. Donny Walsh was the head coach.

'Great, good. Donny's a straight guy though. He remembers you from the old days, liked you a lot. But we got a team heading for the playoffs. With a bit of luck we can lock up home-court advantage throughout the playoffs. It took a while to get the ducks all in a row. It's a balance, you know. Got to keep the ducks on an even keel. Losing Greg really knocked the wind from our sails, but we finally got those ducks back up. Now you come along, see. Clip doesn't tell us why, but he insists we add you to the roster. Fine, Clip is the big chief, no question. But we worry about getting our ducks back sailing straight, you see?'

The mixing of metaphors was making Myron dizzy. 'Sure. I don't want to cause any problems.'

'I know that.' He stood, put the chair back with a sweeping motion. 'You're a good guy, Myron. Always were a straight arrow. We need that now. A team-comes-first kinda guy, am I right?'

Myron nodded. 'A straight-sailing duck.'

'Great, fine. See you out there. And don't worry. You're not going to get in unless it's a blowout.' With that the Kipper hoisted his belt up over the gut and sauntered – almost sashayed – across the room.

Three minutes later, the Kipper shouted out, 'Gather round the board, boys.' No one paid any attention. He repeated this several times, tapping Walkman-entranced players on the shoulders, so that they would hear. It took a full ten minutes to get twelve professional athletes to move less than ten feet. Coach Donny Walsh strode in with great self-importance, took center stage, and began spilling out the tired clichés. This didn't mean he was a bad coach or anything. You play over a hundred games a season it's hard to come up with anything new.

The pep talk lasted a full two minutes. Some of the guys never bothered turning off their Walkmans. TC was busy taking off his jewelry, a task that took great concentration and a team of well-trained technicians. Another minute or two passed and then the locker-room door opened. Everyone removed their Walkmans and headed out. Myron realized they were heading for the court.

Game time.

Myron stood at the end of the line. He swallowed deeply. A cold rush swept through him. As he made his way up the ramp he heard a voice over the loudspeaker scream, 'And nowwwwww, your New Jersey Dragons!' Music blared. The jog quickened into a full trot.

The ovation was thunderous. The players automatically split into two makeshift lines for the lay-up drill. Myron had done this a zillion times before, but for the first time he really thought about what he was doing. When you were a star or a starter, you warmed up casually, loosely, unhurriedly. There was no reason to press it. You had the whole game to show the crowd what you could do. The scrubs – something Myron had never been – handled the warm-ups in one of two ways. Some went all out, slamming reverse dunks, doing windmill moves. In a phrase: showing off. Myron had always found this behavior sort of desperate. Others hung around the superstars, feeding them the ball, playing the mock defender like a boxer with a sparring partner. Cool by association.

Myron got to the front of the lay-up line. Someone passed him the ball. When you're warming up, you are subconsciously convinced that all eyes in the arena are on you, though in point of fact, most people were settling in or chatting or getting food or checking out the crowd and those that were watching couldn't care less what you did. Myron took two dribbles and laid the ball against the glass and in. Sheesh, he thought. The game hadn't started yet and already he didn't know what to do.

Five minutes later the lay-up lines disintegrated and players began to free shoot. Myron glanced into the stands for Jessica. She was not hard to spot. It was like a beacon hit her, like she came forward and the rest of the crowd stepped back, like she was the Da Vinci and the rest of the faces were but a frame. Jessica smiled at him and he felt a warmth spread through him.

With something close to surprise, he realized that this would be the first time Jessica had seen him play in anything but pickup games. They'd met three weeks before Myron's injury. The thought made him pause. And remember. For a brief moment his mind dragged him back. Guilt and pain washed over him until a ball careened off the backboard and smacked him in the head. But the thought remained:

I owe Greg.

The buzzer sounded and the players moved to the bench. Coach Walsh blurted out a few more clichés and made sure each player knew whom they were covering. The players nodded, not listening. TC still glared. Game face, Myron hoped, but didn't really believe it. He also kept an eye on Leon White, Greg's roommate on the road and closest friend on the team. The huddle broke. The players from both sides approached the center circle, greeting one another with handshakes and hand slaps. Once out there, the players on both teams started pointing around, trying to figure out who was covering whom since no one had listened thirty seconds earlier. Coaches from both sides were up, yelling out the defensive assignments until the ball was mercifully tossed in the air.

Basketball is normally a game of momentum shifts,

keeping things fairly close until the final minutes. Not tonight. The Dragons cruised. They led by twelve after one quarter, twenty points by halftime, twenty-six by the end of the third period. Myron started getting nervous. The lead was big enough for him to get in. He hadn't really counted on that. Part of him silently cheered on the Celtics, hoping they could stage enough of a comeback to keep his butt on the aluminum chair. But it was a no-go. With four minutes remaining the Dragons led by twenty-eight points. Coach Walsh shot a glance down the bench. Nine of the twelve players had already gotten in. Walsh whispered something to the Kipper. The Kipper nodded and walked down the bench, stopping in front of Myron. Myron could feel his heart beating in his chest.

'Coach is going to clear the bench,' he said. 'He wants to know if you want to go in.'

'Whatever he wants,' Myron replied, while sending out telepathic messages of no, no, no. But he couldn't tell them that. It wasn't in his nature. He had to play the good trooper, Mr Team-First, Mr Dive-On-The-Grenade-If-That's-What-The-Coach-Wants. He didn't know how else to do it.

A time-out was called. Walsh looked down the bench again. 'Gordon! Reilly! You're in for Collins and Johnson!'

Myron let loose a breath. Then he got mad at himself for feeling such relief. What kind of competitor are you? he asked himself. What kind of a man wants to stay on the bench? Then the truth rose up and smacked him hard in the face:

He was *not* here to play basketball.

What the hell was he thinking? He was here to find Greg Downing. This was just undercover work, that's all.

Like with the police. Just because a guy goes undercover and pretends he's a drug dealer doesn't make him a drug dealer. The same principle applied here. Just because Myron was pretending to be a basketball player didn't make him one.

The thought was hardly comforting.

Thirty seconds later, it started. And it filled Myron's chest with dread.

One voice triggered it. One beer-infested voice rising clearly above all others. One voice that was just deep enough, just different enough, to separate it from the usual cacophony of fandom. 'Hey, Walsh,' the voice cried out. 'Why don't you put in Bolitar?'

Myron felt his stomach plummet. He knew what was coming next. He had seen it happen before, though never to him. He wanted to sink into the floor.

'Yeah!' another voice crowed. 'Let's see the new guy!'

More shouts of agreement.

It was happening. The crowd was getting behind the underdog, but not in a good way. Not in a positive way. In the most blatantly patronizing and mocking way possible. Be-Nice-To-The-Scrub time. We've won the game. We want a few laughs now.

A few more calls for Myron and then . . . the chant. It started low but built. And built. 'We want Myron! We want Myron!' Myron tried not to slouch. He pretended not to hear it, feigning intense concentration on what was happening on the court, hoping his cheeks weren't reddening. The chant grew louder and faster, eventually disintegrating into one word, repeated over and over, mixed with laughter:

'Myron! Myron! Myron!'

He had to defuse it. There was only one way. He

checked the clock. Still three minutes to go. He had to go in. He knew that wouldn't be the end of it, but it would at least quiet the crowd temporarily. He looked down the bench. The Kipper looked back. Myron nodded. The Kipper leaned over to Coach Walsh and whispered something. Walsh did not stand up. He simply shouted, 'Bolitar. In for Cameron.'

Myron swallowed and rose to his feet. The crowd erupted in sarcasm. He headed for the scorer's table, ripping off his sweats. His legs felt stiff and cramped. He pointed to the scorer, the scorer nodded and sounded the buzzer. Myron stepped on the court. He pointed at Cameron. Cameron jogged off. 'Kraven,' he said. The name of the man Myron would defend.

'Now reporting for Bob Cameron,' the loudspeaker began. 'Number 34. Myron Bolitar!'

The crowd went absolutely wild. Hoots, whistles, screams, laughs. Some might think they were wishing him well, but that was not really the case. They were wishing him well the same way you wish a circus clown well. They were looking for pratfalls and darn gone-it, Bolitar was their man!

Myron stepped on the court. This was, he suddenly realized, his NBA debut.

He touched the ball five times before the game ended. Each time it was met with cheer/jeers. He shot only once, from just inside the three point line. He almost didn't want to, knowing the crowd would react no matter what happened, but some things are just too automatic. There was no conscious thought. The ball went in with a happy swish. By now there were only thirty seconds left and thankfully most everyone had had enough and were heading to their cars. The sarcastic applause was minimal. But for those brief seconds when Myron caught the ball, when his fingertips found the groove, when he bent his elbow and cradled the ball half an inch above both palm and forehead, when the arm smoothed into a straight line, when the wrist flowed into a front curl, when the fingertips danced along the ball's surface and created the ideal backspin, Myron was alone. His eyes were focused on the rim, only the rim, never glancing at the ball as it arched its way toward the cylinder. For those few seconds there was only Myron and the rim and the basketball and it all felt very right.

The mood in the locker room was far more animated after the game. Myron managed to meet all of the players except TC and Greg's roommate Leon White, the one man he wanted to get close to most. Figures. He couldn't push it either; that would just backfire. Tomorrow maybe. He'd try again.

He stripped down. The knee began to tighten up, as though somebody had pulled all the tendons too taut. He slapped on an ice pack and fastened it with a stretch wrap. He limped to the showers, dried off, and was just finishing dressing when he realized TC was standing over him.

Myron looked up. TC had his various pierce-jewelry in place. Ear, of course. Three in one, four in the other. One in his nose. He wore black leather pants and a black cut-off mesh tank top, giving one an excellent view of the ring on his left nipple and the one in the belly button. Myron couldn't make out what the tattoos were. They just looked like swirls. TC wore sunglasses now, the wrap-around kind.

'Your jeweler must send you a hell of a Christmas card,' Myron said.

TC replied by sticking out his tongue and revealing another ring near the tip. Myron almost gagged. TC looked pleased by his reaction.

'You new, right?' TC said.

'Right.' Myron held out his hand. 'Myron Bolitar.'

TC ignored the hand. 'You gots to get thumped.'

'Excuse me?'

'Thumped. You the new guy. You gots to get thumped.'

Several other players started chuckling.

'Thumped?' Myron repeated.

'Yeah. You the new guy, right?'

'Right.'

'Then you gots to get thumped.'

More chuckling.

'Right,' Myron said. 'Thumped.'

'There you go.' TC nodded, snapping his fingers, pointed at Myron, left.

Myron finished dressing. Thumped?

Jessica was waiting for him outside the locker-room door. She smiled as he approached, and he smiled back, feeling goofy. She hugged him and gave him a brief kiss. He smelled her hair. Ambrosia.

'Ah,' a voice said. 'Now ain't this just too sweet?'

It was Audrey Wilson.

'Don't talk to her,' Myron said. 'She's the Antichrist.'

'Too late,' Audrey said. She put her hand through Jessica's arm. 'Jess and I are going out now to have a few drinks, talk over old times, that kind of thing.'

'God, you are shameless.' He turned to Jessica. 'Don't tell her anything.'

'I don't know anything.'

'Good point.' Myron said. 'So where are we going?'

'*We* are going nowhere,' Jessica said. She made a motion behind her with her thumb. Win was leaning against the wall, completely still and at ease. 'He said you'd be busy.'

'Oh.' Myron looked over at Win. Win nodded. Myron excused himself and made his way over.

Without preamble, Win said. 'The last cash transaction Greg made was at an ATM machine at eleven oh three P.M. the night he vanished.'

'Where?'

'Manhattan. A Chemical Bank near Eighteenth Street on the West Side.'

'It makes sense,' Myron said. 'Greg gets a call at nine eighteen P.M. from Carla. Carla tells him to meet her in the back booth. So he drives himself to the city and picks up cash before he sees her.'

Win looked at him with flat eyes. 'Thank you for that analysis of the obvious.'

'It's a gift really.'

'Yes, I know,' Win said. 'Moving right along, there are eight saloons within a four block radius of this particular ATM. I limited my search to those. Of the eight only two have what one might term a "back booth." The others had tables or dining facilities sans booths in the rear. Here are the names.'

Myron had long since gotten past asking how Win did it. 'You want me to drive?'

'I can't go,' Win said.

'Why not?'

'I'm going away for a few days.'

'When?'

'I leave from Newark airport in an hour,' Win said.

'This is sudden.'

Win didn't bother responding. The two men headed out the players' entrance. Five kids ran up to Myron and asked for his autograph. Myron obliged. One kid who looked to be around ten years old took back the paper, squinted at Myron's scrawl, and said, 'Who the hell is he?'

Another kid said, 'Some scrub.'

'Hey!' Win snapped. 'That's Mr Scrub to you.'

Myron looked at him. 'Thanks.'

Win made an it's-nothing gesture.

The first kid looked at Win. 'You anybody?'

'I'm Dwight D. Eisenhower,' Win replied.

'Who?'

Win spread his hands. 'Our blessed youth.' He walked away then without saying another word. Win was not big on good-byes. Myron reached his car. When he put the key in the door, he felt a slap on the back. It was TC. He pointed at Myron with a finger holding more jewelry than a Gabor-family reunion. 'Remember,' TC said.

Myron nodded. 'Thumped.'

'Exacto.'

Then he, too, was gone.

Chapter 7

Myron arrived at MacDougal's Pub, the first bar on Win's list. The back booth was empty so he grabbed it. He sat there for a moment, hoping a psychic force would tell him if this was the place where Greg had met up with Carla. He felt nothing – positive or negative. Maybe he should hold a séance.

The waitress came over slowly, as if the effort of crossing the floor was synonymous with wading through deep snow and she should be rewarded for it. Myron warmed her up with one of his patented smiles. The Christian Slater model – friendly yet devilish. Not to be mistaken for the Jack Nicholson model which was devilish yet friendly.

'Hi,' he said.

She put down a Rolling Rock cardboard coaster. 'What can I get you?' she asked, trying to toss up a friendly tone and falling way short. You rarely find a friendly barmaid in Manhattan, except for those born-again waitresses at chains like TGI Friday's or Bennigan's where they tell you their name and that they'll be your 'server' like you might mistake them for something else, like your 'legal consultant' or 'medical advisor.'

'Got any Yoo-Hoo?' Myron asked.

'Any what?'

'Never mind. How about a beer?'

She gave him flat eyes. 'What kind?'

Subtlety was not going to work here. 'Do you like basketball?' he asked her.

Shrug.

'Do you know who Greg Downing is?'

Nod.

'He told me about this place,' Myron said. 'Greg said he was here the other night.'

Blink.

'Did you work last Saturday night?'

Nod.

'Same station? I mean, this booth?'

Quicker nod. Getting impatient.

'Did you see him?'

'No. I got tables. Michelob okay?'

Myron looked at his watch, faked shock. 'Whoops, look at the time. I gotta go.' He gave her two dollars. 'Thanks for your time.'

The next bar on the list was called the Swiss Chalet. Not even close. A dive. The wallpaper was supposed to trick you into believing that the place was wood paneled; the effect may have worked better had the wallpaper not been peeling in so many spots. The fireplace had a flickering, Christmas-light log in it, hardly giving the place the desired ski-lodge warmth. For some reason there was one of those disco mirrored balls in the middle of the bar. No dance floor. No lights. Just the disco mirrored ball – another staple of authentic Swiss chalets, Myron surmised. The place had the stale smell of spilled beer mixed with just a hint of what might have been vomit, the kind of smell only certain bars or frat houses held, the kind where the odor had seeped into the walls like rodents that ended up dying and rotting.

The jukebox blared 'Little Red Corvette' by Prince. Or was it by the Artist Formerly Known As Prince? Wasn't that what he called himself now? But of course when 'Little Red Corvette' had been released he had been Prince. So which was it? Myron tried to reconcile this crucial dilemma, but it began to confuse him like one of those time paradoxes in the *Back to the Future* movies so he gave up.

The place was pretty empty. A guy with a Houston Astros baseball cap and bushy mustache was the sole patron seated at the bar. There was a man and woman semi-necking at a table in the center of the room – the most conspicuous table in the place, as a matter of fact. No one seemed to mind. Another male patron skulked around the back like he was in the adult movie area at his local video store.

Again Myron took the back booth. Again he struck up a conversation with a far more animated waitress. When he reached the part about Greg Downing telling him about the Swiss Chalet, she said, 'Yeah, no kidding? I only seen him in here once.'

Bingo.

'Would that have been Saturday night?'

She scrunched up her face in thought.

'Hey, Joe,' the waitress shouted to the bartender. 'Downing was in here Saturday night, right?'

'Who the fuck wants to know?' Joe shouted back from his spot behind the bar. He looked like a weasel with mousy hair. Weasel and mouse. Nice combination.

'This guy and me, we was just talking.'

Joe Weasel squinted with beady, ferret eyes. The eyes widened. 'Hey, you're the new guy, right? On the Dragons? I saw you on the news. With the dorky name.'

'Myron Bolitar,' Myron said.

'Yeah, right, Myron. That's it. You guys gonna start hanging out here?'

'I don't know.'

'We get a pretty exclusive celebrity clientele,' Joe said, wiping the bar with what looked like a gas station rag. 'You know who was in here once? Cousin Brucie. The disc jockey. Real regular guy, you know.'

'Sorry I missed that,' Myron said.

'Yeah, well we've had other celebs, right, Bone?'

The guy with the Astros hat and bushy mustache pepped up and nodded. 'Like that guy who looked like Soupy Sales. Remember him?'

'Right. Celebrities.'

'Except that wasn't really Soupy Sales. Just someone who looked like him.'

'Same difference.'

Myron said, 'Do you know Carla?'

'Carla?'

'The girl Greg was with.'

'That her name? No, never got a chance to meet her. Didn't meet Greg either. He just kinda ducked in, cognitolike. We didn't bother them.' He sort of puffed out his chest like he was about to salute. 'At the Swiss Chalet, we protect our celebrities.' He pointed at Myron with the dishrag. 'You tell the other guys that, okay?'

72

'Will do,' Myron said.

'Fact, we weren't even sure it was Greg Downing at first.'

'Like with Soupy Sales,' Bone added.

'Right, like that. Except this was really him.'

'Guy looked like Soupy though. Great actor, that Soupy.'

'And what a nickname.'

'Talent all the way round,' Bone agreed.

Myron said, 'Had he ever been in here before?'

'The guy who looked liked Soupy?'

'Moron,' Joe said, snapping the rag at Bone. 'Why the fuck would he want to know about that? He's talking about Greg Downing.'

'How the fuck was I supposed to know? I look like I work for one of those psychic networks or something?'

'Fellas,' Myron tried.

Joe held up a hand. 'Sorry, Myron. Believe me, this don't normally happen here at the Swiss Chalet. We all get along, right, Bone?'

Bone spread his arms. 'Who's not getting along?'

'My point exactly. And no, Myron, Greg isn't one of our regulars. That was his first time here.'

'Same with Cousin Brucie,' Bone added. 'He only came in that one time.'

'Right. But Cousin Brucie liked the place, I could tell.'

'He ordered a second drink. That shoulda told you something.'

'Right you are. Two drinks. Coulda just had one and left. Course, they were only Diet Cokes.'

Myron said, 'How about Carla?'

'Who?'

'The woman Greg was with.'

73

'What about her?'

'Had she been here before?'

'I never seen her here before. Bone?'

Bone shook his head. 'Nope. I woulda remembered.'

'What makes you say that?'

Without hesitation, Joe said, 'Serious hooters.'

Bone cupped his hands and stuck them in front of his chest. 'Major Charlies.'

'Not that she was good looking or anything.'

'Not at all,' Bone agreed. 'Kinda old for a young guy.'

'How old?' Myron asked.

'Older than Greg Downing, that's for sure. I'd say late forties. Bone?'

Bone nodded. 'But a first-rate set of ta-tas.'

'Humongous.'

'Mammoth.'

'Yeah, I think I got that,' Myron interrupted. 'Anything else?'

They looked puzzled.

'Eye color?' Myron tried.

Joe blinked, looked at Bone. 'Did she have eyes?'

'Damn if I know.'

'Hair color?' Myron said.

'Brown,' Joe said. 'Light brown.'

'Black,' Bone said.

'Maybe he's right,' Joe said.

'No, maybe it was on the lighter side.'

'But I'm telling you, Myron. That was some rack. Major guns.'

'Guns of Navarone,' Bone agreed.

'Did she and Greg leave together?'

Joe looked at Bone. Bone shrugged. 'I think so,' Joe said.

'Do you know what time?'

Joe shook his head.

'Bones, you know?' Myron tried.

The bill of the Astros hat jerked toward Myron like a string had been pulled. 'Not Bones, dammit!' he shrieked. 'Bone! No S at the end. Bone! B-O-N-E! No S! And what the fuck do I look like, Big Ben?'

Joe snapped the dishrag again. 'Don't insult a celebrity, moron.'

'Celebrity? Shit, Joe, he's just a scrub. Not like he's Soupy or something. He's a nobody, a zero.' Bone turned to Myron. The hostility was completely gone now. 'No offense, Myron.'

'Why would I take offense?'

'Say,' Joe said, 'you got a photograph? We can put your picture on the wall. You could autograph it to your pals at the Swiss Chalet. We should start like a celebrity wall, you know?'

'Sorry,' Myron said. 'I don't have one on me.'

'Can you send us one? Autographed, I mean. Or bring it next time you come.'

'Er, next time.'

Myron continued to question them but learned nothing more except Soupy Sales's birthday. He left and headed up the block. He passed a Chinese restaurant with dead ducks hung in the window. Duck carcasses, the ideal appetite whetter. Maybe Burger King should hang slaughtered cows in the window. Really draw the kids in.

He tried putting the pieces together a bit. Carla calls Greg on the phone and tells him to meet her at the Swiss Chalet. Why? Why there of all places? Did they not want to be seen? Why not? And who the hell is Carla anyway? How does all this fit into Greg's vanishing act? And what

75

about the blood in the basement? Did they go back to Greg's house or did Greg go home alone? Was Carla the girl he lived with? And if so, why meet here?

Myron was so preoccupied he didn't spot the man until he almost bumped into him. Of course calling him a man might be a bit of an understatement. More like a brick wall doubling as a human being. He stood in Myron's way. He wore one of those pectoral-displaying ribbed T-shirts under an unbuttoned flower-patterned semi-blouse. A gold horn dangled between his near-cleavage. Muscle-head. Myron tried to pass him on the left. The brick wall blocked his path. Myron tried to pass him on the right. The brick wall blocked his path. Myron went back and forth one more time. Brick Wall followed suit.

'Say,' Myron said, 'you know the cha-cha?'

The brick wall showed about as much reaction as one might expect from a brick wall. Then again it wasn't one of Myron's better quips. The man was truly enormous, the size of your average lunar eclipse. Myron heard foot-steps. Another man, this one on the large size but at least of the human variety, came up behind Myron. The second man wore fatigue camouflage pants, a popular new urban fashion trend.

'Where's Greg?' Camouflage Pants asked.

Myron feigned startled. 'What? Oh, I didn't see you.'

'Huh?'

'In those pants,' Myron said. 'You just blended into the background.'

Camouflage didn't like that. 'Where's Greg?'

'Greg?' Snappy retort.

'Yeah. Where is he?'

'Who?'

'Greg.'

76

'Greg who?'

'You trying to be funny?'

'What, you think this is funny?'

Camouflage looked over at Brick Wall. Brick Wall remained completely silent. Myron knew that there was a very real possibility of a physical altercation. He also knew he was good at such things. He also knew – or at least figured – that these two goons were probably good too. Despite Bruce Lee movies, one man defeating two or more quality opponents was nearly impossible. Experienced fighters were not stupid. They worked as a team. They never rushed one at a time.

'So,' Myron said. 'You guys want to catch a beer? Chat this through.'

Camouflage made a scoffing noise. 'We look like guys who like to chat?'

Myron motioned to Brick Wall. 'He does.'

There were three ways to get out of a situation like this unharmed. One was to run, which was always a good option. Problem was, his two adversaries were close enough yet spaced far enough to tackle and/or slow him down. Too risky. Second option: your opponents underestimate you. You act scared and cower and then whammo, you surprise them. Unlikely for Myron. Goons rarely underestimate a guy six-four, two-twenty. Third option: you strike first and hard. By doing this you increase the likelihood of putting one out of commission before the other one can react. This action however required a delicate balance. Until someone strikes, you really cannot say for sure that a physical altercation could not be avoided altogether. But if you wait for someone to strike, this option becomes null and void. Win liked option three. Then again Win liked option three even if there was only one opponent.

Myron never got the chance to make a selection. Brick Wall slammed a fist into the small of Myron's back. Myron sensed the blow coming. He shifted enough to avoid both the kidney and serious damage. At the same time he spun and delivered an elbow strike to Brick Wall's nose. There was a satisfying, crunching noise like a fist closing over a bird's nest.

The victory was short-lived. As Myron had feared, these guys knew what they were doing. Camouflage Pants struck at the same time, connecting where his comrade had failed. Pain erupted in Myron's kidney. His knees buckled but he fought it off. He doubled over toward Brick Wall and threw a back kick, his foot snapping out like a piston. His lack of balance threw off his aim. The blow landed on Camouflage's thigh. It didn't do much damage but it was powerful enough to push him away. Brick Wall was starting to recover. He groped blindly and found Myron's hair. He grabbed and pulled up. Myron pinned the hand with one of his own, digging his fingernails into the sensitive pressure points between the joints. Brick Wall screamed. Camouflage Pants was back. He punched Myron straight in the stomach. It hurt. A lot. Myron knew he was in trouble. He went down to one knee and bounced up, a palm strike at the ready. It connected with Brick Wall's groin. Brick Wall's eyes bulged. He dropped like somebody had pulled a stool out from under him. Camouflage Pants connected with a solid shot to the side of Myron's head. Numbness flowed into Myron's skull. Another blow landed. Myron's eyes began to lose focus. He tried to stand up but his legs wouldn't let him. He felt a kick land on a rib. The world began to spin.

'Hey! Hey, what you doing? Hey, you!'

'Stop it! What the fuck!'

In his haze Myron recognized the voices. Joe and Bone from the bar. Myron took the opportunity to scramble away on all fours. There was no need. Camouflage Pants had already helped Brick Wall to his feet. Both men ran.

Joe and Bone quickly came over and looked down at Myron.

'You okay?' Joe asked.

Myron nodded.

'You won't forget about sending us that autographed picture, will you? Cousin Brucie never sent one.'

'I'll send you two,' Myron said.

Chapter 8

He convinced Joe and Bone not to call the cops. They didn't take much convincing. Most people do not like activities that involve law enforcement. They helped Myron into a taxi. The driver wore a turban and listened to country music. Multiculturalism. Myron spit out Jessica's Soho address and collapsed into the ripped cushions. The driver wasn't interested in conversation. Good.

Myron mentally checked over his body. Nothing broken. The ribs would be bruised at worst. Nothing he couldn't play through. The head was another matter. Tylenol with codeine would help tonight, then he could move down to Advil or something in the morning. There was nothing much you could do for head trauma but give it time and control the pain.

Jessica met him at the door in her bathrobe. He felt, as he often did around her, a little short of breath. She skipped admonishments, drew a bath, helped him undress, crawled in behind him. The water felt good against his skin. He leaned back on her as she wrapped washcloths around his head. He let loose a deep, totally content breath.

'When did you go to medical, school?' he asked.

From behind him Jessica kissed his cheek. 'Feeling better?'

'Yes, Doctor. Much better.'

'You want to tell me about it?'

He did. She listened in silence, her fingertips gently massaging his temples. Her touch was soothing. Myron imagined there were better things in life than being in this tub leaning back against the woman he loved, but for the life of him he couldn't think of any. The pain began to dull and slacken.

'So who do you think they were?' she asked.

'No idea,' Myron said. 'I imagine they're hired goons.'

'And they wanted to know where Greg was?'

'Seems so.'

'If two goons like that were looking for me,' she said, 'I might disappear too.'

The thought had crossed Myron's mind too. 'Yes.'

'So what's your next step?'

He smiled and closed his eyes. 'What? No lectures? No telling me it's too dangerous?'

'Too cliché,' she said. 'Besides, there's something else here.'

'What do you mean?'

'Something about all this you're not telling me.'

'I—'

She put a finger over his lips. 'Just tell me what you plan on doing next.'

He settled back down. Scary how easily she read him. 'I have to start talking to people.'

'Like?'

'His agent. His roommate, a guy named Leon White. Emily.'

'Emily. That would be your old college sweetheart?'

'Uh huh,' Myron said. Quick subject change before she started reading him again. 'How was your evening with Audrey?'

'Fine. We mostly talked about you.'

'What about me?'

Jessica began to stroke his chest. The touch slowly drifted away from being merely soothing. Her fingertips caressed his chest with a feather touch. Gently. Too gently. She was strumming him like Perlman on a violin.

'Uh, Jess.'

She shushed him. Her voice was soft. 'Your ass,' she said.

'My ass?'

'Yep, that's what we talked about.' To emphasize the point her hand cupped a cheek. 'Even Audrey had to admit it was edible, running up and down the court like that.'

'I have a mind too,' Myron said. 'A brain. Feelings.'

She lowered her mouth toward his ear. When her lips touched the lobe, he felt a jolt. 'Who cares?'

'Uh, Jess . . .'

'Shhh,' she said as her other hand slid down his chest. 'I'm the doctor here, remember?'

Chapter 9

The ringing phone jabbed at the base of nerves in the back of his skull. Myron's eyes blinked open. Sunlight knifed through the slit in the curtain. He checked next to him in the bed – first with his hands, then with his eyes. Jessica wasn't there. The phone continued to blare. Myron reached for it.

'Hello.'

'So this is where you are.'

He closed his eyes. The ache in his head multiplied tenfold. 'Hi, Mom.'

'You don't sleep in your home anymore?'

His home was the basement of his parents' house, the same house in which he'd been raised. More and more he was spending his nights at Jessica's. It was probably a good thing. He was thirty-two; he was fairly normal; he had plenty of money. There was no reason to still be living with Mommy and Daddy.

'How's your trip?' he asked. His mother and father

were on some tour of Europe. One of those bus tours that hit twelve cities in four days.

'You think I called at the Vienna Hilton's long distant rates to chitchat about our itinerary?'

'Guess not.'

'You know how much it cost to call from a hotel in Vienna? With all their surcharges and taxes and everything?'

'A lot, I'm sure.'

'I have the rates right here. I'll tell you exactly. Hold on. Al, what did I do with those rates?'

'Mom, it's not important.'

'I had it a second ago. Al?'

'Why don't you tell me when you get home?' Myron suggested. 'It'll give me something to look forward to.'

'Save the fresh remarks for your friends, okay? You know very well why I'm calling.'

'I don't, Mom.'

'Fine, then I'll tell you. One of the other people on this tour – the Smeltmans, very nice couple. He's in the jewelry business. Marvin, his name is. I think. They have a shop in Montclair. We used to drive by it all the time when you were a kid. It's on Bloomfield Avenue, near that movie theater. Remember?'

'Uh huh.' He had no idea what she was talking about but it was easier.

'So the Smeltmans talked to their son on the phone last night. He called them, Myron. He had their itinerary and everything. Just called his parents to make sure they were having a nice time, that kind of thing.'

'Uh huh.' Mom was in decompensation mode. There was no way to stop it. She could go in a heartbeat from the modern, intelligent woman he knew her to be to

84

something out of summer stock *Fiddler on the Roof*. Right now she was Golda heading toward Yenta.

'Anyway the Smeltmans brag how they're on the same trip with Myron Bolitar's parents. Big deal, right? Who knows you anymore? You haven't played in years. But the Smeltmans are big basketball fans. Go figure. Their son used to watch you play or something, I don't know. So anyway the son – I think his name is Herb or Herbie or Ralph, something like that – he tells them you're playing professional basketball. That the Dragons signed you. He says you're making a comeback or something, what do I know? Your father is so embarrassed. I mean, complete strangers are talking about it and your own parents don't even know. We thought the Smeltmans were crazy.'

'It's not what you think,' Myron said.

'What's not what I think?' she countered. 'You shoot around in the driveway a little. Okay, no big deal. But I don't understand. You never even mentioned you were playing again.'

'I'm not.'

'Don't lie to me. You scored two points last night. Your father called Sports Phone. You know what it cost to call Sports Phone from here?'

'Mom, it's no big deal.'

'Listen to me, Myron, you know your father. The man pretends it doesn't mean anything. He loves you no matter what, you know that. But he hasn't stopped smiling since he heard. He wants to fly home right now.'

'Please don't.'

'Don't,' she repeated, exasperated. 'You tell him, Myron. The man is loo-loo, you know that. A crazy person. So tell me what's going on.'

'It's a long story, Mom.'

'But it's true? You're playing again?'

'Only temporarily.'

'What does that mean, "only temporarily"?'

Jessica's Call Waiting clicked in. 'Mom, I gotta go. I'm sorry I didn't tell you earlier.'

'What? That's it?'

'I'll tell you more later.'

Surprisingly she backed off. 'You be careful with your knee.'

'I will.'

He changed over to the other line. It was Esperanza. She didn't bother with hello.

'It's not Greg's blood,' she said.

'What?'

'The blood you found in the basement,' she said. 'It's AB positive. Greg's blood type is O negative.'

Myron had not expected to hear this. He tried to reconcile it in his head. 'Maybe Clip was right. Maybe it was one of Greg's kids.'

'Impossible,' she said.

'Why?'

'Didn't you take basic biology in high school?'

'Eighth grade. But I was too busy staring at Mary Ann Palmiero. What?'

'AB is rare. In order for a kid to have it, his parents have to be A and B or it's impossible. In other words, if Greg is O, then his kids can't be AB.'

'Maybe it's a friend's,' Myron tried. 'Maybe one of the kids had a friend over.'

'Sure,' Esperanza said. 'That's probably it. The kids have some friends over. One of them bleeds all over the place and nobody cleans it up. Oh and then by a strange coincidence Greg vanishes.'

Myron threaded the phone cord through his fingers like his hand was a loom. 'Not Greg's blood,' he repeated. 'Now what?'

Esperanza didn't bother responding.

'How the hell am I supposed to investigate something like this without getting anyone suspicious?' he went on. 'I have to ask people questions, right? They're going to want to know why.'

'I feel very sorry for you,' Esperanza said in a tone that made clear she was anything but. 'I got to get to the office. You coming in?'

'Maybe this afternoon. I'm going to see Emily this morning.'

'Is that the old girlfriend Win told me about?'

'Yes,' Myron said.

'Don't take any chances. Put on a condom now.' She hung up.

Not Greg's blood. Myron didn't get it. As he drifted off to sleep last night he had worked up a neat little theory that went something like this: the hoods were searching for Greg. Maybe they had roughed him up a bit, made him bleed a little. Just to show him they meant serious business. Greg had reacted by running away.

It all sort of fit. It explained the blood in the basement. It explained why Greg suddenly took off. Yep, all a very nice and neat equation: One beating plus one death threat equaled a man on the run.

Problem was, the blood in the basement was not Greg's. Kinda put a damper on the theory. If Greg had been beaten in the basement, then it would have been his blood. Greg would have bled his own blood, not someone else's. In fact, it was very difficult to bleed someone else's blood. Myron shook his head. He needed a shower. A bit more deducing like this and the slaughtered-chicken theory would begin to pick up steam.

Myron soaped himself up, then turned his back to the shower and let the water cascade over his shoulders and down his chest. He toweled off and got dressed. Jessica was on the word processor in the other room. He had learned never to disturb her when the keyboard was clacking. He left a quick note and slipped out. He grabbed the 6 train up to midtown and walked to the Kinney lot on 46th Street. Mario tossed him the keys without glancing up from his paper. He picked up the FDR north at 62nd Street and took it to the Harlem River Drive. There was a slow down for right lane construction, but he made it to the George Washington Bridge in pretty good time. He took Route 4 through a place called Paramus, which was actually a giant mall pretending to also be a township. He veered to the right and passed the Nabisco building on Route 208. He was hoping for a factory Ritz-whiff, but today he got nothing.

As he pulled up to Emily's house, déjà vu swatted him in the back of the head like a father's warning blow. He had been here before, of course, during college breaks in their courting days. The house was brick and modern and fairly huge. It sat in a well-groomed cul-de-sac. The backyard was fenced. He remembered that there was a swimming pool in the back. He remembered that there was also a gazebo. He remembered making love with Emily in the gazebo, their clothes wrapped around ankles, the humidity coating their skin with a thin layer of sweat. The sweet bird of youth.

He parked the car, pulled the key out of the ignition, and just sat there. He had not seen Emily in more than ten years. Much had happened in the ensuing years, but he still feared her reaction to seeing him. The mental image of Emily opening the door, screaming 'Bastard,' then slamming it in his face was one of the reasons he hadn't worked up the nerve to call first.

He looked out the car window. There was no movement on the street. Then again there were only ten houses. He debated his approach and came up with nothing. He checked his watch, but the time didn't register in his head. He sighed. One thing was for sure: he couldn't sit here all day. This was a nice neighborhood, the kind where someone would spot him and call the police. Time to get a move on. He opened the door and stepped out. The development was at least fifteen years old but it still looked new. All the yards were just a little too sparse. Not enough trees and shrubbery yet. The grass looked like a guy with a bad hair transplant.

Myron walked up the brick path. He checked his palms. They were wet. He rang the doorbell. Part of him flashed back to earlier visits, his mind playing along with the long, still-familiar chime of the bell. The door opened. It was Emily.

'Well, well, well,' she said. Myron could not tell if the tone was one of surprise or sarcasm. Emily had changed. She looked a little thinner, a bit more toned. Her face was less fleshy too, accentuating the cheekbones. Her hair was cut shorter and styled. 'If it isn't the good one I let get away.'

'Hi, Emily.' Mr Big Opening.

'Here to propose?' she asked.

'Been there, done that.'

'But you didn't mean it, Myron. I wanted sincerity back then.'

'And now?'

'Now I realize sincerity is overrated.' She flashed him a smile.

'You look good, Emily,' he said. Get Myron on a roll and it's one good line after another.

'So do you,' she said. 'But I'm not going to help you.'

'Help me what?'

She made a face. 'Come on in.'

He followed her inside. The house was full of skylights and cathedral ceilings and white painted walls. Airy. The front foyer was done in some expensive tile. She led Myron to the living room. He sat on a white couch. The floors were beechwood. It was exactly the same as it was ten years ago. Either they had gotten the exact same couches again or their house guests had been exceptionally well behaved. There wasn't a spot on them. The only mess was a pile of newspapers in the corner. Mostly daily tabloids, from the looks of it. A *New York Post* front-page headline read SCANDAL! in huge 72 point print Specific.

An old dog traipsed into the room on rigid legs. It looked like he was trying to wag his tail, but the result was a pitiful sway. He managed to lick Myron's hand with a dry tongue.

'Look at that,' Emily said. 'Benny remembers you.'

Myron stiffened. 'This is Benny?'

She nodded.

Emily's family had bought the overactive puppy for her younger brother Todd when Myron and Emily had first started dating. Myron was there when they brought the puppy home from the breeder. Little Benny had stumbled around with blinking eyes and then peed on this very floor. No one cared. Benny quickly got used to people. He greeted everyone by jumping on them, believing in a way only a dog could that no one would ever do him harm. Benny was not jumping now. He looked very old. He looked a brief step away from death. A sudden sadness swept through Myron.

'You looked good last night,' Emily said. 'It was nice seeing you back on the court.'

'Thanks.' The quips never stop.

'Are you thirsty?' she asked. 'I could make you some lemonade. Like in a Tennessee Williams play. Lemonade for the gentleman caller, except I doubt Amanda Wingfield used a Crystal Light mix.' Before he could answer she disappeared around the corner. Benny looked up at Myron, straggling to see through milky cataracts. Myron scratched the dog's ear. The tail picked up a bit of velocity. Myron smiled sadly at Benny. Benny moved closer, as if he understood how Myron felt and appreciated the sentiment. Emily returned with two glasses of lemonade.

'Here,' she said. She handed him a glass and sat down.

'Thank you.' Myron took a sip.

'So what's next on your agenda, Myron?'

'Next?'

'Another comeback?'

'I don't understand.'

Emily gave him the smile again. 'First you replace Greg on the court,' she said. 'Maybe next you'll want to replace him in the bedroom.'

Myron almost gagged on his lemonade, but he managed to smother the sound. Going for the shock. Classic Emily. 'Not funny,' he said.

'I'm just having a little fun,' she said.

'Yes, I know.'

She put her elbow on the back of the couch and

propped up her head with her hand. 'I see you're dating Jessica Culver,' she said.

'Yep.'

'I like her books.'

'I'll tell her.'

'But we both know the truth.'

'What's that?'

She leaned forward now and took a slow sip from her glass. 'Sex with her isn't as good as it was with me.'

More classic Emily. 'You're sure about that?' he said.

'Very sure,' she replied. 'I'm not being immodest. I'm sure your Ms Culver is quite skilled. But with me it was new. It was discovery. It was impossibly hot. Neither of us can ever recapture that rapture with anyone else. It'd be impossible. It would be like going back in time.'

'I don't compare,' Myron said.

With a smile and a tilt of the head, she said, 'Bullshit.'

'You don't want me to compare.'

The smile was unfazed. 'Come, come now, Myron. You're not going to give me that spiritual crap, are you? You're not going to tell me it's better because you share a deep and beautiful relationship and thus the sex is beyond something physical? That line would be so unbecoming on you.'

Myron did not respond. He didn't know what to say and he didn't feel very comfortable with the conversation. 'What did you mean before?' he asked, shifting gears. 'When you said you wouldn't help me.'

'Exactly what I meant.'

'What won't you help with?'

Again the smile. 'Was I ever stupid, Myron?'

'Never,' he said.

'Do you really think I believed that comeback story? Or

the one about Greg being' – she made quote marks in the air – ' "in seclusion" for an ankle injury? Your visit here just confirms my suspicion.'

'What suspicion?'

'Greg is missing. You're trying to find him.'

'What makes you think Greg is missing?'

'Please, Myron, don't play games with me. You owe me that much at least.'

He nodded slowly. 'Do you know where he is?'

'No. But I hope the bastard is dead and rotting in a hole.'

'Stop mincing words,' Myron said. 'Tell me how you really feel.'

The smile was sadder this time. Myron felt a pang. Greg and Emily had fallen in love. They'd been married. They had two children. What had torn that all apart? Was it something recent . . . or was it something in their pasts, something tainted from the beginning? Myron felt his throat go dry.

'When was the last time you saw Greg?' he asked.

'A month ago,' she said.

'Where?'

'In divorce court.'

'Are you two on speaking terms?'

'I meant what I said before. About him being dead and rotting.'

'I'll take that as a no.'

Emily nodded a suit-yourself.

'If he was hiding, do you have any idea where?'

'Nope.'

'No summer house? No place he liked to get away?'

'Nope.'

'Do you know if Greg had a girlfriend?'

93

'Nope. But I would pity the poor woman.'

'Have you ever heard the name Carla?'

She hesitated. Her index finger tapped her knee, an old gesture so familiar to him it almost hurt to watch. 'Wasn't there a Carla who lived on my floor at Duke?' she asked. 'Yes, Carla Anderson. Sophomore year, wasn't it? Pretty girl.'

'Anything more recent?'

'No.' She sat up, crossed her legs. 'How's Win?'

'The same.'

'One of life's constants,' she said. 'He loves you, you know. I wonder if he's a latent homosexual.'

'Two men can love each other and not be gay,' Myron said.

She arched an eyebrow. 'You really think so?'

He was letting her get to him. Bad mistake. 'Are you aware that Greg was going to sign an endorsement deal?' he asked her.

That got her attention. 'Are you serious?'

'Yes.'

'A big one?'

'Huge from my understanding,' Myron replied. 'With Forte.'

Emily's hands tightened. She would have made fists had her nails not been so long. 'Son of a bitch.'

'What?'

'He waited until the divorce had been finalized and I got squat. Then he signs the deal. That son of a bitch.'

'What do you mean, squat? Greg was still wealthy.'

She shook her head. 'His agent lost it all. Or so he claimed in court.'

'Martin Felder?'

'Yep. Didn't have a penny to his name. Son of a bitch.'

94

'But Greg still works with Felder. Why would he stay with a guy who lost his money?'

'I don't know, Myron.' Her voice was clipped and annoyed. 'Perhaps the son of a bitch was lying. It wouldn't be the first time.'

Myron waited. Emily looked at him. Tears welled in her eyes but she bit them back down. She stood and walked to the other side of the room. Her back was now to him. She looked out the sliding glass doors into the fenced-in yard. The pool was covered with a tarp; random sticks and leaves clung to the aqua. Two children appeared. A boy of about ten chased a girl who looked to be eight. They were both laughing with faces wide and open and a little rosy from either cold or exertion. The boy stopped when he saw his mother. He gave her a big smile and wave. Emily raised her hand and gave a small wave back. The children ran on. Emily crossed her arms like she was hugging herself.

'He wants to take them away from me,' she said in a remarkably calm voice. 'He'll do anything to get them.'

'Like?'

'Like the sleaziest things you can imagine.'

'How sleazy?'

'None of your goddamn business.' She stopped. She still had her back to him. Myron could see her shoulders quake. 'Get out,' she said.

'Emily . . .'

'You want to help him, Myron.'

'I want to find him. There's a difference.'

She shook her head. 'You don't owe him,' she said. 'I know you think you do. It's your way. I saw the guilt in your face back then, and I could still see it the second I opened the front door. It's over, Myron. It had nothing to do with what happened to us. He never found out.'

'Is that supposed to make me feel better?' he asked.

She spun toward him. 'It's not supposed to make you feel better,' she snapped. 'It's not about you. I'm the one who married him. I'm the one who betrayed him. I can't believe you're still beating yourself up about it.'

Myron swallowed. 'He visited me in the hospital. After I got injured. He sat and talked with me for hours.'

'And that makes him a swell guy?'

'We shouldn't have done it.'

'Grow up,' she said. 'It was more than ten years ago. Gone and forgotten.'

Silence.

After some time had passed, Myron looked up at her. 'Could you really lose your kids?' he asked.

'Yes.'

'How far would you go to keep them?'

'As far as I had to.'

'Would you kill to keep them?' Myron asked.

'Yes.' No hesitation.

'Did you?'

'No.'

'Do you have any idea why some goons would be looking for Greg?'

'No.'

'You didn't hire them?'

'If I did,' she said, 'I wouldn't tell you. But if these "goons" want to hurt Greg, I'll do all I can to help them locate him.'

Myron put down the lemonade. 'I guess I better get going.'

She showed him to the door. Before she opened it, she

put a hand on his arm. Her touch burned right through the material. 'It's okay,' she said gently. 'Let it go. Greg never found out.'

Myron nodded.

She took a deep breath and smiled again. Her voice returned to its normal tone. 'It was good to see you again, Myron.'

'Same here,' he said.

'Come back again, will you?' She was trying so hard to be casual. Myron knew it was just an act, one he had seen before. 'Perhaps we can have a quick fling for old times' sake. Couldn't hurt, right?'

One last grasp at the shock. Myron pulled away. 'That's what we said last time,' he said. 'And it still hurts.'

Chapter 10

'It was the night before they got married,' Myron began. He was back at his office. Esperanza sat in front of him. Her eyes were on him, but he didn't know that. He stared at the ceiling, his fingers laced and resting on his chest. He had his chair tilted far back. 'Do you want the details?'

'Only if you want to tell me,' Esperanza said.

He told her. He told her how Emily had called him. He told her how she came to his room. He told her that they'd both had too much to drink. He said that last one as a sort of trial balloon, but a quick glance at Esperanza blew that particular old balloon out of the sky. She interrupted with one question.

'How long after the draft did all this take place?'

Myron smiled at the ceiling. She was so damned perceptive. There was no reason to answer.

'I assume,' Esperanza continued, 'that this little tryst occurred sometime between the pro draft and your injury.'

'You assume correctly.'

'Ah,' she said with a small nod. 'So let me see if I got the true picture now. It's your senior year of college. Your team won the NCAA finals – a point for you. You end up losing Emily and she ends up engaged to Greg – a point for him. The draft comes. Greg is the seventh overall pick; you are the eighth – a point for Greg.'

Myron closed his eyes and nodded. 'You're wondering if I was trying to even the score.'

'Not wondering,' Esperanza corrected. 'The answer is obvious.'

'You're not helping.'

'You want help, go to a shrink,' she said. 'You want the truth, come to me.'

She was right. He took his hands off his chest. Keeping the fingers laced, he placed them behind his head. He put his feet on the desk.

'Did she cheat on you with him?' she asked.

'No.'

'You're sure?'

'Yes. They met after we broke up.'

'Too bad,' she said. 'It would have given you a nice out.'

'Yeah, Pity.'

'So this is why you feel obligated to Greg? Because you slept with his fiancée?'

'That's a big part of it, but there's more to it than that.'

'Like?'

'It's going to sound corny, but there's always been a bond between us.'

'A bond?'

Myron's line of vision traveled from the ceiling to his movie-still wall. Woody Allen and Diane Keaton were enjoying a Manhattan moment in *Annie Hall*. Bogie and

Bergman leaned on Sam's piano back in the days when Paris had been theirs. 'Greg and I were once-in-a-lifetime competitors,' he said. 'And there is a special bond between competitors. Kinda like Magic Johnson and Larry Bird. You become defined by one another. It was like that with Greg and me. It was unspoken, but we both knew the bond was there.'

He stopped. Esperanza waited in silence. 'When I hurt my knee,' Myron continued, 'Greg visited me in the hospital. He showed up the very next day. I woke up from some pain medication and there he was. Sitting with Win. And I instantly understood. Win must have understood too, otherwise he would have thrown him out.'

Esperanza nodded.

'Greg stayed around too. He helped with rehab. That's what I mean by a bond. He was devastated by the news because when I got hurt, it was like a part of him was gone too. He tried to tell me why it meant so much to him, but he couldn't put it into words. It didn't matter. I knew. He just had to be there.'

'And you hurt your knee how long after you'd slept with his new bride?'

'About a month.'

'Did seeing him all the time help or hurt?'

'Yes.'

She said nothing.

'Do you understand now?' he asked. 'Do you see why I have to pursue this? You're probably right. Sleeping with Emily was probably nothing more than payback for not getting drafted before Greg. Just another stupid battle. But what kind of way was that for a marriage to start? I owe Greg Downing. It's that simple.'

'No,' she said. 'It's not that simple.'

'Why not?'

'Because too much of your past is resurfacing. First Jessica—'

'Don't start with that.'

'I'm not,' she said calmly. Her voice was rarely calm when it came to Jessica. 'I'm just stating a fact. Jessica crushed you when she left. You never got over her.'

'But she's back now.'

'Yes.'

'So what's your point?'

'Basketball also crushed you when it left. You never got over it.'

'Sure I did.'

She shook her head. 'First you spent three years trying every possible remedy to fix your knee.'

'I just tried to get better,' he interjected. 'Nothing wrong with that, is there?'

'Nothing. But you were a pain in the ass. You pushed Jessica away. I'm not forgiving her for what she did to you. You didn't ask for that. But you played a part in her leaving.'

'Why are you bringing this all up?'

She shook her head. 'You're the one who's bringing it all up. Your entire past. Jessica and now basketball. You want us to watch you go through all this again, but we won't.'

'Go through what?'

But she didn't answer. Instead she asked, 'Do you want to know why I didn't go see you play last night?'

He nodded, still not facing her. His cheeks felt flush and hot.

'Because with Jessica, at least there's a *chance* you won't get hurt again. There's a chance the witch smartened up.

But with basketball, there is no chance. You can't come back.'

'I can handle it,' he said, hearing those words yet again.

She said nothing.

Myron stared off. He barely heard the phone ring. Neither one of them moved to answer it. 'You think I should drop this?' he asked.

'Yes. I agree with Emily. She's the one who betrayed him. You were just a handy tool. If what happened somehow poisoned their relationship, it was her doing. It was her decision. You don't owe Greg Downing a thing.'

'Even if what you're saying is true,' he said, 'that bond is still there.'

'Bullshit,' Esperanza said. 'That's just a load of pedantic, macho bullshit. You're just proving my point. There's no bond anymore, if there ever was one. Basketball hasn't been a part of your life for a decade. The only reason you think the bond is still there is because you're playing again.'

There was a loud pounding on the door. The frame shook and almost gave way. Myron startled upright. 'Who's manning the phones?' he asked.

Esperanza smiled.

'Oh no.'

'Come in,' Esperanza said.

The door opened. Myron's feet fell to the floor. Though he had seen her many times before, his jaw still dropped open. Big Cyndi ducked in. She was mammoth. Six-five and over three hundred pounds. Cyndi wore a white T-shirt with the sleeves ripped off at the biceps. Her arms were the envy of Hulk Hogan. Her makeup was more garish than it had been in the ring. Her hair was purple spikes; her mascara was also purple though a darker shade than her hair. Her lipstick was a red smear. Cyndi looked like something out of Rocky Horror Picture Show. She was the single most frightening sight Myron had ever seen.

'Hi, Cyndi,' Myron tried.

Cyndi growled. She held up her middle finger, turned, stepped back through the door, closed it.

'What the—'

'She's telling you to pick up line one,' Esperanza said.

'Cyndi's answering phones?'

'Yes.'

'She doesn't talk!'

'In person. On the phone she's very good.'

'Jesus Christ.'

'Pick up the phone and stop whining.'

Myron did so. It was Lisa, their contact at New York Bell. Most people think that only the police can get phone records. Not true. Almost every private eye in the country has a contact at their local phone company. It's just a matter of simply paying someone off. A month's phone record can cost you anywhere from one thousand to five thousand dollars. Myron and Win had met Lisa during their days with the feds. She didn't take money, but they always took care of her in some way or another. 'I got what Win wanted,' Lisa said.

'Go ahead.'

'The call at nine eighteen P.M. came from a public phone located in a diner near Dyckman Street and Broadway,' she said.

'Isn't that up near Two Hundredth Street?'

'I think so. You want the phone number?'

Carla had called Greg from a diner on 200th Street? Weirder and weirder. 'If you have it.'

103

She gave it to him. 'Hope that helps.'

'It does, Lisa. Thanks.' He held up the paper to Esperanza. 'Lookie what I got,' he said. 'A real live clue.'

Chapter 11

To be fair, the Parkview Diner lived up to its name. You did indeed have a view of Lieutenant William Tighe Park across the street; it was smaller than the average backyard with shrubs so high you really couldn't see the landscaped garden within. A wire-mesh fence enclosed the grounds. Hung on the fence in several places were signs that read in big, bold letters: DO NOT FEED THE RATS. No joke. In smaller print the warning was repeated in Spanish: *No Des Comida a Las Ratas*. The signs had been placed there by a group calling itself the Quality of Life Zone. Myron shook his head. Only in New York would this be a problem – people who could not contain themselves from the seductive lure of feeding vermin. Myron glanced again at the sign, then the diner. Rats. Quite the appetite-enhancer.

He crossed the street. Two levels above the Parkview Diner, a dog squeezed his head through the grates of a fire escape and barked at passing pedestrians. The Parkview's green overhang was ripped in several spots. The letters were faded to the point of unintelligibility, and the support pole was bent so far that Myron had to duck to get to the door. There was a poster of a gyro sandwich in the window. Today's specials, according to a blackboard in the same window, included eggplant parmigiana and chicken à la king. The soup was beef consommé. There were permits from the City of New York Department of Buildings stuck on the door like car-inspection decals.

Myron entered and was immediately greeted by the familiar yet nonspecific smell of a Manhattan diner. Fat was in the air. Taking a deep breath felt as if it would clog an artery. A waitress with hair bleached to the point of straw offered him a table. Myron asked her for the manager. Using her pencil she pointed over her shoulder at a man behind the counter.

'That's Hector,' she said. 'He owns the place.'

Myron thanked her and grabbed a soda-fountain stool at the counter. He debated spinning himself in the seat and decided the act might be viewed as immature. Two stools to his right, an unshaven, perhaps homeless man with black Thom McAn sneakers and a tattered overcoat smiled and nodded. Myron nodded and smiled back. The man went back to his coffee. He raised his shoulders and huddled into the drink as though he suspected someone might try to swipe it in mid-sip.

Myron picked up a vinyl menu with cracked binding. He opened it but didn't really read it. There were a lot of worn index cards jammed into protective plastic cases announcing various specials. Worn was an apt description of the Parkview Diner, but it didn't fairly convey the overall impression. There was something welcoming and even clean about this place. The counter gleamed. So did the utensils and the silver milkshake maker and the soda fountain. Most patrons read a newspaper or gabbed with one another as if they were eating at home. They knew their waitress's name, and you could bet your last dollar she didn't introduce herself and tell them she was going to be their server when they first sat down.

Hector the owner was busy at the grill. Almost two P.M. It wasn't the height of the lunch hour, but business was still pretty brisk. He barked out some orders in Spanish, his eyes never leaving the food. Then he turned around with a polite smile, wiped his hands on a rag, and asked Myron if he could help him. Myron asked if he had a pay phone.

'No, sir, I'm sorry,' Hector answered. The Hispanic accent was there, but Hector had worked on it. 'There's one on the street corner. On the left.'

Myron looked at the number Lisa had given him. He read it out loud. Hector did several things at the same time. He flipped burgers, folded over an omelette, checked the french fries. His eyes were everywhere – the cash register, the clientele at both the tables and the counter, the kitchen to his left.

'Oh that,' Hector said. 'It's in the back. In the kitchen.'

'The kitchen?'

'Yes, sir.' Still polite.

'A pay phone in the kitchen?'

'Yes, sir,' Hector said. He was on the short side, thin under his white apron and polyester black pants. His nose had been broken several times. His forearms looked like steel cords. 'It's for my staff.'

'Don't you have a business phone?'

'Of course we do.' His voice spiked up a bit now, as if the question was an insult. 'We do a big takeout and delivery business here. Lots of people order lunch from us. We have a fax machine too. But I don't want my staff tying up the lines, you know? You get a busy signal, you give your business to someone else, yes? So I put a pay phone in the back.'

'I see.' An idea came to Myron. 'Are you telling me customers never use it?'

'Well, sir, if a customer truly insists, I would never refuse him.' The practiced politeness of a good businessman. 'The customer must come first at the Parkview. Always.'

'Has a customer ever insisted?'

'No, sir. I don't think any customers even know we have it.'

'Can you tell me who was using the pay phone at nine eighteen P.M. last Saturday?'

That question got his attention. 'Excuse me?' Myron started to repeat the question but Hector interrupted him. 'Why would you want to know that?'

'My name is Bernie Worley,' Myron said. 'I'm a product supervising agent with AT&T.' *A product what?* 'Somebody is trying to cheat us, sir, and we are not happy about it.'

'Cheat you?'

'A Y511.'

'A what?'

'A Y511,' Myron repeated. You start tossing the bull, your best bet is to just keep tossing. 'It's an electronic monitoring device built in Hong Kong. It's new on the market, but we're onto it. Sold on the streets. Somebody used one on your phone at nine eighteen P.M. on March eighteenth of this year. They dialed Kuala Lumpur and spoke for nearly twelve minutes. The total cost of the call is twenty-three dollars and eighty-two cents, but the fine for using a Y511 will be at least seven hundred dollars with the potential for up to one year in prison. Plus we'll have to remove the phone.'

Hector's face became a mask of pure panic. 'What?' Myron wasn't thrilled with what he was doing – scaring an honest, hard-working immigrant like this – but he knew that the fear of government or big business would work in a situation like this. Hector turned around and shouted something in Spanish to a teenager who looked like him. The teenager took over the grill. 'I don't understand this, Mr Worley.'

'It's a public phone, sir. You just admitted to a product supervising agent that you used the public phones for private use; that is, for your employees only and denying public access. This violates our own code, section one twenty-four B. I wouldn't report it normally, but when you add in the use of a Y511—'

'But I didn't use a Y511!'

'We don't know that, sir.' Myron was playing Mr Bureaucrat to the hilt; nothing made a person feel more impotent. There is no darker pit than the blank stare of a bureaucrat. 'The phone is on your premises,' Myron continued in a bored singsong voice. 'You just explained to me that the phone was only used by your employees—'

'Exactly!' Hector leaped. 'By my employees! Not me!'

'But you own this establishment. You are responsible.' Myron looked around with his best, bored expression – the one he learned while waiting on line at the Division of Motor Vehicles. 'We'll also have to check out the status of all your employees. Maybe we can find the culprit that way.'

Hector's eyes grew big. Myron knew this would hit

home. There wasn't a restaurant in Manhattan that didn't employ at least one illegal alien. Hector's jowls slackened. 'All this,' he said, 'because someone used a pay phone?'

'What someone did, sir, was use an illegal electronic device known as a Y511. What you did, sir, was refuse to cooperate with the product supervising agent investigating this serious matter.'

'Refuse to cooperate?' Hector was grasping at the possible life preserver Myron had offered up. 'No, sir, not me. I want to cooperate. I want to very much.'

Myron shook his head. 'I don't think you do.'

Hector bit down and set his polite meter on extra-strength now. 'No, sir,' he said. 'I want to help very much. I want to cooperate with the phone company. Tell me what I can do to help. Please.'

Myron sighed, gave it a few seconds. The diner bustled. The cash register dinged while the guy who looked homeless with the Thom McAn sneakers picked out greasy coins from a dirty hand. The griddle sizzled. The aroma from the various foods battled each other for dominance with none winning outright. Hector's face grew more and more anxious. Enough, Myron thought. 'For starters, you can tell me who was using the pay phone at nine eighteen P.M. last Saturday.'

Hector held up a finger imploring patience. He shouted something in Spanish to the woman (Mrs Hector maybe?) working the cash register. The woman shouted something back. She closed the drawer and walked toward them. As she drew closer, Myron noticed that Hector was suddenly giving him an odd look. Was he starting to see through Myron's rather husky load of bull-dooky? Perhaps. But Myron looked back at him steadily and Hector quickly backed down. He might be suspicious, but not suspicious enough to risk offending the all-powerful bureaucrat by questioning his authority.

Hector whispered something to the woman. She urgently whispered back. He made an understanding 'ah' noise. Then he faced Myron and shook his head.

'It figures,' he said.

'What?'

'It was Sally.'

'Who?'

'At least I think it was Sally. My wife saw her on the phone around then. But she said she was only on for a minute or two.'

'Does Sally have a last name?'

'Guerro.'

'Is she here now?'

Hector shook his head. 'She hasn't been here since Saturday night. That's what I mean by, figures. She gets me in trouble and then she runs out.'

'Has she called in sick?'

'No, sir. She just up and left.'

'You got an address on her?' Myron asked.

'I think so, let me see.' He pulled out a big carton that read 'Snapple Peach Iced Tea' on the side. Behind him, the griddle hissed when fresh pancake batter touched down upon the hot metal. The files in the box were neat and color coded. Hector pulled one out and opened it. He shuffled through the sheets, found the one he was looking for, and frowned.

'What?' Myron prompted.

'Sally never gave us an address,' Hector said.

'How about a phone number?'

'No.' He looked up, remembering something. 'She said

she didn't have a phone. That's why she was using the one in the back so much.'

'Could you tell me what Ms Guerro looked like?' Myron tried.

Hector suddenly looked uncomfortable. He glanced at his wife and cleared his throat. 'Uh, she had brown hair,' he began. 'Maybe five-four, five-five. Average height, I guess.'

'Anything else?'

'Brown eyes, I think.' He stopped. 'That's about it.'

'How old would you say she was?'

Hector checked the file again. 'According to this, she was forty-five. That sounds about right.'

'How long has she worked here?' he asked.

'Two months.'

Myron nodded, rubbed his chin vigorously. 'It sounds like an operative who goes by the name Carla.'

'Carla?'

'A notorious phone fraud,' Myron continued. 'We've been after her for a while.' He glanced left, then right. Trying to look conspiratorial. 'Have you ever heard her use the name Carla or hear someone call her Carla?'

Hector looked at his wife. She shook her head. 'No, never.'

'Did she have any visitors? Any friends?'

Again Hector checked with his wife. Again the head shook. 'No, none that we ever saw. She kept to herself most of the time.'

Myron decided to push a little further and confirm what he already knew. If Hector balked at this stage, so what? Nothing ventured, nothing gained. He leaned forward; Hector and his wife did likewise. 'This may sound insensitive,' Myron whispered, 'but was this woman large chested?'

Both nods were immediate. 'Very large,' Hector said.

Suspicion confirmed.

He asked a few more questions, but any useful information had already been culled from these waters. Before leaving, he told them that they were in the clear and could continue to violate code section 124B without fear. Hector almost kissed his hand. Myron felt like a louse. *What did you do today, Batman? Well, Robin, I started off by terrorizing a hard-working immigrant's livelihood with a bunch of lies. Holy Cow, Batman, you're the coolest!* Myron shook his head. What to do for an encore – throw empty beer bottles at the dog on the fire escape?

Myron exited the Parkview Diner. He debated going to the park across the street, but suppose he became overcome by a lustful need to feed rats? No, he couldn't risk it. He'd have to stay away. He began to head to the Dyckman Street subway station when a voice stopped him.

'You looking for Sally?'

Myron turned. It was the homeless-looking man with the Thom McAns from the diner. He sat on the pavement, his back leaning against the brick building. He had an empty plastic coffee cup in his hand. Panhandling.

'You know her?' Myron asked.

'She and I . . .' He winked and crossed his fingers. 'We met because of that damn phone, you know.'

'Really.'

Using the wall for support the man stood. His facial hair was whiteish, not full enough to be a beard yet past the stage of a Miami Vice wanna-be. His long hair was black as coal. 'Sally was using my phone all the time. It pissed me off.'

'Your phone?'

'The pay phone in the back,' he said licking his lips. 'It's right by the back door. I hang out in the back alley a lot so I can hear it, you know? It's kind of like my business phone.' Myron couldn't guess his age. His face was boyish but leathered – from the passing years or hard living, Myron couldn't say. His grin was missing a couple of prominent teeth, reminding Myron of that beloved Christmas classic 'All I Want for Christmas Is My Two Front Teeth.' Such a nice song really. No toys, no Sega Genesis video game. The kid just wanted teeth. So selfless really.

'I used to have my own cellular,' the man continued. 'Two of them, as a matter of fact. But they got stolen. And the damn things are so unreliable, especially around the high buildings. And anyone can listen in with the right equipment. Me, I need to keep what I do secret, you see. Spies are everywhere. And they also give you brain tumors. The electrons or something. Brain tumors the size of beach balls.'

Myron kept his face blank. 'Uh huh.' Speaking of tossing the bull.

'So anyway Sally started using it, too. It pissed me off, you know? I mean, I'm a businessman. I got important calls coming in. I can't have the line tied up. Am I right?'

'As rain,' Myron said.

'See, I'm a Hollywood screenwriter.' He stuck out his hand. 'Norman Lowenstein.'

Myron tried to remember the fake name he used with Hector. 'Bernie Worley.'

'Nice to meet you, Bernie.'

'Do you know where Sally Guerro lives?'

'Sure. We used to be . . .' Norman Lowenstein crossed his fingers.

'So I heard. Could you tell me where she lives?'

Norman Lowenstein pursed his lips and used his pointer finger to scratch a spot near his throat. 'I'm not real good with addresses and stuff,' he said. 'But I could take you there.'

Myron wondered how big of a waste of time this was going to be. 'Would you mind?'

'Sure, no problem. Let's go.'

'Which way?'

'The A train,' Norman said. 'Down to One Hundred Twenty-fifth Street.'

They walked toward the subway.

'You go the movies much, Bernie?' Norman asked.

'Much as the next guy, I guess.'

'Let me tell you something about movie-making,' he began, growing more animated. 'It's not all glamour and glitz. It's a dog-eat-dog business like no other, making dreams for people. All the back-stabbing, all that money, all that fame and attention . . . it makes people act funny, you know? I got this screenplay with Paramount right now. They're talking to Willis about it. Bruce Willis. He's really interested.'

'Good luck with it,' Myron said.

Norman beamed. 'Thanks, Bernie, that's real nice of you. I mean it. Real nice. I'd like to tell you what my flick is about, but well, my hands are tied. You know how it is. Hollywood and all the theft out there. The studio wants it kept hush-hush.'

'I understand,' Myron said.

'I trust you, Bernie, it's not that. But the studios insist. I can't blame them really. They got to protect their interests, right?'

'Right.'

'It's an action-adventure flick, that much I can tell you. But with heart too, you know? Not just a shoot-em-up. Harrison Ford wanted in, but he's too old. I guess Willis is okay. He's not my first choice, but what can you do?'

'Uh huh.'

One Twenty-fifth Street was not the nicest stop in the city. It was safe enough during the day, Myron surmised, but the fact that he was now carrying a gun made him feel a tad more secure. Myron did not like 'packing heat' and rarely did so. It was not that Myron was particularly squeamish; it had more to do with comfort. The shoulder holster dug into his armpit and made it itch like he was wearing a tweed condom. But after last night's soiree with Camouflage Pants and Brick Wall, it would be foolhardy to walk around unarmed.

'Which way?' Myron asked.

'Downtown.'

They headed south on Broadway. Norman regaled him with tales of Hollywood. The ins and outs. Myron nodded and kept walking. The farther south they headed, the better the area became. They passed the familiar iron gates of Columbia University, then turned left. 'It's right up here,' Norman said. 'Toward the middle of the block.'

The street was lined with low-rise apartments that were mostly used by Columbia's grad students and professors. Strange, Myron thought, that a diner waitress would live here. But then again nothing else about her involvement in all this made sense – why should where she lived? If she lived here at all, and not, say, with Bruce Willis in Hollywood.

Norman interrupted his thoughts. 'You're trying to help her, right?'

'What?'

Norman stopped walking. He was less animated now. 'All that stuff about being from the phone company. That was all crap, right?'

Myron said nothing.

'Look,' he said, putting his hand on Myron's forearm, 'Hector is a good man. He came to this country with nothing. He works his ass off in that diner. He and his wife and son – they slave there every day. No days off. And every day he's scared someone's going to take it all away from him. All that worry . . . it clouds the thinking, you know? Me, I got nothing to lose so I'm not afraid of anything. Makes it easier to see some stuff. Know what I mean?'

Myron gave a slight nod.

Norman's bright eyes dimmed as a bit of reality swept through him. Myron looked at him, really looked at him, for the first time. He made his eyes stop sweeping by him with barely a notice of age or height or even species. Myron realized that behind the lies and self-delusion lay the dreams of any man, the hopes and wants and needs that are the sole reserve of the human race.

'I'm worried about Sally,' Norman went on. 'Maybe that's clouding my thinking. But I know she wouldn't just up and leave without saying good-bye to me. Sally wouldn't do that.' He stopped, met Myron's eyes with his own. 'You're not from the phone company, are you?'

'No, I'm not.'

'You want to help her?'

'Yes,' Myron said. 'I want to help her.'

He nodded and pointed. 'In here. Apartment two E.'

Myron walked up the stoop while Norman stayed on the street level. He pressed the black button reading 2E. No one answered. No surprise there. He tried the entrance door, but it was locked. You had to be buzzed in.

'You better stay there,' he told Norman. Norman nodded, understanding. These buzzer-protected doors were mild deterrents to crime, but their true purpose was to prevent vagrants from coming in and setting up camp in the lobby. Myron would just wait. Eventually an occupant would leave or enter the building. While said occupant opened the door, Myron would enter as though he belonged. No one would question a man dressed in khakis and a button-down BD Baggies shirt. If Norman stood next to him, however, that same occupant might react differently.

Myron moved down two steps. When he saw two young women approach the door from the inside, he slapped his pockets as though looking for keys. Then he walked purposefully up to the door, smiled, and waited for them to push it open. He need not have bothered with the dramatics. The two young women – college students, Myron guessed – went through the portal without looking up or decelerating their oral activities. Both were talking nonstop, neither listening. They paid absolutely no attention to him. Amazing restraint really. Of course from this angle they couldn't see his ass, so their self-control was not only admirable but somewhat understandable.

He looked back at Norman, who thankfully waved him off. 'You go yourself,' he said. 'I don't want to cause a problem.'

Myron let the door close.

The corridor was pretty much what he expected. It was

painted off-white. No stripes or designs. There were no wall-hangings other than a huge bulletin board that read like a schizophrenic political manifesto. Dozens of leaflets announced everything from a dance sponsored by the Native American Gay and Lesbian Society to poetry readings by a group calling itself the Rush Limbaugh Review. Ah, the college life.

He ascended a stairway lit by two bare bulbs. All this walking and stair climbing were starting to take a toll on his bad knee. The joint tightened up like a rusted hinge. Myron felt himself dragging the leg behind him. He used the railing for support and wondered what the knee would be like when he reached arthritis age.

The floor plan of the building was far from symmetrical. Doors seemed to be placed in the wall as though at random. Off in a corner, a good distance from the other apartments, Myron found the door marked 2E. The positioning made the apartment look like an afterthought, as if someone had spotted some extra space in the back and decided to add an extra room or two. Myron knocked. No answer. No surprise. He checked the corridor. No one in sight. He was thankful that Norman was not here because he wouldn't want someone to witness him breaking in.

Myron was not great at the lock-picking game. He had learned a bit over the years, but picking locks was a bit like playing a video game. You work at it enough, and eventually you move up levels. Myron hadn't worked at it. He didn't like it. He really didn't have much natural talent for it. In most cases, he relied on Win to handle the mechanical stuff, like Barney used to do on *Mission: Impossible*.

He examined the door and felt his heart sink. Even for

New York the dead bolts were nothing short of impressive. Three of them stacked intimidatingly from six inches above the knob to six inches below the top frame. Top of the line stuff. Brand new, judging by the gleam and lack of scratches. This was a tad odd. Was Sally/Carla the extracautious type, or was there a more aberrant reason for such security? Good question. Myron looked at the locks again. Win would have enjoyed the challenge; Myron knew that any effort he made would be fruitless.

He debated kicking in the door when he noticed something. He moved closer and squinted into the door crack. Again something struck him as being odd. The dead bolts were not engaged. Why buy all these expensive locks and not use them? He tried the knob. It was locked, but that one would be easy to get through with the 'loid card.

He took out the card. He couldn't remember the last time he had used it. It looked pristine. Maybe never. He jammed it into the opening. Despite being an old lock it still took Myron almost five minutes to find the right spot to push the lock back. He gripped the knob. The door began to swing open.

It was open barely six inches when the odor attacked.

The bloodcurdling stench popped out into the hallway like pressurized gas. Myron felt his stomach dive and swoop. He gagged a little and felt a weight on his chest. He knew the smell, and dread filled him. He searched his pockets for a handkerchief and came up empty. He blocked his nose and mouth with the crook of his elbow, as if he were doing Bela Lugosi in *Dracula*. He didn't want to go in. He wasn't good at this type of thing. He knew that whatever image lay behind the door would stay with him, would haunt his nights and too often his days too. It would stay with him like a dear friend, tapping him on the shoulder every once in a while when he thought he was alone and at peace.

He pushed the door all the way open. The rancid smell permeated his meager protection. He tried to breathe through his mouth, but the thought of what he was sucking in made that option unbearable.

Fortunately, he didn't have to travel far to find the source of the odor.

Chapter 12

'Whoa, Bolitar, new cologne?'

'Funny, Dimonte.'

NYPD homicide detective Roland Dimonte shook his head. 'Christ, what a stink.' He was out of uniform, but you wouldn't ever call him 'plainclothes.' He wore a green silk shirt and jeans that were too tight and too dark blue. The bottoms were tucked into purple snake-skin boots; the color faded in and out with any angle change, like some psychedelic Hendrix poster from the sixties. Dimonte gnawed on a toothpick, a habit he picked up, Myron surmised, when he spotted himself doing it in the mirror and decided it looked tough. 'You touch anything?' he asked.

'Just the doorknob,' Myron said. He had also checked the rest of the apartment to make sure there weren't any other gruesome surprises. There weren't.

'How did you get in?'

'The door was unlocked.'

'Really?' Dimonte raised an eyebrow and looked back at the door. 'The door is set to lock automatically when you close it.'

'Did I say unlocked? I meant, ajar.'

'Sure you did.' Dimonte did a bit more gnawing, shook his head. He ran his hand through greasy hair. Ringlets clung to his forehead, refusing to give ground. 'So who is she?'

'I don't know,' Myron said.

Dimonte scrunched up his face like a closed fist. Displaying very skeptical. Subtle body language was not Dimonte's forte. 'Little early in the day to be pulling my hardware, ain't it, Bolitar?'

'I don't know her name. It might be Sally Guerro. Then again it might be Carla.'

'Uh-huh.' Toothpick chew. 'I thought I saw you on TV last night. That you were playing ball again.'

'I am.'

The coroner came over. He was tall and thin and his wire-rim glasses looked too big on the elongated face. 'She's been dead awhile,' he pronounced. 'At least four days.'

'Cause?'

'Hard to say for sure. Someone bludgeoned her with a blunt object. I'll know more when I get her on the table.' He looked at the corpse with professional disinterest, then back at Dimonte. 'They're not real, by the way.'

'What?'

He vaguely motioned toward the torso. 'Her breasts. They're implants.'

'Jesus Christ,' Dimonte said, 'you fiddling with dead bodies now?'

The elongated face sagged, his jaw dropping to

somewhere around his navel. 'Don't even joke about that,' the coroner said in a stage whisper. 'You know what rumors like that could do to a guy in my business?'

'Get him promoted?' Dimonte said.

The coroner did not laugh. He gave Myron a wounded look, then Dimonte. 'You think that's funny, huh? God-damn it, this is my career you're fucking around with!'

'Calm down, Peretti, I'm just playing with you.'

'Playing with me? You think my career is some kind of fucking joke? What the hell is wrong with you?'

Dimonte's eyes narrowed. 'Kind of sensitive about all this, Peretti.'

'You have to be in my position,' he said, back straight-ening.

'If you say so.'

'What the hell does that mean?'

' "The lady protests too much, methinks." '

'What?'

'It's Shakespeare,' Dimonte said. 'From *Macbeth*.' Dimonte looked over to Myron.

Myron smiled. '*Hamlet*.'

'I don't give a shit who said it.' Peretti protested. 'You shouldn't mess around with a man's reputation. I don't think any of this is funny.'

'Like I give a rat's ass what you think,' Dimonte said. 'You got anything else?'

'She's wearing a wig.'

'A wig? No kidding, Peretti. The case is as good as solved now. All we need to do is find a killer who hates wigs and fake tits. This is helpful, Peretti. What kind of panties was she wearing, huh? You sniff them yet?'

'I was just—'

'Do me a big favor, Peretti.' Dimonte made himself a

little taller, hitched his pants. Signaling importance. Again the subtlety. 'Tell me when she died. Tell me how she died. Then we'll talk about her fashion accessories, okay?'

Peretti held up his hands in surrender and returned to the body. Dimonte turned to Myron. Myron said, 'The implants and wig might be important. He was right to tell you.'

'Yeah, I know. I just like busting his chops.'

'And the quote is, "Methinks the lady doth protest too much." '

'Uh huh.' Dimonte changed toothpicks. The one in his mouth was frayed like a horse's mane. 'You going to tell me what the fuck is going on, or am I going to drag you downtown?'

Myron made a face. 'Drag me downtown?'

'Don't bust my balls on this, Bolitar, okay?'

Myron forced himself to look at the bloodied corpse. His stomach did back flips. He was starting to get used to the smell, the thought of which was nearly as bad as the smell itself. Peretti was back at it, making a small slit to get to the liver. Myron diverted his gaze. The homicide crew from John Jay was setting up, taking photographs, that kind of thing. Dimonte's partner, a kid named Krinsky, quietly walked around and took notes. 'Why would she make them so big?' Myron wondered out loud.

'What?'

'Her breasts. I can understand the desire to enlarge them. All the pressures in this society. But why make them that big?'

Dimonte said, 'You're shitting me, right?'

Krinsky came over. 'All her stuff is in those suitcases.' He motioned with his hand to two bags on the floor.

Myron had met Krinsky on maybe half a dozen occasions. Talking was not the kid's forte; he seemed to do it as often as Myron picked locks. 'I'd say she was moving out.'

'You got an ID yet?' Dimonte asked.

'Her wallet says her name is Sally Guerro,' Krinsky continued in a soft voice. 'So does one of her passports.'

They both waited for Krinsky to continue. When he didn't, Dimonte shouted, 'What do you mean, one of her passports? How many does she have?'

'Three.'

'Jesus Christ, Krinsky, talk.'

'One is in the name Sally Guerro. One is in the name Roberta Smith. One is in the name Carla Whitney.'

'Give me those.' Dimonte scanned through the various passports. Myron looked over his shoulder. The same woman was in all three pictures, albeit with different hair (ergo the wig) and different Social Security numbers. Judging by the amount of stamps, the woman had traveled extensively.

Dimonte whistled. 'Forged passports,' he said. 'And good ones too.' He turned more pages. 'Plus she has a couple of visits to South America in here. Colombia. Bolivia.' The passports closed with a dramatic snap. 'Well, well, well. Looks like we got ourselves a nice, neat drug hit.'

Myron mulled over that bit of information. A drug hit – could that be part of the answer? If Sally/Carla/Roberta was dealing drugs, it might explain her connection with Greg Downing. She was his source. The meeting on Saturday night was nothing more than a buy. The waitress job was a cover. It also explained her using a pay phone and maintaining powerful door locks – tools of a drug dealer's

126

trade. It made some sense. Of course, Greg Downing did not appear to be a drug user, but he would not be the first person to fool everyone.

Dimonte said, 'Anything else, Krinsky?'

The kid nodded. 'I found a stack of cash in the bedside drawer.' He stopped again.

Dimonte gave him exasperation. 'Did you count it?'

Another nod.

'How much?'

'A little over ten thousand dollars.'

'Ten grand in cash, huh?' That pleased Dimonte. 'Let me see it.'

Krinsky handed it over. New bills, held by rubber bands. Myron watched while Dimonte shuffled through them. All hundreds. The serial numbers were sequential. Myron tried to memorize one of them. When Dimonte finished, he tossed the packet back to Krinsky. The smile was still there.

'Yep,' Dimonte said, 'it looks like things are coming together in a nice, neat, drug-hit package.' He paused. 'Only one problem.'

'What?'

He pointed at Myron. 'You, Bolitar. You're messing up my nice, neat drug-hit. What the hell are you doing—?' Dimonte stopped himself and snapped his fingers. 'Holy shit . . .' His voice sort of drifted off. He slapped the side of his own head. A small spark in his eyes expanded. 'My God!'

Again note the subtlety. 'You have a thought, Rolly?'

Dimonte ignored him. 'Peretti!'

The coroner looked up from the body. 'What?'

'Those plastic tits,' he said. 'Myron noticed they were huge.'

'Yeah, so?'

'How big?'

'What?'

'How big are they?'

'You mean like cup size?'

'Yeah.'

'I look like a lingerie manufacturer? How the fuck would I know?'

'But they're big, right?'

'Right.'

'Really big.'

'You got eyes, don't you?'

Myron watched the exchange in silence. He was trying to follow Dimonte's logic – a most treacherous trail.

'Would you say they were bigger than a water balloon?' Dimonte continued.

Peretti shrugged. 'Depends on the balloon.'

'Didn't you ever make water balloons when you were a kid?'

'Yeah, sure,' Peretti said. 'But I don't remember how big the balloons were. I was a kid then. Everything looks bigger when you're a kid. A couple years ago I went back to my old elementary school to visit my third grade teacher. She still works there, if you can believe it. Her name is Mrs Tansmore. I swear to God the building looked like a goddamn dollhouse to me. It was huge when I was a kid. It was like—'

'All right, moron, let me make this simple.' Dimonte took a deep breath. 'Could they be used for smuggling drugs?'

Silence. Everyone in the room stopped moving. Myron wasn't sure if he just heard the most idiotic thing in the world or the most brilliant. He turned toward Peretti. Peretti looked up, mouth open in fly-catching pose.

'Well, Peretti? Could it be?'

'Could it be what?'

'Could she stick dope in her boobs? Smuggle drugs through customs with them?'

Peretti looked at Myron. Myron shrugged. Peretti turned back to Dimonte. 'I don't know,' he said slowly.

'How can we find out?'

'I'd have to examine them.'

'Then what the fuck you staring at me for? Do it.'

Peretti did as asked. Dimonte smiled at Myron; his eyebrows did a little dance. Proud of his deduction. Myron remained quiet.

'Nope, no way,' Peretti said.

Dimonte wasn't happy with this report. 'Why the hell not?'

'There's hardly any scar tissue,' Peretti said. 'If she were smuggling drugs in there, they'd have to rip the skin open and sew it up. Then they'd have to do it again on this side. There's no sign of that.'

'You're sure?'

'Positive.'

Dimonte said, 'Shit.' Then he glared at Myron and pulled him into a corner. 'Everything, Bolitar. Now.'

Myron had debated how to handle it, but in truth he had no choice. He had to tell. He couldn't keep Greg Downing's disappearance a secret any longer. The best he could hope to do was keep it contained. He suddenly remembered that Norman Lowenstein was waiting outside. 'One second,' he said.

'What? Where the fuck you going?'

'I'll be right back. Just wait here.'

'Like hell.'

Dimonte followed him down the stairs and out onto the stoop. Norman wasn't there. Myron looked up and down the block. No sign of Norman. This was hardly a surprise. Norman probably ran when he saw the cops. Guilty or not, the homeless learn quickly to make themselves scarce when the authorities come calling.

'What is it?' Dimonte asked.

'Nothing.'

'Then start talking. The whole story.'

Myron told him most of it. The story almost knocked the toothpick out of Dimonte's mouth. Dimonte didn't bother asking questions, though he continuously stuck in exclamations of 'Jesus Christ!' and 'Frigging A,' whenever Myron paused. When Myron finished, Dimonte sort of stumbled back and sat on the steps of the stoop. His eyes looked unfocused for a few moments. He gathered himself together, but it took some time.

'In-fuckin—' credible,' he managed.

Myron nodded.

'Are you telling me no one knows where Downing is?'

'If they do, they aren't talking.'

'He just vanished?'

'That's how it appears.'

'And there's blood in his basement?'

'Yes.'

Dimonte shook his head again. He reached down and put his hand on his right boot. Myron had seen him do this before. He liked to sort of pet the boot. Myron had no idea why. Maybe he found the feel of snakeskin soothing. Reminiscent of the womb.

'Suppose Downing killed her and ran,' he said.

'That's a pretty big suppose.'

'Yeah, but it fits,' Dimonte said.

'How?'

'According to what you said, Downing was seen with the victim Saturday night. How much you want to bet that once Peretti gets her on the table we find the time of death around then?'

'Doesn't mean Downing killed her.'

Dimonte increased the speed of his boot-petting stroke. A man on Rollerblades skated by with his dog. The dog looked out of breath, trying to keep up. New product idea: Dog Rollerblades. 'Saturday night, Greg Downing and the victim get together at some gin joint downtown. They leave sometime around eleven o'clock. Next thing we know she's dead and he's vanished.' Dimonte looked up at Myron. 'That points to him killing her and running.'

'It points to a dozen things.'

'Like what?'

'Like maybe Greg witnessed the murder and got scared and ran. Maybe he witnessed the murder and was kidnapped. Maybe he was killed by the same people.'

'So where's his body?' Dimonte asked.

'It could be anywhere.'

'Why not just leave it here with hers?'

'Maybe they killed him someplace else. Or maybe they took his body because he's famous and they didn't want that kind of heat.'

He scoffed at that one. 'You're reaching, Bolitar.'

'So are you.'

'Maybe. Only one way to find out.' He stood. 'We got to get out an APB on Downing.'

'Whoa, hold up a second. I don't think that's a good idea.'

Dimonte looked at Myron as if he were something left

unflushed in a toilet. 'I'm sorry,' he said feigning politeness. 'You must be mistaking me for someone who gives a rat's ass what you think.'

'You're suggesting putting out an APB on a major, beloved sports hero.'

'And you're suggesting I play favorites because he's a major, beloved sports hero.'

'Not at all,' Myron said, his mind racing. 'But imagine what happens when you call out this APB. The press gets it. You start getting that OJ coverage. But there's a difference here. You got squat on Downing. No motive. No physical evidence. Nothing.'

'Not yet I don't,' Dimonte said. 'But it's early—'

'Exactly, it's early. Wait a little while, that's all I'm saying. And handle this one right because the whole world is going to look at everything you do. Tell those bozos upstairs to videotape every step. Leave nothing to chance. Don't let anyone come back later and say you tampered or contaminated something. Get a warrant before you go to Downing's house. Do everything by the book.'

'I can do all that and still put out an APB.'

'Rolly, suppose Greg Downing did kill her. You put out an APB, you know what happens? One, you look single-minded. You look like you got it in your head that Downing was the killer and that was it. Two, you got the press in your face – watching your every move, trying to beat you to the evidence, compromising and commenting on everything you do. Three, you drag Greg in here now and you know what bottom-feeders are stuck to him?'

Dimonte nodded and made a lemon-sucking face. 'Fucking lawyers.'

'A dream team's worth. Before you have anything, they're filing motions and suppressing whatever and, well, you know the routine.'

'Shit,' Dimonte said.

Myron nodded. 'You see what I mean?'

'Yeah, I do,' Dimonte said. 'But there's some stuff you forgot, Bolitar.' He gave Myron big-time toothpick gnawing. 'For example, if I issue an APB your little team investigation goes down the toilet. You lose out.'

'Could be,' Myron said.

Dimonte studied him with a small, uneven smile. 'That doesn't mean what you're saying is wrong. I just don't want you to think I don't see what you're up to.'

'You read me,' Myron said, 'like Vasco da Gama reads a map.'

Dimonte gave him hard eyes for a moment; Myron fought off the desire to roll his in return. 'So here's how we're going to play it. You're going stay on the team and you're going to continue your little investigation. I'm going to try to keep what you told me to myself as long' – he held up a finger for emphasis – 'as long as it benefits my case. If I find enough to haul Downing's ass in here, I put out the APB. And you are going to report everything to me. You are not going to hold back. Any questions?'

'Just one,' Myron said. 'Where do you buy your boots?'

Chapter 13

On the ride to practice, Myron placed a call from the car phone.

'Higgins,' a voice answered.

'Fred? It's Myron Bolitar.'

'Hey, long time, no speak. How you doing, Myron?'

'Can't complain. You?'

'A thrill a minute here at the Treasury Department.'

'Yeah, I bet.'

'How's Win?' Higgins asked.

'The same,' Myron said.

'The guy scares the piss out of me, you know what I mean?'

'Yes,' Myron said, 'I do.'

'You two miss working for the feds?'

'I don't,' Myron said. 'I don't think Win does either. It got too restrictive for him.'

'I hear you. Hey, I read in the papers you're playing ball again.'

'Yep.'

'At your age and with that knee? How come?'

'Long story, Fred.'

'Say no more. Hey, you guys are coming down to play the Bullets next week. Can you get me tickets?'

'I'll do my best.'

'Great, thanks. So what do you need, Myron?'

'The wheres and why of about ten grand in hundred dollar bills. Sequentially wrapped. Serial number B028856011A.'

'How fast you need it?'

'Soon as you can get it.'

'I'll do my best. You take care, Myron.'

'You too, Fred.'

Myron held nothing back at practice. He let it all hang out. The feeling was awesome and overpowering. He entered his own zone. When he shot, it was like an invisible hand carried the ball to the cylinder. When he dribbled, the ball became part of his hand. His senses were heightened like a wolf's in the wilderness. He felt like he'd fallen into some black hole and emerged ten years earlier at the NCAA finals. Even his knee felt great.

Most of practice consisted of a scrimmage between the starting five players and the five who saw the most bench time. Myron played his best ball. His jumper was popping. He came off screens strong and ready to shoot. He even drove straight down the lane twice – into the teeth of the big men's domain – and came away the victor both times.

There were moments he completely forgot about Greg Downing and Carla/Sally/Roberta's mangled corpse and the blood in the basement and the goons who jumped him and yes, even Jessica. An exhilarating rush like no other flooded his veins – the rush of an athlete at his peak. People talked about a runner's high, a euphoria from a gland secretion when your body was pressed to its limit. Myron couldn't relate to that, but he understood the incredible highs and plunging depths of being an athlete. If you played well, your whole body tingled and tears of pure joy came to your eyes. The tingles lasted well into the night when you lay in bed with no chance of sleep and replayed your finest moments, often in slow motion, like an overzealous sportscaster with his finger on the replay button. When you played poorly, you were surly and depressed and stayed that way for hours and even days. Both extremes were way out of proportion with the relevant importance of jamming a ball through a metallic circle or swatting a ball with a stick or throwing a sphere with great velocity. When you played poorly, you tried to remind yourself how stupid it was to get so caught up in something so meaningless. When you hit that rare high, you kept your internal big mouth shut.

As Myron dashed back and forth in the wave of basketball action, a thought sneaked in through the back door of his brain. The thought stayed on the fringes, hiding behind a couch, popping into view every once in a while before ducking back down again. *You can do this*, the thought taunted. *You can play with them.*

Myron's lucky streak continued when it came to his defensive assignment: Leon White, Greg's roomie-on-the-road and best friend. Myron and Leon bonded a bit while playing, the way teammates and even opponents often do. Whispering quick jokes in one another's ear while lined up chest-to-chest for an inbounds pass. Patting the other guy on the back when he made a nice play. Leon was a classy guy on the floor. No trash talk. Even when Myron burned his butt on a fade-away eighteen-footer, Leon offered only words of encouragement.

Coach Donny Walsh blew the whistle. 'That's it, fellas. Take twenty foul shots and go home.'

Leon and Myron exchanged a half-handshake, half-high-five the way only children and professional athletes can. Myron had always loved this part of the game, the almost soldierlike camaraderie; he hadn't had that in years. It felt good. The players partnered themselves up in groups of two – one guy to shoot, one to rebound – and went off to different baskets. Myron lucked out again and hooked up with Leon White. They each snatched a towel and a water bottle and strolled past the bleachers. Several reporters were perched up there for the practice. Audrey was there, of course. She looked at him with an amused smile. He resisted the temptation to stick his tongue out at her. Or his ass. Calvin Johnson had been watching practice too. He wore a suit and leaned against the wall like he was posing for a candid picture. Myron tried to gauge his reaction during the scrimmage, but of course Calvin's expression remained unreadable.

Myron shot first. He stood at the foul line, feet spread shoulder length, his eyes on the front rim. The ball backspun through the hoop.

'I guess we're going to be roommates,' Myron said.

'That's what I heard,' Leon said.

'Probably won't be for very long.' Myron took another shot. Swish. 'When do you think Greg will be back?'

In one motion Leon grabbed the bouncing ball and swooped it back to Myron. 'I don't know.'

'How's Greg feeling? The ankle doing okay?'

'I don't know,' he said again.

Myron took another foul shot. Another swish. His shirt, heavy with sweat, felt right. He grabbed the towel and wiped his face again. 'Have you talked to him at all?'

'No.'

'That's funny.'

Leon passed the ball to Myron. 'What's funny?'

Myron shrugged, took four dribbles. 'I heard you two were tight,' he said.

Leon gave a half-smile. 'Where did you hear that?'

Myron released the ball. Another swish. 'Around, I guess. In the newspapers and stuff.'

'Don't believe everything you read,' Leon said.

'Why's that?'

He bounce-passed the ball to Myron. 'The press loves to build up a friendship between a white player and a black player. They're always looking for that Gale Sayers-Brian Piccolo slant.'

'You two aren't close?'

'Well, we've known each other a long time. I'll say that.'

'But you're not tight?'

Leon looked at him funny. 'Why you so interested?'

'I'm just making conversation. Greg is my only real connection to this team.'

'Connection?'

Myron started dribbling again. 'He and I used to be rivals.'

'Yeah, so?'

'So now we're going to be teammates. It'll be weird.'

Leon looked at Myron. Myron stopped dribbling. 'You think Greg still cares about some old college rivalry?' There was disbelief in his voice.

Myron realized how lame he was sounding. 'It was a

pretty intense thing,' he said. 'At the time, I mean.' Extra lame. Myron didn't look at Leon. He just lined up the shot.

'I hope this don't hurt your feelings or nothing,' Leon said, 'but I've been rooming with Greg for eight years now. I've never heard him mention your name. Even when we talk about college and stuff.'

Myron stopped right before releasing the ball. He looked over at Leon, fighting to keep his face neutral. Funny thing was – much as Myron didn't want to admit it – that did hurt his feelings.

'Shoot already,' Leon said. 'I want to get out of here.'

TC lumbered toward them. He palmed a basketball in each hand with the ease most adults palm grapefruits. He dropped one of the balls and did a handshaking/slapping ritual with Leon. Then he looked over at Myron. His face broke into a big smile.

'I know, I know,' Myron said. 'Thumped, right?'

TC nodded.

'What exactly is thumped?'

'Tonight,' TC said. 'Party at my house. All will be revealed then.'

Chapter 14

Dimonte was waiting for him in the Meadowlands parking lot. He leaned out of his red Corvette. 'Get in.'

'A red Corvette,' Myron said. 'Why aren't I surprised?'

'Just get in.'

Myron opened the door and slid into the black leather seat. Though they were parked with the engine off, Dimonte gripped the steering wheel with both hands and stared in front of him. His face was sheet-white. The toothpick hung low. He kept shaking his head over and over. Yet again, the subtlety. 'Something wrong, Rolly?'

'What's Greg Downing like?'

'What?'

'You fucking deaf?' Dimonte snapped. 'What's he like?'

'I don't know. I haven't spoken to him in years.'

'But you knew him, right? In school. What was he like back then? Did he hang out with perversive types?'

Myron looked at him. 'Perversive types?'

'Just answer the question.'

'What the hell is this? Perversive types?'

Dimonte turned the ignition key. The sound was loud. He hit the gas a bit, let the engine do the rev thing for a while. The car had been jacked up like a race car. The sound was, like, totally rad, man. No women were in the nearby vicinity to hear this human mating call or they would surely be disrobing by now. Dimonte finally shifted into gear.

'Where we going?' Myron asked.

Dimonte didn't answer. He followed the ramp that leads from the arena to Giants Stadium and the horse track.

'Is this one of those mystery dates?' Myron asked. 'I love those.'

'Stop fucking around and answer my question.'

'What question?'

'What's Downing like? I need to know everything about him.'

'You're asking the wrong guy, Rolly. I don't know him that well.'

'Tell me what you do know.' Dimonte's voice left little room for disagreement. His tone was less fake-macho than usual, and there was a funny quake in it. Myron didn't like it.

'Greg grew up in New Jersey,' Myron began. 'He's a great basketball player. He's divorced with two kids.'

'You dated his wife, right?'

'A long time ago.'

'Would you say she was left-wing?'

'Rolly, this is getting too weird.'

'Just answer the goddamn question.' The tone aimed for angry and impatient, but fear seemed to overlap them. 'Would you call her politics radical?'

'No.'

'She ever hang out with perversives?'

'Is that even a word? Perversives?'

Dimonte shook his head. 'Do I look like I'm in the mood for your shit, Bolitar?'

'Okay, okay.' Myron made a surrendering gesture with his hands. The Corvette swerved across the empty stadium lot. 'No, Emily did not hang out with perversives, whatever they are.'

They headed past the racetrack and took the other ramp back toward the arena. It became apparent to Myron that they were just going to circle the Meadowlands' vast expanse of paved lots. 'Let's get back to Downing then.'

'I just told you we haven't talked in years.'

'But you know about him, right? You've been investigating him; you've probably read stuff about him.' Gear shift up. Extra rev power. 'Would you say he was a revolutionary?'

Myron could not believe these questions. 'No, Mr Chairman.'

'Do you know who he hangs out with?'

'Not really. He's supposed to be closest to his teammates, but Leon White – that's his roommate on the road – seemed less than enamored. Oh, here's something that might interest you: after home games, Greg drives a taxi in the city.'

Dimonte looked puzzled. 'You mean he picks up fares and stuff?'

'Yes.'

'Why the fuck does he do that?'

'Greg is a little' – Myron searched for the word – 'off.'

'Uh huh.' Dimonte rubbed his face vigorously, as if he were polishing a fender with a rag. He did this for several seconds, not looking at the road; fortunately, he was in

142

the middle of an empty parking lot. 'Does it make him feel like a regular guy or something? Could that be part of it? Getting closer to the masses?'

'I guess,' Myron said.

'Go on. What about his interests? His hobbies?'

'He's a nature boy. He likes to fish and hunt and hike and boat, that goyish stuff.'

'A back-to-nature type?'

'Sort of.'

'Like maybe an outdoor, communal guy?'

'No. Like maybe an outdoor, loner guy.'

'You have any idea where he might be?'

'None.'

Dimonte hit the gas and circled the arena. He came to a stop in front of Myron's Ford Taurus and put the car in park. 'Okay, thanks for the help. We'll talk later.'

'Whoa, hold up a second. I thought we were working together on this.'

'You thought wrong.'

'You're not going to tell me what's going on?'

His voice was suddenly soft. 'No.'

Silence. The rest of the players were gone by now. The Taurus stood alone in the still, empty lot.

'It's that bad?' Myron said.

Dimonte kept frighteningly still.

'You know who she is, don't you?' Myron went on. 'You got an ID?'

Dimonte leaned back. Again he rubbed his entire face. 'Nothing confirmed,' he muttered.

'You got to tell me, Rolly.'

He shook his head. 'I can't.'

'I won't say anything. You know—'

'Get the fuck out of my car, Myron.' He leaned across Myron's lap and opened the car door. 'Now.'

143

Chapter 15

TC lived in a turn-of-the-century, red brick mansion encircled by a six-foot, matching brick fence on one of the better streets of Englewood, New Jersey. Eddie Murphy lived down the block. So did three Forbes 500 CEOs and several major Japanese bankers. There was a security post by the driveway entrance. Myron gave the security guard his name. The guard checked his clipboard.

'Please park along the drive. The party is out back.' He raised the yellow-and-black striped gate and waved him through. Myron parked next to a black BMW. There were maybe a dozen other cars, all glistening from fresh washes and waxes or perhaps they were all new. Mostly Mercedes Benzes. A few BMWs. A Bentley. A Jag. A Rolls. Myron's Taurus stood out like a zit in a Revlon commercial.

The front lawn was immaculately manicured. Perfectly pruned shrubs guarded and clung to the brick facade. In stark contrast to this majestic setting was the rap music blaring from the speakers. Awful. The shrubs looked pained by the sound. Myron didn't necessarily hate all rap. He knew there was worse music out there – John Tesh and Yanni proved it every day. Some rap songs Myron found engaging and even profound. He also recognized that rap music had not been written for him; he didn't get it all, but he suspected that he wasn't supposed to.

The party was held in the well-lit pool area. The crowd of about thirty mingled about in a fairly subdued fashion. Myron was wearing a blue blazer, a button-down pinstripe shirt, a flower tie, J. Murphy casual loafers. Bolitar the Prep. Win would be so proud. But Myron felt frighteningly underdressed next to his teammates. At the risk of sounding racist, the black guys on the team – there were only two other white players on the Dragons right now – knew how to dress with style. Not Myron's style (or lack thereof), but definitely with style. The group looked like they were readying themselves for a Milan runway walk. Perfectly tailored suits. Silk shirts buttoned to the neck. No ties. Shoes polished like twin mirrors.

TC reclined in a lounge chair by the shallow end of the pool. He was surrounded by a bunch of white guys who looked like college students. They were laughing at his every word. Myron also spotted Audrey in her customary reporter's garb. She had added pearls for the occasion. Really dressing up. He barely had a chance to step toward them when a woman in her late thirties/maybe forty approached him. 'Hello,' the woman said.

'Hi.' The Wordsmith Strikes Again.

'You must be Myron Bolitar. My name is Maggie Mason.'

'Hi, Maggie.' They shook hands. Firm grip, nice smile.

She was dressed conservatively in a white blouse, charcoal-gray blazer, red skirt, and black pumps. Her hair was down and slightly mussed, as if she'd just released her bun. She was slim and attractive and would have been the perfect choice to play the opposing attorney on *L.A. Law*.

She smiled at him. 'You don't know who I am, do you?'

'Sorry, I don't.'

'They call me Thumper.'

Myron waited. When she didn't add anything, he said, 'Uh huh.'

'Didn't TC tell you about this?'

'He mentioned something about getting thump . . .' He stopped midword. She just smiled at him and spread her arms. After some time had passed, he said, 'I don't get it.'

'Nothing to get,' she said matter-of-factly. 'I have sex with all the guys on the team. You're new to the team. It's your turn.'

Myron opened his mouth, closed it, tried again. 'You don't look like a groupie.'

'Groupie.' She shook her head. 'God, I hate that word.'

Myron closed his eyes and pinched the bridge of his nose. 'Let me see if I'm getting this.'

'Go ahead.'

'You've slept with every guy on the Dragons?'

'Yes.'

'Even the married ones?'

'Yes,' she replied. 'Anyone who has been on the team since 1993. That's when I started with the Dragons. I started with the Giants in 1991.'

'Wait a second. You're a groupie for the Giants, too? The football Giants?'

146

'I told you. I don't like the term groupie.'

'What word would you be more comfortable with?'

She tilted her head a little and kept the smile. 'Look, Myron, I'm an investment banker on Wall Street. I work very hard. I like taking cooking classes and I'm a step-aerobics nut. All in all I am pretty normal by this world's standards. I don't hurt anybody. I don't want to get married or have a relationship. But I have this one little fetish.'

'You have sex with professional athletes.'

She held up her index finger. 'Only with the guys on the Giants and Dragons.'

'Nice to see team loyalty,' Myron said, 'in this era of free agency.'

Thumper laughed. 'That's pretty funny.'

'Are you telling me you've slept with every player on the Giants?'

'Just about. I have tickets on the fifty-yard line. After every game, I have sex with two players – one from the defense, and one from the offense.'

'Sort of like the game MVPs?'

'Exactly.'

Myron shrugged. 'Beats getting the game ball, I guess.'

'Yes,' she said slowly. 'It definitely beats getting a game ball.'

Myron rubbed his eyes. *Ground control to Major Tom.* He studied her for a moment. She seemed to be doing the same thing to him. 'So how did you get the nickname Thumper?' he asked.

'It's not what you think.'

'What's not what I think?'

'How I got the nickname. Everyone assumes it has something to do with screwing like a rabbit.'

'And it doesn't?'

'No, it doesn't.' She looked up in the air. 'How do I explain this delicately?'

'You're worried about delicacy?'

She gave him a mildly disapproving look. 'Don't be like that.'

'Like what?'

'Like some right-wing, narrow-minded, Pat Buchanan-type Neanderthal. I have feelings.'

'I didn't say you didn't.'

'No, but you're acting like it. I don't hurt anyone. I'm honest. I'm forward. I'm direct. I control what I do and to whom. And I'm happy.'

'Not to mention disease-ridden,' he heard himself say and immediately regretted it. The words had just slipped out; that happened to him sometimes.

'What?'

'I'm sorry,' he said. 'That was uncalled for.'

But he had hit a nerve. 'The men I have sex with always wear condoms,' she snapped. 'I get tested frequently. I'm clean.'

'I'm sorry. I shouldn't have said anything.'

She didn't stop. 'And I don't sleep with anyone I think might be infected with something. I'm careful that way.'

Myron bit his lip this time. No point. 'My mistake,' he said. 'I didn't mean it; I'm sorry. Please accept my apology.'

Her chest heaved, but she was calm now, 'Okay,' she said with an exhale. 'Apology accepted.'

Her eyes met his again. They smiled at each other for far too long. Myron felt like a game-show contestant. A thought thankfully interrupted the semitrance. 'Did you sleep with Greg Downing?' he asked.

'In 1993,' she said. 'He was one of the first Dragons.'

How that must swell his bosom with pride. 'You still see him?'

'Sure. We're good friends. I'm friends with most of the guys afterwards. Not all, but most.'

'Do you two talk a lot?'

'Sometimes.'

'Recently?'

'Not the past month or two.'

'Do you know if he's seeing anyone?'

Thumper gave him a curious look. 'Why would you want to know about that?'

Myron shrugged. 'Just making conversation.' The Return of Mr Lame.

'It's an odd topic,' she said.

'I guess I've been thinking about him a lot. All this talk about my being on Greg's team and our history together. It just got me thinking.'

'It got you thinking about Greg's love life?' She wasn't buying it.

Myron sort of shrugged and mumbled something even he didn't understand. A laugh broke out from the other side of the pool. A group of his new teammates were enjoying a joke. Leon White was one of them. He met Myron's eye and nodded a hello. Myron nodded back. Myron realized that while no one seemed to be staring at them, all of his teammates had to know why Thumper had approached him. Again he felt like he was back in college, but this time the feeling didn't bring on the same happy nostalgia.

Thumper was busy studying him again, her eyes narrowed and focused. Myron tried to look neutral, but he felt like a doofus. Being so openly inspected did that to him. He tried to meet her gaze.

Thumper suddenly smiled widely and folded her arms. 'I get it now,' she said.

'What?'

'It's obvious.'

'What's obvious?'

'You want revenge,' she said.

'Revenge for what?'

The smile grew a bit, then relaxed. 'Greg stole Emily from you. Now you want to steal someone back.'

'He didn't steal her from me,' Myron said quickly. He heard the defensive tone in his voice and didn't like it. 'Emily and I broke up before they started dating.'

'If you say so.'

'I say so.' Mr Snappy Retort.

She let loose a throaty laugh and put a hand on his arm. 'Relax, Myron. I'm only teasing you.' She looked at him again. All of this eye contact was beginning to give Myron a headache. He stared at her nose instead. 'So are we going to do this?' she asked.

'No,' Myron said.

'If it's the fear of disease—'

'It's not. I'm involved with someone.'

'So?'

'So I don't cheat on her.'

'Who wants you to cheat? I just want to have sex with you.'

'And you think those two things are mutually exclusive?'

'Of course they are,' Thumper said. 'Our having sex should have absolutely no effect on your relationship. I don't want you to stop caring about your girlfriend. I don't want to be a part of your life. I don't even want to be intimate.'

'Gee, you make it sound so romantic,' Myron said.

'But that's just the point. It's not romantic. It's just a physical act. Sure, it feels great, but in the end it's just a physical act. Like shaking hands.'

'Shaking hands,' Myron repeated. 'You should write greeting cards.'

'I'm just telling you how it is. Past civilizations – ones far more intellectually advanced than us – understood that pleasure of the flesh was no sin. Associating sex with guilt is a modern, absurd hang-up. This whole concept of tying sex to possession is something we got from uptight Puritans who wanted to maintain control over their major possession: their wife.'

A history scholar, Myron thought. Nice to see.

'Where is it written,' she continued, 'that two people can't reach heights of physical ecstasy without being in love? I mean, think about how ridiculous that is. It's silly, isn't it?'

'Maybe,' Myron said. 'But I'll still pass, thank you.'

She shrugged a suit-yourself. 'TC will be very disappointed.'

'He'll get over it,' he said.

Silence.

'Well,' she said, clasping her hands together, 'I think I'll mingle. It was nice chatting with you, Myron.'

'A true experience,' Myron agreed.

Myron mingled a bit, too. He hooked up with Leon for a while. Leon introduced him to his wife, a blond sex-pot named Fiona. Very Playmate-like. She had a breathy voice and was one of those women who made even the most casual conversation one long double entendre – so accustomed to using her physical charms that she did not know when to turn them off. Myron chatted with them both briefly and excused himself.

The bartender informed him that they were not stocking any Yoo-Hoo. He took an Orangina instead. Not just orange soda, but Orangina. How European. He took a sip. Pretty good.

A hand slapped Myron's back. It was TC. He had foregone the *GQ*-suit look, opting for white leather pants and a white leather vest. No shirt. He wore dark sunglasses.

'Having a good time?' he asked.

'It's been interesting,' Myron said.

'Come on. I'll show you something.'

They walked in silence up a grassy hill away from the party. The incline grew steadily steeper, the music fainter. The rap had been replaced with an alternative group called the Cranberries. Myron liked their music. 'Zombie' was on right now. Dolores O'Riordan was repeatedly singing, 'In your head, in your head,' until she got tired and moved to repeating the word, 'Zombie, zombie' several hundred times. Okay, the Cranberries could work on their chorus lyrics, but the song still worked. Good stuff.

There were no lights now, but a glow from the ones by the pool provided enough illumination. When they reached the plateau, TC motioned in front of them. 'There.'

Myron looked out, and the sight nearly took his breath away. They were up high enough to get an unimpeded, spectacular view of the Manhattan skyline. The sea of lights seemed to shimmer like beads of water. The George

Washington Bridge looked close enough to touch. They both stood in silence for several moments.

'Nice, huh?' TC said.

'Very.'

He took off his sunglasses. 'I come up here a lot. By myself. It's a good place to think.'

'I would think so.'

They looked off again.

'Thumper talk to you yet?' Myron asked.

TC nodded.

'Were you disappointed?'

'No,' TC said. 'I knew you'd say no.'

'How?'

He shrugged. 'Just a feeling. But don't let her fool you. Thumper's good people. She's probably the closest thing I got to a friend.'

'What about all those guys you were hanging out with?'

TC sort of smiled. 'You mean the white boys?'

'Yeah.'

'Not friends,' he said. 'If tomorrow I stopped playing ball, they'd all look at me like I'm pinching on a loaf on their sofa.'

'Poetically put, TC.'

'Just the truth, man. You in my position, you don't have no friends. Facts of life. White or black, it don't matter. People hang around me because I'm a rich superstar. They figure they can get something for free. That's all.'

'And that's okay with you?'

'Don't matter if it's okay,' TC said. 'It's the way it is. I ain't complaining.'

'Do you get lonely?' Myron asked.

153

'Too many people around to get lonely.'

'You know what I mean.'

'Yeah, I know what you mean.' TC sort of jerked his head from side to side, like he was trying to loosen up his neck before a game. 'Folks always talking about the price of fame, but you wanna know the real price? Forget that privacy shit. So I don't go out to the movies as much. Big fucking deal – where I come from you can't afford to go anyway. The real price is you ain't a person anymore. You're just a thing, a shiny thing like one of those Benzes out there. The poor brothers think I'm a golden ladder with goodies at every step up. The rich white boys think I'm a fancy pet. Like with OJ. Remember those guys who hung out in OJ's trophy room?'

Myron nodded.

'Look, I ain't complaining. Don't get me wrong. This is a whole lot better than pumping gas or working in a coal mine or something. But I always got to remember the truth: the only thing that separates me from any nigger on the street is a game. That's it. A knee going pop, like with what happened to you, and I'm back down there. I always remember that. Always.' He gave Myron hard eyes, letting his words hang in the crisp air. 'So when some hot babe acts like I'm something special, it ain't me she's after. You see what I'm saying? She's blinded by all that money and fame. Everyone is, male or female.'

'So you and I could never be friends?' Myron asked.

'Would you be asking me that if I was just some ignorant fool pumping gas?'

'Maybe.'

'Bullshit,' he said with a smile. 'People bitch about my attitude, you know. They say I act like everybody owes me. Like I'm a prima donna. But they just mad because I

154

see through them. I know the truth. They all think I'm some ignorant nigger – the owners, the coaches, whatever – so why should I respect them? Only reason they even talk to me is because I can slam the ball through the hoop. I'm just a monkey making them money. Once I stop, that's it. I'm just another dumb slice of ghetto shit not fit to sit my black ass on their toilet.' He stopped then, as though out of breath. He looked back at the skyline. The sight seemed to rejuvenate him. 'You ever meet Isiah Thomas?' he asked.

'The Detroit Piston? Yeah, once.'

'I heard him doing this interview one time, must have been when the Pistons won those championships. Some guy asked him what he'd be doing if he wasn't a basketball player. You know what Isiah said?'

Myron shook his head.

'He said he'd be a United States senator.' TC laughed hard and high-pitched. The sound echoed in the still night. 'I mean, is the brother crazy or what? Isiah really believe that shit. A United States senator – who the fuck is he kidding?' He laughed again, but the sound seemed more forced now. 'Me, I know what I'd be. I'd be working in a steel mill, the midnight to ten A.M. shift, or maybe I'd be in jail or dead, I don't know.' He shook his head. 'United States senator. Shit.'

'What about the game?' Myron asked.

'What about it?'

'Do you love playing basketball?'

He looked amused. 'You do, don't you? You buy all that "for the love of the game" bullshit.'

'You don't?'

TC shook his head. The moon reflected off his shaved pate, giving his head an almost mystical glow. 'It was never about that for me,' he said. 'Basketball was just a means to an end. It's about making money. It's about setting me up for life.'

'Did you ever love the game?'

'Sure, I guess I must have. It was a good place to go, you know? But I don't think it was the game – I mean, not the running and jumping and shit. Basketball was just what I was all about. Everywhere else I was just another dumb black boy, but on the basketball court, I was, well, the man. A hero. It's an incredible high, everyone treating you like that. You know what I mean?'

Myron nodded. He knew. 'Can I ask you something else?'

'Go ahead.'

'What's with all the tattoos and rings?'

He smiled. 'They bother you?'

'Not really. I'm just curious.'

'Suppose I just like wearing them,' TC said. 'That enough?'

'Yes,' Myron said.

'But you don't believe it, do you?'

Myron shrugged. 'I guess not.'

'Truth is, I do like them a little. The bigger truth is, it's business.'

'Business?'

'Basketball business. Making money. Lots of it. You know how much money I make in endorsements? A shit load. Why? Because outrageousness sells. Look at Deon. Look at Rodman. The more crazy shit I do, the more they pay me.'

'So it's just an act?'

'A lot of it, yeah. I like to shock, too, just my way. But mostly I do it for the press.'

'But the press is always ripping you apart,' Myron said.

'Don't matter. They write about me, they make me more money. Simple as that.' He smiled. 'Let me clue you in on something, Myron. The press is the dumbest animal on God's green earth. You know what I'm gonna do one day?'

Myron shook his head.

'One day I'll get rid of the rings and shit, and I'll start dressing nice. Then I'll start talking polite, you know, giving them all yes-sirs and yes-ma'ams and start spitting out all that team-effort bullshit they like to hear. You know what'll happen? These same fucks that say I'm destroying the integrity of the game will be kissing my black ass like it's the Blarney Stone. They be talking about how I went through some sort of miraculous transformation. How now I'm a hero. But only thing that's really changed is my act.' TC gave him a big smile.

Myron said, 'You're a piece of work, TC.'

TC turned back to the water. Myron watched him in silence. He hadn't bought all of TC's rationalizations. There was more at work here. TC wasn't lying, but he wasn't exactly telling the truth either – or maybe he couldn't admit the truth even to himself. He hurt. He truly believed no one could love him, and no matter who you are, that hurts. It made you insecure. It made you want to hide and build fences. The sad thing was, TC was at least partially right. Who'd care about him if he wasn't playing professional basketball? If not for his ability to play a child's game, where would he be right now? TC was like the beautiful girl who wanted you to look down deep to find the soul within – but the only reason you'd bother trying was because she was beautiful. Get rid of that physical beauty – become the ugly girl – and nobody gives a damn about scratching the surface to find the beauty within. Get rid of TC's physical prowess and the same thing happens.

In the end, TC was not as off-the-wall as he appeared in public nor was he as put-together as he wanted Myron to think. Myron was no psychologist, but he was sure that there was more to the tattoos and body piercing than making money. They were too physically destructive for so pat an explanation. With TC, there were a lot of factors at work. Being a former basketball star himself, Myron understood some of them; being that Myron and TC came from completely different worlds, there were others he could not so readily grasp.

TC interrupted their joint solitude. 'Now I got a question for you,' he said.

'Shoot.'

'Why you really here?' TC asked.

'Here? As in your house—'

'On the team. Look, man, I saw you play when I was in junior high. In the NCAAs. You were great, okay? But that was a long time ago. You got to know you can't do it anymore. You had to see that at practice today.'

Myron tried not to look stunned. Had he and TC been at the same practice? But of course they had, and of course, TC was right. Didn't Myron remember the days when he was the team's superstar? Didn't he remember scrimmaging against the last five guys who would play their butt off while the starting five screwed around and played with no incentive? Didn't he remember how disillusioned those last five became, fooling themselves into believing they were just as good as the first five when the first five were tired from real games and were just slacking off? And back then, Myron was in college. He played maybe twenty-five games a season – these guys played almost a hundred against vastly superior competition.

Good enough to play with these guys? Who had he been kidding?

'I'm just giving it a shot,' Myron said softly.

'Can't let go, huh?'

Myron said nothing. They fell back into a brief silence.

'Hey, I almost forgot,' TC said. 'I hear you're good friends with a big hotshot at Lock-Horne Securities. That true?'

'Yes.'

'Was he that slice of white bread you talking with after the game?'

Myron nodded. 'His name is Win.'

'You know Thumper works on Wall Street, right?'

'She told me,' Myron said.

'Thumper wants to change jobs. Think your friend could talk to her?'

Myron shrugged. 'I could ask him.' Win would certainly appreciate her outlook on the role of sex in ancient civilizations. 'Who does she work for now?'

'Small outfit. Called Kimmel Brothers. But she needs to move on, you know? They won't make her a partner, even though she busts her butt for them.'

TC said something else but Myron was no longer listening. Kimmel Brothers. Myron remembered the name immediately. When he'd hit the redial button on the phone at Greg's house, a woman had answered and said, 'Kimmel Brothers.' Yet Thumper had just told Myron she hadn't spoken to Greg in a month or two.

Coincidence? Myron thought not.

Chapter 16

Thumper was gone.

'She came for you,' TC said. 'When it didn't happen she split. She got work tomorrow morning.'

Myron checked his watch. Eleven-thirty. Long day. Time for a little shut-eye. He made his good nights and headed for his car. Audrey was leaning against the hood, her arms folded across her chest, her ankles crossed. Pure casual.

'You going back to Jessica's?' she asked.

'Yes.'

'Mind giving me a lift?'

'Hop in.'

Audrey gave him the same smile he had seen back at practice. He had thought at the time she had been impressed with his play; now it was clearer that the amusement was more akin to ridicule than appreciation. He unlocked the doors in silence. She took off her blue blazer and laid it on the backseat; he did likewise. She wore a forest green turtleneck underneath it. She adjusted the neck part, folding it back an extra time. She took off the pearls and jammed them in the front pocket of her jeans. Myron started the car.

'I'm starting to put this thing together,' Audrey said.

Myron did not like the way she said it. Too much authority in her voice. Audrey hadn't needed a lift home, he was sure of that. She wanted to talk to him alone. That worried him. He gave her the good-natured smile and said, 'This doesn't have anything to do with my ass, does it?'

'What?'

'Jessica told me you two were discussing my ass.'

She laughed. 'Well, I hate to admit this,' she said, 'but it did look pretty scrumptious.'

Myron tried not to look too pleased. 'So you doing a story on it?'

'On your ass?'

'Yes.'

'Of course,' she said. 'I was thinking we could give it a big spread.'

Myron groaned.

'You're trying to change the subject,' she said.

'There was a subject?'

'I was telling you how I was putting this thing together.'

'That's a subject?'

He glanced at her. She was sitting with her left knee on the seat and her left ankle tucked under her so her entire body could face him. Audrey had a wide face and a few freckles, though he bet she had a lot more when she was a kid. Remember that tomboy who was kinda cute in your sixth grade class? Here she was all grown up. No beauty certainly. Not in the classic sense. But there was an earthy appeal to Audrey that made you want to reach out and hug her and roll in leaves on a crisp autumn day.

'It shouldn't have taken me so long to figure out,' she continued. 'It's pretty obvious in hindsight.'

'Am I supposed to know what you're talking about?'

'No,' she replied. 'You're supposed to continue to play dumb for a few more minutes.'

'My specialty.'

'Good, then just drive and listen.' Her hands were in constant gesturing motion, peaking and valleying along with her voice. 'See, I was waylaid by the whole poetic irony stuff. That's what I concentrated on. But your backgrounds as rivals is secondary in all this. It's not nearly as important as, say, your past relationship with Emily.'

'I have no idea what you're talking about.'

'You didn't play AAU. You didn't play in any summer league. You play in pickup games at the Y maybe once a week. Your major workout revolves around Master Kwon's place with Win – and they don't have a basketball court.'

'Is there a point?'

Her hands spread in disbelief. 'You haven't been honing your skills. You haven't played anyplace where Clip or Calvin or Donny would have seen you play. So why would the Dragons sign you? It doesn't make sense. Was the move strictly P.R.? Unlikely. The positive bump will be minimum, and if you fail – which, let's face it, is very likely – that good publicity will probably be nullified. Ticket sales are good. The team is doing well. They don't need a publicity stunt right now. So there has to be another reason.' She stopped and readjusted herself on the car seat. 'Enter the timing.'

'The timing?'

'Yes,' she said. 'Why now? Why sign you so late in the season? The answer is obvious really. There is only one thing about the timing that stands out.'

'And that is?'

'Downing's sudden disappearance.'

'He didn't disappear,' Myron corrected. 'He's injured. That's your precious timing. Greg got hurt. A spot opened up. I filled it.'

Audrey smiled and shook her head. 'Still want to play dumb, huh? Fine, go ahead. You're right. Downing is supposed to be injured and in seclusion. Now I'm good, Myron, and for the life of me I can't find this secluded spot of his. I've called in all my best contacts and I can't get anything. Don't you find that a bit odd?'

Myron shrugged.

'Maybe,' she went on, 'if Downing really craved seclusion to fix his injured ankle – an injury which doesn't show up on any game tape, by the way – he could find a way. But if all he's doing is working on an injury, why work so hard at it?'

'So pain in the asses like you don't bother him,' Myron said.

Audrey almost laughed at that one. 'Said with such conviction, Myron. It's almost like you believe it.'

Myron said nothing.

'But let me just add a few more points and then you can stop playing dumb.' Audrey counted them off on ringless, slightly callused fingers. 'One, I know you used to work for the feds. That gives you some background in investigative work. Two, I know Downing has a habit of vanishing. He's done it before. Three, I know Clip's situation with the other owners. The big vote is coming up. Four, I

163

know you visited Emily yesterday and I doubt you were there to restoke the flames.'

'How did you know about that?' Myron asked.

She just smiled and put her hand down. 'Add them up and there's only one conclusion: you are looking for Greg Downing. He's missing again. This time however the timing is much more critical; Clip's ownership vote and the playoffs are coming up. Your job is to find him.'

'You got a hell of an imagination, Audrey.'

'I do at that,' she agreed, 'but we both know I got this right so let's end playing dumb and cut to the heart of it: I want in.'

'Want in.' Myron shook his head. 'You reporters and your lingo.'

'I don't want to give you up,' she continued. Her knee was still up on the seat. Her face was as bright and expectant as a school kid's waiting for the final bell in May. 'I think we should team up. I can help. I got great sources. I can ask questions without worrying about blowing my cover. I know this team inside and out.'

'And what exactly do you want for this help?'

'The full story. I'm the first reporter to know where he is, why he vanished, whatever. You promise to tell only me; I get the full exclusive.'

They passed several sleazy motels and a potpourri of gas stations on Route 4. No-tell motels in New Jersey always gave themselves lofty names that belied their social station. Right now, for example, they were driving past the 'Courtesy Inn.' This fine establishment not only gave you courteous attention, but they gave it to you by the hour at a rate, according to the sign, of $19.82. Not twenty dollars, mind you, but $19.82 – so priced, Myron guessed, because it was also the year they last changed

164

sheets. The CHEAP BEER DEPOT, according to another sign, was the next building on Myron's right. Truth in advertising. Nice to see. The Courtesy Inn could learn a lesson from them.

'We both know I could report it now,' she said. 'It'd still be a pretty good scoop – reporting that Downing wasn't really injured and you're just here to find him. But I'd be willing to trade it in for a larger story.'

Myron thought it over as he paid the toll. He glanced at her expectant face. She looked wild-cyed and wild-haired, kind of like the refugee women coming off the boat in Palestine in the movie *Exodus*. Ready to do battle to claim her homeland.

'You have to make me a promise,' he said.

'What?'

'No matter what – no matter how incredible the story seems – you won't jump the gun. You won't report any of it until he's found.'

Audrey nearly leapt from her seat. 'What do you mean? How incredible?'

'Forget it, Audrey. Report whatever you want.'

'All right, all right, you have a deal,' she said quickly, hands raised in surrender. 'You had to know saying something like that would pique my interest.'

'You promise?'

'Yeah, yeah, I promise. So what's up?'

Myron shook his head. 'You first,' he said. 'Why would Greg vanish?'

'Who knows?' she replied. 'The man is a professional flake.'

'What can you tell me about his divorce?'

'Just that's it's been acrimonious as all hell.'

'What have you heard?'

'They've been battling over the kids. They're both trying to prove the other is an unfit parent.'

'Any details on how they're going about that?'

'No. It's been kept pretty hush-hush.'

'Emily told me Greg had pulled some sleazy tricks,' Myron said. 'Do you know anything about that?'

Audrey chewed on her bottom lip for a few moments. 'I heard a rumor – a very unsubstantiated rumor – that Greg hired a private eye to follow her.'

'Why?'

'I don't know.'

'To film her maybe? Catch her with another man?'

She shrugged. 'It's just a rumor. I don't know.'

'You know the P.I.'s name, or who he works for?'

'Rumor, Myron. Rumor. A pro basketball player's divorce is hardly earth-shattering sports news. I didn't follow it that closely.'

Myron made a mental note to check Greg's files for any payment to an investigation firm. 'How was Greg's relationship with Marty Felder?'

'His agent? Good, I guess.'

'Emily told me Felder had lost Greg millions.'

She shrugged. 'I've never heard anything about that.'

The Washington Bridge was fairly clear. They stayed to the left and took the Henry Hudson Parkway south. On their right, the Hudson River sparkled like a blanket of black sequins; on their left was a billboard with Tom Brokaw displaying his friendly yet firm smile. The caption under his picture read: 'NBC News – Now More Than Ever.' Very dramatic. What the hell did it mean?

'How about Greg's personal life?' Myron continued. 'Girlfriends, that kind of thing?'

'You mean a steady?'

'Yes.'

She ran her fingers through the thick, curling locks, then rubbed the back of her own neck. 'There was this one girl. He kept it kind of secret, but I think they were living together for a while.'

'What's her name?'

'He never told me. I saw them together at a restaurant once. A place called the Saddle River Inn. He didn't look happy to see me.'

'What did she look like?'

'Nothing special from what I remember. She was a brunette. She was sitting so I couldn't tell you height or weight.'

'Age?'

'I don't know. Thirty-ish, I guess.'

'What makes you think they were living together?'

It seemed like an easy question, but she stopped and raised her eyes. 'Leon let something slip once,' she said.

'What did he say?'

'I don't remember anymore. Something about the girl-friend. Then he clammed up.'

'How long ago was this?'

'Three, four months ago. Maybe more.'

'Leon implied that he and Greg weren't really that close, that the media made a bigger deal out of it than it was.'

Audrey nodded. 'There is a tension there now, but I think it's just temporary.'

'Why would there be a tension?'

'I don't know.'

'How long have you noticed the tension?'

'Not long. Within the last two weeks maybe.'

'Anything happen recently between Greg and Leon that you're aware of?'

'Nope. They've been friends for a long time. Friends have disagreements. I didn't take it too seriously.'

Myron let loose a deep breath. Friends did indeed have disagreements, but the timing was curious. 'Do you know Maggie Mason?'

'Thumper? Of course.'

'Were she and Greg close?'

'If you mean did they screw—'

'No, I don't mean that.'

'Well, they screwed. That I'm sure of. Despite what Thumper claims, not every guy on the team has gotten thumped. Some have turned her down. Not many, I admit. But some. She hit on you yet?'

'Just a few short hours ago.'

She smiled. 'I assume you joined the few, the proud, the Unthumped?'

'You assume correctly. But what about her relationship with Greg? Are they close?'

'They're pretty close, I'd say. But Thumper is closest to TC. Those two are very tight. It's not purely sexual either. Don't get me wrong. I'm sure TC and Maggie have had sex and probably still do on occasions. But they're like brother and sister too. It's weird.'

'How do TC and Greg get along?' Myron asked.

'Not bad for team superstars. Not great either.'

'Care to elaborate?'

She paused, gathered her thoughts. 'For five years now, TC and Downing have shared the spotlight. I guess there is a mutual respect for each other on the court, but they don't talk off it. At least, not very much. I'm not saying they dislike each other, but playing basketball is a job like any other. You might be able to stand one another at work, but you don't want to see the person socially.' She looked up. 'Take the Seventy-ninth Street exit.'

'You still live on Eighty-first?'

'Yes.'

Myron took the exit and stopped at a traffic light on Riverside Drive.

'Now it's your turn, Myron. Why did they hire you?'

'It's like you said. They want me to find Greg.'

'What have you learned so far?'

'Not much.'

'So why were you so concerned I'd jump the gun and tell the story early?'

Myron hesitated.

'I promised not to say anything,' she reminded him. 'You have my word.'

Fair is fair. He told her about the blood in Greg's basement. Her mouth dropped open. When he told her about finding Sally/Carla's body, he feared her heart might give out.

'My God,' Audrey said when he finished. 'You think Downing killed her.'

'I didn't say that.'

She fell back against the seat. Her head lolled against the headrest as though her neck could no longer support her. 'Christ, what a story.'

'And one you can't tell.'

'Don't remind me.' She sat back up again. 'Do you think it'll leak soon?'

'It might.'

'Why can't I be the recipient of that leak?'

Myron shook his head. 'Not yet. We got a lid on this so far. You can't be the one to blow it off.'

169

Her nod was grudging. 'Do you think Downing killed her and ran?'

'There is no evidence of that.' He pulled up to her building. 'One last question,' he said. 'Was Greg involved in anything unsavory?'

'Like what?'

'Like is there any reason thugs would be after him?'

Again her excitement was palpable. The woman was like an electric current. 'What do you mean? What thugs?'

'A couple of thugs were watching Greg's house.'

Her face was positively glowing. 'Thugs? You mean like professional gangsters?'

'Probably. I don't know for sure yet. Can you think of anything that would connect Greg to thugs or for that matter, the murder of this woman? Drugs maybe?'

Audrey shook her head immediately. 'It can't be drugs.'

'What makes you so sure?'

'Downing is a health nut, a real Granola head.'

'So was River Phoenix.'

She shook her head again. 'Not drugs. I'm sure of it.'

'Look into it,' he said. 'See what you can come up with.'

'Sure,' she said. 'I'll look into everything we talked about.'

'Try to be discreet.'

'No problem,' she said. She got out of the car. 'Good night, Myron. Thanks for trusting me.'

'Like I had a choice.'

Audrey smiled and closed the car door. He watched her walk into the building. He put the car back in drive and headed back to Seventy-ninth Street. He got back on the parkway and continued south toward Jessica's. He was about to pick up his cellular phone and call her when the phone rang. The dashboard clock read 12:07 A.M. It had to be Jessica.

'Hello?'

It wasn't Jessica. 'Right lane, three cars behind you. You're being followed.'

It was Win.

Chapter 17

'When did you get back?' Myron asked.

Win ignored the question. 'The automobile following you is the same one we spotted at Greg's house. It is registered to a storage facility in Atlantic City. No known mob connections, but that would seem to me to be a safe bet.'

'How long have you been following me?'

Again Win ignored him. 'The two men who jumped you the other night. What did they look like?'

'Big,' Myron said. 'One was absolutely huge.'

'Crew cut?'

'Yes.'

'He's in the car following you. Passenger seat.'

Myron didn't bother asking how Win knew about the thugs jumping him. He had a pretty good idea.

'They've been communicating on the telephone quite a bit,' Win continued. 'I believe they're coordinating with someone else. The phone activity picked up after your stop on Eighty-first Street. Hold on a second. I'll call you right back.' He hung up. Myron checked his rearview mirror. The car was still there, right where Win said it was. A minute later the phone rang again.

'What?' Myron said.

'I just spoke to Jessica again.'

'What do you mean, again?'

Win sighed impatiently. He hated explanations. 'If they are planning to jump you tonight, it is logical to assume it will be by her loft.'

'Right.'

'Ergo, I called her ten minutes ago. I told her to keep an eye out for anything unusual.'

'And?'

'An unmarked white van parked across the street,' Win answered. 'No one got out.'

'So it appears they are going to strike,' Myron said.

'Yes,' Win said. 'Should I preempt it?'

'How?'

'I could disable the car following you.'

'No,' Myron said. 'Let them make their move and see where it leads.'

'Pardon?'

'Just back me up. If they grab me, I may be able to get to the boss.'

Win made a noise.

'What?' Myron asked.

'You complicate the simple,' Win said. 'Would it not be easier to simply take out the two in the car? We could then make them tell us about their boss.'

'It's that "make them" part I have trouble with.'

'But of course,' Win countered. 'A thousand pardons for my lack of ethics. Clearly it is far wiser to risk your

173

own life than to make a worthless goon feel momentary discomfort.'

Win had a way of putting things that made very frightening sense. Myron had to remind himself that the logical was often more terrifying than the illogical – especially where Win was concerned. 'They're just hired help,' Myron said. 'They're not going to know anything.'

Pause. 'Fair point,' Win conceded. 'But suppose they simply shoot you.'

'That wouldn't make any sense. The reason they're interested in me is because they think I know where Greg is.'

'And dead men tell no tales,' Win added.

'Exactly. They want to make me talk. So just follow me. If they take me some place well guarded—'

'I'll get through,' Win said.

Myron did not doubt it. He gripped the steering wheel. His pulse began to race. Easy to dismiss the possibility of getting shot by reasonable analysis; it was another thing to have to park a car down the street from men you knew were out to hurt you. Win would have his eye on the van. So would Myron. If a gun came out before a person, the situation would be handled.

He got off the highway. The streets of Manhattan were supposed to be a nice, even grid. Streets ran north/south and east/west. They were numbered. They were straight. But when you got to Greenwich Village and Soho, it was like a grid painted by Dali. Gone were the numerical roads for the most part, except when they twisted and turned between streets with real-live names. Gone was any pretext of straight or systematized.

Luckily Spring Street was a direct run. A bicyclist sped by Myron, but no one else was out. The white van was parked right where it was supposed to be. Unmarked, just as Jessica had said. The windows were tinted so you couldn't look in. Myron didn't see Win's car, but then again he wasn't supposed to. He moved slowly down the street. He passed the van. When he did, the van started its motor. Myron pulled into a spot toward the end of the block. The van pulled out.

Show time.

Myron parked the car, straightened out the steering wheel, turned the engine off. He pocketed the keys. The van inched forward. He took out his revolver and stuck it under the car seat. It wouldn't do him any good right now. If they grabbed him, they would search him. If they started shooting, shooting back would be a waste of time. Win would either remove the threat or not.

He reached for the door handle. Fear nestled into his throat, but he did not stop. He pulled the handle, opened the door, and stepped out. It was dark. The streetlights in Soho were nearly worthless, like pen beams in a black hole. Lights drifting out from nearby windows provided more of an eerie kindle than real illumination. There were plastic garbage bags out on the street. Most had been torn open; the odor of spoiled food wafted through the air. The van slowly cruised toward him. A man stepped out from a doorway and approached without hesitation. The man wore a black turtleneck under a black overcoat. He pointed a gun at Myron. The van stopped, and the side door slid open.

'Get in, asshole,' the man with the gun said.

Myron pointed at himself. 'You talking to me?'

'Now, asshole. Haul ass.'

'Is that a turtleneck or a dickey?'

The man with the gun moved closer. 'I said, now.'

'It's nothing to get angry about,' Myron said, but he

stepped toward the van. 'If it is a dickey, you can't tell. It's a very sporty look.' When Myron got nervous, his mouth went into overdrive. He knew it was self-destructive; Win had pointed that out to him on several occasions. But Myron couldn't stop himself. Diarrhea of the mouth or some such ailment.

'Move.'

Myron got in the van. The man with the gun did likewise. There were two more men in the back of the van and one man driving. Everyone was in black, except for one guy who looked to be in charge. He wore a blue pinstripe suit. His Windsor-knotted yellow tie was held in place by a gold tie bar at the collar. Euro-chic. He had long, bleached-blond hair and one of those tans that were a little too perfect to come from the sun. He looked more like an aging surfer boy than a professional mobster.

The van's interior had been custom designed, but not in a good way. All the seats had been ripped out except for the driver's. There was a leather couch in the back along one wall where Pinstripe sat alone. A lime-green shag carpet even Elvis would have found too garish ran along the van's floor and up the sides like a poor man's ivy.

The man in the pinstripe suit smiled; his hands were folded in his lap, very much at ease. The van started moving.

The gunman quickly searched Myron. 'Sit, asshole,' he said.

Myron sat on the carpeted floor. He ran his hand over the shag. 'Lime green,' he said to Pinstripe. 'Nice.'

'It's inexpensive,' Pinstripe said. 'That way we don't worry about bloodstains.'

'Thinking of overhead.' Myron nodded coolly, though his mouth felt very dry. 'That's smart business.'

Pinstripe did not bother with a response. He gave the man with the gun and dickey/turtleneck a look that made the man jolt upward. The man cleared his throat.

'This here is Mr Baron,' the gunman told Myron, indicating Pinstripe. 'Everyone calls him the B Man.' He cleared his throat again. He spoke like he'd been rehearsing this little speech, which, Myron surmised, was probably likely. 'He's called the B Man because he enjoys breaking bones.'

'Say, that must woo the women,' Myron said.

The B Man smiled with capped teeth as white as anything in those old Pepsodent commercials. 'Hold his leg out,' he said.

The man with the turtleneck/dickey pressed the gun against Myron's temple hard enough to leave a permanent imprint. He wrapped his other arm around Myron's neck, the inside of his elbow jammed into Myron's windpipe. He lowered his head and whispered, 'Don't even flinch, asshole.'

He forced Myron into a lying position. The other man straddled Myron's chest and pinned the leg to the floor. Myron had trouble breathing. Panic seized him, but he remained still. Any move at this stage would almost inevitably be the wrong one. He'd have to play it out and see where it went.

The B Man moved off the leather couch slowly. His eyes never left Myron's bad knee; his smile was a happy one. 'I'm going to place one hand on the distal femur and the other on your proximal tibia,' he explained in the same tone a surgeon might use with a student. 'My thumbs will then rest on the medial aspect of the patella. When my thumbs snap forward, I will basically rip off your kneecap laterally.' He met Myron's gaze. 'This will tear your medial retinaculum and several other ligaments. Tendons will snap. I fear it will be most painful.'

Myron didn't even try a wisecrack. 'Hey, wait a second,' he said quickly. 'There's no reason for violence.'

The B Man smiled, shrugged. 'Why does there have to be a reason?'

Myron's eyes widened. Fear hardened in his belly. 'Hold on,' he said quickly. 'I'll talk.'

'I know you will,' the B Man replied. 'But first you'll jerk us around a bit—'

'No, I won't.'

'Please don't interrupt me. It's very rude to interrupt.' The smile was gone. 'Where was I?'

'First he'll jerk us around,' the driver prompted.

'That's right, thank you.' He turned the white smile back to Myron. 'First, you'll stall. You'll do a song-and-dance. You'll hope we'll take you someplace where your partner can save you.'

'Partner?'

'You're still friends with Win, aren't you?'

The man knew Win. This was not a good thing. 'Win who?'

'Precisely,' B Man said. 'This is what I mean by being jerked around. Enough.'

He moved closer. Myron started to struggle, but the man jammed the gun in Myron's mouth. It struck teeth and made him gag. The taste was cold and metallic.

'I'll destroy the knee first. Then we'll talk.'

The other man pulled Myron's leg straight while the gunman took the revolver out of Myron's mouth and pressed it back against his temple. Their grips grew a bit tighter. The B Man lowered his hands to Myron's knee, his fingers spread like eagle's talons.

'Wait!' Myron shouted.

'No,' B Man replied calmly.

Myron started to squirm. He grabbed a loading handle on the floor of the van, the kind of thing used to tie down cargo. He held on and braced himself. He didn't have to wait very long.

The crash jarred them. Myron had been ready for it. No one else had. They all went flying, their grips slackening. Glass shattered. The scream of metal hitting metal filled the air. Brakes screeched. Myron held on until the van slowed. Then he curled into a ball and rolled out of harm's way. There were shouts and a door opened. Myron heard a shot being fired. Voices sounded in a cacophony of confusion. The driver ducked out through his door. The B Man followed, leaping like a grasshopper. The side door opened. Myron looked up as Win stepped in with his gun drawn. The man with the turtleneck/dickey had recovered. He picked up his gun.

'Drop it,' Win said.

The man with the turtleneck/dickey didn't. Win shot him in the face. He turned his aim toward the man who had straddled Myron's chest.

'Drop it,' Win said.

The man did. Win smiled at him. 'Fast learner.'

Win's eyes slid smoothly from side to side, never darting. Win barely moved, seeming to glide rather than walk. His movements were short and economical. He returned his eyes to his captive. The one still breathing.

'Talk,' Win said.

'I don't know nothing.'

'Bad answer,' Win said. He spoke with calm authority, his matter-of-fact tone more intimidating than any scream. 'If you know nothing, you are useless to me; if

179

you are useless to me, you end up like him.' He vaguely motioned toward the still form at his feet.

The man held up his hands. His eyes were round and white. 'Hey, wait a sec, okay? It's no secret. Your buddy heard the guy's name. Baron. The guy's name is Baron. But everyone calls him the B Man.'

'The B Man works out of the Midwest,' Win said. 'Who brought him in?'

'I don't know; I swear.'

Win moved the gun closer. 'You're being useless to me again.'

'It's the truth, I'd tell you if I knew. All I know is the B Man flew in late last night.'

'Why?' Win asked.

'It's got something to do with Greg Downing. That's all I know, I swear.'

'How much does Downing owe?'

'I don't know.'

Win moved closer still. He pressed the barrel of the gun between the man's eyes. 'I rarely miss from this distance,' he said.

The man dropped to his knees. Win followed him down with the gun. 'Please.' His voice was a pained plea. 'I don't know nothing else.' His eyes filled with tears. 'I swear to God, I don't.'

'I believe you,' Win said.

'Win,' Myron said.

Win's eyes never left the man. 'Relax,' he said. 'I just wanted to make sure our friend here had confessed all. Confession is good for the soul, is it not?'

The man nodded hurriedly.

'Have you confessed all?'

More nods.

'You're sure?'

Nod, nod.

Win lowered the weapon. 'Go then,' he said. 'Now.'

The man didn't have to be told twice.

Chapter 18

Win looked down at the dead body as though it were a bag of peat moss. 'We best depart.'

Myron nodded. He reached into his pants pocket and took out the cellular phone. A relatively new trick of the trade. Neither he nor Win had hung up after their call. The line was left open; Win had been able to hear everything that had gone on in the van. It worked as well as any bug or walkie-talkie.

They stepped into the cool night. They were on Washington Street. During the day the place was popping with delivery trucks, but at night it was completely silent. Someone would find a nasty surprise in the morning.

Win normally drove a Jaguar, but he had smashed a 1983 Chevy Nova into the van. Totaled. Not that it mattered. Win had several such vehicles he kept out in New Jersey to use for surveillance or activities just east of legal. The car was untraceable. The plates and paperwork were all phony. It would never lead back to anyone.

Myron looked at him. 'A man of your breeding in a Chevy Nova?' He tsk-tsked.

'I know,' Win said. 'Sitting in it almost gave me a rash.'

'If anyone at the club saw you . . .'

Win shuddered. 'Do not even think such a thought.'

Myron's legs still felt shaky and numb. Even as the B Man had reached down for his knee, Myron had known that Win would find a way to get to him. But the thought of how close he'd come to being crippled for life kept plucking at the muscles in his calves and thighs. He kept bending down and touching the bad knee, as if he couldn't believe it was still there. Tears brimmed in his eyes as he looked at Win. Win saw them and turned away.

Myron followed behind him. 'So how do you know this B Man?' he asked.

'He operates out of the Midwest,' Win said. 'He is also a superb martial artist. We met in Tokyo once.'

'What sort of operation does he run?'

'The usual assorted sundries – gambling, drugs, loan sharking, extortion. A bit of prostitution too.'

'So what's he doing here?'

'It appears that Greg Downing owes him money,' Win said, 'probably from gambling. The B Man specializes in gambling.'

'Nice to have a specialty.'

'Indeed. I would assume that your Mr Downing owes them a large sum of money.' Win glanced over at Myron. 'That's good news for you.'

'Why?'

'Because it implies that Downing is on the run rather than dead,' Win said. 'The B Man is not wasteful. He wouldn't kill someone who owes him a lot of money.'

'Dead men pay no debts.'

'Precisely,' Win said. 'On top of that, he is clearly looking for Downing. If he killed him, he wouldn't need you to find him.'

Myron considered this for a moment. 'It sort of meshes with what Emily told me. She said Greg had no money. Gambling might explain that fact.'

Win nodded. 'Kindly fill me in on what else has occurred in my absence. Jessica mentioned something about finding a dead woman.'

Myron told him everything. As he spoke, new theories rushed forward. He tried to sort through them and organize them a bit. When he finished the recap, Myron went right into the first one.

'Let's assume,' he said, 'that Downing does owe a lot of money to this B Man. That might explain why he finally agreed to sign an endorsement deal. He needs the money.'

Win nodded. 'Go on.'

'And let's also assume the B Man is not stupid. He wants to collect, right? So he would never really hurt Greg. Greg makes him money through his physical prowess. Broken bones would have an adverse effect on Greg's financial status and thus his ability to pay.'

'True,' Win said.

'So let's say Greg owes them a lot of money. Maybe the B Man wanted to scare him in another way.'

'How?'

'By hurting someone close to him. As a warning.'

Win nodded again. 'That might work.'

'And suppose they followed Greg. Suppose they saw him with Carla. Suppose they figured that Greg and Carla were close.' Myron looked up. 'Wouldn't killing her be a hell of a warning?'

Win frowned. 'You think the B Man killed her to warn Downing?'

'I'm saying it's possible.'

'Why wouldn't he just break some of her bones?' Win asked.

'Because the B Man wasn't personally on the scene yet, remember? He got in last night. The murder would have been the work of hired muscle.'

Win still didn't like it. 'Your theory is improbable, at best. If the murder was indeed a warning, where is Downing now?'

'He ran away,' Myron said.

'Why? Because he was afraid for his own life?'

'Yes.'

'And did he run away immediately after learning Carla was dead?' Win asked. 'On Saturday night?'

'That would be most logical.'

'He was frightened off then? By the murder?'

'Yes,' Myron said.

'Ah.' Win stopped and smiled at Myron.

'What?' Myron asked.

'Pray tell,' Win began with a lilt in his voice, 'if Carla's body was just discovered today, how did Downing know about the murder last Saturday night?'

Myron felt a chill.

'For your theory to hold up,' Win continued, 'Greg Downing would have to have done one of three things. One, he witnessed the murder; two, he stumbled into her apartment after the murder; three, he committed the murder himself. Furthermore, there was a great deal of cash in her apartment. Why? What was it doing there? Was this money to help pay back the B Man? If so, why didn't his men take it? Or better yet, why didn't Downing take it back when he was there?'

Myron shook his head. 'So many holes,' he said. 'And we still haven't come up with what connection there is between Downing and this Carla or Sally or whatever her name is.'

Win nodded. They continued walking.

'One more thing,' Myron said. 'Do you really think the mob would kill a woman just because she happened to be with Greg at a bar?'

'Very doubtful,' Win agreed.

'So basically, that whole theory is blown to hell.'

'Not basically,' Win corrected. 'Entirely.'

They kept walking.

'Of course,' Win said, 'Carla could have been working for the B Man.'

An icy finger poked at Myron. He saw where Win was going but he still said, 'What?'

'Perhaps this Carla woman was the B Man's contact. She collected for him. She was meeting Downing because he owed a great deal of money. Downing promises to pay. But he doesn't have the money. He knows they are closing in on him. He has stalled long enough. So he goes back to her apartment, kills her, and runs.'

Silence. Myron tried to swallow, but his throat felt frozen. This was good, this talking it through. It helped. His legs were still rubbery from the incident, but what really bothered him now was how easily he had forgotten the dead man lying in the van. True, the man was probably a professional scum bag. True, the man had jammed the barrel of a gun into his mouth and had not dropped his weapon when Win told him to. And true, the world was probably a better place without him. But in the past

Myron would have still felt some remorse for this fellow human being; in all honesty, he didn't now. He tried to muster some sympathy, but the only thing he felt sad about was that he didn't feel sad.

Enough self-analysis. Myron shook it off and said, 'There are problems with that scenario too.'

'Such as?'

'Why would Greg kill her? Why not just run off before the back-booth meeting?'

Win considered this. 'Fair point. Unless something happened during their meeting to set him off.'

'Like what?'

Win shrugged.

'It all comes back to this Carla,' Myron said. 'Nothing about her adds up. I mean, even a drug dealer doesn't have a setup like hers – working as a diner waitress, hiding sequentially numbered hundred dollar bills, wearing wigs, having all those fake passports. And on top of that, you should have seen Dimonte this afternoon. He knew who she was and he was in a panic.'

'You contacted Higgins at Treasury?' Win asked.

'Yes. He's tracing those serial numbers.'

'That could help.'

'We also need to get a hold of the telephone records from the Parkview Diner. See who Carla called.'

They fell back into silence and kept walking. They didn't want to hail a taxi too close to the scene.

'Win?'

'Yes?'

'Why didn't you want to go to the game the other night?'

Win kept on walking. Myron kept pace. After some

time, Win said, 'You've never watched a replay of it, have you?'

He knew he meant the knee injury. 'No.'

'Why not?'

Myron shrugged. 'No point.'

'No, there is a point.' Win kept walking.

'Mind telling me what that is?' Myron said.

'Watching what happened to you might have meant dealing with it. Watching it might have meant closure.'

'I don't understand,' Myron said.

Win nodded. 'I know.'

'I remember you watched it,' Myron said. 'I remember you watched it over and over.'

'I did that for a reason,' Win said.

'For vengeance.'

'To see if Burt Wesson injured you on purpose,' Win corrected.

'You wanted to pay him back.'

'You should have let me. Then you might have been able to put it behind you.'

Myron shook his head. 'Violence is always the answer for you, Win.'

Win frowned. 'Stop sounding melodramatic. A man committed a vile act upon you. Squaring things would have helped put it behind you. It's not about vengeance. It's about equilibrium. It's about man's basic need to keep the scales balanced.'

'That's your need,' Myron said, 'not mine. Hurting Burt Wesson wouldn't have fixed my knee.'

'But it might have given you closure.'

'What does that mean, closure? It was a freak injury. That's all.'

Win shook his head. 'You never watched the tape.'

188

'It wouldn't have mattered. The knee was still ruined. Watching a tape wouldn't have changed that.'

Win said nothing.

'I don't understand this,' Myron continued. 'I went on after the injury. I never complained, did I?'

'Never.'

'I didn't cry or curse the gods or do any of that stuff.'

'Never,' Win said again. 'You never let yourself be a burden on any of us.'

'So why do you think I needed to relive it?'

Win stopped and looked at him. 'You've answered your own question, but you choose not to hear it.'

'Spare me the Kung-Fu-grasshopper philosophical bullshit,' Myron shot back. 'Why didn't you go to the game?'

Win started walking again. 'Watch the tape,' he said.

Chapter 19

Myron didn't watch the tape. But he had the dream.

In the dream he could see Burt Wesson bearing down on him. He could see the gleeful, almost giddy violence in Burt's face as he drew closer and closer. In the dream, Myron had plenty of time to step out of harm's way. Too much time really. But in this dream – as in many – Myron could not move. His legs would not respond, his feet mired in thick, dream-world quicksand while the inevitable approached.

But in reality, Myron had never seen Burt Wesson coming. There had been no warning. Myron had been pivoting on his right leg when the blinding collision befell him. He heard rather than felt a snap. At first there had been no pain, just wide-eyed astonishment. The astonishment had probably lasted less than a second, but it was a frozen second, a snapshot Myron only took out in dreams. Then came the pain.

In the dream Burt Wesson was almost on him now.

Burt was a huge man, an enforcer-type player, the basket-ball equivalent of a hockey goon. He did not have much talent, but he had tremendous bulk and he knew how to use it. It had gotten him far, but this was the pros now. Burt would be cut before the start of the season – poetic irony that neither he nor Myron would play in a real professional basketball game. Until two nights ago any-way.

In the dream Myron watched Burt Wesson approach and waited. Somewhere in his subconscious, he knew that he would awaken before the collision. He always did. He lingered now in that cusp between nightmare and being awake – that tiny window where you are still asleep but you know it is a dream and even though it may be terrifying, you want to go on and see how it will end because it is only a dream and you are safe. But reality would not keep that window open for long. It never did. As Myron swam to the surface, he knew that whatever the answer was, he would not find it in any nocturnal voyage to the past.

'Phone for you,' Jessica said.

Myron blinked his eyes and rolled onto his back. Jessica was already dressed. 'What time is it?' he asked.

'Nine.'

'What? Why didn't you wake me?'

'You needed the sleep.' She handed him the phone. 'It's Esperanza.'

He took it. 'Hello.'

'Christ, don't you ever sleep in your own bed?' Esper-anza said.

He was hardly in the mood. 'What is it?'

'Fred Higgins from Treasury is on the line,' she said. 'I thought you'd want it.'

'Pass it through.' A click. 'Fred?'

'Yeah, how you doing, Myron?'

'I'm okay. You got anything on those serial numbers?'

There was a brief hesitation. 'You stumbled into some heavy shit, Myron. Some very heavy shit.'

'I'm listening.'

'People don't want this out, you understand? I had to jump through all kinds of hoops to get this.'

'Mum's the word.'

'Okay then.' Higgins took a deep breath. 'The bills are from Tucson, Arizona,' he said. 'More specifically, First City National Bank of Tucson, Arizona. They were stolen in an armed bank heist.'

Myron shot up in the bed. 'When?'

'Two months ago.'

Myron remembered a headline, and his blood turned cold.

'Myron?'

'The Raven Brigade,' Myron managed. 'That was one of theirs, right?'

'Right. You ever work on their case with the feds?'

'No, never.' But he remembered. Myron and Win had worked on cases with a special and almost contradictory nature: high profile with the need for undercover. They had been perfect for such situations – who, after all, would suspect a former basketball star and a rich, Main Line prep of being undercover agents? They could travel in whatever circles they wanted to and not raise suspicion. Myron and Win didn't have to create a cover; their reality was the best one the agency had. But Myron was never full-time with them. Win was their fair-haired boy; Myron was more a utility fielder Win called in when he thought it necessary.

But of course he knew about the Raven Brigade. Most people with even a passing familiarity with sixties extremism knew about them. Started by a charismatic leader named Cole Whiteman, the Ravens had been yet another splinter group of the Weather Underground. They were very much like the Symbionese Liberation Army, the group that kidnapped Patty Hearst. The Ravens, too, attempted a high-profile kidnapping, but the victim ended up dead. The group had gone underground. Four of them. Despite the FBI's best efforts, the four escapees – including Cole Whiteman, who with his Win-like blond hair and Waspy background never looked the part of an extremist – had remained hidden for nearly a quarter century.

Dimonte's bizarre questions about radical politics and 'perversives' no longer seemed so bizarre.

'Was the victim one of the Ravens?' Myron asked.

'I can't say.'

'You don't have to,' Myron said. 'I know it was Liz Gorman.'

There was another brief hesitation. Then: 'How the hell did you know that?'

'The implants,' Myron said.

'What?'

Liz Gorman, a fiery redhead, had been one of the founding members of the Raven Brigade. During their first 'mission' – a failed attempt to burn down a university chemistry lab – the police had picked up a code name on the scanner: CD. It was later revealed that the male members of the Brigade called her CD, short for Carpenter's Dream, because she was 'flat as a board and easy to screw.' Sixties radicals, for all their so-called progressive thoughts, were some of the world's biggest sexists. Now the implants made sense. Everyone Myron had inter-viewed remembered one thing about 'Carla' – her cup size. Liz Gorman had been famous for her flat chest – what better disguise than oversized breast implants?

'The feds and cops are cooperating on this one,' Higgins said. 'They're trying to keep this quiet for a while.'

'Why?'

'They got her place under surveillance. They're hoping to maybe draw out another member.'

Myron felt completely numb. He had wanted to learn more about the mystery woman and now he had: she was Liz Gorman, a famous radical who had not been seen since 1975. The disguises, the various passports, the im-plants – they all added up now. She wasn't a drug dealer, she was a woman on the run.

But if Myron had hoped learning the truth about Liz Gorman would help clarify his own investigation, he had been sadly mistaken. What possible connection could there be between Greg Downing and Liz Gorman? How had a professional basketball player gotten enmeshed with a wanted extremist who had gone underground when Greg was still a kid? It made absolutely no sense.

'How much did they get in the bank heist?' Myron asked.

'Hard to say,' Higgins answered. 'About fifteen thou-sand in cash, but they also blew open the safe-deposit boxes. Over a half million in goods have been declared for insurance purposes, but a lot of it is bullshit. A guy gets robbed, all of a sudden he was keeping ten Rolexes in the box instead of one – trying to rip off the insurance company, you know how it is.'

'On the other hand,' Myron said, 'anyone keeping illegal dollars in there wouldn't declare it. They'd just have to swallow the loss.' Back to drugs and drug money. The extremists in the underground needed resources. They'd been known to rob banks, blackmail former followers who had gone mainstream, deal drugs, whatever. 'So it could have been even more.'

'Right, hard to say.'

'You got anything else on this?'

'Nothing,' Higgins said. 'It's being kept sealed tight, and I'm not in the loop. I can't tell you how hard it was to get this, Myron. You owe me big.'

'I already promised you the tickets, Fred.'

'Courtside?'

'I'll do my best.'

Jessica came back into the room. When she saw Myron's face, she stopped and looked a question at him. Myron hung up and told her. She listened. Remembering Esperanza's crack, Myron realized that he had now spent four nights in a row here – a postbreakup world and Olympic record. He worried about that. It wasn't that he didn't like staying here. He did. It wasn't that he feared commitment or any of that other drivel; to the contrary, he craved it. But part of him was still afraid – old wounds that wouldn't heal and all that.

Myron had a habit of exposing too much of himself. He knew that. With Win or Esperanza it was okay. He trusted them absolutely. He loved Jessica with all his heart, but she had hurt him. He wanted to be tentative. He wanted to hold back, to not leave himself so open, but the heart don't know from stop. At least, Myron's didn't. Two primal internal forces were at odds here: his natural instinct to give all he had when it came to love vs. the survival instinct of pain avoidance.

'This whole thing,' Jessica said when he had finished, 'is just too weird.'

'Yep,' he said. They had barely talked last night. He had assured her that he was all right and they had both gone to sleep. 'I guess I should thank you.'

'For what?'

'You were the one who called Win.'

She nodded. 'After those goons jumped you.'

'I thought you said you weren't going to interfere.'

'Wrong. I said I wasn't going to try to stop you. There's a difference.'

'True enough.'

Jessica started chewing on her bottom lip. She was wearing jeans and a Duke sweatshirt several sizes too large on her. Her hair was still wet from a recent shower. 'I think you should move in,' she said.

Her words hit him square in the jaw. 'What?'

'I didn't mean to just blurt it out like that,' she said. 'I'm not very good at beating around the bush.'

'That's my job anyway,' he said.

She shook her head. 'You pick the strangest times to be crude.'

'Yeah, I'm sorry.'

'Look, I'm not good at this stuff, Myron. You know that.'

He nodded. He knew.

She tilted her head to the side, shrugged, smiled nervously. 'It's just that I like having you here. It feels right.'

His heart soared and sung and quivered in fear. 'It's a big step.'

'Not really,' she said. 'You're here most of the time anyway. And I love you.'

'I love you, too.'

The pause lingered a bit longer than it should. Jessica jumped into it before it could do irreparable harm. 'Don't say anything now,' she said, rushing the words out in a gush. 'I want you to think about it. It was a dumb time to bring it up, with all this stuff going on. Or maybe that's why I chose now, I don't know. But don't say anything. Just think about it. Don't call me today. Or tonight. I'm going to your game, but then I'm taking Audrey out for a few drinks. It's her birthday. Sleep at your house tonight. Maybe we'll talk tomorrow, okay? Tomorrow?'

'Tomorrow,' Myron agreed.

Chapter 20

Big Cyndi sat at the reception desk. 'Sat.' was probably the wrong word. Talk about the proverbial camel trying to squeeze through the eye of the needle. The desk's four legs were off the floor, the top teetering on Big Cyndi's knees like a seesaw. Her coffee mug disappeared into fleshy hands that resembled couch cushions. Her short spikes of hair had more of a pinkish hue today. Her makeup reminded him of a childhood incident involving melted Crayola crayons. She wore white lipstick, like something out of an Elvis documentary. Her size-3XL T-shirt read CLUB SODA NOT SEALS. It took Myron a few seconds to get it. Politically correct but cute.

Usually she growled when she saw Myron. Today she smiled sweetly and batted her eyes at him. The sight was far more frightening, like Bette Davis in *Whatever Happened to Baby Jane*, only on steroids. Big Cyndi pointed up her middle finger and bounced it up and down.

'Line one?' he tried.

She shook her head. The up and down gesture became more hurried. She looked up at the ceiling. Myron followed her gaze but he saw nothing. Cyndi rolled her eyes. The smile was frozen on her face, like a clown's.

'I don't get it,' he said.

'Win wants to see you,' she said.

It was the first time Myron had heard her voice, and it startled him. She sounded like one of those perky hostesses on a cable shopping network, the one where people call up and describe in far too much detail how much their lives were improved by purchasing a green vase shaped like Mount Rushmore.

'Where's Esperanza?' he asked.

'Win's cute.'

'Is she here?'

'Win seemed to think it was important.'

'I'm just—'

'You're going to see Win,' Cyndi interrupted. 'You're certainly not checking up on your most valued associate.' The sweet smile.

'I'm not checking up. I just want to know—'

'Where Win's office is. It's two stories up.' She made a sound with her coffee that some might loosely label, 'slurping.' Moose in the tri-state area scattered in search of mates.

'Tell her I'll be back,' Myron said.

'But of course.' She batted her eyelashes. They looked like two tarantulas in death throes. 'Have a nice day.'

Win's corner office faced Fifty-second Street and Park Avenue. Major league view for Lock-Horne Securities' golden boy. Myron sank into one of the lush burgundy leather chairs. There were several paintings of fox hunts on the richly paneled walls. Dozens of manly men on horseback, dressed in black hats, red blazers, white pants, black boots, rode out armed with only rifles and dogs to chase down a small furry creature until they caught and killed it. Ah, gamesmanship. A tad overkill maybe. Like using a flamethrower to light a cigarette.

Win typed on a laptop computer that looked lonely on the mono-expanse he called a desk. 'I found something of interest on the computer disks we made at Greg's house.'

'Oh?'

'It appears our friend Mr Downing had an e-mail address with America Online,' Win said. 'He downloaded this particular piece of mail on Saturday.' Win spun the laptop around so Myron could read the screen:

Subj:	Sex!
Date:	3–11 14:51:36 EST
From:	Sepbabe
To:	Downing22

Meet you tonight at ten. The place we discussed. Come. I promise you the greatest night of ecstasy imaginable.
—F

Myron looked up. 'Greatest night of ecstasy imaginable?'

'She has quite the writing flair, no?' Win said.

Myron made a face.

Win put a sincere hand to his heart. 'Even if she could not live up to such a promise,' he continued, 'one has to admire her ability to take risk, her dedication to her craft.'

'Uh huh,' Myron said. 'So who is F?'

'There is no profile for the screen name Sepbabe on line,' Win explained. 'That doesn't mean anything, of course. Many users don't have a profile. They don't want everyone knowing their real name. I would assume however that F is yet another alias for our dearly departed friend Carla.'

'We have Carla's real name now,' Myron said.

'Oh?'

'Liz Gorman.'

Win arched an eyebrow. 'Pardon?'

'Liz Gorman. As in the Raven Brigade.' He told Win about Fred Higgins's call. Win leaned back in his chair and steepled his fingers. As usual his face gave away nothing.

When Myron finished, Win said, 'Curiouser and curiouser.'

'It comes down to this,' Myron said. 'What connection could there possibly be between Greg Downing and Liz Gorman?'

'A strong one,' Win said, nodding toward the screen. 'The possibility of the greatest night of ecstasy imaginable, if one is to buy into the hyperbole.'

'But with Liz Gorman?'

'Why not?' Win almost sounded defensive. 'You shouldn't discriminate on the basis of age or implants. It wouldn't be right.'

Mr Equal Rights. 'It's not that,' Myron said. 'Let's pretend that Greg has the hots for Liz Gorman, even though nobody described her as much of a looker . . .'

'You're so shallow, Myron,' Win said with a disenchanted shake of the head. 'Did you ever consider the possibility that Greg saw beneath that? She did, after all, have large breasts.'

'As usual when discussing sex,' Myron replied, 'you've missed the point.'

'Which is?'

'How would they have hooked up in the first place?'

Win steepled his fingers again, bouncing the tips against his nose. 'Ah,' he said.

'Right, ah. Here's a woman who's been living underground for more than twenty years. She's traveled all over the world, probably never staying in one spot for very long. She was in Arizona robbing a bank two months ago. She's working as a waitress in a tiny diner on Dyckman Street. How does this woman hook up with Greg Downing?'

'Difficult,' Win allowed, 'but not impossible. There is plenty of evidence to support that.'

'Like?'

Win motioned to the computer screen. 'This e-mail is talking about last Saturday night, for one – the same night Greg and Liz Gorman met in a New York City bar.'

'In a dive bar,' Myron corrected. 'Why there? Why not go to a hotel or her place?'

'Perhaps because it is out of the way. Perhaps, as you implied, Liz Gorman would want to keep out of the public eye. Such a bar might be a good alternative.' He stopped steepling and lightly drummed his fingers on the desk. 'But you, my friend, are forgetting something else.'

'What?'

'The woman's clothes in Greg's house,' Win said. 'Your investigation has led us to conclude that Downing has a lover he was keeping secret. The question, of course is: why? Why would he work so hard to keep a love affair clandestine? One possible explanation is that the secret love was the infamous Liz Gorman.'

Myron wasn't sure what to think. Audrey had seen Greg at a restaurant with a woman that did not fit Liz

Gorman's description. But what did that mean? It might have been another date. It might have been something innocent. It might have been a side affair, who knows? Still, Myron had trouble buying a romantic entanglement involving Greg Downing and Liz Gorman. Something about it just didn't wash. 'There must be a way of tracing down this screen name and finding out the user's real identity,' he said. 'Let's make sure it checks back to Liz Gorman or one of her aliases.'

'I'll see what I can do. I don't have any contacts with America Online, but someone we know must.' Win reached behind him. He opened up the paneled door on his minifridge. He tossed Myron a can of Yoo-Hoo and poured himself a Brooklyn Lager. Win never drank beer, only lager. 'Greg's money has been difficult to locate,' he said. 'I'm not sure there is very much.'

'That would fit into what Emily said.'

'However,' Win continued, 'I did find one major with-drawal.'

'How much?'

'Fifty thousand dollars in cash. It took some time because it came out of an account that Martin Felder holds for him.'

'When did he withdraw it?'

'Four days before he disappeared,' Win said.

'Paying off a gambling debt?'

'Perhaps.'

Win's phone rang. He picked it up and said, 'Articu-late. Okay, put it through.' Two seconds later he handed the phone to Myron.

'For me?' Myron asked.

Win gave him flat eyes. 'No,' he said. 'I'm handing you the phone because it's too heavy for me.'

Everyone's a wiseass. Myron took the phone. 'Hello?'

'I got a squad car downstairs.' It was Dimonte in full bark. 'Get your ass in it now.'

'What's wrong?'

'I'm at fucking Downing's house, that's what's wrong. I had to practically suck off a judge to get the warrant.'

'Nice imagery, Rolly.'

'Don't fuck with me, Bolitar. You said there was blood in the house.'

'In the basement,' Myron corrected.

'Well, I'm in the basement right now,' he countered. 'And it's as clean as a baby's ass.'

Chapter 21

The basement was indeed clean. No blood anywhere.

'There's got to be traces,' Myron said.

Dimonte's toothpick looked like it was about to snap between his clenched teeth. 'Traces?'

'Yeah. With a microscope or something.'

'With a . . .' Dimonte flapped his arms, his face crimson. 'What the hell good is traces going to do me? They don't prove a damn thing. You can't test traces.'

'It'll prove there was blood.'

'So what?' he shouted. 'You go through any house in America with a microscope and you're bound to find traces of blood. Who the fuck cares?'

'I don't know what to tell you, Rolly. The blood was there.'

There were maybe five lab cops – no uniforms, no marked cars – going through the house. Krinsky was there too. The videocamera in his hand was off right now. He also had what looked like manila files jammed into his armpit. Myron motioned to them. 'That the coroner's report?'

Roland Dimonte stepped in to block Myron's view. 'That ain't none of your business, Bolitar.'

'I know about Liz Gorman, Rolly.'

The toothpick hit the floor on that one. 'How the hell . . . ?'

'It's not important.'

'The fuck it ain't. What else do you know? If you're holding out on me, Bolitar—'

'I'm not holding out on you, but I think I can help.'

Dimonte narrowed his eyes. Senor Suspicious. 'Help how?'

'Just tell me Gorman's blood type. That's all I want to know. Her blood type.'

'Why the hell should I?'

'Because you're not a total numb nut, Rolly.'

'Don't give me that shit. Why do you want to know?'

'Remember I told you about finding blood in the basement?' Myron said.

'Yeah.'

'I left something out.'

Dimonte gave him the glare. 'What?'

'We tested some of the blood.'

'We? Who the fuck is . . .' His voice trailed off. 'Oh Christ, don't tell me that psycho-yuppie is in on all this?'

To know Win was to love him. 'I'd like to make a little trade.'

'What kind of trade?'

'You tell me the blood type in the report. I tell you the blood type we found in the basement.'

'Fuck you, Bolitar. I can arrest your ass for tampering with evidence in a police investigation.'

206

'What tampering? There was no investigation.'

'I could still nail your ass for breaking and entering.'

'If you could prove it. And if Greg were around to press charges. Look, Rolly—'

'AB positive,' Krinsky said. He ignored Dimonte's renewed glare and continued. 'It's fairly rare. Four percent of the populace.'

They both turned their attention to Myron. Myron nodded. 'AB positive. It's the same.'

Dimonte put up both hands and scrunched his face into perplexed. 'Whoa, hold up here. Just what the fuck are you trying to say? That she was killed down here and moved?'

'I'm not saying anything,' Myron said.

'Cause we didn't see any evidence of the body being moved,' Dimonte went on. 'None at all. Not that we were looking for it. But the bleeding pattern – I mean, if she was killed down here, there wouldn't have been so much blood like that at her apartment. You saw the mess there, right?'

Myron nodded.

Dimonte's eyes darted aimlessly. Myron could practically sees the gears inside his head grinding to a halt. 'You know what that means, don't you, Bolitar?'

'No, Rolly, why don't you enlighten me?'

'It means the killer came back here after the murder. It's the only explanation. And you know who all this is starting to point to? Your pal Downing. First we found his fingerprints in the victim's apartment—'

'What's this?'

Dimonte nodded. 'That's right. Downing's fingerprints were by the door frame.'

'But not inside?'

'Yeah, inside. Inside the door frame.'

'But nowhere else?'

'What the hell's the difference? The fingerprints prove he was at the scene. What more do you need? Anyway, here's how it must have happened.' He stuck a new toothpick in his mouth. New toothpick for a new theory. 'Downing kills her. He comes back to his house to pack or something. He's in a rush so he leaves a little mess in the basement. Then he runs away. A few days later he comes back and cleans it up.'

Myron shook his head. 'Why come down to the basement in the first place?'

'The laundry room,' Dimonte answered. 'He was coming down here to wash his clothes.'

'The laundry room is upstairs off the kitchen,' Myron said.

Dimonte shrugged. 'So maybe he was getting a suitcase.'

'They're in the bedroom closet. This is just a kids' playroom, Rolly. Why did he come down here?'

That stopped Dimonte for a moment. It stopped Myron too. None of this made much sense. Had Liz Gorman been killed here and dragged to her apartment in Manhattan? That didn't seem to make much sense based on the physical evidence. Could she have been injured down here?

Whoa, hold the phone.

Maybe the attack started here. Maybe there had been a scuffle in the basement. In the course of subduing or knocking her out, blood was spilled. But then what? Did the killer stick her in a car and drive to Manhattan? And then – what? – on a fairly active street, the killer parked a car, dragged her injured body up the stairs, entered her apartment, killed her?

Did that make any sense?

From the first level a voice cried down, 'Detective! We found something! Quick!'

Dimonte wet his lips. 'Turn on the video,' he told Krinsky. Videotaping all the relevant moments. Just like Myron had told him. 'Stay here, Bolitar. I don't want to have to explain your ugly mug being on the film.'

Myron followed but at a discreet distance. Krinsky and Dimonte headed up the stairs into the kitchen. They turned left. The laundry room. Vinyl yellow wallpaper with white chicks blanketed all four walls. Emily's taste? Probably not. Knowing Emily she'd probably never even seen the inside of a laundry room.

'Over here,' someone said. Myron stayed back. He could see that the dryer had been pushed away from the wall. Dimonte bent down and looked behind it. Krinsky arched over to make sure the whole thing was being filmed. Dimonte stood back up. He was trying like hell to look grim – a smile wouldn't look good on film – but he was having a rough time of it. He snapped on a pair of rubber gloves and lifted the item into view.

The baseball bat was covered with blood.

Chapter 22

When Myron got back to the office, Esperanza was at the reception desk.

'Where's Big Cyndi?' Myron asked.

'Having lunch.'

The image of Fred Flintstone's car tipping over from the weight of his Bronto-ribs flashed in front of Myron's eyes.

'Win filled me in on what's been going on,' Esperanza said. She wore an aqua-blue blouse open at the throat. A gold heart on a slender chain dangled proudly against the dark skin of her sternum. Her always-mussed hair was slightly entangled in big hoop earrings. She pushed the hair back with one finger. 'So what happened at the house?'

He explained about the cleaned-up blood and the baseball bat. Esperanza usually liked to do other things while she listened. She wasn't right now. She stared square into his eyes. When she looked at you like that, there was such intensity it was sometimes hard to look back.

'I'm not sure I understand,' she said. 'You and Win found blood in the basement two days ago.'

'Right.'

'Since then, someone cleaned up that blood – but they left behind the murder weapon?'

'So it appears.'

Esperanza considered this for a moment. 'Could it have been a maid?'

'The police already checked on that. She hasn't been there in three weeks.'

'Do you have a thought?'

He nodded. 'Someone is trying to frame Greg. It's the only logical explanation.'

She arched a skeptical eyebrow. 'By planting and then cleaning up blood?'

'No, let's start from the beginning.' He grabbed the chair and sat in front of her. He had been going over it in his mind the whole ride back, and he wanted to talk it out. In the corner on his left, the fax machine sounded its digitally primordial screech. Myron waited for the sound to subside. 'Okay,' he said, 'first I'm going to assume that the killer knew Greg was with Liz Gorman that night – maybe he followed them, maybe he was waiting for them near her apartment. Whatever, he knows they were together.'

Esperanza nodded, stood. She walked over to the fax machine to check the incoming transmission.

'After Greg leaves, the killer murders Liz Gorman. Knowing that Downing would make a good fall guy, he takes some blood from the murder scene and plants it at Greg's house. That will raise suspicion. To put the icing on the cake, the killer also takes the murder weapon and plants it behind the dryer.'

'But you just said the blood was cleaned up,' she interjected.

'Right. Here's where it gets a little tricky. Suppose, for example, I wanted to protect Greg Downing. I go into his house and find the blood. Now remember, I want to protect Greg from a murder rap. So what would I do?'

She squinted at the fax coming through. 'Clean up the blood.'

'Exactly.'

'Wow, thanks. Do I get a gold star? Get on with it already.'

'Just bear with me, okay? I would see the blood and clean it up. But – and here's the important part – the first time I was in that house I *never* saw the bat. That's not just in this example. That's real life. Win and I only saw the blood in the basement. No baseball bat.'

'Hold on,' she said. 'You're saying someone cleaned up the blood to protect Greg from a murder rap but didn't know about the bat?'

'Right.'

'Who?'

'I don't know.'

Esperanza shook her head. She moved back to her desk and hit some keys on her computer keyboard. 'It doesn't add up.'

'Why not?'

'Suppose I'm madly in love with Greg Downing,' she said, moving back to the fax machine. 'I'm in his house. For some reason I can't fathom, I'm in his kids' playroom. Doesn't matter where I am. Imagine I'm in my own apartment. Or I'm visiting your house. I could be anywhere.'

'Okay.'

'I see blood on the floor or on the walls or wherever.' She stopped, looked at him. 'What conclusion would you logically expect me to draw?'

Myron shook his head. 'I don't understand what you're saying.'

Esperanza thought a moment. 'Suppose you left here right now,' she began, 'and went back to the bitch's loft.'

'Don't call her that.'

'Whatever. Suppose when you walked in, you found blood on her walls. What would be your first reaction?'

Myron nodded slowly. Now he saw what she was getting at. 'I'd be worried about Jessica.'

'And your second reaction? After you found out she was okay?'

'Curiosity, I guess. Whose blood is it? How did it get there? That sort of thing.'

'Right,' she said with a quick nod. 'Would you think to yourself, "Gee, I better clean it up before the bitch gets accused of murdering somebody"?'

'Stop calling her that.'

Esperanza waved him off. 'Would you think that or not?'

'Not in that circumstance, no,' Myron said. 'So in order for my theory to hold water—'

'Your protector had to know about the murder,' she finished for him, back checking her computer for something. 'He or she would also have to know that Greg was somehow involved.'

Myron's head spun with possibilities. 'You think Greg killed her,' he said. 'You think he went back to his house after the murder and left behind some traces of the crime – like blood in the basement. Then he sent this protector back to the house to help cover his tracks.'

213

Esperanza made a face. 'Where the hell did you come up with that?'

'I just—'

'That's not what I think at all,' Esperanza said. She stapled the fax pages together. 'If Greg sent someone to get rid of the evidence, the weapon would be gone too.'

'Right. So that leaves us where?'

Esperanza shrugged, circled something on the fax page with a red marker. 'You're the great detective. You figure it out.'

Myron thought about it a moment. Another answer – one he prayed was wrong – came to him all at once. 'There's another possibility,' he said.

'What?'

'Clip Arnstein.'

'What about him?'

'I told Clip about the blood in the basement.' Myron said.

'When?'

'Two days ago.'

'How did he react?'

'He freaked, pretty much,' Myron said. 'He's also got motive – any scandal will destroy his chances of keeping control of the Dragons. Hell, that's why he hired me. To keep any trouble contained. Nobody else even knew about the blood in the basement.' Myron stopped. He leaned back and ran it through his mind again. 'Of course I haven't had a chance to tell Clip about Liz Gorman's murder. He didn't even know the blood wasn't Greg's. All he knew was that there was blood in the basement. Would he go that far just on that? Would he still risk covering it all up if he didn't know anything about Liz Gorman?'

Esperanza gave him a small smile. 'Maybe he knows more than you think,' she said.

'What makes you say that?'

She handed him the fax. 'It's the list of long distance calls made from the pay phone at the Parkview Diner,' she said. 'I already cross-checked it with my computer Rolodex. Look at the number I circled.'

Myron saw it. A call lasting twelve minutes had been made from the Parkview Diner four days before Greg's disappearance. The phone number was Clip's.

Chapter 23

'Liz Gorman called Clip?' Myron looked up at Esperanza. 'What the hell is going on?'

Esperanza shrugged. 'Ask Clip.'

'I knew he was keeping something from me,' he went on, 'but I don't get it. How does Clip fit into this equation?'

'Uh huh.' She shuffled through some papers on her desk. 'Look, we got a ton of work to do. I mean, sports agent work. You have a game tonight, right?'

He nodded.

'So ask Clip then. In the meantime, we're just going around in circles here.'

Myron scanned the sheet. 'Any other numbers jump out at you?'

'Not yet,' she said. 'But I want to talk about something else for a minute.'

'What?'

'We have a problem with a client.'

'Who?'

'Jason Blair.'

'What's wrong?'

'He's pissed off,' she said. 'He's not happy with me handling his contract negotiations. He said he hired you, not some' – she made quote marks in the air with her fingers – ' "scantily clad wrestler with a nice ass." '

'He said that?'

'Yep. Nice ass. Didn't even notice my legs.' Esperanza shook her head.

Myron smiled. 'So what happened?'

Behind them the elevator dinged. Only one hit this part of the floor. The elevator opened directly into the reception area of MB SportsReps. Classy, or so he had been told. When the doors opened, two men came out. Myron recognized them right away. Camouflage Pants and Brick Wall. They were both armed. They aimed their guns at Myron and Esperanza. B Man stepped out behind them like he'd just been introduced on the Leno show. Big smile, acknowledging-the-crowd wave.

'How's the knee, Myron?' he asked.

'Better than your van.'

B Man laughed at that one. 'That Win,' he mused. 'The man is always a surprise. How did he know when to hit us?'

No reason not to tell. 'We kept the cellular phones on.'

B Man shook his head. 'Ingenious really. I'm very impressed.' He wore one of those suits that are just a tad too shiny and a pink tie. His shirt was french-cuffed and monogrammed with four letters: B MAN. Taking the nickname thing a little far. A thick, ropelike gold bracelet encircled his right wrist.

'How did you get up here?' Myron asked.

'Do you really think a few rent-a-cops are going to stop us?'

'I'd still like to hear,' Myron said.

B Man shrugged. 'I called Lock-Horne Securities and told them I was looking for a new financial advisor for my millions. An anxious young peon told me to come right up. I hit the twelfth floor on the elevator instead of the fifteenth.' He spread his hands. 'So here I am.' He smiled at Esperanza. What with the too-white teeth and the tan, it looked like he switched on a night-light.

'And who is this fetching creature?' he asked with a wink.

'My,' Esperanza said, 'what woman doesn't love to be called a creature?'

B Man laughed again. 'The little lady has gumption,' he said. 'I like that. I really do.'

'Like I care,' Esperanza said.

More laughter. 'May I indulge you a moment, Miss . . . ?'

'Money Penny,' she finished for him. She said it with her best Sean Connery imitation. No Rich Little, but not bad either.

Another laugh from the B Man. The man was half-hyena. 'Would you please call Win down here? On the speakerphone if you don't mind. Tell him to come down unarmed.'

She looked at Myron. Myron nodded. She dialed. Over the speakerphone, Win offered up another, 'Articulate.'

Esperanza said, 'Some bottled blond with a bottled tan is down here to see you.'

'Ah, I've been expecting him,' Win said. 'Hello, B Man.'

'Hello, Win.'

'I assume you are in well-armed company.'

'That I am, Win,' B Man said. 'If you try anything, your friends won't make it out alive.'

' "Won't make it out alive"?' Win repeated. 'I expected better from you, B Man, really. I'll be down in a second.'

'Come unarmed, Win.'

'Not a chance. But there will be no violence. That I promise you.' The phone clicked off. For several moments everyone looked at one another as if wondering who was going to take the lead.

'I don't trust him,' B Man said. He pointed to Brick Wall. 'Take the girl in the other room. Duck down behind a desk or something. You hear any shooting, you blow her head off.'

The Brick Wall nodded.

B Man directed his attention to Camouflage Pants. 'Keep your gun on Bolitar.'

'Right.'

B Man took out his own weapon. When the elevator dinged, he squatted and aimed. The doors slid open, but it wasn't Win. Big Cyndi emerged from the elevator, not unlike a dinosaur emerging from its egg.

'Jesus Christ!' Camouflage Pants said. 'What the hell is that?'

Big Cyndi growled.

'Who is she, Bolitar?' B Man demanded.

'My new receptionist.'

'Tell her to wait in the other room.'

Myron nodded to her. 'It's okay. Esperanza's in there.'

Cyndi growled again, but she listened. She walked past the B Man on her way to Myron's office. His gun looked like a disposable lighter next to her. She opened the door, snarled one last time, and closed it.

Silence.

'Jesus Christ,' Camouflage Pants said again.

They waited approximately thirty seconds before the elevator dinged again. B Man got back into his squat and aimed. The doors slid open. Win stepped out. He looked mildly annoyed when he saw the weapon aimed his way. His voice was clipped. 'I told you there would be no violence.'

'You have information we need,' B Man said.

'I'm well aware of that.' Win replied. 'Now put that gun away and we'll talk civilly.'

The B Man kept his weapon on Win. 'You armed?'

'Of course.'

'Hand over your weapon.'

'No,' Win said. 'And it's not weapon. It's weapons. Plural.'

'I said—'

'And I heard you, Orville.'

'Don't call me that.'

Win sighed. 'Fine, *B Man*.' He shook his head as he said it. 'You are making this far more difficult than it has to be.'

'What's that supposed to mean?'

'It means that for an intelligent fellow, you too often forget that brute strength is not the only course. There are situations that call for restraint.'

Win lecturing on restraint, Myron thought. What next? Xaviera Hollander lecturing on monogamy?

'Think about what you've already done,' Win said. 'First, you have Myron roughed up by a pair of amateurs—'

'Amateurs!' Camouflage Pants didn't like that. 'Who you calling—'

'Shut up, Tony,' B Man said.

'You hear what he called me? An amateur?'

'I said, shut up, Tony.'

But Tony The Pants wasn't through yet. 'Hey, I got feelings too, B Man.'

The B Man gave him hard eyes. 'Your left femur, if you don't shut up.'

Tony closed his mouth.

The B Man looked back to Win. 'Sorry about the interruption.'

'Apology accepted.'

'Go on.'

'As I was saying,' Win continued, 'first you try to rough Myron up. Then you try to kidnap and cripple him. All for naught.'

'Not for naught,' B Man countered. 'We need to know where Downing is.'

'And what makes you think Myron knows?'

'You were both at his house. Then all of a sudden Bolitar is on Downing's team. As a matter of fact, he takes his place on the roster.'

'So?'

'So I'm not stupid. You two know something.'

'And what if we do?' Win said, hands spread. 'Why didn't you just ask? Did you ever even consider that possibility? Did you ever think that maybe the best course of action would be simply to ask?'

'I did ask!' Camouflage Pants jumped in. He was defensive now. 'On the street! I asked him where Greg was. He gave me lip.'

Win looked at him. 'Were you ever in the military?' he asked.

Pants seemed confused. 'No.'

'You are a worthless punk,' Win said in the same tone he might use when discussing a mixed stock report. 'A pitiful ectoplasm such as yourself wearing army fatigues is an affront to any man or woman who has ever experienced real combat. If I ever happen across you again donning any similar garb, I will hurt you severely. Do I make myself clear?'

'Hey—'

'You don't know this guy, Tony,' B Man interrupted. 'Just nod and shut up.'

Camouflage Pants looked hurt but he did as he was told.

Win turned his attention back to the B Man. 'We can help each other out in this situation,' he said.

'How?'

'It just so happens that we, too, are searching for the elusive Mr Downing. That is why I wish to make a proposal.'

'I'm listening.'

'First,' Win said, 'stop aiming the weapons at us.'

B Man gave him a funny look. 'How do I know I can trust you?'

'If I wanted you dead,' Win answered, 'I would have killed you last night.'

The B Man thought it over, nodded, lowered his weapon. He signaled Camouflage Pants, who then did likewise. 'Why didn't you?' B Man asked. 'I probably would have killed you in the same situation.'

'That's what I mean about brute force,' Win said. 'About being wasteful. We need each other here. If I had killed you, I wouldn't be able to make this proposal today.'

'Fair enough. The floor is yours.'

'I assume that Mr Downing owes you a rather hefty sum.'

'Very hefty sum.'

'Fine,' Win said. 'You tell us what you know. We find him, no cost to you. When we do find him, you promise not to hurt him if he pays up.'

'And if he doesn't pay up?'

Win grinned and held his hands out, palms up. 'Who are we to interfere with the way you conduct your business?'

B Man thought about it, but not for very long. 'Okay, I can live with that,' he said. 'But I don't talk with the hired help around.' He turned to Camouflage. 'Go sit in the other room.'

'Why?'

'Because if someone decides to torture you, you'll know nothing.'

That answer seemed to make perfect sense to Camouflage. He went into Myron's office without another word.

'Why don't we sit?' Win suggested.

They did so. B Man crossed his legs and started right in. 'Downing is your basic gamble-a-holic,' he began. 'He had pretty good luck for a long time. That's a bad thing when a man has the itch. When his luck changed – as it must in the long run – he kept thinking he could win it back. They all do. When they have the sort of money that Downing has, I let them go. Let them dig their own grave. It's good for business. But at the same time, you have to keep an eye out. There is a fine line working here. You don't want them to end up digging to China either.' He turned and looked at Myron. 'You know what I'm saying?'

Myron nodded. 'China.'

'Right. Anyway, Downing started losing big. I'm talking very big here. He was never a prompt payer, but he was always good for it. I sometimes let the tab run as high as two-fifty or even three.'

'Hundred thousand?' Myron asked.

'Yeah.' B Man smiled. 'You don't know any gamblers, do you?'

Myron kept silent. He wasn't about to tell this slime bucket his life story.

'It's as bad as alcohol or heroin,' B Man went on. 'They can't stop themselves. In some ways, it's even worse. People drink and do drugs to escape despair. Gambling has that element, too, but it also offers you the friendly hand of hope. You always got hope when you gamble. You always believe that you're just one bet away from turning it all around. It's a catch-twenty-two. If you got hope, you keep on gambling. But with gambling, there's always hope.'

'Very deep,' Win said. 'Let's get back to Greg Downing.'

'Simply put, Greg stops paying his tab. It runs up to half a million. I start putting some pressure on him. He tells me he's flat broke, but I shouldn't worry because he's signing some big endorsement deal that will net him zillions.'

The Forte deal, Myron thought. Greg's sudden change of heart about endorsement money made more sense now.

'I asked him when this endorsement money will be coming in. He tells me in about six months. Six months? On a half million dollar debt and growing? I told him that's not good enough. He'd have to pay up now. He said he didn't have the money. So I ask for a show of good faith.'

Myron knew where this was going. 'He shaved points.'

'Wrong. He was *supposed* to shave points. The Dragons were favored by eight over Charlotte. Downing was going to see to it that the Dragons won by less than eight. No big deal.'

'He agreed?'

'Sure he did. The game was on Sunday. I dumped a ton on Charlotte. A ton.'

'And Greg never played,' Myron finished for him.

'You got it,' B Man said. 'The Dragons won by twelve. Okay, I figure Greg got hurt. Like the papers say. A freak injury, that's not his fault. Don't get me wrong. He's still responsible for what I lost. Why should I pay for his freak injury?' He paused to see if anyone was going to argue with his logic. No one bothered. 'So I waited for Downing to call me, but he never did. I'm owed close to two million by now. Win, you know I can't just sit back with that kind of thing, right?'

Win nodded.

'When was the last time Greg made a payment to you?' Myron asked.

'It's been a while. I don't know. Five, six months maybe.'

'Nothing more recent?'

'Nothing.'

They talked a bit more. Esperanza, Big Cyndi, Camouflage, and Brick Wall came back into the room. Win and B Man changed the topic to martial art buddies they had in common. A few minutes later B Man and his entourage left. When the elevator door closed, Big Cyndi turned and smiled widely at Esperanza. Then she began to skip in a circle. The floor shook.

Myron looked a question at Esperanza.

'That big guy,' Esperanza said, 'the one who was with us in the other room.'

'What about him?'

'He asked Cyndi for her phone number.'

Big Cyndi continued skipping with childlike abandon. The occupants of the floor beneath them were probably diving for cover like it was the last day of Pompeii. He turned to Win. 'Did you catch the fact that Greg hadn't paid anything in months?'

Win nodded. 'Clearly the fifty thousand dollars he withdrew before his disappearance was not to pay off gambling debts.'

'So what was it for?'

'To run, I imagine.'

'So he knew at least four days before the fact that he was going to take off,' Myron said.

'It would appear so.'

Myron thought about that for a moment. 'Then the timing of the murder can't just be a coincidence. If Greg planned to disappear, it can't be a coincidence that the day he takes off is the day Liz Gorman gets killed.'

'Doubtful,' Win agreed.

'You think Greg killed her?'

'The clues point in that direction,' Win said. 'I mentioned to you that the money had come from an account handled by Marty Felder. Perhaps Mr Felder has an answer.'

Myron wondered about that. Big Cyndi suddenly stopped skipping. She hugged Esperanza and made a la-la noise. Young love. 'If Felder knew Greg was going into

226

hiding,' Myron said, 'why would he leave those messages on Greg's machine?'

'Perhaps to throw us off. Or perhaps he did not know Greg's intent.'

'I'll call him,' Myron said. 'See if I can make an appointment for tomorrow.'

'You have a game tonight, do you not?'

'Yes.'

'What time?'

'Seven-thirty.' Myron checked his watch. 'But I need to leave pretty soon if I want to talk to Clip first.'

'I'll drive,' Win said. 'I'd like to meet this Mr Arnstein.'

After they left, Esperanza went through the messages on the voice mail. Then she straightened out her desk. Her two photographs – one of her bearded collie Chloe getting Best in Breed at the Westchester Dog Show; the other of her as Little Pocahontas and Big Cyndi as Big Chief Mama, holding up their FLOW (Fabulous Ladies Of Wrestling) tag-team title belts – had been knocked askew by Cyndi's knees.

As she stared at the photographs, something Myron said kept needling her. He was worried about timing. The timing of the murder. The timing of Downing's disappearance. But what about Liz Gorman's timing? What about the timing of her arrival in New York City? The bank in Tucson was robbed two months ago; Liz Gorman also started working for the Parkview Diner two months ago. A criminal on the run would want to get far away from the crime scene, yes, but to a place as populated as New York City? Why?

The more Esperanza thought about it, the more she grew bewildered. There had to be a cause and effect at work here. There had to be something about the bank heist that made Liz Gorman come out this way. Esperanza chewed on this for another minute or two. Then she picked up the phone and called one of Myron and Win's closest contacts at the bureau.

'They need everything you got on the Raven Brigade bank heist in Tucson,' Esperanza said. 'Can you send me a copy of the file?'

'You'll have it by tomorrow morning.'

Chapter 24

Win and Myron shared a somewhat unusual passion for Broadway musicals. Right now, the stereo system in Win's Jag was pumping out the soundtrack from *1776*. A Continental Congressman cried out, 'Somebody better open up a window!' This led to a fierce argument over the merits of opening said window (it was 'hot as hell in Philadelphia') vs. keeping them closed ('too many flies'). Interspersed in this argument, people were telling John Adams to sit down. History.

'Who played the original Thomas Jefferson?' Win asked. He knew the answer. Life with Myron's friends was a nonstop quiz show.

'Movie version or stage?'

Win frowned. 'I don't do movie versions.'

'Ken Howard,' Myron answered.

'Correct. What is Mr Howard's most famous role?'

'The coach on the *White Shadow*.'

'Correct again. The original John Adams?'

'William Daniels.'

'Best known as?'

'The obnoxious surgeon on *St. Elsewhere*.'

'The actress who portrayed Martha Jefferson?'

'Betty Buckley. Best known as Abby on *Eight Is Enough*.'

Win smiled. 'You are good.'

Myron stared out the window, the buildings and cars blurring into one pulsating mass, and thought about Jessica. Moving in with her. There was no reason not to. He loved her. She loved him. More than that, she had made the first move – the first time he could remember such a thing. In most relationships, one partner has more control than the other. It was just the natural order of things. Perfect balance was a hard thing to find. In their case, Jessica currently had the upper hand. Myron knew that – if he hadn't, Esperanza's constant references to his being 'whipped' would surely have made him aware. It didn't mean he loved her more or Jessica loved him less. Or maybe it did. Myron wasn't sure anymore. What he did know for sure was that moments where Jessica made the move – where she was the one exposing herself – were rare. Myron wanted to embrace it, encourage it. He had waited a long time for her to say such words to him. But something held him back. Like with TC, there were a lot of factors pushing and pulling at him.

His mind churned through the pros and cons, but no conclusions spewed forward. What he really wanted was to bounce his thoughts off someone. He deliberated best that way – by thinking out loud with a close friend. The problem was, who? Esperanza, his most dependable confidante, hated Jessica. Win . . . well, when it came to matters of the heart, Win was simply not your man;

something in that nether region had shorted out a long time ago.

Still Myron heard himself say, 'Jessica asked me to move in.'

For a moment Win said nothing. Then: 'Do you get a full share of the playoff money?'

'What?'

'You joined the team late. Have you worked out what share of the playoff money you'll be getting?'

'Don't worry. It's taken care of.'

Win nodded. His eyes remained on the road. The speedometer hovered around eighty, a swiftness Route 3 was not built to bear. Win swerved lanes constantly. Myron had gotten somewhat used to Win's driving over the years, but he still kept his eyes averted from the front windshield.

'Are you staying for the game?' Myron asked.

'That depends.'

'On?'

'On if this Thumper will be there,' Win replied. 'You said she was seeking employment. Perhaps I can interrogate her at the same time.'

'What will you say?'

'That,' Win said, 'is a dilemma we both face. If you ask her about Downing's call, you blow your cover. If I ask her, she'll want to know the whys and wherefores. Either way, unless this Thumper is brain dead, she will be suspicious. Moreover, if she knows anything significant, she will most probably lie.'

'So what do you suggest?'

Win tilted his head as though in deep thought. 'Perhaps I'll bed her,' he concluded. 'Then I can make her talk while lost in the throes of passion.'

'She only sleeps with men on the Giants or the Dragons,' Myron said. Then he frowned and added, 'Bed her?'

Win shrugged. 'Just suggesting an alternative to whipping her with a rubber hose,' he said. 'Unless, of course, she's into that kind of thing.'

'Any other suggestions?'

'I'm working on it.' They took the exit to the Meadowlands in silence. On the CD player, Abigail Adams was telling John Adams that women in Massachusetts needed pins. Win hummed along with the music for a moment. Then he spoke. 'As far as Jessica goes' – he took one hand off the wheel and sort of waved it – 'I'm not one to ask about such things.'

'I know.'

'You were miserable the first time she left,' he added. 'I don't know why you would risk going through that again.'

Myron looked at him. 'You really don't, do you?'

Win said nothing.

'That's sad, Win.'

'Yes,' he replied. 'So very tragic.'

'I'm serious,' Myron said.

Win put a dramatic forearm to his brow. 'Oh, what woe that I may never experience the depths of misery you plunged to when Jessica left. Pity this child.'

'You know there's more to it than that.'

Win put down the arm, shook his head. 'No, my friend, there is not. What was real was your pain. The rest of what you felt is the stuff of cruel delusion.'

'You really feel that way?'

'Yes.'

'About all relationships?'

Win shook his head. 'I never said that.'

'How about our friendship? Is that a cruel delusion too?'

'This isn't about us,' Win said.

'I'm just trying to understand—'

'There is nothing to understand,' Win interrupted. 'Do what you believe is best. As I said, I am not the one with which to have this discussion.'

Silence. The arena loomed in front of them. For years, it had been called the Brendan Byrne Arena, named for the unpopular governor who had been in office when the complex had been built. Recently, however, the sports authority needed to raise funds, so the name had been changed to the Continental Airlines Arena – not exactly musical, but then again the old name didn't exactly make you want to break out in song either. Brendan Byrne and his past lackeys cried foul over this affront. What a disgrace, they shouted with grave indignation. This was Governor Byrne's legacy. How could they sell him out like this? But Myron didn't have a problem with the name change. Which would you rather do – tax the people to collect twenty-seven million dollars or bruise a politician's ego? No contest when you thought about it.

Myron glanced over at Win. Win's eyes were on the road, his fingers tightly wrapped around the wheel. Myron's mind flashed back to the morning after Jessica left five years ago. He'd been moping around his house alone when Win knocked on the door. Myron opened it.

Without preamble, Win said, 'Come on. I'll hire you a girl. You need to get laid.'

Myron shook his head.

'Are you certain?'

'Yes,' Myron said.

'Do me a favor then.'

'What?'

'Don't go out and get drunk,' Win said. 'That would be such a cliché.'

'And what, getting laid isn't?'

Win pursed his lips together. 'But at least it's a good cliché.'

Then Win turned around and left. That had been it. They had never broached the subject of his relationship with Jessica again. It'd been a mistake to have brought it up now. Myron should have known better.

There were reasons Win was the way he was. Myron looked now at his friend and truly did pity him. From Win's vantage point, his life had been one long lesson in how to take care of himself. The results weren't always pretty, but they were usually effective. Win had not severed off his feelings or anything that dramatic, nor was he as robotic as he sometimes wanted people to think. But Win had learned not to trust or depend on others very much. There were not many people he cared about, but those he did were cherished with an intensity few ever experienced. The rest of the world meant very little to him.

'I'll get you a seat near Thumper's,' Myron said softly.

Win nodded, pulled into a parking spot. Myron gave his name to Clip's secretary and they were shown into his office. Calvin Johnson was already there, standing to Clip's right. Clip was behind his desk. He looked older today. His cheeks were grayer; and the skin around his jowls seemed looser. When he stood, it seemed to take more effort.

Clip eyed Win for a moment. 'This must be Mr Lockwood.'

He even knew about Win – again well prepared. 'Yes,' Myron said.

'He's helping us with our problem?'

'Yes.'

Introductions were made. Hands were shaken. Rear ends were seated. As was his custom in such situations, Win remained silent. His eyes slid from one side of the room to the other, taking in everything. He liked to study people for a while before speaking to them, especially in their home environment.

'So,' Clip began, forcing up a tired smile, 'what have we got?'

'When you first approached me,' Myron began, 'you were afraid I'd uncover something unsavory. I'd like to know what that something was.'

Clip tried to look amused. 'Nothing personal, Myron,' he began with a light chuckle, 'but if I knew that, I wouldn't have needed to hire you.'

Myron shook his head. 'Not good enough.'

'What?'

'Greg has disappeared before.'

'So?'

'So you never suspected anything unsavory then,' Myron said. 'Why now?'

'I told you. I have the owners' vote coming up.'

'That's your only concern?'

'Of course not,' Clip said. 'I'm worried about Greg too.'

'But you never hired anyone to find him before. What are you afraid of?'

Clip shrugged. 'Probably nothing. I'm just covering all my bases. Why? What have you found out?'

Myron shook his head. 'You never cover all your bases, Clip. You're a risk-taker. Always were. I've seen you trade popular, proven veterans for untested draft picks. I've seen you risk going for the steal rather than hoping your defense holds. You've never been afraid to lean over that edge, to risk it all.'

Clip smiled thinly. 'The problem with that strategy,' he said, 'is that you lose too. Sometimes you lose a lot.'

'What did you lose this time?' Myron asked.

'Nothing yet,' he said. 'But if Greg doesn't come back, it might cost my team a championship ring.'

'That's not what I meant. There's something more going on.'

'I'm sorry,' Clip said, spreading his hands. 'I really don't know what you're talking about. I hired you because it was the logical thing to do. Greg vanished. Now true, he's vanished before, but never this late in the season and never when we were so close to a championship. This simply isn't like him.'

Myron glanced over at Win. Win appeared to be bored.

'Do you know a woman named Liz Gorman?' Myron tried.

In the corner of his eye, Myron saw Calvin sit up a bit.

'No,' Clip said. 'Should I?'

'How about a woman named Carla or Sally?'

'What? You mean have I ever known a woman named—'

'Recently. Or any woman involved in some way with Greg Downing.'

Clip shook his head. 'Calvin?' Calvin also shook his head, but the shake was a little too lingering. 'Why do you ask?' Clip demanded.

'Because that's whom Greg was with the night he vanished,' Myron said.

Clip sat up, his words coming scattergun. 'Have you located her? Where is she now? Maybe they're together.'

Myron looked at Win again. This time, Win nodded

236

ever so slightly. He'd caught it too. 'She's dead,' Myron said.

Any traces of color on Clip's face drained away. Calvin remained silent, but he crossed his legs. A big move for ol' Frosty. 'Dead?'

'Murdered, to be more specific.'

'Oh my God . . .' Clip's eyes leapt from one face to another, as though seeking some sort of answer or solace there. He found none.

'Are you sure you don't know the names Liz Gorman, Carla, or Sally?' Myron asked.

Clip opened his mouth, closed it. No sound came out. He tried again. 'Murdered?'

'Yes.'

'And she was with Greg?'

'He's the last known person to see her alive. His fingerprints are at the murder scene.'

'The murder scene?' His voice trembled, his eyes dazed. 'My God, the blood you found in the basement,' he said. 'The body was at Greg's house?'

'No. She was killed in her apartment in New York.'

Clip looked puzzled. 'But I thought you found blood in Greg's basement. In the playroom.'

'Yes. But that blood is gone now.'

'Gone?' Clip sounded both confused and annoyed. 'What do you mean, gone?'

'I mean somebody cleaned it up.' He looked straight at Clip. 'I mean somebody entered Greg's house in the past two days and tried to snuff out an unsavory scandal.'

Clip startled up at that one. Life came back into the eyes. 'You think it was me?'

'You were the only one I told about the blood. You wanted to keep the discovery secret.'

'I left that up to you,' Clip countered. 'I said I thought it was the wrong move, but I'd respect your decision. Of course, I would want to avoid a scandal. Who wouldn't? But I would never do something like that. You know me better than that, Myron.'

'Clip,' Myron said, 'I have the dead woman's phone records. She called you four days before the murder.'

'What do you mean she called me?'

'Your office number is in the phone records.'

He started to say something, stopped, started again. 'Well, maybe she called here, but that doesn't mean she spoke to me.' His tone was far from convincing. 'Maybe she spoke to my secretary.'

Win cleared his throat. Then he spoke for the first time since entering the office. 'Mr Arnstein?' he said.

'Yes.'

'With all due respect, sir,' Win continued, 'your lies are growing tiresome.'

Clip's mouth dropped. He was used to underlings kissing his rear, not to being called a liar. 'What?'

'Myron has a great deal of respect for you,' Win said. 'That's admirable. People do not earn Myron's respect easily. But you know the dead woman. You talked to her on the phone. We have proof.'

Clip's eyes narrowed. 'What kind of proof?'

'The phone records, for one—'

'—but I just told you—'

'And your own words, for another,' Win finished.

He slowed down, his expression wary. 'What the hell are you talking about?'

Win steepled his fingers. 'Earlier in this conversation, Myron asked you if you knew Liz Gorman or a woman named Carla or Sally. Do you recall that?'

'Yes. I told him no.'

'Correct. And then he told you – and I quote his exact words because they are relevant – "that's whom Greg was with the night he vanished." Awkward phrasing, I admit, but with a purpose. Do you recall your next two queries, Mr Arnstein?'

Clip looked lost. 'No.'

'They were – and again I quote exact words – "Have you located *her* yet? Where is *she* now?" ' Win stopped.

'Yeah, so?'

'You said, *her*. Then you said, *she*. Yet Myron asked you if you knew Liz Gorman or Carla or Sally. From his wording, wouldn't it be natural to assume he was referring to three different women? A *they* rather than a she or her? But you, Mr Arnstein, immediately concluded that these three names belonged to one woman. Don't you find that odd?'

'What?' But Clip's anger was all bluster now. 'You call that evidence?'

Win leaned forward. 'Myron is being well compensated for his efforts here. For that reason, I would normally recommend that he continue working for you. I would advise him to mind his own business and take your money. If you wish to muck up your own investigation, who are we to interfere? Not that Myron would listen. He is a nosy man. Worse, he has this warped sense of doing right, even when it is not required.'

Win stopped, took a breath, leaned back again. Instead of steepling his fingers, he gently bounced the tips against one another. All eyes were on him. 'The problem is,' he continued, 'a woman has been murdered. On top of that, someone has tampered with a crime scene. Someone has also vanished and may very well be a murderer or another victim. In other words, it is now far too dangerous to remain in such a situation with blinders on. The potential costs outweigh the possible benefits. As a businessman, Mr Arnstein, you should understand that.'

Clip remained silent.

'So let us get to it, shall we?' Win spread his hands, then resteepled. 'We know the murder victim spoke to you. Either tell us what she said, or we shake hands and part company.'

'She spoke to me first.' It was Calvin. He shifted in his seat. He avoided Clip's eyes, but there was no need. Clip did not seem upset by the outburst. He sank farther down in his chair, a balloon continuing to deflate. 'She used the name Carla,' Calvin continued.

With a small nod, Win settled back into his chair. He had done his part. The reins were back in Myron's hands.

'What did she say?' Myron asked.

'She said she had some kind of dirt on Greg. She said she could destroy the franchise.'

'What was the dirt?'

Clip came back into the fold. 'We never found out,' he chimed in. Clip hesitated a moment – to buy time or gather himself, Myron wasn't sure which. 'I didn't mean to lie to you, Myron. I'm sorry. I was just trying to protect Greg.'

'You spoke to her too?' Myron asked.

Clip nodded 'Calvin came to me after she called. The next time she called we both spoke to her. She said she wanted money in exchange for silence.'

'How much?'

'Twenty thousand dollars. We were supposed to meet on Monday night.'

'Where?'

'I don't know,' Clip said. 'She was going to tell us the locale on Monday morning, but she never called.'

Probably because she was dead, Myron thought. Dead people rarely made phone calls. 'And she never told you her big secret?'

Clip and Calvin looked a question at each other. Calvin nodded. Then Clip turned back to Myron. 'She didn't have to,' Clip said with resignation. 'We already knew.'

'Knew what?'

'Greg gambled. He owed a lot of money to some very bad people.'

'You already knew about his gambling?'

'Yes,' Clip said.

'How?'

'Greg told me.'

'When?'

'About a month ago,' Clip said. 'He wanted help. I . . . I've always been something of a father figure to him. I care about him. I care about him very much.' He looked up at Myron, his eyes raw with pain. 'I care about you too, Myron. That's what makes this so hard.'

'Makes what so hard?'

But he shook it off. 'I wanted to help him. I convinced him to start seeing somebody. A professional.'

'Did he listen?'

'Greg started with the doctor just last week. A psychiatrist who specializes in gambling addictions. We also talked about him signing an endorsement deal,' he added. 'To pay off the gambling debt.'

'Did Marty Felder know about the gambling?' Myron asked.

'I can't say for certain,' Clip said. 'The doctor told me about the amazing lengths gamblers go to keep their addiction a secret. But Marty Felder handled most of Greg's money. If he didn't know, I'd be surprised.'

Behind Clip's head was a poster of this year's team. Myron looked at it a moment. The co-captains, TC and Greg, were kneeling in front. Greg smiled widely. TC sneered in typical fashion. 'So even when you first hired me,' Myron said, 'you suspected Greg's disappearance had something to do with his gambling.'

'No.' Then thinking further, Clip added. 'At least not in the way you think. I never thought Greg's bookie would harm him. I figured the Forte deal bought him time.'

'Then in what way?'

'I worried about his sanity.' Clip motioned to Greg's image on the poster behind him. 'Greg is not the most balanced person to begin with, but I wondered how much the pressure from the gambling debt weighed on his already questionable sanity. He loved his image, you know, strange as that might sound. He loved being a fan favorite more than the money. But if his fans learned the truth, who knows how they'd react? So I wondered if all of this pressure was too much for him. If maybe he had snapped.'

'And now that a woman is dead,' Myron asked, 'what do you think?'

Clip shook his head vehemently. 'I know Greg better than anyone. When he feels trapped, he runs away. He wouldn't kill anyone. I believe that with all my heart. He is not a violent man. Greg learned the dangers of violence a long time ago.'

No one spoke for several moments. Myron and Win both waited for Clip to elaborate. When he didn't, Win said, 'Mr Arnstein, do you have anything else to tell us?'

'No. That's all.'

Win rose without another word or gesture and walked out of the office. Myron sort of shrugged and started after him.

'Myron?'

He turned back to Clip. The old man was standing now. His eyes looked moist.

'Have a good game tonight,' he said softly. 'It's only a game, after all. Remember that.'

Myron nodded, discomfited yet again by Clip's demeanor. He jogged ahead and caught up with Win.

'Do you have my ticket?' Win asked.

Myron handed it to him.

'Describe this Thumper person please.'

Myron did. When they reached the elevator, Win said, 'Your Mr Arnstein is still not telling us the truth.'

'Anything concrete or just a hunch?'

'I don't do hunches,' Win said. 'Do you believe him?'

'I'm not sure.'

'You are fond of Mr Arnstein, are you not?'

'Yes.'

'Even though he has already admitted lying to you?'

'Yes.'

'Then let me present you with an interesting scenario,' Win said. 'Who, besides Greg, has the most to lose if his gambling addiction becomes public knowledge? Who, besides Greg, would have the greatest motive to keep Liz Gorman silent? And finally, if Greg Downing was about to become a terrible embarrassment to the franchise – to the point of devaluating if not destroying Clip Arnstein's chances of maintaining control – who would have the best motive to make sure Greg Downing disappeared?'

Myron did not bother answering.

Chapter 25

The seat next to Thumper was open. Win took it and gave
her the full-wattage smile.

'Good evening,' he said.

She smiled back. 'Hello.'

'You must be Ms Mason.'

She nodded. 'And you are Windsor Horne Lockwood
III. I recognize you from the picture in *Forbes*.'

They shook hands, their eyes meeting. Their hands
released one another; their eyes didn't. 'A pleasure to
meet you, Ms Mason.'

'Please call me Maggie.'

'Yes, fine.' Win upped the smile for a moment. A
buzzer sounded on the court. The first quarter was over.
He saw Myron stand up to let his teammates sit. Seeing
him dressed in a uniform on an NBA court hit Win in a
very weird, unpleasant way. He didn't like to watch.
He turned back toward Thumper. She looked at him
expectantly.

'I understand that you are seeking employment with my firm,' Win said.

'Yes.'

'Do you mind if I ask you a few questions?'

'Please do.' She motioned a welcome with her hand.

'You are currently employed by Kimmel Brothers, are you not?'

'Yes.'

'How many traders do they currently engage?' Win asked.

'Less than ten,' she said. 'We're very small.'

'I see.' Win did the steepling, feigning consideration of her words. 'Do you work there on weekends?'

'Sometimes.'

'Weekend evenings?'

Her eyes narrowed just slightly, then relaxed back into place. 'Sometimes,' she repeated.

'How about last Saturday night?'

'Pardon me?'

'You know Greg Downing, do you not?'

'Of course but—'

'As you are no doubt aware,' Win continued, 'he has been missing since last Saturday night. Interestingly enough, the last call Mr Downing made from his home was to your office. Do you recall that phone call?'

'Mr Lockwood—'

'Please. Call me Win.'

'I don't know what you're trying to do here—'

'It's quite simple really,' Win interrupted. 'Last night, you told my associate Mr Bolitar that you had not spoken to Greg Downing in several months. Yet, as I have just told you, I have information that contradicts your statement. So there is a discrepancy here – a discrepancy that may cause some to view you, Ms Mason, as less than honest. I cannot have that at Lock-Horne Securities. My employees must be beyond reproach. For that reason, I'd like you to explain this contradiction.'

Win took out a bag of peanuts from his coat pocket. He shelled a few in the neatest manner imaginable, swept the shells with small movements into a second bag, then placed the peanuts into his mouth one at a time.

'How do you know Mr Downing called my office?' Thumper asked.

'Please,' Win said with a side glance. 'Let us not waste time with trivialities. His call is an established fact. You know it. I know it. Let us move beyond it.'

'I didn't work last Saturday night,' she said. 'He must have been calling somebody else.'

Win frowned. 'I grow weary of your tactics, Ms Mason. As you just admitted to me, yours is a small firm. I could call your employer, if you wish. I am sure he would be glad to tell Mr Windsor Horne Lockwood III if you were there or not.'

Thumper sat back in her chair, folding her arms across her chest, looking out at the game. The Dragons were up 24 to 22. Her eyes followed the course of the ball down the court. 'I have nothing more to say to you, Mr Lockwood.'

'Ah. No longer interested in a job?'

'That's right.'

'You misunderstand,' Win said. 'I don't mean just with Lock-Horne Securities. I mean with anybody, including your current employer.'

She turned to him. 'What?'

'There are two options here,' Win said. 'Let me spell them out for you clearly, so that you choose the one most suitable for you. One, you tell me why Greg Downing called you on Saturday night. You tell me why you lied to Myron about it. You tell me everything you know about his disappearance.'

'What disappearance?' she interrupted. 'I thought he was injured.'

'Option two,' Win went on. 'You continue to either stay silent or lie to me, in which case I will begin to circulate a rumor within our industry vis-à-vis your integrity. More specifically, I will let it be known that there are federal authorities looking into serious allegations of embezzlement.'

'But . . .' she started, stopped. 'You can't do that.'

'No?' He made an amused face. 'I am Windsor Horne Lockwood III. My word on such matters will not be questioned. You, on the other hand, will have difficulty finding employment as a hat check girl in a roadside Denny's when I'm through.' He smiled and tilted the bag her way. 'Peanut?'

'You're insane.'

'And you are normal,' Win countered. He looked down at the court. 'Say, that young towel boy is wiping a player's sweat off the floor. That must be worth' – he gave a big shrug – 'oh, I don't know. Fellatio at the very least, wouldn't you say?'

Win smiled at her sweetly.

'I'm leaving.' She started to stand.

'Would you sleep with me?' he asked.

She looked at him in horror. 'What?'

'Would you sleep with me? If you're very good, I may consider employing you at Lock-Horne.'

Her teeth were clenched. 'I'm not a prostitute,' she hissed.

'No, you are not a prostitute,' Win said, loud enough so that a few heads turned. 'But you are a hypocrite.'

'What are you talking about?'

Win motioned to her seat. 'Please sit down.'

'I'd rather not.'

'And I'd rather not have to shout.' He motioned again. 'Please.'

With wary eyes she did as he asked. 'What do you want?'

'You find me attractive, do you not?'

She made a face. 'I think you are the most repulsive man I have—'

'I am just speaking only about looks here,' Win said. 'The physical, remember? As you told Myron just last night, having sex is merely a physical thing. Like shaking hands – though with an analogy like that I question your partners' prowess. Now, at the risk of appearing immodest, I know that I am not physically unattractive. When you think back over the many Giants and Dragons you've bedded in your stellar career, surely there must be at least one that was less physically attractive than *moi*.'

Her eyes squinted. She looked intrigued and horror-stricken at the same time. 'Perhaps,' she allowed.

'Yet you will not sleep with me. That, my dear, is hypocritical.'

'How so?' Thumper countered. 'I'm an independent woman. I choose.'

'So you've told me,' Win said. 'But why do you choose only Giants and Dragons?' When she hesitated a bit too long, he smiled and wagged his finger. 'You should at least be honest as to why you made that particular choice.'

'You seem to know a lot about me,' Thumper said. 'Why don't you tell me?'

'Fine. You immediately announce this bizarre rule about Dragons and Giants and whatnot. You set limits. I do not. If I find a woman attractive, that is enough. But you need this random team affiliation. You use it as a fence to separate you.'

'Separate me from what?'

'Not from what. Whom. From so-called freewheeling sluts. As you just pointed out to me, you are not a prostitute. You choose, dammit. You are no slut.'

'That's right, I'm not.'

He smiled. 'But what is a slut? A woman who sleeps around? Well, no. That's what you do. You wouldn't criticize a fellow sister to the cause. So what exactly is a slut? Well, by your definition, there is no such thing. Except, of course, you needed to deny being a slut when I questioned you. Why?'

'Don't make it out to be more than it is,' Thumper said. 'Slut carries with it a negative connotation. That's the only reason I got defensive.'

Win spread his hands. 'But why should there be any negative connotation? If a slut is, by definition, a so-called loose woman, a woman who sleeps around, why not embrace the term with both legs? Why put up these fences? Why create these artificial limits? You use your team affiliations to announce your independence. But it announces the opposite. It announces that you are unsure and insecure.'

'And that's why I'm a hypocrite?'

'Of course. Go back to my request to sleep with you. Either sex is a purely physical act, in which case my brusque behavior with you now should have no bearing on it, or sex is something more than physical. Which is it?'

She smiled, gave a quick head shake. 'You're an interesting man, Mr Lockwood. Maybe I will sleep with you.'

'No good,' he said.

'What?'

'You'll be doing it simply to prove I'm wrong. That, my dear, is as pathetic and insecure as what you are currently doing. But we are getting sidetracked. That is my fault, I apologize. Are you going to tell me about your conversation with Greg Downing, or do I destroy your reputation?'

She looked dazed. It was what he wanted.

'Of course there is option three,' Win continued, 'which closely follows option two. That is, on top of having your reputation destroyed you face a murder charge.'

That made her eyes widen. 'What?'

'Greg Downing is a serious suspect in a murder investigation. If it is discovered that you in some way helped him, that would make you an accessory.' He stopped, frowned. 'But to be frank, I don't think the D.A. will get a conviction. No matter. I'll start with your reputation. We'll see how it goes from there.'

Thumper looked at him steadily. 'Mr Lockwood?'

'Yes.'

'Go fuck yourself,' she said.

Win rose. 'Undeniably a better option than present company.' He smiled and bowed. If he had a hat, he would have tipped it. 'Good day.'

He moved away, head high. There was, of course, a method to such madness. She would not talk. He knew that almost immediately. She was both smart and loyal. A dangerous albeit admirable combination. But what he had said would jar her. Even the best amongst us would panic or at the very least act. He would wait outside and follow her.

He checked the scoreboard. Midway through the second quarter. He had no interest in watching any more of this game. But as he reached the gate, a buzz came over the loudspeaker and then a voice said, 'Now coming in for Troy Erickson, Myron Bolitar.'

Win hesitated. Then he took another step for the exit. He did not wish to watch. But he stopped again and, still standing, he faced the court.

Chapter 26

Myron sat at the far end of the bench. He knew that he wasn't going to play, but his chest was still wrapped in the steel bands of pregame jitters. In his younger days Myron had enjoyed the pressure of big-time competition, even when the jitters reached a level of near paralysis. They never lasted long after the opening tip. Once he had physical contact with an opponent or chased down a loose ball or shot a fade-away jumper, the butterflies flew off, the crowd's cheers and jeers dissolving into something akin to office background music.

Pregame jitters hadn't been a part of Myron's existence for over a decade, and he knew now what he'd always suspected: this nerve-jangled high was directly connected to basketball. Nothing else. He had never experienced anything similar in his business or personal life. Even violent confrontations – a perverted high if ever there was one – were not exactly like this. He had thought this uniquely sports-related sensation would ebb away with age and maturity, when a young man no longer takes a small event like a basketball game and blows it into an entity of near biblical importance, when something so relatively insignificant in the long run is no longer magnified to epic dimensions through the prism of youth. An adult, of course, can see what is useless to explain to a child – that one particular school dance or missed foul shot would be no more than a pang in the future. Yet here Myron was, comfortably ensconced in his thirties and still feeling the same heightened and raw sensations he had known only in youth. They hadn't gone away with age. They'd just hibernated – as Calvin had warned him – hoping for a chance to stir, a chance that normally never came in one man's lifetime.

Were his friends right? Was this all too much for him? Had he not put this all behind him? He spotted Jessica in the stands. She was watching the action, that funny look of concentration on her face. She alone seemed unconcerned by his return, but then again, she had not been a part of his life in his basketball heyday. Did the woman he love not understand, or did she—?

He stopped.

When you are on the bench, an arena can be a small place. He saw, for example, Win speaking with Thumper. He saw Jessica. He saw the other players' wives and girlfriends. And then, entering from a gate dead straight in front of him, he saw his parents. His eyes quickly fled back to the court. He clapped his hands and yelled out encouragement to his teammates, pretending to be interested in the outcome of the game. His mom and dad. They must have flown in early from their trip.

He risked a quick glance. They sat near Jessica now, in the family and friends section. His mom was staring back at him. Even from the distance he could see the lost look in her glassy eyes. Dad's eyes darted about, his jaw taut, as though he were summoning up a little extra before looking at the court straight on. Myron understood. This was all too familiar, like an old family film coming to life. He looked away again.

Leon White came out of the game. He grabbed an empty seat next to Myron. A towel boy draped his sweat top around his shoulders and gave him a squeeze bottle. Leon guzzled some Gatorade, his body glistened with sweat.

'Saw you talking with Thumper last night,' Leon said.

'Yeah.'

'You get some?'

Myron shook his head. 'I remain thump-less.'

Leon chuckled. 'Anyone tell you how she got that nick-name?'

'No.'

'When she gets into it – I mean, when she gets really fired up – she's got this habit of thumping her leg up and down. Left leg. Always her left leg, you know. So she's like on her back and you're pumping her for all you're worth and then all of a sudden her left leg starts bopping up and down. You hear thump-thump, get it?'

Myron nodded. He got it.

'So if she don't do that – if a guy don't get Thumper thumping – it's like you haven't done your duty. You can't show your face. You hang your head.' Then he added, 'It's a pretty serious tradition.'

'Like lighting a menorah on Hanukkah,' Myron said.

Leon laughed. 'Well, not exactly.'

'You ever been thumped, Leon?'

'Sure, once.' Then he quickly added, 'But that was before I was married.'

'How long you been married?'

'Me and Fiona been married a little over a year.'

Myron's heart plummeted down an elevator shaft. Fiona. Leon's wife's name was Fiona. He looked up in the stands at the flashy, well-rounded blonde. Fiona began with the letter F.

'Bolitar!'

Myron looked up. It was Donny Walsh, the head coach. 'Yeah?'

'Go in for Erickson.' Walsh said it like the words were fingernail clippings he needed to spit out. 'Take the off guard spot. Put Kiley at the point.'

Myron looked at his coach as if he were speaking Swahili. It was the second quarter. The score was tied.

'What the fuck you waiting for, Bolitar? For Erickson. Now.'

Leon slapped his back. 'Go, man.'

Myron stood. His legs felt like strung-out Slinkys. Thoughts of murder and disappearances fled like bats in a spotlight. He tried to swallow but his mouth was bone dry. He jogged over to the scorer's table. The arena spun like the bed of a drunk. Without conscious thought he discarded his sweats on the floor like a snake changing skin. He nodded at the scorer. 'For Erickson,' he said. Ten seconds later, a buzzer sounded. 'Now coming in the game for Troy Erickson, Myron Bolitar.'

He jogged out, pointing to Erickson. His teammates looked surprised to see him. Erickson said, 'You got Wallace.' Reggie Wallace. One of the game's best shooting guards. Myron lined up next to him and prepared. Wallace studied him with an amused smile.

'SWB alert,' Reggie Wallace called out with a mocking laugh. 'Goddamn SWB alert.'

Myron looked at TC. 'SWB?'

'Slow White Boy,' TC told him.

'Oh.'

Everyone else was breathing deeply and coated with sweat. Myron felt stiff and unprepared. His eyes swung back to Wallace. The ball was about to be inbounded. Something caught Myron's eye and he looked up. Win stood near an exit. His arms crossed. Their eyes met for a brief second. Win gave a half nod. The whistle blew. The game began.

Reggie Wallace began the trash talk immediately. 'You got to be kidding me,' he said. 'Old-timer, I'm gonna make you my woman.'

'Dinner and a movie first,' Myron said.

Wallace looked at him. 'Lame retort, old man.'

Hard to argue.

Wallace lowered himself to a ready position. He shook his head. 'Shit. Might as well have my grandma cover me.'

'Speaking of making someone your woman,' Myron said.

Wallace looked at him hard, nodded. 'Better,' he said.

The Pacers inbounded the ball. Wallace tried to post Myron up under the basket. This was a good thing. Physical contact. Nothing unclasped those steel bands like battling for position. Their bodies bounced against one another with small grunts. At six-four, two-twenty, Myron held his ground. Wallace tried digging back with his butt, but Myron held firm, putting a knee into Wallace's backside.

'Man,' Wallace said, 'you are so strong.'

And with that, he made a move Myron barely saw. He spun off Myron's knee so quickly that Myron barely had time to turn his head. Seeming to use Myron for leverage, Wallace leaped high in the air. From Myron's vantage point, it looked like an Apollo spacecraft heading straight out of the arena. He watched helplessly as Wallace's outstretched hands grasped the lob pass at rim level. He seemed to pause in midair, then continue rising as though gravity itself had decided to freeze frame the moment. When Reggie Wallace finally began to descend, he pulled the ball behind his head before throwing it through the cylinder with frightening force.

Slam dunk.

Wallace landed with both arms spread for applause. His taunting chased Myron up court. 'Welcome to the NBA, has-been. Or never-was. Or whatever the fuck you are. Oh, man, was that pretty or what? How did I look going up? Be honest. Bottom of my sneakers look sweet, don't they? I'm so pretty. So very pretty. How did it feel when I slammed it in your face? Come on, old-timer, you can tell me.'

Myron tried to tune him out. The Dragons came down and missed a quick shot. The Pacers grabbed the rebound and headed back up court. Wallace faked going back inside and popped way out past the three point circle. He caught the pass and shot in one motion. The ball went in with a swish. Three pointer.

'Whoa, old man, did you hear that sound?' Reggie Wallace went on. 'That swish? There is no sweeter sound on earth. You hear me? No sweeter sound at all. Not even a woman crying out in orgasm.'

Myron looked at him. 'Women have orgasms?'

Wallace laughed. 'Touché, old-timer. Touché.'

Myron checked the clock. He'd been in for thirty-four seconds and his man had scored five points. Myron did some quick math. At that rate, Myron could hold Reggie Wallace to under six hundred points per game.

The boos started soon after. Unlike his youth, the crowd sounds did not fade into the background. They were not one indistinguishable blur of sound, a home-court cheer to perhaps ride upon the way a surfer picks up a wave. Or a boo in a rival's arena – something you expect and even thrive on in a perverse way. But to hear your own fans boo your specific performance, to hear your home crowd turn against you – Myron had never experienced that before. He heard the crowd now as never before, as a collective entity of derision and as distinct voices making ugly catcalls. 'You suck, Bolitar!' 'Get that stiff outta there!' 'Blow out your other knee and sit down!' He tried to ignore them but each catcall punctured him like a dagger.

Pride took over. He would not let Wallace score. The mind was willing. The heart was willing. But as Myron soon saw, the knee was not. He was simply too slow. Reggie Wallace scored six more points off Myron that period for a total of eleven. Myron scored two off an open jumper. He took to playing what he used to call 'appendix' basketball; that is, certain players on the floor are like your appendix – they're either superfluous or they hurt you. He tried to stay out of the way and hit TC down low. He kept passing and moving away from the ball. When he saw a big opening and drove the lane near the end of the quarter, the Pacers' big center swatted the shot into the crowd. The boos were thunderous. Myron looked up. His mom and dad were still as two statues. One box over, a group of well-dressed men were cupping their hands around their mouths and starting a 'Bolitar Sucks' chant. Myron saw Win move quickly toward them. Win offered his hand to the cheer's leader. The leader took it. The leader went down.

But the odd thing was, even as Myron stunk up the joint, even as he continued to get beaten on defense and play ineffectively on offense, the old confidence remained. He wanted to stay in the game. He would still look for an opening, relatively unshaken, a man in denial, a man ignoring the mounting evidence that a crowd of 18,812 (according to the loudspeaker) could plainly see. He knew his luck would change. He was a little out of shape, that was all. Soon it would all turn around.

He realized how much that sounded like B Man's description of a compulsive gambler's rationale.

The half ended not long after that. As Myron headed off the court, he looked up again at his parents. They stood and smiled down at him. He smiled and nodded back. He looked toward the group of well-dressed booers. They were nowhere to be seen. Neither was Win.

Nobody spoke to him at halftime, and Myron didn't get in the rest of the game. He suspected that Clip had been behind his playing. Why? What had Clip been trying to prove? The game ended in a two-point victory for the Dragons. By the time they got into the locker room and began changing, Myron's performance was forgotten. The media surrounded TC, who had played a brilliant game, scoring thirty-three points and grabbing eighteen rebounds. TC slapped Myron's back when he walked past him but said nothing.

Myron unlaced his sneakers. He wondered if his parents were going to wait for him. Probably not. They would figure he would want to be alone. His parents, for all their butting in, were actually pretty good at knowing when to make themselves scarce. They'd wait for him at home, staying up all night if they had to. To this day, his father stayed awake watching TV on the couch until Myron got home. Once Myron put the key in the lock, his father feigned sleep, his reading glasses still perched at the end of his nose, the newspaper lying across his chest. Thirty-two years old and his father still waited up for him. Christ, he was too old for that anymore, wasn't he?

Audrey peered tentatively around the corner and waited. Only when he signaled with a beckoning wave did she approach. She stuck her pad and pencil in her purse and shrugged. 'Look at the bright side,' she said.

'And that is?'

'You still have a great ass.'

'It's these pro shorts,' Myron said. 'They really mold and hold.'

'Mold and hold?'

He shrugged. 'Hey, happy birthday.'

'Thanks,' Audrey said.

' "Beware the Ides of March," ' Myron pronounced in dramatic fashion.

'The Ides are the fifteenth,' Audrey said. 'Today is the seventeenth.'

'Yeah, I know. But I never skip an opportunity to quote Shakespeare. Makes me look smart.'

'Brains and a good ass,' Audrey said. 'Who cares if you have no lateral movement?'

'Funny,' Myron said, 'Jess never complains about that.'

'At least not to your face.' Audrey smiled. 'Nice to see you so chipper.'

He returned the smile, shrugged.

Audrey looked around to make sure no one was in earshot. 'I got some info for you,' she said.

'On?'

'On the private eye in the divorce case.'

'Greg hired one?'

'Either him or Felder,' she replied. 'I have a source who does electronics work for ProTec Investigations. They do all of Felder's work. Now my source doesn't know all the details, but he helped set up a videotaping at the Glenpointe Hotel two months ago. You know the Glenpointe?'

Myron nodded. 'The hotel on Route 80? Maybe five miles from here?'

'Right. My source doesn't know what it was for or what ended up on it. He just knows the work was for the Downing divorce. He also confirmed the obvious: this thing is usually done to catch a spouse in *flagrante delicto*.'

Myron frowned. 'This was two months ago?'

'Yep.'

'But Greg and Emily were already separated by then,' Myron said. 'The divorce was practically finalized. What would be the point?'

'The divorce, yes,' she agreed. 'But the child custody battle was just starting.'

'Yeah, but so what? She was a near-single woman having a sexual encounter. That kind of thing hardly proves parental unfitness in this day and age.'

Audrey shook her head. 'You are so naive.'

'What do you mean?'

'A tape of a mother getting it on with some buck at a motel, doing lord-knows-what? We still live in a sexist society. It would be bound to influence a judge.'

Myron mulled it over, but it just wouldn't mesh. 'First of all, you're assuming the judge is both male and a Neanderthal. Second' – he sort of held up his hands and shrugged – 'it's the nineties for crying out loud. A woman separated from her husband having sex with another man? Hardly earth-shattering stuff.'

'I don't know what else to tell you, Myron.'

'You got anything else?'

'That's it,' she said. 'But I'm working on it.'

'Do you know Fiona White?'

'Leon's wife? Enough to say hello. Why?'

'She ever model?'

'Model?' She sort of chuckled. 'Yeah, I guess you'd call it that.'

'She was a centerfold?'

'Yep.'

'You know what month?'

'No. Why?'

He told her about the e-mail. He was fairly sure now that Ms F was Fiona White, that Sepbabe was short for September babe, the month, he bet, that she was a center-fold. Audrey listened raptly. 'I can check it out,' she said when he finished. 'See if she was a September playmate.'

'That would help.'

'It would explain a lot,' Audrey continued. 'About the tension between Downing and Leon.'

Myron nodded.

'Look, I gotta run. Jess is getting the car around back. Keep me posted.'

'Right, have fun.'

He finished up, toweled off, started dressing. He thought about Greg's secret girlfriend, the one who had been staying at his house. Could it possibly be Fiona

White? If so, that would also explain the need for secrecy. Could Leon White have found out about it? That seemed logical based on his antagonism toward Greg. So where did that leave us? And how did this all tie in with Greg's gambling and Liz Gorman's blackmail scheme?

Whoa, hold the phone.

Forget gambling for a moment. Suppose Liz Gorman had something else on Greg Downing, a revelation equally if not potentially more explosive than laying down a few bets. Suppose she had somehow found out that Greg was having an affair with his best friend's wife. Suppose she had decided to blackmail Greg and Clip with this information. How much would Greg pay to keep his fans and teammates from learning about his betrayal? How much would Clip pay to keep that particular warhead from detonating in the midst of a championship run?

It was worth looking into.

Chapter 27

Myron stopped at the traffic light that divided South Livingston Avenue and the JFK Parkway. This particular intersection had barely changed in the past thirty years. The familiar brick facade of Nero's Restaurant was on his right. It had originally been Jimmy Johnson's Steak House, but that had to be at least twenty-five years ago. The same Gulf station occupied another corner, a small firehouse another, undeveloped land on the last.

He turned onto Hobart Gap Road. The Bolitar family had first moved to Livingston when Myron was six weeks old. Little had changed in comparison to the rest of the world. The familiarity of seeing the same sights over so many years was less comforting now than numbing. You didn't notice anything. You looked but you never saw.

As he turned up the same street where his dad had first taught him to ride that two-wheeler with a Batman reflector on the back, he tried to pay true heed to the homes that had surrounded him all of his life. There had been changes, of course, but in his mind it was still 1970. He and his parents still referred to the neighboring homes by their original owners, as though they were Southern plantations. The Rackins, for example, hadn't lived in the Rackin House for over a decade. Myron didn't know anymore who lived in the Kirschner Place or the Roth House or the Parkers'. Like the Bolitars, the Rackins and the Kirschners and the rest had moved in when the construction was new, when you could still see some remnants of the Schnectman farm, when Livingston was considered the boonies, as far away from New York City at twenty-five miles as western Pennsylvania. The Rackins and the Kirschners and the Roths had lived a big chunk of their lives here. They'd moved in with infant children, raised them, taught them how to ride bicycles on the same streets Myron had learned on, sent them to Burnet Hill elementary school, then Heritage Junior High, finally Livingston High School. The kids had gone off to college, visiting only on college breaks. Not long after, wedding invitations went out. A few started displaying photos of grandchildren, shaking their heads in disbelief at how time flew. Eventually the Rackins and the Kirschners and the Roths felt out of place. This town designed to raise kids held nothing for them anymore. Their familiar homes suddenly felt too big and too empty, so they put them on the market and sold them to new young families with infant children who would too soon go off to Burnet Hill elementary school, then Heritage Junior High, and finally Livingston High School.

Life, Myron decided, was not that different from one of those depressing life insurance commercials.

Some neighborhood old-timers had managed to hang on. You could usually tell which houses belonged to them because – in spite of the fact that the children were grown – they had built additions and nice porches and kept their lawns well groomed. The Brauns and the Goldsteins were two who had done just that. And of course, Al and Ellen Bolitar.

Myron pulled his Ford Taurus into the driveway, his headlights sweeping across the front yard like searchlights during a prison break. He parked up on the blacktop not far from the basketball hoop. He turned off the ignition. For a moment he just stared at the basket. An image of his father lifting him so he could reach the basket appeared before him. If the image had come from memory or imagination, he could not say. Nor did it matter.

As he moved toward the house, outside lights came on via a motion detector. Though the detectors had been installed three years ago, they were still a source of unbridled awe for his parents, who considered this technological advance on a par with the discovery of fire. When the motion detectors were first put up, Mom and Dad spent blissful hours in disbelief testing the mechanism, seeing if they could duck under its eye or walk super-slowly so that the detector would not sense them. Sometimes in life, it's the simple pleasures.

His parents were sitting in the kitchen. When he entered, they both quickly pretended they were doing something.

'Hi,' he said.

They looked at him with tilted heads and too-concerned eyes. 'Hi, sweetheart,' Mom said.

'Hi, Myron,' Dad said.

'You're back from Europe early,' Myron said.

Both heads nodded like they were guilty of a crime.

Mom said, 'We wanted to see you play.' She said it gently, like she was walking on thin ice with a blowtorch.

'So how was your trip?' Myron asked.

'Wonderful,' Dad said.

'Marvelous,' Mom added. 'The food they served was just terrific.'

'Small portions though,' Dad said.

'What do you mean, small portions?' Mom snapped.

'I'm just commenting, Ellen. The food was good, but the portions were small.'

'What, did you measure it or something? What do you mean small?'

'I know a small portion when I see one. These were small.'

'Small. Like he needs larger portions. The man eats like a horse. It wouldn't kill you to lose ten pounds, Al.'

'Me? I'm not getting heavy.'

'Oh no? Your pants are getting so tight you'd think you were starring in a dance movie.'

Dad winked at her. 'You didn't seem to have any problem taking them off on the trip.'

'Al!' she shrieked, but there was a smile there too. 'In front of your own child! What's wrong with you?'

Dad looked at Myron, arms spread. 'We were in Venice,' he said in a way of explanation. 'Rome.'

'Say no more,' Myron said. 'Please.'

They laughed. When it died out his mother spoke in a hushed tone.

'You okay, sweetheart?'

'I'm fine,' he said.

'Really?'

'Really.'

'I thought you did some good things out there,' Dad

267

said. 'You hit TC for a couple of nice passes on the post. Real nice passes. You showed smarts.'

Count on Dad to find the silver lining. 'I bit the big one,' Myron said.

Dad gave a staunch head shake and said, 'You think I'm saying this just to make you feel good?'

'I know you're saying this just to make me feel good.'

'It doesn't matter,' Dad said. 'It never mattered. You know that.'

Myron nodded. He did know. He had witnessed pushy fathers all his life, men who tried to live hollow dreams through their offspring, forcing their sons to carry a burden they themselves could never carry. But not his father. Never his father. Al Bolitar had never needed to fill his son with grandiose stories of his athletic prowess. He never pushed him, possessing the wondrous ability to appear almost indifferent while making it clear he cared intensely. Yes, this was a direct contradiction – sort of a detached attachment – but somehow Dad pulled it off. Sadly, it was unusual for Myron's generation to admit to such wonderment. His generation had remained un-defined – shoehorned between the Beat Generation of Woodstock and the Generation X of MTV, too young when *thirty-something* had ruled the airwaves, too old now for *Beverly Hills, 90210*, or *Melrose Place*. Mostly, it seemed to Myron, he was part of the Blame Generation, where life was a series of reactions and counterreactions. In the same way those pushy fathers put everything on their sons, the sons came right back and blamed their future failures on the fathers. His generation had been taught to look back and pinpoint exact moments when their parents had ruined their lives. Myron never did. If he looked back – if he studied his parents' past feats – it was only to try to unravel their secret before he had children of his own.

'I know what it looked like tonight,' he said, 'but I really don't feel that bad.'

Mom sniffled. 'We know.' Her eyes were red. She sniffled again.

'You're not crying over—'

She shook her head. 'You've grown up. I know that. But when you ran out on the court again like that, for the first time in so long . . .'

Her voice died out. Dad looked away. The three of them were all the same. They were drawn to nostalgia like starlets to paparazzi.

Myron waited until he was sure his voice would be clear. 'Jessica wants me to move in with her,' he said.

He expected protests, at least from his mother. Mom had not forgiven Jessica for leaving the first time; Myron doubted that she ever would. Dad, as was his way, acted like a good news reporter – neutral, but you wondered what opinion he was making under those balanced questions.

Mom looked at Dad. Dad looked back and put a hand on her shoulder. Then Mom said, 'You can always come back,' she said.

Myron almost asked for a clarification, but he stopped himself and simply nodded. The three of them gathered around the kitchen table and began to talk. Myron made himself a grilled cheese. Mom didn't do it for him. Dogs were domesticated, she believed, not people. She never cooked anymore, which Myron took as a positive thing. Her doting was all verbal, and that was all right with him.

They told him about their trip. He briefly and very vaguely sketched out why he was playing pro basketball again. An hour later he headed into his room in the basement. He had lived here since he was sixteen, the year his sister had gone off to college. The basement was subdivided into two rooms – a sitting area he almost never used except for company and hence kept clean, and a bedroom that looked very much like a teenager's. He crawled into bed and looked at the posters on the wall. Most had been up since his adolescence, the colors faded, the corners frayed near the thumbtacks.

Myron had always loved the Celtics – his father had grown up near Boston – and so his two favorite posters were of John Havlicek, the Celtics star of the sixties and seventies, and Larry Bird, the team's star of the eighties. He looked now from Havlicek to Bird. Myron was supposed to have been the next poster on the wall. It had been his boyhood dream. When the Celtics drafted him, it barely surprised him. A higher power was at work. It had been preordained that he would be the next Celtics legend.

Then Burt Wesson slammed into him.

Myron put his hands behind his head. His eyes adjusted to the light. When his phone rang, he reached for it absently.

'We have what you're looking for,' an electronically altered voice said.

'Excuse me?'

'The same thing Downing wanted to buy. It'll cost you fifty thousand dollars. Get the money together. We'll call you with instructions tomorrow night.'

The caller hung up. Myron tried hitting star-six-nine to ring back, but the call was from out of the area. He lowered his head back to the pillow. Then he stared at the two posters and waited for sleep to claim him.

Chapter 28

Martin Felder's office was on Madison Avenue in midtown, not far from Myron's own. The agency was called Felder Inc., the clever name making it very apparent that Marty wasn't on Madison Avenue as a hotshot advertising exec. A sprightly receptionist was all too happy to show Myron the way to Marty's office.

The door was already open. 'Marty, Myron is here to see you.'

Marty. Myron. It was one of those kind of offices. Everyone was a first name. Everyone was dressed in that new, neat-casual look. Marty, who Myron guessed was in his mid-fifties, wore one of those blue jean shirts with a bright orange tie. His thinning gray hair was plastered down, almost a comb over but not quite. His pants were Banana Republic green and crisply pressed. His orange socks matched the tie and his shoes looked like Hush Puppies.

'Myron!' he exclaimed, pumping Myron's hand. 'Great to see you.'

'Thanks for seeing me so soon, Marty.'

He waved a dismissing hand. 'Myron, please. For you, anytime.' They'd met a few times at different sporting and sports representative events. Myron knew that Marty had a solid reputation as a guy who was – to coin a cliché – tough but fair. Marty also had a knack for getting great media coverage for both himself and his athletes. He'd written a couple of how-to-succeed books which helped enhance his name recognition as well as his rep. On top of that, Marty looked like your favorite, self-effacing uncle. People liked him instantly.

'Can I get you a drink?' he asked. 'Caffè latte perhaps?'

'No thanks.'

He smiled, shook his head. 'I've been planning on calling you for the longest time, Myron. Please, have a seat.'

The walls were bare except for bizarre sculptures twisted out of neon light. His desk was glass, the built-in shelves fiberglass. There were no visible papers. Everything shone like the inside of a spaceship. Felder gestured to a chair in front of the desk for Myron; then he took the other chair in front of the desk. Two equals chatting it up. No desk to use as a divider or intimidator.

Felder started right in. 'I don't have to tell you, Myron, that you are quickly making a name for yourself in this field. Your clients trust you absolutely. Owners and managers respect and fear' – he emphasized the fear part – 'you. That's rare, Myron. Very rare.' He slapped his palms on his thighs and leaned forward. 'Do you enjoy being in sports representation?'

'Yes.'

'Good,' he said with a sharp nod. 'It's important to like what you're doing. Choosing a profession is the most important decision you'll ever make – more important even than choosing a spouse.' He looked up at the ceiling. 'Who was it that said, you may tire of your relationship with people but never of a job you love?'

'Wink Martindale?' Myron said.

Felder chuckled and offered up a shy, caught-himself smile. 'Guess you didn't come here to hear me drone on about my own personal philosophies,' he said. 'So let me put my cards on the table. Just flat out say it. How would you like to come work for Felder Inc.?'

'Work here?' Myron said. Job Interview Rule #1: Dazzle them with sparkling repartee.

'Here's what I'd like to do,' Felder said. 'I want to make you a senior vice president. Your salary would be generous. You'd still be able to give all your clients the personal Bolitar attention they've come to expect, plus you'll have all the resources of Felder Inc. at your command. Think about it, Myron. We employ over one hundred people here. We have our own travel agency to handle all those arrangements for you. We have – well, let's call them what they are, shall we? – gofers who can deal with all those details that are so necessary in our business, freeing you up to tackle important tasks.' He raised a hand as if to stop Myron, though Myron hadn't moved. 'Now I know you have an associate, Miss Esperanza Diaz. She'd come aboard too, of course. At a higher salary. Plus I understand she's finishing up law school this year. There'll be plenty of room for advancement here.' He gestured with his hands before adding, 'So what do you think?'

'I'm very flattered—'

273

'Don't be,' Felder interrupted. 'It's a sound business decision for me. I know good stock when I see it.' He leaned forward with a sincere smile. 'Let someone else be the client's errand boy, Myron. I want to free you up to do what you do best – recruit new clients and negotiate deals.'

Myron had no interest in giving up his company, but the man knew how to make it sound attractive. 'May I think about it?' he asked.

'Of course,' Felder said, raising his hands in surrendered agreement. 'I don't want to pressure you, Myron. Take your time. I certainly don't expect an answer today.'

'I appreciate that,' Myron said, 'but I actually wanted to talk to you about another matter.'

'Please.' He leaned back, folded his hands on his lap, smiled. 'Go right ahead.'

'It's about Greg Downing.'

The smile didn't budge, but the light behind it flickered a bit. 'Greg Downing?'

'Yes. I have a few questions.'

Still smiling. 'You realize, of course, that I cannot reveal anything that may fall under what I consider privileged.'

'Of course,' Myron agreed. 'I was wondering if you could tell me where he is.'

Marty Felder waited a beat. This was no longer a sales pitch meeting. It was now a negotiation. A good negotiator is frighteningly patient. Like a good interrogator, he must above all else be a listener. He must make his opponent do the talking. After several seconds, Felder asked, 'Why do you want to know that?'

'I need to speak with him,' Myron said.

'May I ask what this is about?'

'I'm afraid it's confidential.'

They looked at each other, both faces open and friendly, but now they were two card sharks who didn't want to show their hands. 'Myron,' Felder began, 'you have to understand my position here. I don't feel comfortable divulging this type of information without having at least some hint as to why you want to see him.'

Time to jar something loose. 'I didn't join the Dragons to make a comeback,' Myron said. 'Clip Arnstein hired me to find Greg.'

Felder's eyebrows dropped to half mast. 'Find him? But I thought he went into seclusion to heal an ankle injury.'

Myron shook his head. 'That was the story Clip told the press.'

'I see.' Felder put a hand to his chin and nodded slowly. 'And you're trying to locate him?'

'Yes.'

'Clip hired you? He chose you himself? It was his idea?'

Myron answered in the affirmative. There was a faint smile on Felder's face now, like he was enjoying an inside joke. 'I'm sure Clip already told you that Greg had done this kind of thing before.'

'Yes,' Myron said.

'So I don't see why you should be all that concerned,' Felder said. 'Your help is appreciated, Myron, but it is really not necessary.'

'You know where he is?'

Felder hesitated. 'Again, Myron, I ask you to put yourself in my position. If one of your clients wanted to stay hidden, would you go against his wishes or respect his rights?'

Myron smelled a bluff. 'That would depend,' he said.

'If the client was in big trouble, I'd probably do whatever I could to help him.'

'What sort of big trouble?' Felder asked.

'Gambling, for one. Greg owes a lot of money to some awfully unpleasant fellows.' Still no reaction from Felder. In this case, Myron read it as a good thing. If most people had just heard that a client owed money to mobsters, they would show some sort of surprise. 'You know about his gambling, don't you, Marty?'

Felder's words were slow, as if he were weighing each one separately with a hand scale. 'You are still new in this business, Myron. With that comes a certain enthusiasm that is not always well placed. I am Greg Downing's sports representative. That gives me certain responsibilities. It is not a carte blanche to run his life. What he or any other client does on his own time is not, should not, and cannot be my concern. For all our sakes. We care about every client, but we are not parental substitutes or life managers. It's important to learn this early on.'

The Cliff Notes summary: he knew about the gambling.

Myron asked, 'Why did Greg withdraw fifty thousand dollars ten days ago?'

Again Felder showed no reaction. He was either beyond being surprised by what Myron knew or he had the ability to shut off any connection between his brain and facial muscles. 'You know I can't discuss that with you – or even confirm that such a withdrawal took place.' He slapped his palms against his thighs again and mounted a smile. 'Do us both a favor, Myron. Think about my offer and drop this other matter. Greg will pop up soon. He always does.'

'I wouldn't be so sure,' Myron said. 'He's in real trouble this time.'

'If you are talking about his alleged gambling debts—'

Myron shook his head. 'I'm not.'

'Then what?'

So far, the man had given Myron nothing. Letting on that he knew about the gambling problem was a lay-up. He had realized Myron knew about it. To deny it would make him look either incompetent for not knowing or dishonest for making a strong denial. Marty Felder was shrewd. He would not misstep. Myron tried shifting direction. 'Why did you videotape Greg's wife?'

He blinked. 'Pardon?'

'ProTec. That's the name of the agency you hired. They set up a videotape surveillance at the Glenpointe Hotel. I'd like to know why.'

Felder looked almost amused. 'Help me understand this, Myron. First you say that my client is in deep trouble. You claim you want to help him. Then you start making allegations about a videotape. I'm having trouble following you.'

'I'm just trying to help your client.'

'The best thing you can do for Greg is to tell me all you know. I am his advocate, Myron. I am truly interested in doing what's best for him – not what might be best for the Dragons or Clip or anybody else. You said he was in trouble. Tell me how.'

Myron shook his head. 'First you tell me about the videotape.'

'No.'

There you have it. Top-notch negotiating getting down to basics. Soon they'd be sticking tongues out at each other, but for now both faces remained pleasant. They were playing the waiting game. Who would be the first to crack? Myron ran down the situation in his mind. The cardinal rule of negotiating: Don't lose sight of what you want and what your opponent wants. Okay. So what did Felder have that Myron wanted? Information on the fifty thousand dollars, the videotape, and maybe some other stuff. What did Myron have that Felder wanted? Not much. Myron had made him curious when he mentioned big trouble. Felder might already know what trouble Greg was in, but he would still want to know what Myron knew. End analysis: Myron needed the information more. He would have to move. Time to up the ante. And no more delicacy.

'I don't have to be the one asking you these questions,' Myron said.

'What do you mean?'

'I could have a homicide detective ask them.'

Felder barely moved, but his pupils expanded in a funny way. 'What?'

'A certain homicide detective is this close' – Myron held up his thumb and index finger close together – 'to putting out an APB on Greg.'

'A homicide detective?'

'Yes.'

'But who was killed?'

Myron shook his head. 'First the videotape.'

Felder was not a man to jump. He refolded his hands on his lap, looked up, tapped his foot. He took his time, considering the pros and cons, the costs and benefits, all that. Myron half-expected him to start charting graphs.

'You never practiced as an attorney, did you, Myron?'

Myron shook his head. 'I passed the bar. That's about it.'

'You're lucky,' he said. He sighed and made a tired gesture with his hands. 'You know why people make all the jokes about lawyers being scum? It's because they are. It's not their fault. Not really. It's the system. The system encourages cheating and lying and basic scummy behavior. Suppose you were at a Little League game. Suppose you told the kids that there were no umpires today – that they were to umpire themselves. Wouldn't that lead to some pretty unethical behavior? Probably. But then tell the little tykes that they must win, no matter what. Tell them that their only obligation is to winning and that they should forget about things like fair play and sportsmanship. That's what our judicial system is like, Myron. We allow for deceit in the name of an abstract greater good.'

'Bad analogy,' Myron said.

'Why's that?'

'The part about no umpires. Lawyers have to face judges.'

'Not many of them. Most cases are settled before a judge sees it. You know that. But no matter, my point is made. The system encourages attorneys to lie and distort under the guise of the client's best interest. That best-interest crap has become an all-purpose excuse for anything goes. It's ruining our judicial system.'

'Fascinating, really,' Myron said. 'And all this relates to the videotape . . . ?'

'Very directly,' Felder said. 'Emily Downing's lawyer lied and distorted the truth. She did it to an unethical and unnecessary extreme.'

'Are you talking about the child custody case?' Myron asked.

'Yes.'

'What did she do?'

He smiled. 'I'll give you a hint. This particular claim is made now in one out of every three child custody cases in the United States. It has become almost standard practice, tossed about like rice was at the actual wedding, though it destroys lives.'

'Child abuse?'

Felder did not bother with an answer. 'We felt that we needed to quell these malicious and dangerous untruths. To balance the scales, so to speak. I'm not proud of that. None of us are. But I'm not ashamed either. You can't fight fair if your opponent insists on using brass knuckles. You must do what you can to survive.'

'What did you do?'

'We videotaped Emily Downing in a rather delicate situation.'

'When you say delicate, what exactly do you mean?'

Felder stood up and took a key from his pocket. He unlocked a cabinet and pulled out a videotape. Then he opened another cabinet. A TV and VCR faced them. He placed the tape in the machine and picked up the remote. 'Your turn now,' he said. 'You said Greg was in big trouble.'

It was time for Myron to give a little. Another cardinal rule of negotiation: don't be a pig and just take. It'll backfire in the long run. 'We believe a woman may have been blackmailing Greg,' he said. 'She has several aliases. Usually Carla but she may have used the names Sally or Liz. She was murdered last Saturday night.'

That one stunned him. Or at least he acted stunned. 'Surely the police don't suspect Greg—'

'Yes,' Myron said.

'But why?'

Myron kept it vague. 'Greg was the last person seen with her the night of the murder. His fingerprints were at the murder scene. And the police found the murder weapon at his house.'

'They searched his house?'

'Yes.'

'But they can't do that.'

Already playing the ready-to-distort lawyer. 'They got a warrant,' Myron said. 'Do you know this woman? This Carla or Sally?'

'No.'

'Do you have any idea where Greg is?'

'None.'

Myron watched him, but he couldn't tell if he was lying or not. Except in very rare instances, you can never tell if a person is lying by watching their eyes or their body language or any of that stuff. Nervous, fidgety people tell the truth too, and a good liar could look as sincere as Alan Alda at a telethon. So-called 'students of body language' were usually just fooled with more certainty. 'Why did Greg take out fifty thousand dollars in cash?' Myron asked.

'I didn't ask,' Felder said. 'As I just explained to you, such matters were not my concern.'

'You thought it was for gambling.'

Again Felder didn't bother responding. He lifted his eyes from the floor. 'You said this woman was blackmailing him.'

'Yes,' Myron said.

He looked at Myron steadily. 'Do you know what she had on him?'

'Not for sure. The gambling, I think.'

Felder nodded. With his eyes looking straight ahead, he

pointed the remote control at the television behind him and pressed some buttons. The screen brightened into gray static. Then a black and white image appeared. A hotel room. The camera seemed to be shooting from the ground up. No one was in the room. A digital counter showed the time. The setup reminded Myron of those tapes of Marion Barry smoking a crack pipe.

Uh oh.

Could that be it? Having sex would hardly be grounds to show unfitness as a parent, but what about drugs? What better way to balance the scales, as Felder had put it, than to show the mother smoking or snorting or shooting up in a hotel room? How would that work on a judge?

But as Myron was about to see, he was wrong.

The hotel room door opened. Emily entered alone. She looked around tentatively. She sat on the bed, but then got back up. She paced. She sat down again. She paced again. She checked the bathroom, came right back out, paced. Her fingers picked up whatever object they could find – hotel brochures, room services menus, a television guide.

'Is there any sound?' Myron asked.

Marty Felder shook his head no. He was still not looking at the screen.

Myron watched transfixed as Emily continued to go through her nervous ritual. Suddenly she froze in place and turned to the door. Must have heard a knock. She approached tentatively. Looking for Mr Goodbar? Probably, Myron surmised. But when Emily turned the knob and let the door swing open, Myron realized he was wrong again. It was not Mr Goodbar who entered the hotel room.

It was Ms Goodbar.

The two women talked for a bit. They had a drink from the room's minibar. Then they began to undress. Myron's stomach coiled. By the time they moved to the bed, he had seen more than enough.

'Turn it off.'

Felder did so, still not looking at the screen. 'I meant what I said before. I'm not proud of that.'

'What a guy,' Myron said.

So now he understood Emily's ferocious hostility. She had indeed been taped in *flagrante delicto* – not with another man, but with a woman. Certainly no law against it. But most judges would be influenced. It was the way of the world. And speaking of the way of the world, Myron knew Ms Goodbar by another nickname:

Thumper.

Chapter 29

Myron walked back to his office, wondering what it all meant. For one thing, it meant that Thumper was more than a harmless diversion in all this. But what exactly was she? Had she set up Emily or had she, too, been taped unaware? Were they steady lovers or participants in a one-night stand? Felder claimed he didn't know. On the tape, the two women hadn't appeared to be all that familiar with each other – at least, not in the small portion he had watched – but he was hardly an expert on the subject.

Myron cut east on 50th Street. An albino wearing a Mets cap and yellow boxer shorts on the outside of ripped jeans played an Indian sitar. He was singing the seventies classic 'The Night Chicago Died' in a voice that reminded Myron of elderly Chinese women in the back of a laundromat. The albino also had a tin cup and a stack of cassettes. A sign read 'The Original Benny and His Magical Sitar, only $10.' The original. Oh. Wouldn't want that imitation albino, sitar, AM seventies music, no sir.

Benny smiled at him. When he reached the part of the song where the son learns a hundred cops are dead – maybe even the boy's fathers – Benny began to weep. Moving. Myron stuffed a dollar into the cup. He crossed the street, his thoughts reverting back to the videotape of Emily and Thumper. He wondered now about the relevance. He'd felt like a dirty voyeur for watching the tape in the first place, and now he felt that way for rehashing it in his mind. It was, after all, probably no more than a bizarre aside. What possible connection could there be in all this to the murder of Liz Gorman? None that he could see; then again he still had trouble seeing how Liz Gorman fit in with Greg's gambling or how she fit in at all.

Still, the video undoubtedly raised a few fairly major issues. For one thing, there was the abuse allegations made against Greg. Was there anything to them, or as Marty Felder had indicated, was Emily's attorney just playing hardball? And hadn't Emily told Myron she would do anything to keep her kids? Even kill. How did Emily react when she learned about the videotape? Spurred on by this awful violation, how far would Emily go?

Myron entered his office building on Park Avenue. He exchanged a brief elevator smile with a young woman in a business suit. The elevator reeked of drugstore cologne, the kind where some guy decides that taking a shower is too time-consuming so he opts for sprinkling himself with enough cologne to glaze a wedding cake. The young woman sniffed and looked at Myron.

'I don't wear cologne,' he said.

She didn't seem convinced. Or perhaps she was condemning the gender in general for this affront. Understandable under these circumstances.

'Try holding your breath,' he said.

She looked at him, her face a seaweed green.

When he entered his office, Esperanza smiled and said, 'Good morning.'

'Oh no,' Myron said.

'What?'

'You've never said good morning to me before. Ever.'

'I have, too.'

Myron shook his head. '*Et tu*, Esperanza?'

'What are you talking about?'

'You heard about what happened last night. You're trying to be – dare I say it? – nice to me.'

The fire in her eyes flamed up. 'You think I give a shit about that game? That you got your butt burned at every turn?'

Myron shook his head. 'Too late,' he said. 'You care.'

'I do not. You sucked. Get over it.'

'Nice try.'

'What, nice try? You sucked. S-U-C-K-E-D. A pitiful display. I was embarrassed to know you. I hid my head in shame when I came in.'

He bent down and kissed her cheek.

Esperanza wiped it off with the back of her hand. 'Now I got to get a cootie shot.'

'I'm fine,' he said. 'Really.'

'Like I care. Really.'

The phone rang. She picked it up. 'MB SportsReps. Why yes, Jason, he is here. Hold on a moment.' She put a hand over the receiver. 'It's Jason Blair.'

'The vermin who said you had a nice ass?'

She nodded. 'Remind him about my legs.'

'I'll take it in my office.' A photograph on the top of a stack of papers on her desk caught his eye. 'What's this?'

'The Raven Brigade file,' she said.

He picked up a grainy photo of the group taken in 1973, the only shot of the seven of them together. He quickly found Liz Gorman. He hadn't gotten a good look at her, but from what he saw, there was no way anyone would ever imagine that Carla and Liz Gorman were one and the same. 'Mind if I keep this for a few minutes?' he asked.

'Suit yourself.'

He moved into his office and picked up the phone. 'What's up, Jason?'

'Where the fuck have you been?'

'Not much. How about you?'

'Don't play smart guy with me. You put that little lady on my contract and she fucked it all up. I got half a mind to leave MB.'

'Calm down, Jason. How did she fuck it up?'

His voice cracked with incredulity. 'You don't know?'

'No.'

'Here we are, hot in the middle of negotiating with the Red Sox, right?'

'Right.'

'I want to stay in Boston. We both know that. But we have to make a lot of noise like I'm leaving. That's what you said to do. Make them think you want to switch teams. To up the money. I'm a free agent. This is what we got to do, right?'

'Right.'

'We don't want them to know I want to be on the team again, right?'

'Right. To a degree.'

'Fuck to a degree,' he snapped. 'The other day my neighbor gets a mailing from the Sox, asking him to renew his season tickets. Guess whose picture is on the brochure saying I'm gonna be back? Go ahead. Guess.'

'Would that be yours, Jason?'

'Damn straight mine! So I call up little Miss Nice Ass—'

'She's got great legs too.'

'What?'

'Her legs. She's not that tall, so they're not very long. But they're nicely toned.'

'Will you quit fucking around here, Myron? Listen to me. She tells me the Sox called up and asked if they could use my picture in the ad, even though I wasn't signed. She tells them to go ahead! Go right fucking ahead! Now what are those Red Sox assholes supposed to think, huh? I'll tell you what. They think I'm gonna sign with them no matter what. We lost all our leverage because of her.'

Esperanza opened the door without knocking. 'This came in this morning.' She tossed a contract on Myron's desk. It was Jason's. Myron began to skim through it. Esperanza said, 'Put the pea brain on the speakerphone.'

Myron did.

'Jason.'

'Oh Christ, Esperanza, get the fuck off the line. I'm talking to Myron here.'

She ignored him. 'Even though you don't deserve to know, I finalized your contract. You got everything you wanted and more.'

That slowed him down. 'Four hundred thou more per year?'

'Six hundred thousand. Plus an extra quarter million on the signing bonus.'

'How the . . . what . . . ?'

'The Sox screwed up,' she said. 'Once they printed your picture in that mailer, the deal was as good as done.'

'I don't get it.'

'Simple,' she said. 'The mailer went out with your picture on it. People bought tickets based on that. Meanwhile I called the front office and said that you'd decided to sign with the Rangers down in Texas. I told them the deal was almost final.' She shifted in the chair. 'Now, Jason, pretend you are the Red Sox for a moment. What are you going to do? How are you going to explain to all those ticket holders that Jason Blair, whose picture was on your latest mailer, won't be around because the Texas Rangers outbid them?'

Silence. Then: 'To hell with your ass and legs,' Jason said. 'You got the most gorgeous set of brains I ever laid eyes on.'

Myron said, 'Anything else, Jason?'

'Go practice, Myron. After the way you played last night, you need it. I want to talk over the details with Esperanza.'

'I'll take it at my desk,' Esperanza said.

Myron put him back on hold. 'Nice move,' he said to her.

She shrugged. 'Some kid in the Sox marketing department screwed up. It happens.'

'You read it very well.'

Her tone was exaggerated monotone. 'My heaving bosom is swelling with pride.'

'Forget I said anything. Go take the call.'

'No, really, my goal in life is to be just like you.'

Myron shook his head. 'You'll never have my ass.'

'There's that,' she agreed before leaving.

Left alone, Myron picked up the Raven Brigade photo. He located the three members still at large – Gloria Katz, Susan Milano, and the Raven's enigmatic leader and most famous member, Cole Whiteman. No one had drawn the press's attention and ire more than Cole Whiteman. Myron had been in elementary school when the Ravens went into hiding, yet he still remembered the stories. For one thing, Cole could have passed for Win's brother – blond, patrician-featured, well-to-do family. While everyone else in the picture was scraggly and long haired, Cole was fresh shaven with a conservative haircut, his one sixties concession being sideburns that went down a tad too far. Hardly your Hollywood-cast, radical leftist. But as Myron had learned from Win, looks could often be deceiving.

He put down the photograph and dialed Dimonte's line at One Police Plaza. After Dimonte snarled a hello, Myron asked him if he had anything new.

'You think we're partners now, Bolitar?'

'Just like Starsky and Hutch,' Myron said.

'God, I miss those two,' Dimonte said. 'That hot car. Hanging out with Fuzzy Bear.'

'Huggy Bear,' Myron said.

'What?'

'His name was Huggy Bear, not Fuzzy Bear.'

'Really?'

'Time's short, Rolly. Let me help if I can.'

'You first. What have you got?'

Another negotiation. Myron told him about Greg's gambling. Figuring that Rolly had the phone records too, he also told him about the suspected blackmail scheme. He didn't tell him about the videotape. It wouldn't be fair, not until he spoke to Emily first. Dimonte asked a few questions. When he was satisfied, he said, 'Okay, what do you want to know?'

'Did you find anything else at Greg's house?'

'Nothing,' Dimonte said. 'And I mean, nothing.

Remember how you told me you found some feminine doodads in the bedroom? Some woman's clothes or lotions or something?'

'Yes.'

'Well, someone got rid of them too. No sign of any female apparel.'

So, Myron thought, the lover theory rears its ugly head once again. The lover comes back to the house and cleans up the blood to protect Greg. Then she covers her own tracks too, making sure that their relationship remains a secret. 'How about witnesses?' Myron asked. 'Anybody in Liz Gorman's building see anything?'

'Nope. We canvassed the whole neighborhood. No one saw nada. Everybody was studying or something. Oh, another thing: the press picked up the murder. The story hit the morning editions.'

'You gave them her real name?'

'You crazy? Of course not. They think it's just another breaking and entering homicide. But get this. We got an anonymous tip called in this morning. Someone suggested we check out Greg Downing's house.'

'You're kidding.'

'Nope. Female voice.'

'He's being set up, Rolly.'

'No shit, Sherlock. By a chick nonetheless. And the murder didn't exactly make a big news splash. It was stuck in the back pages like every other unspectacular homicide in this cesspool. Got a little extra juice because it was so close to a college campus.'

'Have you looked into that connection?' Myron asked.

'What connection?'

'Columbia University being so close by. Half of the sixties movements started there. They must still have some sympathizers in the ranks. Maybe someone there helped Liz Gorman.'

Dimonte gave a dramatic sigh. 'Bolitar, do you think all cops are morons?'

'No.'

'You think you're the only one who thought of that?'

'Well,' Myron said, 'I have been called gifted.'

'Not in today's sports section.'

Touché. 'So what did you find out?'

'She rented the place from some whacko, fanatic, leftist, commie, pinko so-called Columbia professor named Sidney Bowman.'

'You're so tolerant, Rolly.'

'Yeah, well, I lose touch when I keep missing those ACLU meetings. Anyway, this pinko won't talk. He says she just rented from him and paid in cash. We all know he's lying. The feds grilled him, but he got a team of faggot, liberal lawyers down here to spring him. Called us a bunch of Nazi pigs and stuff.'

'That's not a compliment, Rolly. In case you don't know.'

'Thanks for clueing me in. I got Krinsky tailing him right now, but he's got nothing. I mean, this Bowman's not a retard. He's got to know we're watching.'

'What else have you got on him?'

'Divorced. No kids. He teaches a class in existential, worthless-in-the-real-world bullshit. According to Krinsky he spends most of his time helping the homeless. That's supposed to be his daily ritual – hanging out with hobos in parks and shelters. Like I said, a whacko.'

Win entered the office without knocking. He headed straight for the corner and opened the closet door, revealing a full-length mirror. He checked his hair. Patted it though every strand was perfect. Then he spread his legs a bit and put his arms straight down. Pretending to be gripping a golf club. Win slowly began to turn into a backswing, watching his motion in the mirror, making sure the front arm remained straight, the grip relaxed. He did this all the time, sometimes stopping in front of store windows while walking down the street. This was the golf equivalent, Myron surmised, to the weight lifters who flex whenever they happen past their reflection. It was also annoying as all hell.

'Got anything else, Rolly?'

'No. You?'

'Nothing. I'll talk to you later.'

'Can hardly wait, Hutch,' Dimonte said. 'You know something? Krinsky's so young he doesn't even remember the show. Sad, ain't it?'

'Today's youth,' Myron said. 'They got no culture.'

Myron hung up. Win continued to study his shot in the mirror. 'Fill me in please,' he said. Myron did. When he finished, Win said, 'This Fiona, the ex-playmate. She sounds like a perfect candidate for a Windsor Horne Lockwood III interrogation.'

'Uh huh,' Myron said. 'But why don't you first tell me about the Windsor Horne Lockwood III interrogation of Thumper?'

Win frowned at the mirror, adjusted his grip. 'She is rather closed mouthed,' he said. 'So I took a distinctive tack.'

'What tack is that?'

Win told him about their conversation. Myron just shook his head. 'So you followed her?'

'Yes.'

'And?'

'And there is not much to report. She went to TC's house after the game. She slept over. No calls of any consequence were made from his residence. Either she was not rattled by our conversation, or she doesn't know anything.'

'Or,' Myron added, 'she knew she was being followed.'

Win frowned again. He either didn't like Myron's suggestion or he'd spotted a problem with his swing. Probably the latter. He turned away from the mirror and glanced at Myron's desk. 'Is that the Raven Brigade?'

'Yes. One of them looks like you.' Myron pointed to Cole Whiteman.

Win studied it for a moment. 'While the man is indeed handsome, he lacks both my sense of style and my striking, debonair good looks.'

'Not to mention your humility.'

Win put out his hand. 'Then you understand.'

Myron looked at the picture again. He thought again about what Dimonte said about Professor Sidney Bowman's daily routine. Then it came to him all at once. Ice flooded his veins in a gush. In his mind he changed around Cole's features a bit, imagined distortions from plastic surgery and twenty years of aging. It didn't fit exactly, but it was close enough.

Liz Gorman had disguised herself by perverting her most distinguishing characteristic. Wouldn't it make sense to assume that Cole Whiteman had done the same?

'Myron?'

He looked up. 'I think I know where to find Cole Whiteman.'

Chapter 30

Hector was not thrilled to see Myron back at the Parkview Diner.

'We think we found Sally's accomplice,' Myron said.

Hector cleaned the counter with a rag.

'His name is Norman Lowenstein. Do you know him?'

Hector shook his head.

'He's a homeless man. He hangs out in the back and uses your pay phone.'

Hector stopped cleaning. 'You think I'd let a homeless man in my kitchen?' he said. 'And we don't even have a back. Take a look.'

The answer did not surprise Myron. 'He was sitting at the counter when I was here the other day,' he tried. 'Unshaven. Long black hair. Tattered beige overcoat.'

Still working the rag over the Formica, Hector nodded. 'I think I know who you mean. Black sneakers?'

'Right.'

'He comes in a lot. But I don't know his name.'

'Did you ever see him talk to Sally?'

Hector shrugged. 'Maybe. When she was his waitress. I really don't know.'

'When was he here last?'

'I haven't seen him since the day you came in,' Hector said.

'And you never met him?'

'No.'

'Or know anything about him?'

'No.'

Myron wrote down his phone number on a scrap of paper. 'If you see him, please call. There's a thousand dollar reward.'

Hector studied the phone number. 'This your work number? At AT&T?'

'No. It's my personal phone.'

'Uh huh,' Hector said. 'I called AT&T after you left last time. There's no such thing as Y511 and there's no employee named Bernie Worley.' He did not look particularly upset, but he wasn't dancing the hula either. He just waited, watching Myron with steady eyes.

'I lied to you,' Myron said. 'I'm sorry.'

'What's your real name?' he asked.

'Myron Bolitar.' He gave the man one of his cards. Hector studied it for a moment.

'You're a sports agent?'

'Yes.'

'What does a sports agent have to do with Sally?'

'It's a long story.'

'You shouldn't have lied like that. It wasn't right.'

'I know,' Myron said. 'I wouldn't have done it if it wasn't important.'

Hector put the card in his shirt pocket. 'I have

customers.' He turned away. Myron debated explaining further, but there was no point.

Win was waiting for him on the sidewalk. 'Well?'

'Cole Whiteman is a homeless man who calls himself Norman Lowenstein.'

Win waved down a taxi. A driver in a turban slowed down. They got in. Myron told him where to go. The driver nodded; as he did, his turban buffed the taxi's ceiling. Sitar music blew forth from the front speakers, plucking at the air with razor-sharp nails. Awful. It made Benny and His Magical Sitar sound like Itzhak Perlman. Still it was preferable to Yanni.

'He looks nothing like that old picture,' Myron said. 'He's had plastic surgery. He grew his hair and dyed it jet black.'

They waited at a traffic light. A blue TransAm pulled up next to them, one of those souped up models that hip-hopped up and down while playing music loud enough to crack the earth's core. The taxi actually started shaking from the decibel level. The light turned green. The Trans-Am sped ahead.

'I started thinking about how Liz Gorman had disguised herself,' Myron continued. 'She'd taken her defining attribute and stood it on its head. Cole was the well-bred, clean-cut, rich boy. What better way to stand that on its head than to become an unkempt vagrant?'

'A *Jewish*, unkempt vagrant,' Win corrected.

'Right. So when Dimonte told me that Professor Bowman liked to hang out with the homeless, something clicked.'

The turban barked, 'Route.'

'What?'

'Route. Henry Hudson or Broadway.'

'Henry Hudson,' Win replied He glanced over at Myron. 'Continue.'

'This is what I think happened,' Myron said. 'Cole Whiteman suspected Liz Gorman was in some kind of trouble. Maybe she hadn't called him or met up with him. Something. The problem was, he couldn't check it out himself. Whiteman hasn't survived underground all these years by being stupid. He knew that if the police found her, they'd set a trap for him – the way they're doing right now.'

'So,' Win said, 'he gets you to go in for him.'

Myron nodded. 'He hangs around the diner, hoping to hear something about "Sally." When he overhears me talking to Hector, he figures I'm his best bet. He gives me this weird story about how he knows her from using the phone at the diner. Claimed they were lovers. The story didn't really mesh, but I didn't bother questioning it. Anyway, he takes me to her place. Once I'm inside, he hides and waits to see what happens. He sees the cops come. He probably even sees the body being taken out – all from a safe distance. It confirms what he probably suspected all along. Liz Gorman is dead.'

Win thought about it a moment. 'And now you think Professor Bowman may be contacting him when he visits with the homeless?'

'Yes.'

'So our next goal is to find Cole Whiteman.'

'Yes.'

'Amongst the wretched unbathed in some godforsaken shelter?'

'Yes.'

Win looked pained 'Oh, goodie.'

'We could try to set a trap for him,' Myron said. 'But I think it'll take too long.'

'Set a trap how?'

'I think he's the one who called me on the phone last night,' Myron said. 'Whatever blackmail scheme Liz Gorman was running, it's natural to think that Whiteman was in on it too.'

'But why you?' Win asked. 'If he has dirt on Greg Downing, why would you be the target of his extortion?'

It was a question that had been gnawing at Myron too. 'I'm not sure,' he said slowly. 'The best guess I can come up with is that Whiteman recognized me at the diner. He probably figures that I'm closely connected to Greg Downing. When he couldn't reach Greg, he decided to try me.'

Myron's cellular phone rang. He flicked it on and said hello.

'Hey, Starsky.' It was Dimonte.

'I'm Hutch,' Myron said. 'You're Starsky.'

'Either way,' Dimonte said, 'I think you'll want to get your butt over to the precinct pronto.'

'You got something?'

'Only if you call a picture of the killer leaving Gorman's apartment something,' Dimonte said.

Myron almost dropped the phone. 'For real?'

'Yep. And you'll never guess what.'

'What?'

'It's a she.'

Chapter 31

'Here's the deal,' Dimonte said. They were threading their way through a veritable United Nations of cops, witnesses, and whatnots. Win was waiting outside. He didn't like cops, and they didn't exactly feel like taking him out for ice cream. Best for all if he kept his distance. 'We got a partial image of the perp on a videotape. Problem is, it's not enough to make an ID. I thought maybe you'd recognize her.'

'What kind of videotape?'

'There's a shipping garage on Broadway between One Hundred Tenth and One Hundred Eleventh streets, east side of the block,' Dimonte said. He remained a pace ahead of Myron, moving briskly. He kept turning behind him to make sure Myron was keeping up. 'They handle home electronics. You know how that is – every worker steals like it's a Constitutional right. So the company set up surveillance cameras all over the place. Videotape everything.' Still moving he shook his head, awarded

Myron a toothpick-less smile and added, 'Good old big brother. Every once in a while somebody tapes a crime instead of a bunch of cops beating up a perp, you know what I'm saying?'

They entered a small interrogation room. Myron looked into a mirror. He knew it was one-way glass – so did anybody with even a passing knowledge of cop shows or movies. Myron doubted anybody was on the other side, but he stuck his tongue out just in case. Mr Mature. Krinsky was standing by a television and a VCR. For the second time today, Myron was going to watch a video. He trusted this one would be more tame.

'Hey, Krinsky,' Myron said.

Krinsky barely nodded. Mr Loquacious.

Myron looked over at Dimonte. 'I still don't see how a shipping garage camera could have gotten the killer on tape.'

'One of the cameras is by the truck entrance,' Dimonte explained. 'Just to make sure nothing falls off the truck as it's leaving, if you know what I mean. The camera catches part of the sidewalk. You can see people walking by.' He leaned up against the wall and motioned Myron to sit in a chair. 'You'll see what I mean.'

Myron sat. Krinsky hit the play button. Black and white again. No sound again. But this time the shot was from above. Myron saw the front end of a truck and behind it, a glimpse of the sidewalk. Not many people walked by; the ones that did were barely more than distant silhouettes.

'How did you come up with this?' Myron asked.

'With what?'

'This tape.'

'I always check for this stuff,' Dimonte said, hitching

up his pants by belt loops. 'Parking garages, storage houses, any of those places. They all have surveillance cameras nowadays.'

Myron nodded. 'Good work, Rolly. I'm impressed.'

'Wow,' Dimonte said, 'now I can die happy.'

Everyone's a wiseass. Myron turned his attention back to the screen. 'So how long is each tape?'

'Twelve hours,' Dimonte replied. 'They change them at nine A.M. and P.M. Eight camera set-up. They keep each tape for three weeks. Then they tape over them.' He pointed his fingers. 'Here she comes now, Krinsky.'

Krinsky pressed a button and the tape froze.

'The woman who just entered the picture. On the right. Heading south, which would be away from the scene.'

Myron saw a blurry image. He couldn't see a face or even gather much about her height. She wore high heels and a long overcoat with a frilly neck. Hard to tell much about her weight either. The hair however was familiar. He kept his tone neutral. 'Yeah, I see her.'

'Look at her right hand,' he said.

Myron did. There was something dark and long in it. 'I can't make it out.'

'We got it blown up. Krinsky.'

Krinsky handed Myron two large black and white photographs. The woman's head was enlarged in the first one, but you still couldn't see any facial features. In the second picture, the long, dark object in her hand was clearer.

'We think it's a plastic garbage bag wrapped around something,' Dimonte said. 'Kind of an odd shape, wouldn't you say?'

Myron looked at the photo and nodded. 'You figure it's covering up a baseball bat.'

302

'Don't you?'

'Yeah,' Myron said.

'We found plastic garbage bags just like that one in Gorman's kitchen.'

'And probably half the kitchens in New York City,' Myron added.

'True enough. Now look at the date and time on the screen.'

On the top left-hand side of the screen, a digital clock read 02:12.32 A.M. The date was early Sunday morning. Just hours after Liz Gorman had been at the Swiss Chalet bar with Greg Downing.

'Did the camera get her coming the other way?' Myron asked.

'Yeah, but it's not too clear. Krinsky.'

Krinsky hit the rewind button. Several seconds later, he stopped and the picture came back on. The time now read 01:41.12. A little more than thirty minutes earlier.

'Coming now,' Dimonte said.

The image almost flew past. Myron only recognized the woman by the long overcoat with the frilly neck. This time, she was carrying nothing in her hand. Myron said, 'Let me see the other part again. All the way through.'

Dimonte nodded at Krinsky. Krinsky found it and hit play. While Myron still couldn't see the woman's face, her walk was another matter. And a person's walk could be fairly distinctive. Myron felt his heart crawl up into his throat.

Dimonte was studying him through squinting eyes. 'You recognize her, Bolitar?'

Myron shook his head. 'No,' he lied.

Chapter 32

Esperanza liked to make lists.

With the Raven Brigade file in front of her, she jotted down the three most important factors in chronological order:

1) The Raven Brigade robs a bank in Tucson.

2) Within days, at least one of the Ravens (Liz Gorman) was in Manhattan.

3) Soon after, Liz Gorman made contact with a high profile professional basketball player.

It didn't flow.

She opened the file and briefly scanned the 'brigade's' history. In 1975 the Ravens had kidnapped Hunt Flootworth, the twenty-two-year-old son of publishing giant Cooper Flootworth. Hunt had been a classmate at San Francisco State of several of the Ravens, including both Cole Whiteman and Liz Gorman. The famous Cooper Flootworth, never one to sit around idly and let others handle his affairs, hired mercenaries to rescue his son.

During their raid, young Hunt was shot at point-blank range in the head by one of the Ravens. No one knew which one. Of all the brigade members at the scene, four managed to escape.

Big Cyndi skipped into the office. The vibrations rolled Esperanza's pens off the desk.

'Sorry,' Cyndi said.

'It's okay.'

'Timmy called me,' Cyndi said. 'We're going out Friday night.'

Esperanza made a face. 'His name is Timmy?'

'Yeah,' Cyndi said. 'Isn't that sweet?'

'Adorable.'

'I'll be in the conference room,' Cyndi said.

Esperanza turned back to the file. She flipped ahead to the Tucson bank heist – the group's first in more than five years. The robbery took place as the bank was closing. The feds believed one of the security guards was in on it, but so far they had nothing more than the guard's left-leaning background. About $15,000 in cash was taken, but the robbers took the time to blow the safe deposit boxes. Risky. The feds theorized that the Ravens had somehow found out that drug money was stored there. The bank cameras showed two people dressed head to toe in black with black ski masks. No fingerprints or hairs or fibers. Nada.

Esperanza read through the file again, but nothing new exploded from the pages. She tried to imagine what the past twenty years had been like for the surviving Ravens, constantly on the run, never sleeping in the same place very long, leaving and reentering the country, relying on old sympathizers you were never sure you could completely trust. She grabbed her piece of paper and made some more notes:

Liz Gorman ———> Bank Robbery ———> Blackmail

Okay, she thought, follow the arrows. Liz Gorman and the Ravens needed funds, so they robbed the bank. That worked out. It explained the first arrow. That was a gimme anyway. The real problem was that second connection:

Bank Robbery ———> Blackmail.

Simply put, what about the bank robbery had led her to the East Coast and her scheme to blackmail Greg Downing? She tried to write down possibilities.

1) Downing was involved in the bank robbery.

She looked up. It was possible, she surmised. He needed the money for gambling debts. He might do something illegal. But this hypothesis still did not answer the biggest question in all this: how did they meet? How did Liz Gorman and Greg Downing hook up in the first place?

That, she felt, was the key.

She wrote a number two. And waited.

What other link could there be?

Nothing came to mind so she decided to try it from the opposite end. Start with the blackmail and go back. In order to blackmail Downing, Liz Gorman had to have stumbled across something incriminating. When? Esperanza drew another arrow:

Bank Robbery <———> Blackmail

Esperanza felt something like a tiny pinprick. The bank robbery. Something they found at the bank robbery led to the blackmail scheme.

She quickly shuffled through the file, but she already knew that it wasn't there. She picked up the phone and dialed. When the man answered, she said, 'Do you have a list of the people who were renting safe-deposit boxes?'

'Somewhere, I guess,' he replied. 'Why, you need it?'

'Yes.'

Deep sigh. 'All right, I'll start looking. But tell Myron he owes me for this. Owes me big.'

When Emily opened the door, Myron said, 'Are you alone?'

'Why, yes,' she replied with a coy smile. 'What do you have in mind?'

He shoved past her. Emily stumbled back, her mouth an open circle of surprise. He headed straight for the foyer closet and opened it.

'What the hell are you doing?'

Myron did not bother answering. His hands pushed hangers left and right in a frenzy. It didn't take long. He pulled the long overcoat with the frilly neck into view. 'Next time you commit a murder,' he said, 'dispose of the clothes you wore.'

She took two steps back, her hand fluttering toward her mouth. 'Get out,' she hissed.

'I'm giving you one chance to tell the truth.'

'I don't care what you're giving. Get the fuck out of my house.'

He held up the coat. 'You think I'm the only one who knows? The police have a videotape of you at the murder scene. You were wearing this coat.'

Her body slackened. Her face looked like she'd been on the receiving end of a palm strike to the solar plexus.

Myron lowered the coat to his side. 'You planted the murder weapon at your old house,' he said. 'You smeared blood in the basement.' He turned and half-pounced into the living room. The pile of tabloids was still there. He pointed at it. 'You kept searching the papers for the story. When you read about the body being found, you made an anonymous call to the police.'

He glanced back at Emily. Her eyes were unfocused and glazed.

'I kept wondering about the playroom,' Myron said. 'Why, I kept asking myself, would Greg go down there of all places after the murder? But of course that was the point. He wouldn't. The blood could remain undetected for weeks if need be.'

Emily made two fists at her sides. She shook her head, finally finding her voice. 'You don't understand.'

'Then tell me.'

'He wanted my kids.'

'So you framed him for murder.'

'No.'

'This isn't the time to lie, Emily.'

'I'm not lying, Myron. I didn't frame him.'

'You planted the weapon—'

'Yes,' she interrupted, 'you're right about all that. But I didn't frame him.' Her eyes closed and reopened, almost like she was doing a minimeditation. 'You can't frame somebody for something they did.'

Myron stiffened. Emily stared at him stone faced. Her hands were still tightened into small balls. 'Are you saying Greg killed her?'

'Of course.' She moved toward him, taking her time, using the seconds the way a boxer uses an eight count after a surprise left hook. She took the coat from his hands. 'Should I really destroy it, or can I trust you?'

'I think you better explain first.'

'How about some coffee?'

308

'No,' Myron said.

'I need some. Come on. We'll talk in the kitchen.'

She kept her head high and walked the same walk Myron had watched on the tape. He followed her into a bright white kitchen. The kitchen gleamed in tiled splendor. Most people probably thought the decor was to die for; Myron thought it resembled a urinal at a fancy restaurant.

Emily took out one of those new coffee presses people were using. 'You sure you won't have some? It's Starbucks. Kona Hawaiian blend.'

Myron shook his head. Emily had regained her senses now. She was back in control; he'd let her stay there. A person in control talks more and thinks less.

'I'm trying to figure out where to begin,' she said, adding hot water to the press. The rich aroma immediately filled the air. If this was a coffee commercial, one of them would be saying 'Ahhhh' right about now. 'And don't tell me to begin at the beginning or I'll scream.'

Myron held up his hands to show he would do no such thing.

Emily pushed a little on the plunger, met resistance, pushed again. 'She came up to me one day in the supermarket of all places,' she said. 'Out of the blue. I'm reaching for some frozen bagels, and this woman tells me she has uncovered something that could destroy my husband. She tells me that if I don't pay up, she's going to call the papers.'

'What did you say?'

'I asked her if she'd need a quarter for the phone.' Emily chuckled, stopped pressing, stood upright. 'I figured it was a joke. I told her to go ahead and destroy the bastard. She just nodded and said she'd be in touch.'

309

'That was it?'

'Yep.'

'When was this?'

'I don't know. Two, three weeks ago.'

'So when did you hear from her next?'

Emily opened a cabinet and took out a coffee mug. The mug had a picture of some cartoon character. The words WORLD'S GREATEST MOM was emblazoned on the side. 'I'm making enough for two,' she said.

'No thank you.'

'You sure?'

'Yes,' Myron said. 'What happened next?'

She bent down and peered into the coffee press like it was a crystal ball. 'A few days after this, Greg did something to me . . .' She stopped. Her tone was different now, the words coming slower and with more care. 'It's like I told you last time you were here. He did something awful. The details aren't important.'

Myron nodded but said nothing. No reason to raise the videotape now and knock her off stride. Facilitate her – that was the key.

'So when she came back and told me Greg was willing to pay big for her silence, I told her I'd pay more to make her talk. She told me it would cost a lot. I told her I didn't care how much. I tried to appeal to her as a woman. I went so far as to tell her about my situation, how Greg was trying to take my kids away from me. She seemed to sympathize, but she also made it clear that she couldn't afford to be philanthropic. If I wanted the information, I'd have to pay up.'

'Did she tell you how much?'

'One hundred thousand dollars.'

Myron held back a whistle. Serious double dipping. Liz

Gorman's strategy was probably to keep collecting from both of them, bleeding them both for as long as she thought it was safe. Or maybe she was hitting hard and fast because she knew she would have to go underground again. Either way, it made sense from Liz Gorman's perspective to collect from all interested parties – Greg, Clip, and Emily. Take money for silence. Take money to sing. Blackmailers have the loyalty of election-year politicians.

'Do you know what she had on Greg?' he asked.

Emily shook her head. 'She wouldn't tell me.'

'But you were prepared to pay her a hundred grand?'

'Yes.'

'Even though you didn't know what it was for?'

'Yes.'

Myron gestured with both hands. 'How did you know she wasn't just a crackpot?'

'The truth? I didn't know. But I was going to lose my kids, for chrissake. I was desperate.'

And, Myron thought, Emily had shown that desperation to Liz Gorman who, in turn, took full advantage of it. 'So you still have no idea what she had on him?'

Emily shook her head. 'None.'

'Could it have been Greg's gambling?'

Her eyes narrowed in confusion. 'What about it?'

'Did you know Greg gambled?'

'Sure. But so what?'

'Do you know how much he gambled?' Myron asked.

'Just a little,' she said. 'A trip to Atlantic City once in a while. Maybe fifty dollars on a football game.'

'Is that what you thought?'

Her eyes moved over his face, trying to read it. 'What are you saying?'

Myron looked out the back window. The pool was still

covered, but some of the robins had returned from the yearly aliya to the south. A dozen or so crowded a bird feeder, heads down, wings flapping happily like dog tails. 'Greg is a compulsive gambler,' Myron said. 'He's lost away millions over the years. Felder didn't embezzle money – Greg lost it gambling.'

Emily gave him a little head shake. 'That can't be,' she said. 'I lived with him for almost ten years. I would have seen something.'

'Gamblers learn how to hide it,' Myron said. 'They lie and cheat and steal – anything to keep on betting. It's an addiction.'

Something in her eyes seemed to spark up. 'And that's what this woman had on Greg? The fact that he gambled?'

'I think so,' Myron said. 'But I can't say for sure.'

'But Greg definitely gambled, right? To the point where he lost all his money?'

'Yes.'

The answer kindled Emily's face with hope. 'Then no judge in the world would award him custody,' she said. 'I'll win.'

'A judge is more likely to give the kids to a gambler than a murderer,' Myron said. 'Or someone who plants false evidence.'

'I told you already. It's not false.'

'So you say,' Myron said. 'But let's get back to what happened with the blackmailer. You were saying she wanted a hundred grand.'

Emily moved back to her coffee press. 'That's right.'

'How were you to pay her?'

'She told me to wait by a pay phone outside a Grand Union supermarket on Saturday night. I was supposed to get there at midnight and have the money ready. She called at midnight on the dot and gave me an address on One Hundred Eleventh Street. I was supposed to get there at two in the morning.'

'So you drove to One Hundred Eleventh Street at two in the morning with one hundred thousand dollars?' He tried not to sound too incredulous.

'I could only raise sixty thousand,' she corrected.

'Did she know that?'

'No. Look, I know this all sounds crazy, but you don't understand how desperate I was. I would have done anything at this point.'

Myron understood. He had seen up-close how far mothers would go. Love twists; maternal love twists absolutely. 'Go on,' he said.

'When I turned the corner, I saw Greg come out of the building,' Emily said. 'I was stunned. He had his collar up, but I could still see his face.' She looked up at Myron. 'I was married to him a long time, but I've never seen his face like this.'

'Like what?'

'So filled with terror,' she replied. 'He practically sprinted toward Amsterdam Avenue. I waited until he turned the corner. Then I approached the door and pressed her apartment button. Nobody answered. I started pressing other buttons. Somebody finally buzzed me in. I went upstairs and knocked on her door for a while. Then I tried the knob. It was unlocked. So I opened the door.'

Emily stopped. A trembling hand brought the cup up to her lips. She took a sip.

'This is going to sound awful,' she went on, 'but I didn't see a dead human being lying there. I only saw my last hope of keeping my kids.'

'So you decided to plant evidence.'

Emily put down the cup and looked at him. Her eyes were clear. 'Yes. And you were right about everything else, too. I chose the playroom because I knew he'd never go down there. I figured that when Greg got back home – I didn't know he'd run – the blood would be safe. Look, I know I went too far, but it's not like I was lying. He killed her.'

'You don't know that.'

'What?'

'He might have stumbled across the body the same way you did.'

'Are you serious?' Her tone was sharp now. 'Of course Greg killed her. The blood on the floor was still fresh. He was the one who had everything to lose. He had motive, opportunity.'

'Just as you do,' Myron said.

'What motive?'

'You wanted to set him up for murder. You wanted to keep your children.'

'That's ridiculous.'

'Do you have any proof your story is true?' Myron asked.

'Do I have what?'

'Proof. I don't think the police are going to buy it.'

'Do you buy it?' she asked him.

'I'd like to see proof.'

'What do you mean, proof?' she snapped 'Like what? It's not like I took pictures.'

'Any facts that back up your story?'

'Why would I kill her, Myron? What possible motive could I have? I needed her alive. She was my best chance of keeping my kids.'

'But let's assume for a moment that this woman did indeed have something on Greg,' Myron said. 'Something concrete. Like a letter he wrote or a videotape' – he watched for a reaction – 'or something like that.'

'All right,' she said with a nod. 'Go ahead.'

'And suppose she double-crossed you. Suppose she sold the incriminating evidence to Greg. You admit Greg was there before you. Maybe he paid her enough so that she'd back out of your agreement. Then you go into her apartment. You find out what she's done. You realize your one chance at keeping your kids is gone. So you kill her and pin it on the man who had seemed to have the most to gain from her death: Greg.'

Emily shook her head. 'That's nuts.'

'You hated Greg enough,' Myron continued. 'He played dirty with you; you'd play dirty back.'

'I didn't kill her.'

Myron took another look at the robins, but they were gone. The yard looked barren now, stripped of any life. He waited a few seconds before he turned back toward her. 'I know about the videotape of you and Thumper.'

A quick bolt of anger hit Emily's eyes. Her fingers clutched the coffee mug. Myron half-expected her to throw it at him. 'How the hell . . . ?' Then her grip suddenly slackened. She backed away. She sort of shrugged into a slouch. 'It doesn't matter.'

'It must have made you furious,' he said.

She shook her head. A small sound like a chuckle escaped from her lips. 'You just don't get it, do you, Myron?'

'Don't get what?'

'I wasn't looking for revenge. The only thing that mattered was that the tape could take away my kids.'

'No, I do get it,' Myron countered. 'You'd do anything to keep your kids.'

'I didn't kill her.'

Myron shifted gears. 'Tell me about you and Thumper,' he said.

Emily snorted a derisive laugh. 'I didn't think you were that type, Myron.'

'I'm not.'

She picked up her coffee mug and took a deep sip. 'Did you watch the whole tape from beginning to end?' she asked in a tone somewhere between flirtatious and furious. 'Did you hit the slow motion button a few times, Myron? Rewind and replay certain parts over and over? Drop your pants to your knees?'

'No to all of the above.'

'How much did you see?'

'Just enough to know what was going on.'

'Then you stopped?'

'Then I stopped.'

She regarded him from behind the mug. 'You know something? I actually believe you. You're that kind of goody two-shoes.'

'Emily, I'm trying to help.'

'Help me or Greg?'

'Help get to the truth. I assume you want that too.'

She shrugged noncommittally.

'So when did you and Thumper . . . ?' He made vague coming-together motions with his hand.

She laughed at his discomfort. 'It was the first time,' she replied. 'In all respects.'

'I'm not judging—'

'I don't care if you are or not. You want to know what

happened, right? It was my first time. That little whore set me up.'

'How?'

'What do you mean, how?' she countered. 'You want me to go into details – how many drinks I had, how I was feeling lonely, how her hand started up my leg?'

'I guess not.'

'Then let me give you the quick capsule: she seduced me. We'd flirted innocently a few times in the past. She invited me to the Glenpointe for drinks. It was like a dare on myself – I was drawn and repelled, but I knew I wouldn't go through with it. One thing led to another. We went upstairs. End of capsule.'

'So you're saying Thumper knew you were being filmed?'

'Yes.'

'How do you know? Did she say anything?'

'She didn't say anything. But I know.'

'How?'

'Myron, please stop asking so many goddamn questions. I just know, okay? How else would anyone know to set up a camera in that room? She set me up.'

That made sense, Myron thought. 'But why would she do it?'

Her face registered her exasperation. 'Christ, Myron, she's the team whore. Didn't she fuck you yet? Or no, let me guess. You refused, right?'

Emily stormed away into the living room and collapsed on a couch. 'Get me the aspirin,' she said. 'They're in the bathroom. In the medicine chest.'

Myron shook out two tablets and filled a cup with water. When he came back, he said, 'I have to ask you about one more thing.'

She sighed. 'What?'

'I understand you made allegations against Greg,' he said.

'My attorney made allegations.'

'Were they true?'

She put the pills on her tongue, took some water, swallowed. 'Some of them.'

'How about the ones about him abusing the children?'

'I'm tired, Myron. Can we talk more later?'

'Were they true?'

Emily looked into Myron's eyes, and a cold gust of air blew across his heart. 'Greg wanted to take my kids away from me,' she said slowly. 'He had money, power, prestige on his side. We needed something.'

Myron broke the eye contact. He walked toward the door. 'Don't destroy that coat.'

'You have no right to judge me.'

'Right now,' he said, 'I don't want to be near you.'

Chapter 33

Audrey was leaning against his car. 'Esperanza told me you'd be here.'

Myron nodded.

'Jesus, you look like hell,' she said. 'What happened?'

'Long story.'

'And one that you will soon tell me in riveting detail,' Audrey added. 'But I'll go first. Fiona White was indeed a Miss September in 1992 – or as that particular rag calls it, the September Babe-A-Rama.'

'You're kidding.'

'Nope. Fiona's turn-ons include moonlit walks on the beach and cozy nights by a fireplace.'

He smiled in spite of himself. 'My, what originality.'

'Her turn-offs include shallow men who only care about looks. And men with back hair.'

'Did they list her favorite movies?'

'*Schindler's List*,' Audrey said. 'And *Cannonball Run II*.'

He laughed. 'You're making this up.'

'All except the part about being the September Babe-A-Rama in 1992.'

Myron shook his head. 'Greg Downing and his best friend's wife,' he sighed. In a way, the news sort of buoyed him. Myron's ten-year-old indiscretion with Emily no longer seemed quite so bad. He knew that he shouldn't find comfort in such logic, but man takes solace where he can find it.

Audrey motioned toward the house. 'So what's up with the ex?'

'Long story.'

'You said that already. I got time.'

'I don't.'

She held up her palm like a cop directing traffic. 'Not fair, Myron. I've been a good girl. I've been running your errands and keeping my big mouth shut. Not to mention the fact that I got zippo from you for my birthday. Please don't make me start with the exposure threats again.'

She was right. Myron gave her an abbreviated update, leaving out two parts: the Thumper videotape (no reason anyone had to know about that) and the fact that Carla was the infamous Liz Gorman (it was simply too big a story; no reporter could be trusted to keep it off the record).

Audrey listened intently. Her page-boy cut had grown a little too long in the front. Hairs dangled close to her eyes. She kept sticking out her lower lip and blowing strands off her forehead. Myron had never before seen this particular gesture done by anybody over the age of eleven. It was kind of sweet.

'Do you believe her?' Audrey asked, motioning again to Emily's house.

'I'm not sure,' he replied. 'Her story sort of makes sense. She had no motive to kill the woman, except to frame Greg and that's reaching.'

Audrey tilted her head as if to say, maybe yes – maybe no.

'What?' he asked.

'Well,' she began, 'isn't there a chance that we're looking at this from the wrong perspective?'

'What do you mean?'

'We assume that this blackmailer had dirt on Downing,' Audrey said. 'But maybe she had dirt on Emily.'

Myron stopped, looked back at the house as though it held some answers, looked back at Audrey.

'According to Emily,' Audrey went on, 'the blackmailer approached her. But why? She and Greg aren't together anymore.'

'Carla didn't know that,' Myron replied. 'She figured Emily was his wife and would want to protect him.'

'That's one possibility,' Audrey agreed. 'But I'm not sure it's the best one.'

'Are you saying that they were blackmailing her, not Greg?'

Audrey turned her palms skyward. 'All I'm saying is that it could work the other way too. The blackmailer might have had something on Emily – something Greg would want to use against her in the child custody case.'

Myron folded his arms and leaned against the car. 'But what about Clip?' he asked. 'If they had something on Emily, why would he be interested?'

'I don't know.' Audrey shrugged. 'Maybe she had dirt on both of them.'

'Both of them?'

'Sure. Something that could destroy them both. Or

maybe Clip thought whatever it was – even if it was about Emily – would distract Greg.'

'Any guesses?'

'Not a one,' Audrey said.

Myron mulled it over for a few seconds, but nothing came to him. 'There's a chance,' he said, 'we'll find out tonight.'

'How?'

'The blackmailer called. He wants to sell me the information.'

'Tonight?'

'Yep.'

'Where?'

'I don't know yet. He's going to call. I got my home line forwarded to the cellular.'

As if on cue, the cellular rang. Myron took it out of his pocket.

It was Win. 'The dear professor's schedule was posted on his office door,' he said. 'He is in class for another hour. After that, he has open office hours so the kiddies can whine about grades.'

'Where are you?'

'On Columbia's campus,' Win replied. 'By the way, Columbia women are fairly attractive. I mean, for the Ivy Leagues and all.'

'Glad you haven't lost your powers of observation.'

'Indeed,' Win said. 'Have you finished speaking to our girl?'

Our girl was Emily. Win did not trust cellular phones with names. 'Yes,' he said.

'Goodie. What time should I expect you then?'

'I'm on my way.'

Chapter 34

Win was sitting on a bench near the Columbia gate on
116th Street. He was wearing Eddie Bauer khakis, Top-
Siders without socks, a blue button-down Oxford, and a
power tie.

'I'm blending in,' Win explained.

'Like a Hasid at Christmas mass,' Myron agreed. 'Is
Bowman still in class?'

Win nodded. 'He should be exiting that door in ten
minutes.'

'Do you know what he looks like?'

Win handed him a faculty handbook. 'Page two ten,' he
said. 'So tell me about Emily.'

Myron did. A tall brunette dressed in a black, skintight
cat suit strolled by with her books pressed up against
her chest. Julie Newmar on Batman. Win and Myron
watched her closely. Meow.

When Myron finished, Win didn't bother with any

questions. 'I have a meeting at the office,' he said as he stood. 'Do you mind?'

Myron shook his head and sat down. Win left. Myron kept his eye on the door. Ten minutes later students began to file out the door. Two minutes after that, Professor Sidney Bowman followed suit. He had the same unkempt, academic beard as in the photo. He was bald but kept his fringe hair ridiculously long. He wore jeans, Timberland boots, and a red flannel shirt. He was either trying to look like a working stiff or Jerry Brown on the campaign trail.

Bowman pushed up his spectacles and kept walking. Myron waited until he was out of sight before following. No rush. The good professor was indeed heading for his office. He crossed the grassy commons and disappeared into yet another brick building. Myron found a bench and sat down.

An hour passed. Myron watched the students and felt very old. He should have brought a newspaper. Sitting for an hour without reading material meant he had to think. His mind kept conjuring up new possibilities and then dismissing them. He knew he was missing something, could see it bobbing in the distance, but every time he reached out it ducked back down below the surface.

He suddenly remembered that he had not checked Greg's answering machine today. He took out his cellular phone and dialed the number. When Greg's voice came on, he pressed 317, the code numbers Greg had programmed into the machine. There was only one message on the tape, but it was a doozy.

'Don't fuck with us,' the electronically altered voice said. 'I've spoken to Bolitar. He's willing to pay. Is that what you want?'

End of message.

Myron sat very still. He stared at a brick, ivyless wall. He listened to a tone for a few seconds and did nothing. What the hell . . . ?

'. . . *He's willing to pay. Is that what you want?*'

Myron pressed the star button to have the message replayed. Then he did it again. He probably would have listened for a fourth time, had Professor Bowman not suddenly appeared at the door.

Bowman stopped to chat with a couple of students. The conversation grew animated, all three displaying fervent, academic earnest. College. Continuing their undoubtedly weighty discourse, they walked off campus and down Amsterdam Avenue. Myron pocketed the phone and kept his distance. At 112th Street, the group separated. The two students continued south. Bowman crossed the street and headed toward the Cathedral of St John the Divine.

St John the Divine's was a massive structure and interestingly enough, the largest cathedral in the world in terms of cubic square feet (St Peter's in Rome is considered a basilica by this statistic, not a cathedral). The edifice was like the city that housed it: awe-inspiring yet worn. Towering columns and gorgeous stained-glass windows were surrounded by signs like HARD HAT AREA (though it dated back to 1892, St John the Divine's has never been completed) and THE CATHEDRAL IS PATROLLED AND ELECTRONICALLY MONITORED FOR YOUR PROTECTION. Wooden planks plugged holes in the granite facade. On the left side of this architectural wonder were two prefab aluminum storage barracks that brought back memories of the opening credits of *Gomer Pyle*. On the right was the Children's Sculpture Garden featuring the Peace Fountain, an enormous sculpture that inspired several moods, none of them peaceful. Images of severed heads and limbs, lobster claws, hands reaching out from the dirt as though trying to escape hell, a man twisting the neck of a deer all whirled together to create an atmosphere that was more Dante meets Goya than languid tranquillity.

Bowman headed down the driveway on the cathedral's right. Myron knew that there was a homeless shelter down that way. He crossed the street and tried to keep his distance. Bowman passed a group of apparently homeless men – all dressed in threadbare synthetics and pants with plunging butt-lines. Some waved and called out to Bowman. Bowman waved back. Then he disappeared through a door. Myron debated what to do. There was no choice really. Even if it meant blowing his cover, he had to go in.

He passed the men, nodded, smiled. They nodded and smiled back. The shelter entrance was a double black door with chintzy lace curtains. Not far from it were two signs – one reading SLOW CHILDREN AT PLAY and the other CATHEDRAL SCHOOL. A homeless shelter and a children's school side by side – an interesting yet working combo. Only in New York.

Myron entered. The room was packed with frayed mattresses and men. A smell like a used bong after an all-nighter singed his nostril hairs. Myron tried not to make a face. He spotted Bowman talking to several men in one corner. None of them was Cole Whiteman aka Norman Lowenstein. Myron glanced about the unshaven faces and hollow eyes, his gaze swinging left to right.

They spotted each other at exactly the same time.

From across the room, their eyes locked for perhaps a second, but that was long enough. Cole Whiteman turned and ran. Myron followed, threading his way through the throngs. Professor Bowman spotted the disturbance. Eyes afire, he jumped in Myron's path. Myron lowered his shoulder and flattened him without breaking stride. Just like Jim Brown. Except Jim Brown had to do it against guys like Dick Butkus and Ray Nitschke opposed to a fifty-year-old college professor who probably didn't weigh 180 even with the soft gut. Still.

Cole Whiteman disappeared out a back door, slamming it behind him. Myron went through it not long after. They were outside now, but only briefly. Whiteman disappeared up a metal stairway and back into the main chapel. Myron followed. The inside was very much like the outside – spectacular examples of art and architecture mixed in with the tattered and tacky. The pews, for example, were cheap folding chairs. Lush tapestries hung upon granite walls with seemingly no organization. Ladders were melded into thick columns.

Myron spotted Cole heading back out a nearby door. He sprinted after him, his heels echoing up through the giant arched ceiling. They were back outside. Cole headed down below the cathedral and through heavy fire doors. A sign read A.C.T. PROGRAM. It looked like a basement school or daycare center. Both men raced down a hallway lined with beat-up, metallic lockers. Cole turned right and disappeared behind a wooden door.

When Myron pushed the door open, a darkened stairway greeted him. He heard footsteps below him. He trotted down, the light from above dwindling with each step. He was descending deep into the cathedral's subdwelling now. The walls were cement and clammy to the touch. He wondered if he was entering a crypt or tomb or something equally creepy, if indeed there was equally creepy. Did American cathedrals have crypts, or was that only in Europe?

By the time he reached the bottom step, Myron was bathed in darkness, the light from above little more than distant glint. Great. He stepped into a black hole of a room. He cocked his head, listening for a sound like a dog on a hunt. Nothing. He felt for a light switch. Again nothing. The room had a bone-chilling, windless cold. A damp smell permeated his surroundings. He didn't like it down here. He didn't like it at all.

He inched forward blindly, his arms outstretched like Frankenstein's monster. 'Cole,' he called out. 'I just want to talk to you.'

His words echoed hard before fading out like a song on the radio.

He kept going. The room was still as . . . well, as a tomb. He had moved about five feet when his outstretched fingers hit something. Myron kept his hand on the smooth, cold surface. Like marble, he thought. He traced down. It was a statue of some sort. He felt the arm, the shoulder, to the back, down a marble wing. He wondered if it was some kind of tombstone decoration and quickly withdrew his hand.

He stayed perfectly still and tried to listen again. The only sound was a rushing in his ears, like seashells were pressed against them. He debated going back upstairs, but there was no way he could do that. Cole knew now that his identity was in danger. He would go into hiding again and not resurface. This was Myron's only chance.

He took another step, leading now with his foot. His toe hit something hard and unyielding. Marble again, he figured. He circled around it. Then a sound – a scurrying sound – made him freeze in his tracks. It had come from the ground. Not a mouse. Too big for a mouse. He cocked his head again and waited. His pulse raced. His eyes were just beginning to adjust to the darkness, and he could make out a few shadowy, tall figures. Statues. Lowered heads. He imagined the serene expressions of religious art on their faces, looking down at him with the knowledge they were embarking on a journey to a better place than the one in which they dwelled.

He took another step, and cold fingers of flesh grabbed his ankle.

Myron screamed.

The hand pulled and Myron fell hard against the cement. He kicked his leg loose and scrambled backward. His back slammed into more marble. A man giggled madly. Myron felt the hairs on the nape of his neck stand up. Another man giggled Then another. Like a group of hyenas were encircling him.

Myron tried to get to his feet, but midway up, the men suddenly pounced. He didn't know how many. Hands dragged him back to the floor. He threw a blind fist and connected square into a face. Myron heard a crunching sound and a man fell. But others reached their target. He found himself sprawled on the wet cement, fighting blindly and frantically. He heard grunts. The stench of body odor and alcohol was suffocating, inescapable. The hands were everywhere now. One ripped off his watch. One grabbed his wallet. Myron threw another punch. It hit ribs. Another grunt and another man fell.

Somebody turned on a flashlight and shone it into his eyes. It looked like a train heading toward him.

'Okay,' a voice said, 'back off him.'

The hands slid off like wet snakes. Myron tried to sit up.

'Before you get any cute ideas,' the voice behind the flashlight said, 'take a look at this.'

The voice put a gun in front of the flashlight.

Another voice said, 'Sixty bucks? That's fuckin' all? Shit.'

Myron felt the wallet hit him in the chest.

'Put your hands behind your back.'

He did as the voice asked. Someone grabbed the forearms, pulling them closer together, tearing at the shoulder tendons. A pair of handcuffs were snapped on his wrists.

'Leave us,' the voice said. Myron heard the rustling movements. The air cleared. Myron heard a door open, but the flashlight in his eyes prevented him from seeing anything. Silence followed. After some time passed, the voice said, 'Sorry to do this to you, Myron. They'll let you go in a few hours.'

'How long you going to keep running, Cole?'

Cole Whiteman chuckled. 'Been running a long time,' he said. 'I'm used to it.'

'I'm not here to stop you.'

'Imagine my relief,' he said. 'So how did you figure out who I was?'

'It's not important,' Myron said.

'It is to me.'

'I don't have any interest in bringing you down,' Myron said. 'I just want some information.'

There was a pause. Myron blinked into the light 'How did you get involved in all this?' Cole asked.

'Greg Downing vanished. I was hired to find him.'

'You?'

'Yes.'

Cole Whiteman laughed deep and hearty. The sound bounced around like balls of Silly Putty, the volume reaching a frightening crescendo before mercifully fading away.

'What's so funny?' Myron asked.

'Inside joke.' Cole stood, the flashlight rising with him. 'Look, I have to go. I'm sorry.'

More silence. Cole flicked off the flashlight, plunging Myron back into total blackness. He heard footsteps receding.

'Don't you want to know who killed Liz Gorman?' Myron called out.

The footsteps continued unimpeded. Myron heard a switch and a dim lightbulb came on. Maybe forty watts. It didn't come close to fully illuminating the place, but it was a hell of an improvement. Myron blinked away black spots left over from the flashlight assault and examined his surroundings. The room was jammed with marble statues, lined and piled up without reason or logic, some tilted over. It wasn't a tomb, after all. It was some bizarre, church-art storage room.

Cole Whiteman came back over to him. He sat cross-legged directly in front of Myron. The white stubble was still there – thick in some spots, completely missing in others. His hair jutted up and out in every direction. He lowered the gun to his side.

'I want to know how Liz died,' he said softly.

'She was bludgeoned with a baseball bat,' Myron said.

Cole's eyes closed. 'Who did it?'

'That's what I'm trying to find out. Right now, Greg Downing is the main suspect.'

Cole Whiteman shook his head. 'He wasn't there long enough.'

Myron felt a knot in his stomach. He tried to lick his lips but his mouth was too dry. 'You were there?'

331

'Across the street behind a garbage can. Like Oscar the fucking Grouch.' His lips smiled, but there was nothing behind it. 'You want no one to notice you? Pretend you're homeless.' He stood up in one fluid motion, like some kind of yoga master. 'A baseball bat,' he said. He pinched the bridge of his nose, turned away, and lowered his chin to his chest. Myron could hear small sobs.

'Help me find her killer, Cole.'

'Why the fuck should I trust you?'

'Me or the police,' Myron said. 'It's up to you.'

That slowed him. 'The cops won't do shit. They think she's a murderer.'

'Then help me,' Myron said.

He sat back down on the floor and inched a bit closer to Myron. 'We're not murderers, you know. The government labeled us that and now everyone believes it. But it's not true. You understand?'

Myron nodded. 'I understand.'

Cole gave him a hard look. 'You patronizing me?'

'No.'

'Don't patronize me,' Cole said. 'You want me to stay and talk, don't you dare patronize me. You stay honest – I'll stay honest.'

'Fine,' Myron said. 'But then don't hand me the "we're not killers, we're freedom fighters" line. I'm not in the mood for a verse of "Blowin' in the Wind."'

'You think that's what I'm talking about?'

'You're not being prosecuted by a corrupt government,' Myron said. 'You kidnapped and killed a man, Cole. You can dress it up in all the fancy language you want, but that's what you did.'

Cole almost smiled. 'You really believe that.'

'Wait, don't tell me; let me guess,' Myron said. He

332

feigned looking up in thought. 'The government brain-washed me, right? This whole thing has been a CIA plot to crush a dozen college students who threatened to undermine our government.'

'No,' he said. 'But we didn't kill Hunt.'

'Who did?'

Cole hesitated. He looked up and blinked back what looked like tears. 'Hunt shot himself.'

His reddening eyes looked to Myron for a reaction. Myron remained still.

'The kidnapping was a hoax,' Cole went on. 'The whole thing was Hunt's idea. He wanted to hurt his old man so he figured what better way than to take his money and then embarrass the shit out of him? But then those assholes surprised us and Hunt chose another revenge.' Cole's breathing grew deep and erratic. 'He ran outside with the gun. He screamed, "Fuck you, Dad." Then he blew his own head off.'

Myron said nothing.

'Look at our history,' Cole Whiteman said, his voice a semiplea. 'We were a harmless group of stragglers. We protested at antiwar rallies. We got stoned a lot. We never committed one act of violence. None of us even had a gun, except for Hunt. He was my roommate and best friend. I could never hurt him.'

Myron didn't know what to believe; more to the point, he didn't have time now to worry about a twenty-year-old homicide. He waited for Cole to continue, to let him talk out the past, but Cole remained still. Finally, Myron tried to update the subject. 'You saw Greg Downing go into Liz Gorman's building?'

Cole nodded slowly.

'She was blackmailing him?'

333

'Not just her,' he corrected. 'It was my idea.'

'What did you have on Greg?'

Cole shook his head. 'Not important.'

'She was probably killed over it.'

'Probably,' Cole agreed. 'But you don't need to know the specifics. Trust me.'

Myron was in no position to push it. 'Tell me about the night of the murder.'

Cole scratched at his stubble hard, like a cat on a post. 'Like I said,' he began, 'I was across the street. When you live underground, you have certain rules you live by – rules that have kept us alive and free for the last twenty years. One of them is that after we commit a crime, we never stay together. The feds look for us in groups, not individuals. Since we've been in the city, Liz and I have made sure we were never together. We only communicated by pay phone.'

'What about Gloria Katz and Susan Milano?' Myron asked. 'Where are they?'

Cole smiled without mirth or humor. Myron saw the missing teeth and wondered if they were part of the disguise or something more sinister. 'I'll tell you about them another time,' he said.

Myron nodded. 'Go on,' he said.

The lines in Cole's face seemed to deepen and darken in the bare light. He took his time before continuing. 'Liz was all packed and ready to go,' he said finally. 'We were going to score the cash and get out of the city, just like I planned. I was just waiting across the street for her signal.'

'What signal?'

'After all the money was collected, she'd flicker the lights three times. That meant she'd be down in ten minutes. We were going to meet at One Hundred Sixteenth Street and take the One train out of here. But the signal never came. In fact, her light never went off at all. I was afraid to go check on her for obvious reasons. We got rules about that, too.'

'Who was Liz supposed to collect from that night?'

'Three people,' Cole said, holding up the pointer, middle man, and ring man. 'Greg Downing' – he dropped ring man – 'his wife what's-her-name—'

'Emily.'

'Right, Emily.' The middle finger went down. 'And the old guy who owns the Dragons.' His hand made a fist now.

Myron's heart contracted. 'Wait a second,' he said. 'Clip Arnstein was supposed to show up?'

'Not supposed to,' Cole corrected. 'He did.'

A black coldness seeped into Myron's bones. 'Clip was there?'

'Yes.'

'And the other two?'

'All three showed up. But that wasn't the plan. Liz was supposed to meet Downing at a bar downtown. They were going to make the transaction there.'

'A place called the Swiss Chalet?'

'Right.'

'But Greg showed up at the apartment too?'

'Later on, yeah. But Clip Arnstein arrived first.'

Win's warning about Clip came back to him. You like him too much. You're not being objective. 'How much was Clip supposed to pay?'

'Thirty thousand dollars.'

'The police only found ten thousand in her apartment,'

Myron said. 'And those bills were from the bank robbery.'

Cole shrugged. 'Either the old man didn't pay her or else the killer took the money.' Then, thinking it through a little more he added, 'Or maybe Clip Arnstein killed her. But he seems kind of old, don't you think?'

Myron didn't answer. 'How long was he inside?'

'Ten, fifteen minutes.'

'Who came by next?'

'Greg Downing. I remember he had a satchel. I figured it had the money in it. He was in and out fast – couldn't have been more than a minute. And he still had the satchel on him when he came out. That's when I started to worry.'

'Greg could have killed her,' Myron said. 'It doesn't take long to hit someone with a baseball bat.'

'But he wasn't carrying a bat,' Cole said. 'The satchel wasn't big enough for one. And Liz had a bat in her apartment. She hated guns, so she kept it for protection.'

Myron knew that no bat had been found at Gorman's apartment. That meant the killer must have used Liz's. Could Greg have gone upstairs, entered her apartment, found the bat, killed her with it, ran out – all in such a short time?

It seemed doubtful.

'What about Emily?' Myron asked.

'She came in last,' Cole said.

'How long was she there?'

'Five minutes. Something like that.'

Time enough to gather the evidence to plant. 'Did you see anybody else go in and out of the building?'

'Sure,' Cole said. 'Lot of students live there.'

'But we can assume that Liz was already dead by the time Greg Downing arrived, right?'

'Right.'

'So the question is, who do you remember going in between the time she got back from the Swiss Chalet and the time Greg arrived? Besides Clip Arnstein.'

Cole thought about it and shrugged. 'Mostly students, I guess. There was a real tall guy—'

'How tall?'

'I don't know. Very.'

'I'm six-four. Taller than me?'

'Yeah, I think so.'

'Was he black?'

'I don't know. I was across the street and the light wasn't too good. I wasn't watching that closely. He might have been black. But I don't think he's our man.'

'Why do you say that?'

'I watched the building until the next morning. He never came back out. He must have lived there or at least stayed with someone overnight. I doubt the killer would've hung around like that.'

Tough to argue, Myron thought. He tried to process what he was hearing in a cold, computerlike way, but the circuits were starting to overload. 'Who else did you remember seeing? Anybody stand out?'

Cole thought again, his eyes wandering aimlessly. 'There was one woman who went in not long before Greg got there. Now that I think of it, she left before he got there too.'

'What did she look like?'

'I don't remember.'

'Blond, brunette?'

Cole shook his head. 'I only remember her because she

337

wore a long coat. The students all wear windbreakers or sweatshirts or something like that. I remember thinking she looked like an adult.'

'Was she carrying anything? Did she—'

'Look, Myron, I'm sorry. I gotta get moving.' He stood and looked down at Myron with a hollow, lost expression. 'Good luck finding the son of a bitch,' he said. 'Liz was a good person. She never hurt anyone. None of us did.'

Before he could turn away, Myron asked, 'Why did you call me last night? What were you going to sell me?'

Cole smiled sadly and began to walk away. He stopped before he reached the door and turned back around. 'I'm alone now,' he said. 'Gloria Katz was shot in the initial attack. She died three months later. Susan Milano died in a car crash in 1982. Liz and I kept their deaths a secret. We wanted the feds searching for four of us, not two. We thought it would help us stay hidden. So you see, there is only one of us left now.'

He had the bone-weary look of a survivor who wasn't so sure the dead weren't the lucky ones. He rambled back over toward Myron and unlocked the handcuffs. 'Go,' he said.

Myron rose, rubbing his wrists. 'Thank you,' he said.

Cole merely nodded.

'I won't tell anyone where you are.'

'Yeah,' Cole said. 'I know.'

Chapter 35

Myron sprinted to his car and dialed Clip's number. Clip's secretary answered and told him that Mr Arnstein was not in at the moment. He asked her to transfer the call to Calvin Johnson. She put him on hold. Ten seconds later, the call was put through.

'Hey, Myron,' Calvin said, 'what's up?'

'Where's Clip?'

'He should be here in a couple of hours. By game time anyway.'

'Where is he now?'

'I don't know.'

'Find him,' Myron said. 'When you do, call me back.'

'What's going on?' Calvin asked.

'Just find him.'

Myron disconnected the call. He opened the car window and took deep breaths. It was a few minutes after six. Most of the guys would already be at the arena warming up. He headed up Riverside Drive and crossed the George Washington Bridge. He dialed Leon White's number. A woman answered.

'Hello?'

Myron disguised his voice. 'Is this Mrs Fiona White?' he asked.

'Yes, it is.'

'Would you like to subscribe to *Popular Mechanics*? We have a special going on for a limited time.'

'No, thank you.' She hung up.

Conclusion: Fiona White, the Sepbabe and promisor of night ecstasy, was home. Time to pay her a little visit.

He took Route 4 and got off at Kindermack Road. Five minutes later, he was there. The house was a semi-nouveau ranch with orange-tinged brick and diamond-shaped windows. This particular architectural look was all the rage for maybe a two-month span in 1977, and it had aged about as well as the leisure suit. Myron parked in the driveway. On either side of the cement walkway were low-rise iron fences with plastic ivy snaked through them. Classy.

He rang the bell. Fiona White opened the door. Her green, flower-print blouse hung open over a white leotard. Her bleached-blonde hair was tied in a bun that was falling apart, spare strands dangling down over her eyes and ears. She looked at Myron and frowned. 'Yes?'

'Hi, Fiona. I'm Myron Bolitar. We met the other night at TC's house.'

The frown was still there. 'Leon isn't here.'

'I wanted to talk to you.'

Fiona sighed and crossed her arms under the ample bosom. 'What about?'

'Can I come inside?'

'No. I'm busy right now.'

'I think it would be better in private.'

'This is private,' she said, her face unyielding. 'What do you want?'

Myron shrugged, conjured up his most charming smile, saw it would take him nowhere. 'I want to know about you and Greg Downing.'

Fiona White's arms dropped to her side. She suddenly looked horror-stricken. 'What?'

'I know about your e-mail to him. Sepbabe. You were supposed to meet last Saturday for the' – Myron made quote marks with his fingers – ' "greatest night of ecstasy imaginable." Do you recall that?'

Fiona White went to close the door. Myron stuck his foot in the way.

'I've got nothing to say to you,' she said.

'I'm not trying to expose you.'

She pushed the door against his foot. 'Get out.'

'I'm just trying to find Greg Downing.'

'I don't know where he is.'

'Were you having an affair with him?'

'No. Now leave.'

'I saw the e-mail, Fiona.'

'Think what you want. I'm not talking to you.'

'Fine,' Myron said, moving back and throwing up his hands. 'I'll talk to Leon instead.'

Her cheeks flushed. 'Do whatever you want,' she said. 'I did not have an affair with him. I did not see him last Saturday night. I don't know where he is.'

She slammed the door.

Gee, that went well.

Myron headed back to his car. As he reached the door, a black BMW with tinted windows rocketed up the street and screeched to a halt in the driveway. The driver's door opened and Leon flew out like an escaped bird.

'What the fuck you doing here?' he snapped.

'Take it easy, Leon.'

'Fuck take it easy,' he shouted. Leon ran up and stuck his face within an inch of Myron's. 'What the fuck you doing around here, huh?'

'I came by to see you.'

'Bullshit.' The spittle hit Myron's cheeks. 'We're supposed to be at the arena in twenty minutes.' He pushed Myron in the chest. Myron stumbled back. 'Why you here, huh?' Leon pushed again. 'What are you sniffing after?'

'Nothing.'

'You think you'd find my wife alone?'

'It's nothing like that.'

Leon lined himself up for another push. Myron was ready. When Leon's hand reached him, Myron's right forearm shot across his body, pinning Leon's hands helplessly against Myron's chest. Myron bent at the waist, bending Leon's wrists back the wrong way. The pressure forced Leon to drop to one knee. Myron's right hand slid until it met Leon's left. He grabbed it and quickly executed an elbow lock. Leon winced.

'You calm?' Myron asked.

'Motherfucker.'

'That doesn't sound like calm, Leon.' Myron applied a little pressure to the elbow. Joint locks were about controlled pain. They worked by bending joints in ways they were never intended to bend. The more the bend, the more the pain. But go too far and the joint dislocated or a bone broke. Myron was careful.

'Greg is missing again,' Myron said. 'That's why I'm on the team. I'm supposed to find him.'

Leon was still on his knees, his arm locked and upright. 'So what does that have to do with me?'

'You two have had a falling out,' Myron said. 'I want to know why.'

Leon looked up at him. 'Let go of me, Myron.'

'If you attack me again—'

'I won't. Just let go already.'

Myron waited another second or two, then did as Leon asked. Leon rubbed his arm and stood. Myron eyed him.

Leon said, 'You're here because you think Greg and Fiona were getting it on.'

'Were they?'

He shook his head. 'Not from a lack of trying though.'

'What do you mean?'

'He's supposed to be my best friend. But he's not. He's just another fucking superstar who takes what he wants.'

'Including Fiona.'

'He tried. Tried like hell. But she's not like that.'

Myron said nothing. Not his place.

'Guys are always hitting on Fiona,' he went on. 'Because of the way she looks. And the whole racial thing. So when I saw you here when you figured I wouldn't be around . . .' He shrugged into silence.

'Did you ever confront Greg?' Myron asked.

'Yeah,' he said. 'A couple of weeks ago.'

'What did you say to him?'

Leon's eyes narrowed, suddenly wary. 'What does this have to do with finding him?' he asked, suspicious now. 'You trying to pin this on me?'

'Pin what on you?'

'You said he's disappeared. You trying to pin that on me?'

'I'm just trying to find out where he is.'

'I got nothing to do with it.'

'I didn't say you did. I just want to know what happened when you confronted him.'

'What do you think happened?' Leon countered. 'The motherfucker denied it. He made this big point of swearing he'd never sleep with any married woman – especially his best friend's wife.'

Myron sort of gulped at that one. 'But you didn't believe him.'

'He's a superstar, Myron.'

'That doesn't make him a liar.'

'No, but it makes him something different. Guys like Greg and Michael Jordan and Shaq and TC . . . they ain't like the rest of us. They got their own thing going. Everyone else is a fucking underling to them. The whole planet is set up to cater to their whims, you know what I'm saying?'

Myron nodded. In college he had been one of those who got to breathe the rarefied air of superstardom. He thought again about the bonds superstars shared. He and Greg had not exchanged more than five words before Greg visited him in the hospital, but there had been a bond. They both knew. Superstars share that rarefied air with very few. As TC had told him, it does indeed isolate in a very bizarre, often unhealthy way.

And with that thought came something of a revelation. Myron took a step back.

He'd always thought that if Greg was in trouble, he'd go to his closest friend for help. But that wasn't the case. If Greg had indeed stumbled across the dead body and panicked, if he had seen all his problems – the gambling debts, the threat of exposure, the divorce, the child custody case, the blackmail, the probability of being a suspect in a murder – closing in on him, who would he go to for help?

He'd go to the guy who understood him best.

He'd go to the guy who could best relate to the unique troubles of superstardom.

He'd go to the guy who shared that rarefied air with him.

Chapter 36

Myron wasn't sure what to do next.

In truth, he had nothing more than a suspicion. There was no proof. No real evidence. But it could potentially answer a lot of questions. Why, for example, had Thumper helped set up Emily on videotape? By all accounts, she was not particularly close to Greg.

But she was to TC.

Again the superstar bond. Greg had feared losing his kids in a custody battle. That's about as big a worry as a person can have. So whom did he turn to for help?

TC.

When Win had leaned on Thumper last night, letting her know that he was searching for Greg, whom had she warned?

TC.

No proof, of course. But it felt very right.

Myron could now put a lot of it together. Greg was under incredible strain – not the best situation for a man of his questionable mental fortitude to be ensnared. What had gone through his mind when he saw Liz Gorman dead on the floor? He'd have to have known that he would be the prime suspect in her murder. As Emily had pointed out, Greg had motive, opportunity, and was at the murder scene. Emily saw that. It was why she set him up. Greg must have seen it too.

So what did he do?

He ran.

Seeing Liz Gorman dead had been the final straw. But Greg had also known that he could not do it alone. People would be looking for him this time. He needed help. He needed time and space.

So whom did Greg reach out to?

The guy who understood him best. Who could relate to the unique troubles of superstardom. Who shared that rarefied air with him.

Myron stopped at a red light. He was close, so god-damn close. TC was helping Greg hide; he was sure of it. But of course, TC was only part of the solution. None of this answered the central question in all this:

Who killed Liz Gorman?

He put his mind on rewind and reviewed the night of the murder. He thought about Clip being the first of the three to arrive. In many ways, Clip was now his best suspect. But Myron still saw big problems with that scenario. What was Clip's motive, for example? Yes, Liz Gorman's information may have been detrimental to the team. The information may have even been potent enough for him to lose the vote. But would Clip pick up a baseball bat and murder a woman over that? People kill for money and power all the time. Would Clip?

But there was still a larger problem at work here, one

that Myron could not get around no matter how hard he tried. Emily was the one who planted the blood and murder weapon at Greg's house. That was established and that made sense. Okay, fine. We know who planted the evidence . . .

. . . but who cleaned it up?

There were only three logical choices: 1) Greg Downing, 2) someone trying to protect Greg, or 3) the killer.

But it couldn't have been Greg. Even if you accept the semi-impossible premise that Greg went back into his house after going into hiding, how did he find the blood? Did he just happen to go down into the playroom? No. It was too ridiculous. The only way Greg would have gone down there was if he'd known the blood had been planted.

Myron froze.

That was it. Whoever had cleaned up the blood had known what Emily had done. They didn't just stumble across it by accident. So how did they find out? From Emily? Uh uh, no way. Emily would be the last person to say anything. Could she have been spotted in the act? Again, the answer was a resounding no. If that had been the case, the bat would have been removed too. More to the point, the blood would have been cleaned up right away – *before* Myron and Win found it. The timing of the clean-up was crucial – it'd happened after Myron and Win had revealed their discovery. That meant Myron and Win were the leak.

So who had they told?

The finger pointed back to Clip.

He turned on Route 3 and entered the Meadowlands complex. The arena loomed before him like a large UFO on a white landing pad. Did Clip Arnstein murder Liz

Gorman and clean up the blood? Myron wrestled with the possibility, but he didn't like it. How had Clip gotten inside Greg's house? There were no signs of forced entry. Had he picked the lock? Doubtful. Did he have a key? Doubtful. Did he hire a professional? Still doubtful. Clip hadn't even let a private investigator do a simple credit card check on Greg for fear word would get out. Whom would he trust to clean up the blood of a person he murdered?

And something else still jabbed at Myron with a sharpened, steel point: the woman's clothes in the bedroom. They had been packed away too. Why would Clip remove all traces of a secret girlfriend? Why would anybody?

The different scenarios swirled in Myron's head like rubber ducks in a whirlpool. He concentrated again on the mystery girlfriend. Could it have been Fiona White? She wasn't talking, but Myron firmly believed that she was not the one. How could Fiona have lived with Greg and kept it hidden from a husband as obsessively jealous as Leon? Perhaps there had been some entanglement between Greg and Fiona – a casual fling in a motel room or something – but Myron no longer believed even that. The more he thought about it, the 'greatest night of sexual ecstasy' epistle was more of a come-on than the talk of two familiar lovers. It seemed more logical that Greg was telling Leon the truth when he said he would never sleep with another man's wife. The thought gave Myron's old shame new life.

A commercial came on the radio. A very hip man and a very hip woman were enjoying a Molson's Golden far too much. They spoke in low voices and laughed at each other's lame jokes. Myron switched it off.

He still had more questions than answers. But when he

picked up his cellular phone to check Greg's answering machine, his fingers began to tremble. Something tightened his chest, making it hard to breathe. This feeling, however, was not like pregame jitters. In fact, it was the furthest thing from them.

Chapter 37

Myron rushed by Clip's secretary.

'He's not in there,' she cried.

Ignoring her, he opened the office door. The lights were off and the room was empty. He spun back toward the secretary. 'Where is he?'

The secretary, a classic battle-ax who had probably been with Clip since the Coolidge Administration, put her hands on her hips. 'I don't have the slightest idea,' she huffed.

Calvin Johnson came out of the adjoining office. Myron approached him. He waited until they were inside Calvin's office and the door was closed. 'Where is he?'

Calvin held up his hands. 'I don't know. I tried his house, but there was no answer.'

'Does he have a car phone?'

'No.'

Myron shook his head and began pacing. 'He lied to me,' Myron said. 'The son of a bitch lied.'

'What?'

'He met with the blackmailer.'

Calvin raised an eyebrow. He moved to the chair behind his desk and sat down. 'What are you talking about?'

'The night she was murdered,' Myron said, 'Clip went to her apartment.'

'But she wasn't supposed to meet with us until Monday,' Calvin said.

'Did you hear her say that?'

Calvin plucked at his chin with his thumb and pointer. The track lights from above his desk reflected off the receding forehead. His face remained the ever placid pool. 'No,' he said slowly. 'Clip told me.'

'He lied to you.'

'But why?'

'Because he's hiding something.'

'Do you know what?'

'No,' Myron said. 'But I intend to find out tonight.'

'How?'

'The blackmailer still wants to sell,' Myron said. 'I'm his new buyer.'

Calvin tilted his head. 'I thought you said the blackmailer was dead.'

'She had a partner.'

'I see,' Calvin said with a slow nod. 'And you're meeting tonight?'

'Yep. But I don't know when or where. He's supposed to call.'

'I see,' Calvin said again. He made a neat fist and coughed into it. 'If it's something damaging. I mean, something that could affect the outcome of the vote tomorrow . . .'

'I'll do whatever is right, Calvin.'

'Of course. I didn't mean to imply otherwise.'

Myron rose. 'Let me know when he gets here.'

'Sure.'

Myron entered the locker room. TC was in his pre-game pose – sprawled on a chair in the corner with a Walkman plugged into his ears, his eyes blazing straight ahead and unmoving. He did not acknowledge Myron. Leon was also there. He, too, studiously avoided Myron's gaze. Not surprising.

Audrey approached. 'How did it go with—?'

Myron shook his head to silence her. She nodded, understanding. 'You okay?' she asked.

'Fine.'

'You think they can hear us?'

'I'm not taking any chances.'

Audrey looked left, then right. 'You find something new?'

'Plenty,' Myron said. 'You should have your story tonight. And then some.'

The gleam in her eye expanded. 'You know where he is?'

Myron nodded. The locker room door opened. Calvin popped his head in. He leaned over and spoke to the Kipper for a moment. When he left, Myron noticed that he turned right, which led to the exit, as opposed to left which would have taken him back to his office.

The cellular phone in Myron's pocket rang. He looked up at Audrey. Audrey looked back. He moved closer to the corner and picked it up.

'Hello?'

An electronically altered voice said, 'You got the money?'

'You got lousy timing,' Myron said.

'Answer my question.'

Leon pulled up his gym shorts. TC stood and bobbed his head in rhythm to the music.

'I have it,' Myron said. 'I also have a game tonight.'

'Forget the game. Do you know Overpeck Park?'

'The one in Leonia? Yeah, I know it.'

'Turn in the right side off Route Ninety-five. Then go down a quarter mile and make another right. You'll see a cul-de-sac. Park there and look for a flashlight. Approach with both your hands raised.'

'Do I get to say a password?' Myron asked. 'I loves passwords.'

'Fifteen minutes. Don't be late. And for the record, I know your superhero partner is in his Park Avenue office. I have a man watching it. If he leaves between now and then, the deal is off.'

Myron turned off the phone. It was coming to a head now. In fifteen minutes it would all be over – one way or another. 'Could you hear?' he asked.

Audrey nodded. 'Most of it.'

'There's going to be some weird stuff going down,' Myron said. 'I need an unbiased journalist to record it. You want to come along?'

She smiled. 'That was a rhetorical question, right?'

'You'll have to keep on the floor in the backseat,' he went on. 'I can't risk having you spotted.'

'No problem,' she said. 'It'll remind me of my high school dates.'

Myron turned toward the door. His nerves were as frayed as an old horse whip. He tried to look nonchalant as they exited. Leon was lacing up his sneakers. TC remained still, but this time his eyes followed them out.

Chapter 38

Rain beat down, blackening the pavement. Cars were just starting to enter the arena lot in force. Myron took the back exit over the New Jersey Turnpike and onto the northbound lanes just past the final toll booth. He veered to the right, staying on Route 95.

'So what's going on?' Audrey asked.

'The man I am about to meet,' he said, 'killed Liz Gorman.'

'Who's Liz Gorman?'

'The blackmailer who was murdered.'

'I thought her name was Carla.'

'That was an alias.'

'Wait a minute. Isn't Liz Gorman the name of some sixties radical?'

Myron nodded. 'It's a long story; I don't have time to go into details. Suffice to say the guy we're about to meet was part of the blackmail scheme. Something went awry. She ended up dead.'

'Do you have evidence?' Audrey asked.

'Not really. That's what I need you for. You have your microcassette player?'

'Sure.'

'Let me have it.'

Audrey reached into her purse and handed it up front.

'I'm going to try to get him to talk,' Myron said.

'How?'

'By pushing the right buttons.'

She frowned. 'You think he'll fall for that?'

'Yeah, I do. If I push the right ones.' He picked up the car phone. 'I have two separate phones here: the car phone and the cellular in my pocket. I'm going to dial the car phone with the cellular and keep the line open. This way, you can listen in. I want you to take down every word. If something happens to me, go to Win. He'll know what to do.'

She leaned forward and nodded. The windshield wipers whipped shadows across her face. The rain picked up its tempo, glistening the road in front of them. Myron took the next exit. A sign reading Overpeck Park greeted them a quarter mile later.

'Get down,' he said.

She disappeared from view. He made the right turn. Another sign told him the park was closed. He ignored it and proceeded ahead. It was too dark to see anything, but he knew there were woods on his left and a horse stables straight ahead. He made the first right. The car's head-lights danced across a picnic area, illuminating tables, benches, garbage cans, a swing set, a sliding board. He reached the cul-de-sac and stopped the car. He killed the lights, turned off the engine, and dialed the car's number on his cellular. He answered with the car's speakerphone so Audrey could listen in. Then he waited.

For several minutes nothing happened. The rain pelted down on the roof like tiny pebbles. Audrey remained still in the back. Myron put his hands back on the wheel and felt his grip tighten. He could hear his heart thumping in his chest.

Without warning, a beacon of light sliced through the night like a reaper's scythe. Myron shaded his eyes with his hand and squinted. He slowly opened the car door. The wind had picked up now, spraying the rain into his face. He hefted himself out of the car.

A male voice, distorted by the elements, shouted, 'Put your hands up.'

Myron raised them above his head.

'Open your coat. I know you're carrying a gun in a shoulder holster. Take it out with two fingers and toss it onto the seat of the car.'

Keeping one hand in the air, Myron unbuttoned his coat. He was already drenched from the rain, his hair matted against his forehead. He took out the gun and put it on his car seat.

'Close the door.'

Again Myron obeyed the voice.

'Do you have the money?'

'First I want to see what you brought,' Myron said.

'No.'

'Hey, be reasonable here. I don't even know what I'm buying.'

A brief hesitation. 'Come closer.'

Myron stepped toward the light, ignoring the symbolism. 'Whatever you're selling,' he said, 'how do I know you haven't made copies?'

'You don't,' the voice said. 'You'll have to trust me.'

'Who else knows about this?'

'I'm the only one,' the voice said, 'who is still alive.'

Myron picked up the pace. His hands were still in the air. The wind whipped into his face. His clothes were sopping. 'How do I know you won't talk?'

'Again, you don't. Your money buys my silence.'

'Until someone ups the bid.'

'No. I'm leaving after this. You won't hear from me again.' The flashlight flickered. 'Please stop.'

Ten feet in front of him stood a man wearing a ski mask. He had a flashlight in one hand and a box in the other. He nodded at Myron and lifted the box. 'Here.'

'What is it?'

'First, the money.'

'For all I know, the box is empty.'

'Fine. Go back to your car and leave then.' The man in the ski mask turned around.

'No, wait,' Myron said. 'I'll get the money.'

The ski mask faced Myron again. 'No games.'

Myron headed back to the car. He had moved about twenty paces when he heard the gunshots. Three of them. The noises did not startle him. He slowly turned around. The man with the ski mask was down. Audrey was running toward the still body. She was carrying Myron's gun.

'He was going to kill you,' Audrey cried. 'I had to shoot.'

Audrey kept running. When she reached the still body, she ignored it and scooped up the box. Myron slowly walked toward her.

'Open it,' he said.

'Let's get out of this rain first. The police—'

'Open it.'

She hesitated. No thunder bellowed. No lightning struck.

'You were right before,' Myron said.

Audrey looked puzzled. 'About what?'

'I was looking at this the wrong way.'

'What are you talking about?'

Myron took another step toward her. 'When I asked myself who knew about the blood in the basement,' he began, 'I only remembered Clip and Calvin. I forgot I told you. When I wondered why Greg's lover would have to keep her identity a secret, I thought about Fiona White and Liz Gorman. Again I forgot about you. It's hard enough for a woman to get respect as a female sports reporter. Your career would be ruined if anybody found out you were dating one of the players you covered. You had to keep it quiet.'

She looked at him, her face a wet, white blank.

'You're the only one who fits, Audrey. You knew about the blood in the basement. You had to keep a relationship with Greg a secret. You had a key to his house so access would be no problem. And you were the one who had a motive to clean up the blood in order to protect him. After all, you killed to protect him. What's cleaning up some blood?'

She brushed her hair away from her eyes and blinked into the rain. 'You can't seriously believe that I—'

'That night after TC's party,' Myron interrupted, 'when you told me how you had put it all together. I should have wondered then. Sure, my joining the team was unusual. But only somebody with a personal connection – somebody who truly knew that Greg had vanished and why – would have been able to come up with it so fast. You were the mystery lover, Audrey. And you don't know where Greg is either. You cooperated with me not because you wanted the story, but because you wanted to find Greg. You're in love with him.'

'That's ridiculous,' she said.

'The police will comb the house, Audrey. They'll find hairs.'

'That doesn't mean anything,' she said. 'I interviewed him a couple of times—'

'In his bedroom? In his bathroom? In his shower?' Myron shook his head. 'They'll also comb the murder scene now that they know about you. There'll be evidence there too. A hair or something.' He took another step toward her. Audrey raised the gun with a quivering hand.

'Beware the Ides of March,' Myron said.

'What?'

'You were the one who pointed it out to me. The ides are the fifteenth of March. Your birthday was the seventeenth. March seventeenth. Three-one-seven. The code Greg set on his answering machine.'

She pointed the gun at his chest. 'Turn off the tape recorder,' she said. 'And the phone.'

Myron reached into his pocket and did as she asked.

Tears and rain mixed together and cascaded down her cheeks. 'Why couldn't you just keep your mouth shut?' she wailed. She pointed to the still body on the wet grass. 'You heard what he said: no one else knows. All the blackmailers are dead. I could have destroyed this thing' – she held up the box – 'once and for all. I wouldn't have had to hurt you. It would have finally been over.'

'And what about Liz Gorman?'

Audrey made a scoffing noise. 'That woman was nothing more than a conniving blackmailer,' she said. 'She couldn't be trusted. I told Greg that. What was to stop her from making copies and bleeding him dry? I even went to her house that night and pretended I was an ex-girlfriend with an ax to grind. I told her I wanted to buy a copy. She said sure. Don't you see? Paying her off would do no good. There was only one way to keep her quiet.'

He nodded. 'You had to kill her.'

'She was just a low-life criminal, Myron. She'd robbed a bank, for chrissake. Greg and I . . . we were perfect together. You were right about my career. I had to keep our relationship a secret. But not much longer. I was going to get transferred to another beat. Baseball. The Mets or Yankees. Then we could be open about it. It was going so well, Myron, and then this low-life bitch comes along . . .' Her voice drifted off with a hard shake of the head. 'I had to think about our future,' she said. 'Not just Greg's. Not just mine. But our baby's too.'

Myron's eyes closed in pain. 'You're pregnant,' he said softly.

'Now do you see?' Her wide-eyed enthusiasm was back, though it took on a more twisted dimension now. 'She wanted to destroy him. Destroy us. What choice did I have? I'm not a killer but it was either us or her. And I know how it looks – Greg running off and not telling me. But it's just the way he is. We've been together for more than six months. I know he loves me. He just needed time.'

Myron swallowed. 'It's over now, Audrey.'

She shook her head and held the gun with both hands. 'I'm sorry, Myron. I don't want to do it. I'd almost rather die first.'

'It doesn't matter.' Myron took another step. She moved back. The gun trembled in her hand. 'They're blanks,' he said.

Her eyes squinted in confusion. The man in the ski mask sat up like Bela Lugosi in an old Dracula film. He pulled off the mask and showed his badge. 'Police,' Dimonte shouted. Win and Krinsky came over the crest. Audrey's mouth formed a perfect circle. Win had made the fake blackmailer call; Myron had set his cellular phone's volume on high to be sure Audrey overheard it. The rest was easy.

Dimonte and Krinsky made the arrest. Myron watched, no longer feeling the rain. After Audrey was put into the back of a cruiser, he and Win walked toward the car.

'Superhero partner?' Myron said.

Win shrugged.

Chapter 39

Esperanza was still in the office when the fax machine rang. She crossed the room and watched the machine begin to spew out paper. The facsimile was addressed to her attention, from the FBI:

Re: FIRST CITY NATIONAL BANK – TUCSON, ARIZONA
Subject: Renters of Safe-Deposit Boxes.

She'd been waiting for this transmission all day.

Esperanza's theory on the blackmail plot had gone something like this: The Raven Brigade robbed the bank. They hit the safe-deposit boxes. People keep all kinds of things in those. Money, jewelry, important documents. That was what hooked the timing together. Simply put, the Raven Brigade had found something in one of those boxes that was damaging to Greg Downing. Then they hatched their little blackmail scheme.

The names came out in alphabetical order. Esperanza read down the list while the paper was still being transmitted. The first page ended in the Ls. No name was familiar. The second page ended in the Ts. No name was familiar. On the third page, when she reached the Ws, her heart leaped into her throat. Her hand fluttered to her mouth, and for a moment she feared that she might scream.

It took several hours to sort through the mess. Statements had to be taken. Explanations made. Myron told Dimonte practically the whole story. He left out the videotape of Thumper and Emily. Again, it was nobody's business. He also left out the part about meeting up with Cole Whiteman. Myron somehow felt he owed him. For her part, Audrey would not talk at all, except to ask for a lawyer.

'Do you know where Downing is?' Dimonte asked Myron.

'I think so.'

'But you don't want to tell me.'

Myron shook his head. 'He's not your business.'

'Ain't that the truth,' Dimonte agreed. 'Go on. Get out of here.'

They were downtown at One Police Plaza. Myron and Win walked out in the city night. Large municipal structures consumed the neighboring area. Modern bureaucracy in its most extreme and intimidating form. Even this late at night, you could visualize lines of people heading out the door.

'It was a good plan,' Win said.

'Audrey is pregnant.'

'I heard.'

'Her baby will be born in jail.'

'Not your doing.'

'She thought it was her only way out,' Myron said.

Win nodded. 'She saw a blackmailer who stood in the way of all her dreams. I'm not so sure I would have behaved any differently.'

'You don't commit murder to stave off life's inconveniences,' Myron said.

Win didn't argue, but he didn't agree either. They kept walking. When they reached the car, Win said, 'So where does that leave us?'

'With Clip Arnstein,' Myron said. 'He has some explaining to do.'

'You want me to come along?'

'No. I want to talk to him alone.'

Chapter 40

By the time Myron arrived at the arena, the game was over. Cars tapped the exits, making it hard to go the opposite way. Myron managed to weave through. He showed his ID to the guard and drove into the players' lot.

He ran to Clip's office. Someone called his name. He ignored it. When he reached the outer office door, he tried the knob. It was locked. He was tempted to break it down.

'Yo, Myron.'

It was one of the towel boys. Myron forgot the kid's name. 'What's up?' he said.

'This came for you.'

The kid handed Myron a manila envelope.

'Who dropped this off?' Myron asked.

'Your uncle.'

'My uncle?'

'That's what the guy said.'

Myron looked at the envelope. His name was scrawled

across the front in giant block letters. He tore it open and turned it upside down. First, a letter slid out. He shook again and a black cassette tape fell into the palm of his hand. He put the cassette down and unfolded the letter:

Myron,
   I should have given this to you at the cathedral. I'm sorry I didn't, but I got too caught up in Liz's murder. I wanted you to concentrate on catching the killer, not on this tape. I was afraid it would distract you. I still think it will, but that doesn't give me the right to keep it from you. I just hope you stay focused enough to find the bastard who killed Liz. She deserves justice.
   I also wanted to tell you that I'm thinking about turning myself in. Now that Liz is gone, there's no reason to keep hiding. I spoke to some old lawyer buddies about it. They've already started reaching out to all the mercenaries Hunt's father hired. They're sure one of them will corroborate my story. We'll see.
   Don't listen to this tape alone, Myron. Listen to it with a friend.
      Cole

Myron folded the letter. He had no idea what to think. He glanced down the corridor. No sign of Clip. He jogged toward the exit. Most of the players had already left the arena. TC, of course. Last in, first out. Myron got in his car and turned the key. Then he stuck the tape into the car's player and waited.

Esperanza tried dialing Myron's car phone. No answer. Then his cellular. Same deal. He always carried his cellular. If he wasn't picking up, it was because he didn't want to. She quickly dialed Win's cellular. He picked up on the second ring.

'Do you know where Myron is?' she asked.

'He went to the arena.'

'Go find him, Win.'

'Why? What's wrong?'

'The Raven Brigade robbed the safe-deposit boxes. That's where they got the information they used to black-mail Downing.'

'What did they find?'

'I don't know,' she said, 'but I have a list of the people who rented the boxes.'

'So?'

'One was rented to a Mr and Mrs B. Wesson.'

Silence.

Win said, 'Are you sure it's the same B. Wesson who injured Myron?'

'I already checked,' she said. 'The B stands for Burt, listed on his application as a thirty-three-year-old high school basketball coach. It's him, Win. It's the same Burt Wesson.'

Chapter 41

Nothing.

Myron fiddled with the volume knob. Static feedback screeched through the car speakers. He turned it down a second, then back up. He heard muffled sounds, but he had no idea what they were. Then the sounds faded away.

Silence.

Two minutes of blank tape passed before Myron finally heard voices. His ears perked up, but he couldn't make out much. Then the voices grew a little louder, a little clearer. He leaned closer to the speaker and suddenly he heard a gruff voice with frightening clarity:

'*You have the money?*'

A hand reached into Myron's chest, grabbed his heart, and squeezed. He hadn't heard the voice in ten years, but recognition was instantaneous. It was Burt Wesson. What the hell—?

Then the second voice jarred him like a body blow:

'*I got half now. A thousand dollars now. You get the other half when he goes down . . .*'

Myron's entire body shuddered. A flash of rage unlike anything he had ever known warmed and then engulfed him. His hands tightened into fists. Tears forced their way forward. He remembered wondering why the black-mailers had contacted him to buy the dirt on Greg; he remembered Cole Whiteman's laugh and Marty Felder's ironic smile when they'd learned that he'd been hired to find Greg Downing; he remembered the voice on Greg's answering machine saying, 'He's willing to pay. Is that what you want?'; and most of all, he remembered Greg's pained face at the hospital all those years ago. It hadn't been a bond that brought Greg to Myron's bedside.

It'd been guilt.

'*Don't hurt him too bad, Burt. I just want Bolitar banged up for a few games . . .*'

Something in the deep recesses of Myron's mind snapped like a dry twig. Without conscious thought, Myron shifted into reverse.

'*Look, I really need the money. Can't you give me another five hundred? They're going to cut me soon. It's my last scrimmage and then I'm unemployed . . .*'

He straightened out his car and shifted into drive. His foot pressed down upon the pedal. The speedometer climbed. Myron's face twisted into a mask of incognizant fury. Tears sheeted down his cheeks but no sound came with them. He drove without really seeing.

When he reached the Jones Road exit, Myron wiped his face with his sleeve. He turned into TC's driveway. The security gate blocked his path.

The guard stepped out of his little hut. Myron waved

him closer to the car. When the guard was fully out of the box, Myron showed the gun.

'Move and I'll blow your head off.'

The guard's hands went up. Myron got out of the car and opened the gate. He ordered the guard inside the car. The car roared up the driveway. Myron slammed on the brake just feet before the front door. He jumped out on the run and without hesitating, he kicked in TC's front door. He ran into the den.

The television was on. TC looked up, startled. 'What the fuck—?'

Myron bounded across the room, grabbed TC's arm, twisted it behind his back.

'Hey—'

'Where is he?' Myron demanded.

'I don't know what—'

Myron pulled up on the arm. 'Don't make me break it, TC. Where is he?'

'What the fuck are you—?'

Myron silenced him by pushing the arm farther up his back. TC cried out, his huge frame bent at the waist to lessen the pressure. 'Last time I ask,' Myron said. 'Where's Greg?'

'I'm here.'

Myron let go and spun toward the voice. Greg Downing stood in the doorway. Myron did not hesitate. Letting out a guttural scream, he pounced.

Greg put up his hands, but it was like quieting a volcano with a squirt gun. Myron's fist landed square in Greg's face. Greg toppled back from the assault. Myron fell on him, his knee landing in his ribs. Something cracked. He straddled Greg's chest and threw another punch.

'Stop!' TC shouted, 'You're gonna kill him.'

Myron barely heard him.

He cocked his other fist, but TC was on him before he could throw it. Myron rolled with the tackle, digging his elbow into TC's solar plexus. When they hit the wall, the air whooshed out of TC, his eyes bulging as he gasped for air. Myron rose. Greg was scrambling away. Myron vaulted over the couch. He grabbed Greg by the leg and pulled him toward him.

'You fucked my wife!' Greg shouted. 'You think I didn't know? You fucked my wife!'

The words slowed Myron, but they didn't stop him. Through his tears, he threw another punch. Greg's mouth filled with blood. Myron cocked his fist again. A hand of iron reached out and grabbed his arm, holding it in place.

'Enough,' Win said.

Myron looked up, his face distorted by confusion and rage. 'What?'

'He's had enough.'

'But it's like you said,' Myron pleaded. 'Wesson did do it on purpose. Greg hired him.'

'I know,' Win said. 'But he's had enough.'

'What the hell are you talking about? If it was you—'

'I'd probably kill him,' Win finished for him. He looked down and something flickered in his eyes. 'But you wouldn't.'

Myron swallowed. Win nodded again and let go of Myron's wrist. Myron let his arm fall to his side. He got off Greg Downing.

Greg sat up, coughing blood into his hand. 'I followed Emily that night,' Greg managed through the hacks. 'I saw you two . . . I just wanted payback, that's all. You weren't supposed to get hurt that bad.'

372

Myron swallowed and breathed deeply. The adrenaline rush would soon ebb, but for now it was still there. 'You been hiding here since the beginning?'

Greg touched part of his face, winced, then nodded 'I was afraid they'd think I killed that woman,' he said. 'And I had the mob chasing me and the custody battle and my girlfriend is pregnant.' He looked up. 'I just needed some time.'

'Do you love Audrey?'

Greg said, 'You know?'

'Yes.'

'Yeah,' Greg said, 'I love her a lot.'

'Then give her a call,' Myron said. 'She's in jail.'

'What?'

Myron didn't elaborate. He'd hoped throwing that in Greg's face would give him some sort of perverse pleasure, but it didn't. All it did was remind him that he was far from blameless in this.

He turned and walked away.

Myron found Clip alone in that same corporate sky-box they'd met in when this all began. He was looking down at the empty court, his back to Myron. He didn't move when Myron cleared his throat.

'You knew all along,' Myron said.

Clip said nothing.

'You went to Liz Gorman's apartment that night,' Myron continued. 'She played the tape for you, didn't she?'

Clip clasped his hands behind his back. Then he nodded.

'That's why you hired me. This wasn't all a coincidence. You wanted me to find out the truth.'

'I didn't know how else to tell you.' Clip finally turned and faced Myron. His eyes were dazed and hazy. All color was gone from his face. 'It wasn't an act, you know. The emotion at the press conference . . .' He lowered his head, gathered himself, raised it again. 'You and I lost touch after your injury. I wanted to call you a thousand times, but I understood. You wanted to stay away. The injury never leaves the great ones, Myron. I knew it would never leave you.'

Myron opened his mouth but nothing came out. His entire being felt exposed and raw. Clip came closer. 'I thought this would be a way for you to learn the truth,' Clip said. 'I also hoped this would be something of a catharsis. Not a complete one. Like I said, it never leaves the great ones.'

For several moments, they both just stood and stared.

'You told Walsh to play me the other night,' Myron said.

'Yes.'

'You knew I wouldn't be able to match up.'

Clip nodded slowly.

Myron felt the tears come back to his eyes. He blinked them down.

Clip set his jaw. There were tiny tremors in his face, but he stood rigid. 'I wanted to help you,' he said, 'but my reasons for hiring you were not all altruistic. I knew, for example, that you'd always been a team player. You loved that aspect of basketball, Myron – being part of a team.'

'So?'

'My plan included making you feel like a member of the team. A real member. So much so that you would never hurt us.'

Myron understood. 'You figured that if I bonded with my teammates, I wouldn't blow the whistle when I learned the truth.'

'It's not in your nature,' Clip said.

'But it will come out,' Myron said. 'There's no way to avoid it now.'

'I know that.'

'You could lose the team.'

Clip smiled, shrugged. 'There are worse things,' he said. 'Just as you now know there are worse things than never being able to play again.'

'I always knew,' Myron said. 'I just maybe needed a reminder.'

Chapter 42

He and Jessica sat on the couch in her loft. He told her
everything. Jess hugged her knees and rocked back and
forth. Her eyes looked pained.

'She was my friend,' Jessica said.

'I know.'

'I wonder.'

'What?'

'What would I have done in the same situation? To
protect you.'

'You wouldn't have killed.'

'No,' she said. 'I guess not.

Myron watched her. She looked on the verge of tears.
He said, 'I think I learned something about us in all this.'

She waited for him to elaborate.

'Win and Esperanza didn't want me to play again. But
you never tried to stop me. I was afraid that maybe you
didn't understand me as well as they do. But that wasn't
the case at all. You saw what they couldn't.'

Jessica studied his face with a penetrating gaze. She let go of her knees and slid her feet to the floor. 'We've never really talked about this before,' she said.

He nodded.

'The truth is, you never mourned the end of your career,' Jessica went on. 'You never showed weakness. You stuffed it all in some internal suitcase and moved on. You tackled everything else in your life with a smothering desperation. You didn't wait. You seized whatever was left and pressed it against you, afraid your whole world was as fragile as that knee. You rushed off to law school. You ran off and helped Win. You frantically clung to whatever you could.' She stopped.

'Including you,' he finished.

'Yes. Including me. Not just because you loved me. Because you were afraid of losing more than you already had.'

'I did love you,' he said. 'I still do.'

'I know. I'm not trying to put this all on you. I was an idiot. It was mostly my fault. I admit that. But your love back then bordered on the desperate. You channeled your grief into a grasping need. I was afraid of suffocating. I don't want to sound like an amateur shrink, but you needed to mourn. You needed to put it behind you, not suppress it. But you wouldn't face it.'

'You thought my playing again would make me face it,' he said.

'Yes.'

'It's not like this was a cure-all.'

'I know,' she said. 'But I think it helped you let go a little.'

'And that's why you think now is a good time for me to move in.'

Jessica swallowed hard. 'If you want,' she said. 'If you feel ready.'

He looked up in the air and said, 'I'll need more closet space.'

'Done,' she whispered. 'Whatever you want.'

She snuggled into him. He put his arms around her, pulled her close, and felt very much at home.

It was a sweltering morning in Tucson, Arizona. A big man opened his front door.

'Are you Burt Wesson?'

The big man nodded. 'Can I help you with something?'

Win smiled. 'Yes,' he said. 'I think you can.'

Don't miss
the breathtaking new thriller from
HARLAN COBEN

Available now
in Orion Hardback and eBook
Read on for a preview

www.orionbooks.co.uk

Kat Donovan spun off her father's old stool, readying to leave O'Malley's pub, when Stacy said, "You're not going to like what I did."

The tone made Kat stop mid-stride. "What?"

O'Malley's used to be an old-school cop bar. Kat's grandfather had hung out here. So had her father and their fellow NYPD colleagues. Now it had been turned into a yuppie, preppy, master-of-the-universe, poser ass-hat bar, loaded up with guys who sported crisp white shirts under black suits, two-day stubble, manscaped to the max to look un-manscaped. They smirked a lot, these soft men, their hair moussed to the point of over-coif, and ordered Ketel One instead of Grey Goose because they watched some TV ad telling them that was what real men drink.

Stacy's eyes started darting around the bar. Avoidance. Kat didn't like that.

"What did you do?" Kat asked.

"Whoa," Stacy said.

"What?"

"A Punch-Worthy at five o'clock."

Kat swiveled to the right to take a peek.

"See him?" Stacy asked.

"Oh yeah."

Décor-wise, O'Malley's hadn't really changed much over the years. Sure, the old console TVs had been replaced by a host of flat screens showing too wide a variety of games—who cared about how the Edmonton Oilers did?—but outside of that, O'Malley's had kept the cop feel and that was what appealed to these posers, the faux authenticity, moving in and pushing out what made this place hum, turning it into some Disney Epcot version of what it had once been.

Kat was the only cop left in here. The others now went home after their shifts, or to AA meetings. Kat still came and tried to sit quietly on her father's old stool with the ghosts, especially tonight, with her father's murder haunting her anew. She just wanted to be here, to feel her father's presence, to—corny as it sounded—gather strength from it.

But the douchebags wouldn't let her be, would they?

This particular Punch-Worthy—shorthand for any guy deserving a fist to the face—had committed a classic punch-worthy sin. He was wearing sunglasses. At eleven o'clock at night. In a bar with poor lighting. Other punch-worthy indictments included wearing a chain on your wallet, do-rags, unbuttoned silk shirts, an overabundance of tattoos (special category for those sporting tribal symbols), dog tags when you didn't serve in the military, and really big white wristwatches.

4

Sunglasses smirked and lifted his glass toward Kat and Stacy.

"He likes us," Stacy said.

"Stop stalling. What won't I like?"

When Stacy turned back toward her, Kat could see over her shoulder the disappointment on Punch-Worthy's glistening-with-overpriced-lotion face. Kat had seen that look a zillion times before. Men liked Stacy. That was probably something of an understatement. Stacy was frighteningly, knee-knockingly, teeth-and-bone-and-metal-meltingly hot. Men became both weak-legged and stupid around Stacy. Mostly stupid. Really, really stupid.

This was why it was probably a mistake to hang out with someone who looked like Stacy—guys often concluded that they had no shot when a woman looked like that. She seemed unapproachable.

Kat, in comparison, did not.

Sunglasses honed in on Kat and began to make his move. He didn't so much walk toward her as glide on his own slime.

Stacy suppressed a giggle. "This is going to be good."

Hoping to discourage him, Kat gave the guy flat eyes and a disdainful frown. Sunglasses was not deterred. He bebopped over, moving to some sound track that was only playing in his own head.

"Hey, babe," Sunglasses said. "Is your name Wi-Fi?"

Kat waited.

"Because I'm feeling a connection."

Stacy burst out laughing.

Kat just stared at him. He continued.

"I love you small chicks, you know? You're kinda adorable. A spinner, am I right? You know what would look good on me? You."

5

"Do these lines ever work?" Kat asked him.

"I'm not done yet." Sunglasses coughed into his fist, took out his iPhone, and held it up to Kat. "Hey, babe, congrats—you've just moved to the top of my to-do list."

Stacy loved it.

Kat said, "What's your name?"

He arched an eyebrow. "Whatever you want it to be, babe."

"How about Ass Waffle?" Kat opened her blazer, showing the weapon on her belt. "I'm going to reach for my gun now, Ass Waffle."

"Damn, woman, are you my new boss?" He pointed to his crotch. "Because you just gave me a raise."

"Go away."

"My love for you is like diarrhea," Sunglasses said. "I just can't hold it in."

Kat stared at him, horrified.

"Too far?" he said.

"Oh man, that's just gross."

"Yeah, but I bet you never heard it before."

He'd win that bet. "Leave. Now."

"Really?"

Stacy was nearly on the floor with laughter.

Sunglasses started to turn away. "Wait. Is this a test? Is Ass Waffle, like, a compliment or something?"

"Go."

He shrugged, turned, spotted Stacy, figured why not. He looked her long body up and down and said, "The word of the day is legs. Let's go back to your place and spread the word."

Stacy was still loving it. "Take me, Ass Waffle. Right here. Right now."

"Really?"

"No."

Ass Waffle looked back at Kat. Kat put her hand on the butt of her gun. He held up his hands and slinked away.

Kat said, "Stacy?"

"Hmm?"

"Why do these guys keep thinking they have a chance with me?"

"Because you look cute and perky."

"I'm not perky."

"No, but you look perky."

"Seriously, do I look like that much of a loser?"

"You look damaged," Stacy said. "I hate to say it. But the damage . . . it comes off you like some kind of pheromone that douche bags can't resist."

They both took a sip of their drinks.

"So what won't I like?" Kat asked.

Stacy looked back toward Ass Waffle. "I feel bad for him now. Maybe I should throw him a quickie."

"Don't start."

"What?" Stacy crossed her show-off long legs and smiled at Ass Waffle. He made a face that reminded Kat of a dog left in a car too long. "Do you think this skirt is too short?"

"Skirt?" Kat said. "I thought it was a belt."

Stacy liked that. She loved the attention. She loved picking up men because she thought that a one-night stand with her was somehow life changing for them. It was also part of her job. Stacy owned a private investigation firm with two other gorgeous women. Their specialty? Catching (really, entrapping) cheating spouses.

"Stacy?"

"Hmm?"

"What won't I like?"

"This."

Still teasing Ass Waffle, Stacy handed Kat a piece of paper. Kat looked at the paper and frowned:

KD8115

HottestSexEvah

"What is this?"

"KD8115 is your user name."

Her initials and badge number.

"HottestSexEvah is your password. Oh, and it's case sensitive."

"And these are for?"

"A website. YouAreJustMyType.com."

"Huh?"

"It's an online dating service."

Kat made a face. "Please tell me you're joking."

"It's upscale."

"That's what they say about strip clubs."

"I bought you a subscription," Stacy said. "It's good for a year."

"You're kidding, right?"

"I don't kid. I do some work for this company. They're good. And let's not fool ourselves. You need someone. You want someone. And you aren't going to find him in here."

Kat sighed, rose, and nodded to the bartender, a guy named Pete who looked like a character actor who always played the Irish bartender—which is what, in fact, he was. Pete nodded back, indicating that he'd put the drinks on Kat's tab.

"Who knows?" Stacy said. "You could end up meeting Mr. Right."

Kat started for the door. "But more likely, Mr. Ass Waffle."

Kat typed in "YouAreJustMyType.com", hit the RETURN button, and filled in her new user name and the rather embarrassing password. She frowned when she saw the moniker at the top of the profile that Stacy had chosen for her:

"Cute and Perky!"

"She left off *damaged*," Kat muttered under her breath.

It was past midnight, but Kat wasn't much of a sleeper. She lived in an area far too upscale for her—West 67th Street off Central Park West, in the Atelier. A hundred years ago, this and its neighboring buildings, including the famed Hotel des Artistes, had housed writers, painters, intellectuals—artists. The spacious old-world apartments faced the street, the smaller artist studios in the back. Eventually the old art studios were converted into one-bedroom apartments. Kat's father, a cop who watched his friends get rich doing nothing but buying real estate, had tried to find his way in. A guy whose life Dad had saved sold him the place on the cheap.

Kat had first used it as an undergrad at Columbia University. She had paid for her Ivy League education with a NYPD scholarship. According to the life plan, she was then supposed to go to law school and join a big white-shoe firm in New York City, finally breaking away from the cursed family legacy of police work.

Alas, it hadn't worked out that way.

A glass of red wine sat next to her keyboard. Kat drank too much. She knew that was a cliché—a cop who drank too much—but sometimes the clichés are there for a reason. She functioned fine. She didn't drink on the job. It didn't really affect her life in any noticeable way, but if Kat made calls or even decisions late at night, they tended to be, er, sloppy ones. She had learned over the years to turn off her mobile phone and stay away from e-mail after ten P.M.

Yet here she was, late at night, checking out random dudes on a dating website.

Stacy had uploaded four photographs to Kat's page. Kat's profile picture, a head shot, had been cropped from a bridesmaid group photo taken at a wedding last year. Kat tried to view herself objectively, but that was impossible. She hated the picture. The woman in the photograph looked unsure of herself, her smile weak, almost as though she was waiting to be slapped or something. Every photograph—now that she went through the painful ritual of viewing them—had been cropped from group pictures, and in every one, Kat looked as though she were half wincing.

Okay, enough of her own profile.

On the job, the only men she met were cops. She didn't want a cop. Cops were good men and horrible husbands. She knew that only too well. When Grandma got terminally ill, her grandfather, unable to handle it, ran off until, well, it was too late. Pops never forgave himself for that. That was Kat's theory, anyway. He was lonely and while he had been a hero to many, Pops chickened out when it counted most and he couldn't live with that and his service revolver was sitting right there, right on the same top shelf in the kitchen where he'd always kept it, and so one night, Kat's grandfather reached up and took his piece down from the shelf and sat by himself at the kitchen table and . . .

Ka-boom.

Dad, too, would go on benders and disappear for days at a time. Mom would be extra cheery when this happened—which made it all the more scary and creepy—either pretending Dad was on an undercover mission or ignoring his disappearance altogether, literally out of sight, out of mind, and then, maybe a week later, Dad would waltz in with a fresh shave and a smile and a dozen roses for Mom, and everyone would act like this was normal.

YouAreJustMyType.com. She, the cute and perky Kat Donovan, was on an internet dating site. Man oh man, talk about the best-laid plans. She lifted the wine glass, made a toasting gesture toward the computer screen, and took too big a gulp.

The world sadly was no longer conducive to meeting a life partner. Sex, sure. That was easy. That was, in fact, the expectation, the elephant in the date room, and while she loved the pleasures of the flesh as much as the next gal, the truth was, when you went to bed with someone too quickly, rightly or wrongly, the chances of a long-term relationship took a major hit. She didn't put a moral judgment on this. It was just the way it was.

Her computer dinged. A message bubble popped up:

We have matches for you! Click here to see someone who might be perfect for you!

Kat finished the glass of wine. She debated pouring another, but really, enough. She took stock of herself and realized an obvious yet unspoken truth: She wanted someone in her life. Have the courage to admit that to yourself, okay? Much as she strove to be independent,

Kat wanted a man, a partner, someone in her bed at night. She didn't pine or force it or even make much of an effort. But she wasn't really built to be alone.

She began to click through the profiles. You got to be in it to win it, right?

Pathetic.

Some men could be eliminated with a quick glance at their profile photograph. It was key, when you thought about it. The profile portrait each man had painstakingly chosen was, in pretty much every way, the first (very controlled) impression. It thus spoke volumes.

So: If you made the conscious choice to wear a fedora, that was an automatic no. If you chose not to wear a shirt, no matter how well built you were, automatic no. If you had a Bluetooth in your ear—gosh, aren't *you* important?—automatic no. If you had a soul patch or sported a vest or winked or made hand gestures or chose a tangerine-hued shirt (personal bias) or balanced your sunglasses on top of your head, automatic no, no, no. If your profile name was ManStallion, SexySmile, RichPrettyBoy, LadySatisfier—you get the gist.

Kate clicked open a few where the guy looked . . . approachable, she guessed. There was a sad, depressing sameness to all the write-ups. Every person on the website enjoyed walks on a beach and dining out and exercising and exotic travel and wine tasting and theater and museums and being active and taking chances and grand adventures—yet they were equally content with staying home and watching a movie, coffee and conversation, cooking, reading a book, the simple pleasures. Every guy claimed that the most important quality they looked for in a woman was a sense of humor—right, sure—to the point where Kat wondered whether "sense of humor" was a euphemism for "big boobs." Of course, every man also listed preferred body type as athletic, slender *and* curvy.

That seemed more accurate, if not downright wishful.

The profiles never reflected reality. Rather than being what you are, they were a wonderful if not futile exercise in what you *think* you are or what you want a potential partner to think you are—or most likely, the profiles (and man, shrinks would have a field day) simply reflect what you want to be.

The personal statements were all over the place, but if she had to use one word to sum them up, it would probably be *treacle*. The first read, "Every morning, life is a blank canvas waiting to be painted"—click. Some aimed for honesty by telling you repeatedly that they were honest. Some faked sincerity. Some were highfalutin or showboating or insecure or needy. Just like real life, when Kat thought about it. Most were simply trying too hard. The stench of desperation came off the screen in squiggly, bad-cologne waves. The constant soulmate talk was, at best, off-putting. In real life, Kat thought, none of us can find someone we want to go out with more than once, yet somehow we believe that on YouAreJustMyType.com we will instantly find a person we want to wake up next to for the rest of our lives.

Delusional—or does hope spring eternal?

That was the flip side. It was easy to be cynical and poke fun, but when she stepped back, Kat realized something that pierced her straight through the heart: Every profile was a life. Simple, yep, but behind every cliché-ridden, please-like-me profile was a fellow human being with dreams and aspirations and desires. These people hadn't signed up, paid their fee, or filled out this information idly. Think about it: Every one of these lonely people came to this website—signed in and clicked on profiles—hoping it would be different this time, hoping against hope that finally they would meet the one person who, in the end, would be the most important person in their lives.

Wow. Just let that realization roll over you for a moment.

Kat had been lost in this thought, clicking through the profiles at a constantly increasing velocity, the faces of these men—men who had come here in the hopes of finding "the one"—blurring into a fleshy mess from the speed, when she spotted his picture.

For a second, maybe two, her brain didn't quite believe what her eyes had seen. It took another second for the finger to stop clicking the mouse button, another for the profile pictures tumbling by to slow down and come to a halt. Kat sat and took a deep breath.

It couldn't be.

She had been surfing at such a rapid pace, thinking about the men behind the photographs, their lives, their wants, their hopes. Her mind—and this was both Kat's strength and weakness as a cop—had been wandering, not necessarily concentrating on what was directly in front of her yet being able to get a sense of the big picture. In law enforcement, it meant that she was able to see the possibilities, the escape routes, the alternate scenarios, the figure lurking behind the obstacles and obfuscations and hindrances and subterfuge.

But that also meant that sometimes Kat missed the obvious.

She slowly started to click the back arrow.

It couldn't be him.